Father's Day
A Slice of Life

Greg Slominski

Father's Day: A Slice of Life
All rights reserved.
Copyright © 2019 Greg Slominski
All rights reserved.
SDC Publishing, LLC
All rights reserved.
Library of Congress Registration Number:
TXu 1-580-858

ISBN: 9781087824345

PREFACE

Remember… Remember when you were young.

Remember!

Remember when you were young and it was summer? Adults melted in humid sun-drenched days. To us kids, the heat fueled boundless energy. Remember how a day felt? Life coursed through our veins!

Shake off "adult" and remember.

Heartbeat quicker yet?

Summer was all about play and you didn't want the day to end. Argh! Just the thought of the day ending seemed a travesty. Play all day at whatever entertained you and your friends… basketball, dodge ball, kickball, tag, red rover, hide and seek. Life was the moment—this moment-- revealed an instant at a time. And we experienced it in all its glory.

When friends weren't around there were a thousand places and mysteries to discover on your bike, your freedom machine. My bike was a chopper, some called them banana bikes. It got the name chopper because the chrome handlebars jutted high like customized Harleys and banana bike because the long narrow seat accommodated two. Mine was green and came with bright green and white plastic tassels streaming from the rubber-coated handgrips. The tassels danced in the air as the bike zoomed streets and fields. Before I outgrew the bike, the handlebar tassels were worn clean off. The original seat and tires changed countless times.

Remember the feeling of freedom – the wind in your hair? No bike helmets back then. And no gears, just one speed that built thighs no exercise machine ever will!

There wasn't a summer day we'd give up on. We frolicked as a swarm of kids bounding from one yard to the next, one activity to the next. Rain or shine, we'd play until supper. After supper we'd be back out, engaged to the hilt. Kick the can, freeze tag, ghost tag, or just swinging and sharing our most intimate feelings.

During hide and seek we'd shout the phrase "Ollie, Ollie in com free!" not knowing what the heck it meant except it drew the kids to base. I was all grown up when I finally realized that was bastardized old English: "All ye all ye in come free!" That chant's passed through the centuries kid to kid long after the first inciter turned to dust.

We were kids, still shy of an age when the allure of the opposite sex took hold of us. We noted and admired the difference in the sexes, filing the realization for future reference, but we were kids and this was the season of our lives for wide-open play. For now, carefree romping came naturally. We were at one with the universe… stardust on a mission of joy and discovery.

Feel it?

Night rolled in. Play continued. The sun gave way to evening and we'd insist it was still too bright to come in. At twilight eyes adjusted guided by stars and imagination. Surrender neither day nor night! Time was too precious to waste, to stop playing, to yield to the practical demand of parents.

Night was magical! Dusk settled, air cooled, dew formed and smells changed. Eyes widened and senses came alive! The settling dampness gave a musky odor to the world and we played with new energy, directed no longer by sight but rather hearing smell and touch. Our ears perked up a notch, and our nostrils flared, bringing in the world around us. And touch – never forget touch. The differences between little boys and little girls enchanted the night. A casual touch at night during tag held a million possibilities.

Remember? Can you feel it like you used to?

It took a dad's booming voice, loud enough to startle the whole neighborhood, to bring me home. Adults – clueless, yet in charge – finally prevailed.

I asked my dad one night as I came in the house; "When do you get summer vacation?"

"I don't."

"And you're OK with that?"

I mumbled quite alarmed at the apparent lack of parental wisdom as I headed upstairs. "That seems strange! Adults create the rules and you don't give yourself all summer off? What could be more important than enjoying life?

"When I get older, I'll change the rules and give adults the summer off too!"

We were just kids, but we knew how sacred each day, each night, each moment. We lived to the fullest and were sometimes too tired to take a bath. Might clean up a bit, but then again, there were times we'd just crash all sweaty and dirty-- crash asleep on top of our sheets without undressing. Wasted. Blessedly wasted from draining the essence of creation.

Can you feel it in your heart again? Remember wide-open play? Try! Get there... we need you! You'll need the energy to keep up.

It is hard to imagine that feeling once we become adults. I got a glimpse again.

The feeling of intense joy coursing through a kid's veins is what teenagers try to regain as they cruise the strip in their cars on Friday night. That feeling of being totally alive is what young lovers briefly rekindle in each other's arms. But as kids it was ours, a precious gift we didn't seek. I got a glimpse again. I remember what it felt like because I'm in love again.

Trouble is-- she's not my wife.

So pin your ears back. Let your smile pull back your cheeks and open your nostrils, because it is nighttime, we're playing tag, and you're it.

INTRODUCTION

Please note the following disclaimer:
    WARNING: Do Not Try This At Home!

An emotional stuntman performed the absurd matters of the heart portrayed by the lead character. Any attempt to conduct your life in a similar manner will likely cause excruciating heartbreak and torment loved ones.

The book was written to help you know yourself, know others, and most importantly deepen your appreciation relationships with the opposite sex. The idea was to display wisdom and provide insights into love. I used my own life as fodder where wisdom was in short supply, so the book evolved into a humorous testament on how *not* to love in the 21st Century.

The journey explores many subjects surrounding love and the feelings of attraction, most notably unrequited love. I was forty-two and a half years old when I heard the word "unrequited" for the first time and realized many people experience this troubling challenge. Unrequited love is a one-way love, unanswered and unreturned. It is the kind of love you have when you're head over heels in love with someone who sees you as a friend. It's a widespread phenomenon.

Let's go check in on the Bean and laugh, cry, learn, and love.

May the Bean's journey help you rediscover a lost chunk of your heart.

Glimpse of Lunch

Twenty-three years is too long to go without feasting upon the face of your lover.

Her eyes enchanted the way the Queen of Sheba mesmerized. Glowing vibrant, she enthralled me from the start. Her eyes sparkled like effervescent conduits-- waterfalls from her soul cascading into mine. Tumbling rapturously in her presence, I swirled in an agitated whirlpool as my heart came alive and beat with new purpose. Consumed by her large brown eyes glistening with joy and wonderment, I soaked in her beauty.

I'd been captivated by her beauty years ago when we first met. I found myself similarly smitten years later over lunch.

It was beautiful day, mid-afternoon on a Thursday, June 12th. Late spring was usually muggy and hot around these parts. But fortune favored. The air felt more like late September as we casually dined on an elevated patio overlooking a lake.

It had been twenty-three years since we'd been on a date and twenty years since our last brief encounter. The realization drew a gasp. How could I have missed a moment being with her!

An honest gesture brought us together again. I'd contacted the Department of Health's Environmental Services after receiving an invitation to attend a meeting and learned of her employment. She no longer carried her maiden name, so I assumed she was happily married or as close to that ideal as mere mortals achieve. Just business. Innocent.

She'd been married once and now divorced. I was married once and still married.

For the first forty-five minutes I swam in the pools of her eyes as we spoke across the small outdoor table in Raleigh. Her smile radiated and I felt at peace-- blessed like a flower waking up to the springs precious possibilities.

The sun shifted and she reached into her purse for sunglasses. I barely caught my mouth gaping in dismay as I lost the chance to look into her eyes. I spent the rest of the time listening intensely and taking in her cheeks and the gentle fall of her neck and shoulders.

We wandered the width and breadth of the lost decades. Her mellow voice rang through my head like the gentle vibration that follows the percussion of a large bell. Clear, strong and soothing, it danced through my ears and tapped dormant emotions. Her voice resonated in an unexpected manner, giving me a warm feeling-- of finally being home.

My mind reeled at the discrepancy. Twenty years? It felt more like a long weekend since we'd been together, not half our lives. The woman who sat before me was as beautiful today as she was in college. My head knew I had a wife, and three wonderful kids, and that I lived in Lynchburg. But my heart realized that I loved Alexandra as much today as I did then.

As time did a quick rewind, Alexandra explained her favorite drink was shade-grown coffee. From that moment on, I was the Bean. Until then, our friendship hadn't been the kind that would produce a nickname. We'd been friends in college, nothing more.

But it wasn't my doing that kept us just friends. From the very first day we met, I wanted us to be a couple.

The Back Row

"Caledonia! What makes your big head so hard!" John Lee Hooker.

My friend Mark burdened my new 1980 Chevrolet Chevette hatchback with his clean laundry and a box of school supplies. College break and holiday trips home were punctuated with clean laundry and foodstuffs to restock our meager dorm rooms. This one was no different. This Christmas and New Year's break was mild, like North Carolina usually is blessed. We loaded the car in short sleeves.

"New ride! Nice color." Mark slid his hand along the deep blue paint of the passenger door as he opened it.

"They call it midnight blue." I said with a young man's pride of his first car.

Mark studied the color, "Reminds me of those Mercedes sedans."

I acknowledged his complement with a nod. "A tad cheaper but the color's regal!"

"So how was N.A.S.A? Didn't you work at Cape Canaveral or Houston?"

"Huntsville."

"Huntsville?"

"Alabama, Marshall Space Flight Center-- its part of the Redstone Arsenal. America's home of the rocket."

"Oh." Marks's interest waned instantly but he continued politely, "Learn anything? How about one thing?"

"Plan-Do-Check-Act."

Mark looked befuddled.

"Think of it as the scientific method on the go. Make an educated guess, test the hell out of it, refine the guess and do it again. That is pretty much what NASA is all about."

"Easy enough." Braced for a more technical answer, Mark relaxed into the passenger seat and shifted his legs into a comfortable position.

With supplies stowed around us like westward bound pioneers in a Conestoga, we departed on our journey to State.

Mark was a member of a group of friends playfully called the "Back Row." The name dated back to high school. The moniker arose because many of us sat on the back row in our advanced math class.

Making friends was easy for me; keeping them was hard. My family moved about every year so I'd lost every buddy. I keenly appreciated the value of these guys, the Back Row, as we transitioned from high school to college.

"How were school and Raleigh?" I asked.

"School was ok, didn't fail anything. Social life sucked."

"Same as last year?"

"Not better. How about Alabama?"

A broad smile enveloped me; "Mark… the weather does something to women. Warms them into Southern Bells."

Anticipation increased his stare.

"Locals and transplants alike were all real friendly. Dated a girl from Colorado and one from Canada. Warm and friendly."

"Wow! Better than Raleigh!"

"Hey, you'll love this, I got into jazz and blues clubs! Great scene."

"Jazz and blues!"

Mark was the avid musician in the Back Row playing french horn, trumpet and coronet. He stayed with it at State marching in the band.

"Yep! Saw local bands and national acts too.

"Hey, let's put our newfound N.A.S.A knowledge to work?"

"Plan… Do… um this and that?"

"Plan, Do, Check, Act." I corrected. "The social life in Raleigh is rotten you say. Huntsville was better, so what does that tell us?"

"We should have gone to Auburn?"

"Well possibly. Auburn's a bit farther south. But let's not give up on NC State just yet."

Mark nodded with a frown and a tight-lipped smile.

"If we want something better than a social life that sucks, we can't settle for what we've become accustomed to. Got to improve our lot!"

"Right!" Mark's enthusiastic response bubbled with unending bachelor hope.

"Won't get better on its own. It's a sign of insanity to continue to do the same thing but expect different."

Mark nodded and flipped on the radio as we made headway into our seventy-five minute haul back to campus, bobbing his head to the tunes.

"Can you change quickly? Can I change quickly?" I questioned.

"Uh… no!"

"Right. Let's look for something else. Tweak another variable of the social scene."

Mark remained engaged but not getting warmer.

I prompted, "How about the places we hang out in Raleigh? Bars are smoke filled. They smell like stale beer."

Mark added, "They keep the lights off because they're nothing but empty rooms painted black. The volume is so loud you can't talk to a girl once you get her attention."

"Exactly. On the other hand, the blues and jazz clubs I visited in Huntsville offered air I could breathe without gagging. I could talk and enjoy the evening without permanent hearing loss. Unimaginative guys own college bars motivated by the profit gained by leading students toward a future of deaf alcoholism! What can you expect in an environment like that?"

Mark answered flatly, "Strikeout."

"After strikeout, after strikeout. Exactly! Year after year after year if you don't change something! If we don't change something.

"Here's the plan, we need to change something and run the experiment again. It isn't you. It isn't me. Well, if it's one of us, it's you."

Wide eyed, mark looked over and laughed.

"I mean neither of us is going to be movie stars based on appearance alone."

"Appearance alone? Yeah, guess I better start studying."

We laughed the plight of the ordinary.

"Hard to change you and me. So change the music, change the beat, the scenery. You're the music guy, when we get back to State, your job is to find a new place to meet girls."

"Yes sir, captain!"

Two hours later we were unpacked and milling in Clay and Mark's room. Clay found a place for new Christmas gifts. A large hot plate and a hot air popcorn popper with a large yellow cover occupied his concern. The new appliances threatened to occupy way too much of the cramped room. Clay busied himself stashing socks and other laundry that Mark had shuttled from home. I lounged across one of the two single beds. Mark commanded the other. Décor highlights consisted of posters of Led Zeppelin and a wacked out black light poster of a stoned mouse with M Eye Sea Kay E Why written over his head that I could never seem to interpret.

Mark sat up as he glancing through the newspaper, "Hey, there's a new place. Crazy Zacks."

We exchanged a blank look.

Clay offered without looking up from drawing the last bundle of rolled socks, "Oh that's the new Beach music place down Hillsboro Street."

Mark and I silently mouthed "Beach music?" with faces drawn in distain.

"Is that like blues or jazz?" I admitted complete ignorance on the subject.

Mark bobbed his shoulders and turned to Clay for insight. Clay added "I don't know. But I hear the girls like it."

Mark ceased scanning the paper. His head rose and our eyes convened in the center of the room like we were engrossed in a séance. Clay so slowly slid the wooden drawer closed, turned, and only then realized the gravity of his proclamation.

"I'll drive."

How We Met

"Under the boardwalk, down by the sea..." The Drifters

I drove up in my sparkling blue sophomore wheels. Mark, Clay, and Bob, all Back Row guys, un-piled ready to try the club specializing in the melodious strains of "beach music" for the usual reason. We wanted to meet girls.

That didn't take long. There was a small line queuing near the door. Immediately in front of us a gaggle of five girls convened. They talked about being students at a local all-girls' college.

There were three such hallowed schools in Raleigh, Peace, St. Mary's, and Meredith. Each school was a natural magnet for State's male students. These young starletts attended the picturesque Meredith.

All five girls were attractive, but one radiant young lady stood out. She was... amazing! Quiet but confident, pretty, with gently tanned skin, dark hair, and beautiful eyes, she emanated an elegant panache. A beam of sunlight shone down and singled her out. It was love at first sight, instant corporal and emotional harmony. I felt infinitely alive and completed by her presence.

The pavement seemed to move like an escalator drawing me closer to her. A distortion of senses-- I shook my head.

Agitation arose amongst the ladies. A rift separated the group. Voices rose, despite effort to keep the commotion secret, and the tight formation spread disassociating the outcast. The line was moving now, and the girls drew near the ticket window where an attendant checked IDs and collected a small cover charge.

The radiant girl didn't have her ID.

She hadn't forgotten her proof of age, she was just too young. A person had to be eighteen to enter a place that served beer and she was a month shy. Maybe she hoped no one at the club would check. Maybe it was just the freshman naiveté. But the older girl that drove them wasn't a freshman, and she wouldn't interrupt her evening's plans by carting this young back school.

I immediately offered, "Hi. I'm Brian. Couldn't help but overhear. Seems you have a little problem. I'll be happy to drive you back to your dorm."

The Meredith driver looked infinitely relieved and disappeared. My guys shrugged knowing I'd be back to collect them. The remaining girls buzzed talking it over. The beautiful young lady gauged trust in a quickly shortening list of other options.

"OK." She nodded acceptingly. "My name is Alexandra."

We headed back to her school. She guided me through the streets of the petite campus and thanked me when we arrived in front of her dorm.

"Might your nickname Sasha?"

"Why yes!" She sat back in her seat impressed, if I caught the brief display of feeling correctly. "How did you know?" She relaxed and finally graced me with a look that didn't wander.

"Chance acquaintance with a Russian girl while I lived overseas. My Dad was in the Army. We traveled. After a football game I met a Russian girl. She was introduced as Alexandra but quickly confided that her friends called her Sasha."

Alexandra offered warmly "Well, how about that. I lived overseas growing up too! My father was in the Navy. And only two people regularly call me Sasha, my maternal grandmother and my mom. None of my friends at school know me by that name."

A smile must have crossed my face. Grandma, Mom, and me.

Sasha began her challenge of finding a girl on campus whose ID looked enough like her to fool the beach club's gatekeeper. Spring semester classes hadn't started; few students were back from the holiday break.

Sasha offered me an excuse to depart. "This may take a while." She said holding the door.

"I'll wait. Take your time."

In her absence, the thought crossed my mind: "Why doesn't she just wait a few months until she's legal?" But it seemed like a harmless tweaking of authority. I'd done something similar a year ago. That night I walked into a sandwich shop a month before I turned eighteen and ordered a beer. I got about two sips down before the manager carded us at the table. I relinquished the beer. Kindly the manager didn't ask us to leave.

Sasha returned dejected after fifteen minutes.

"Hey, I'm happy to continue waiting… for you."

"Really? She perked up, "I'll try another dorm."

She emerged with an ID and took a seat. The inexpensive upholstery barely made a sound as she alighted. "Does it look like me?"

I laughed at the lack of resemblance, "No, but it will probably suffice. A pretty girl isn't going to get turned away. They want you in there to liven up the place. If it doesn't work, I'll drive you back to your dorm. Fair enough?"

She agreed with a nod.

When we got back to the club we split up. She hadn't come to meet me, though I was delighted to have met her. It wasn't quite so large an establishment that she could hide. We joined each other a few times that night and danced.

That wonderfully spontaneous chance meeting led to many precious dates.

The Talk

Growing up was tough. Coming of age, hormones, half kid and half adult. As middle and high school students we saw ourselves as increasing independent, yet we were blind to how impressionable we were. For me, the hardest part of adolescence was becoming sexually awake but feeling socially restrained from acting. God, that was tough. Stuck between a rock and a hard place!

Parental wisdom was bestowed during "The Talk" while I was in what was then called junior high.

Mom's version came first. Mom was motivated by my older sister's remark displaying a woeful lack of biological acumen.

During a romantic TV movie scene my sister covered her eyes, "Kissing will get that girl pregnant!"

Mom and I looked at each in disbelief. In my sensitive brotherly way I derided, "No it won't you idiot!"

Mom approached the learning opportunity more constructively.

Mom addressed us separately, sister first. My sister emerged sullen faced fully in denial that man and woman, especially our parents, could do anything so ghastly. She strode past me down the hall encased in the ashen face reserved for funeral homes. I puckered for another snide comment but mom cut me off with a sharp look and the "your next" inviting finger.

Mom was raised in rural eastern North Carolina and her advice was influenced by her Dixie upbringing. She described the man's role in dating with a detached, almost revered, manner. A calm trance enveloped her and generations of farmwomen that knew youthful fleeting romance followed by hard work. Eons of laborious lives spoke through her. "Let the girl make the first contact. If she wants to hold hands, she'll touch your arm or slip her hand in your hand. Same goes for kissing. If she wants to be kissed, she'll lean close… you'll know."

I listened to her words and pondered the urges that had taken hold inside. I'd stayed "out of trouble" through a combination of self-control and fear of the unknown. But even at my young age self-discipline was sorely tested by the mere presence of the fairer gender.

The biological urge to close ranks with girls and reproduce grows within a teenage boy with the patience of a stampeding bull buffalo. Guys want to charge into the fertile pasture and graze! Yet society and wisdom preaches restraint. Mom put the control, the signal to initiate contact, into the girl's domain. Her way proved a good check to the compulsion that gathered in my loins. Giving the girl control made me keep the brakes on until I got a hint of a green light. That one little talk, motherly advice, kept me from pushing myself on girls. Over the next few years, her advice left me dry after many dates when I might otherwise have tasted sweet lips. I panted plenty, awash in passion, checked like a hound dog driven mad lunging against a restraining chain staked to moral ground. I suffered that way, as many well-raised boys do.

Dad shared his side of "The Talk" a year or two later during tenth grade. Dad was great at "dad" things but remained quiet on matters of the heart. He was very supportive of the athletic events and academic pursuits. We didn't talk about emotions or take quiet walks together. Talking about feelings and relationships wasn't the strong point of The Greatest Generation. But out of the blue early one Saturday afternoon something important perched in his mind. He suggested, "Let's take a walk."

With dad, most statements came across like orders. Such were the ways of being an infantry officer and a dad. Even when he was being sensitive, it felt like a salute was in order.

In tenth grade we lived in Teheran, Iran. Most Army tours of duty were for one or two years. We were in the second year of this assignment, settled in a nice rented house situated as far north in the capital city as roads and terrain allow.

Teheran spreads out on a massive plateau that butts up to the Elburz Mountains. Like the topography of Denver Colorado, the mountains form a sheer rise, confining urban growth. We lived on the gentle rise of the first foothill. The road ceased about three blocks north, turning into a pedestrian trail that wound upward.

Dad hung a left as we departed the gated house, heading for the cool mountain air.

There aren't many more important conversations a father and son can have. He didn't rush it.

"Do you know… the basics… about conception?"

I'd never seen him troubled so, almost stumbling in step and words.

With understated certainty, I offered "Yes, I think so."

Half the weight disappeared off his shoulders. With reestablished confidence his curiosity grew, "Where and when did you learn?"

"Remember back at Fort Ord, our neighbor Col. Heinz? They had a son about five years older than me. He filled me in."

He nodded recollecting the duty assignment and neighbors.

"GI Joes, playing in foxholes, and the birds and the bees."

He nodded remembering the older boy and the clarity that such a friend would cover more ground that action figures.

In hindsight, it seems natural to learn the facts from a guy. But it would have been a far more compelling memory to be schooled by a girl!

I added, "Didn't think much at all about it at the time. The whole dual-purpose penis thing was beyond my comprehension as a third grader. Guess you have to grow into some facts to appreciate."

Dad offered a genuine smile.

I gave a quick rundown to convince him the natural science facts were solid.

He nodded satisfied and then launched words of restraint rather than coaching success. "When I was your age, guys felt the same urges you do. Some guys got lost in girls."

I waited for him to continue, but he held a thoughtful pause through many strides up hill. The surrounded pines and other evergreens enveloped us adding a sense of privacy to our otherwise open discussion.

I looked in the woods left and right following hard on his heels. "Lost in girls?"

The allure of a vagina was tempting beyond reason, but it could a guy get lost in there?

"Lost in girls. They lost their heads over girls. They got so hung up…" He stopped momentarily, looking much farther away than the surroundings allowed, "They couldn't get enough of them and they lost all focus."

Dad started walking again, "Those guys didn't amount to much in life. They never regained their composure."

I relaxed logging it as emotional loss, a spiritual loss. Not a navigational error.

I looked with different eyes on dad that instant. He spoke as if he had been on the brink. Good friends had gone astray. Some guys failed to pass transformation from boy to man without irreparable damage.

That was heavy! This was for real-- a true test of character. A guy could become so enamored, so infatuated, that he lost direction and set out with a singular goal that might yield sexual pleasure, but leave him without reason or greater purpose.

"Wow! That is a surprise. News to me boys got lost in girls, in the pleasures of sex, in your generation. I never imagined folks-- - dads-- would have given up on their studies, athletics, and all for girls."

Centered within the generation that has received much acclaim, dad gazed down from his taller and wiser perspective. He added flatly, "Women were as attractive to us then as they are to you now."

Ah, the cherished gifts of the female, I smiles to myself. Forty years ago a skirt was still a skirt and a smooth calf exposed by a playful wind yanked at boys' hearts as much as hip hugger jeans fashions torment today.

We shared a long glance and nodded in unison as we stepped in stride.

Dad's advice reassured. I comforted in the assumption that these teenage years were the most tortuous. He lived through it. I realized turbulent times would calm.

Strange thing though. I never imagined troubled days might reappear, say mid-life.

I added "I know guys who were already sexually active and show traces of being lost in girls."

Like the would-be addict who must shun the needle the first time to save his life, I wondered if once I embraced my desire, would I survive the thrill? Or would I be lost? As we strolled, I thought of those rare young couples that dated steadily in high school and appeared to balance relationships with other interests and responsibilities. I confided, "Dad, there are some boys and girls that seem to get along great. I see them in the school halls. That's what I want."

I wanted a healthy relationship that nourished the soul and, through playful responsible contact, a relationship that soothed the urges. I wanted nourishing and playful, but no way would I admit the randy part to him that day or any thereafter.

The constant emotional upheaval suffered by Army dependents played into all military brats lives. Moving nearly every year caused painful separation from friends. It also created a resilient spirit and emotional detachment. I made a conscious decision as a young teenager to ignore-- as much as humanly possible-- the storming rage of hormones. I vowed to reserve forming "girlfriend'" relationships until I would not be pulled away by the next move. So I didn't date in high school.

There was a corollary to this sexual restraint. Not quite as important as the restraining order itself, but another piece of Southern tradition. Somewhere along the way mom and dad instilled the notion of "taking home the girl that you brought to the dance." That line of guidance said it was wrong to flirt around. When you date, remain true. As I grew older, and bolder, and able to mesh with women without fear of losing myself, I folded the corollary restraint into my personality. I dated only one girl at a time and remained faithful.

Feelings for Alexa

"Girl, you really got me goin'. You got me so I don't know
what I'm doin'." The Kinks.

It's delightfully easy to remember feelings for Sasha. Young and in love-- infatuated beyond sleep. No task however mundane occurred without the mind fixing. Eat, drink, walk, each occurred with the scent of her emblazoned. A psychological study reported men in their late teens think of girls and sex at least once every seventeen seconds. About right.

The trouble with such vigorous and recurring thoughts spurred by biological urge is how they butt up against social values and ethics. Guys are unable to purge themselves from mental desire for very long unless they are fully engaged in deep contemplative study or athletic endeavors. And these other activities, meaningful though they may be, are only a temporary respite from the predominant matter in our lives, thoughts of young ladies!

"Novelty is another name for desire. We always take
pleasure in whatever is new. The sexual impulse makes our
actions unpredictable. Commencing out of curiosity, the thirst for
satisfaction soon appears." Karma Sutra

If it's been awhile since you've been completely wrapped up in someone let me remind you.

You can't get that person off your mind. Brain in overdrive, new synapses and neurons constantly develop to handle all the amorous thoughts. Emotional brain kicks into overdrive leaving skid marks on reason and restraint. The hunger that builds is insatiable. Your mind wanders when it should be focusing on the world around you -- but your love *is* the only world you want.

Let me tell you about Sasha, starting with her skin. It was somewhere between the color of cinnamon cappuccino and… perfection. I'd like a double grade, or "Venti" of that please!

Starbucks offers a "Venti," or "20 ounces" in Italian. That's two tens, and if "ten" is a perfect girl, venti sums up Sasha. Her flawless tan was genetic predisposition more than a function of sunlight. Her skin struck the fine balance between Caucasian and perhaps Polynesian ancestors. It seemed to cry for me to touch it. Touch and hold, caress, touch and hold. Yep, it was far more than every seventeen seconds!

Her beauty was all fulfilling. There was no comparison to Sasha. The measurement of another woman's height, waist, breast size, or beauty had no relevance of and by itself. I could not assimilate another woman's beauty on its own accord -- once I'd seen Sasha, the only measurement that really mattered was how a woman compared to her.

My beloved's beauty wasn't only in her face. Her physique was ideal, the epitome of grace, strength, and splendor. If Webster put a picture of Sasha beside the word "svelte," the editors could save a thousand words and sell more dictionaries.

She had perfectly rounded, strong but graceful, shoulders. Her torso tapered to her waist in an appealing fashion. Her build was strong, but not suggesting hard labor. Rather, her physique indicated that she'd run and played as a kid, growing up a tomboy. All this youthful activity left her lean, yet pleasantly filled out in all the right places. Her waist rounded into hips in a most delightful way.

We played tennis once, and I can assure you that her legs were as beautiful as any you could hope to find. The smooth skin of her thighs retained the color of creamed coffee all year long. Her young body bounded on the court in perfect harmony. I was breathless but not from the level of play.

Raised as an Army brat who'd put his feelings on hold until getting to college, I was delighted to learn that Sasha was the daughter of a career Navy man. She'd traveled her whole life, and lived overseas too. Similar backgrounds reassured. We were opposites-- boy vs. girl; Army vs. Navy; but similar in experience. It felt so right, like it was meant to be. Written in the stars.

Thinking of Sasha was both pleasurable and painful. It was a mental condition that I coined "Sasha on the Brain," or S.O.T.B. Sasha on the Brain was a case of being smitten.

> "Every individual seeks variations of feelings; change, novelty, the taste for beauty, are all part of man's nature… At the moment which it is obtained, a thing gives you immediate satisfaction, but if you do not obtain it at once, you tend to idealize it." Karma Sutra

I'm not crazy. Trust me on this. She was "All That" and more.

As you see the Bean's love for Sasha unfold keep in mind I was not chasing women left and right. There are only two women I've wanted to share my life with. One is Sasha. The other is my wife.

Just thought you should know.

The Bean in a Nutshell

June-05

Sasha and I went our separate ways while in college. Neither of us knew where the other was for decades. A mutual friend reacquainted us.

Hosting a tour for the Department of Health's Environmental Group in the late 1990s introduced me to her organization. The Environmental Group did health and human safety and environmental impact studies. As such, it needed input from industry. Few companies felt altruistic enough to invite government study teams and regulators into their facilities. My invitation was rare and appreciated. It helped advance one Department of Health scientist's career.

Years later I received an e-mail from him again. He wanted feedback from industry on another issue and invited me to a meeting. "Come down to the Raleigh office or attend via a phone link." He invited.

In our discussion we talked about NC State and Lynchburg College where I'd gotten my MBA. He quickly focused on my time in Raleigh and said he had a co-worker who had lived in Raleigh. Guess who?

I became speechless when he mentioned her name. "Say hello to her for me." was all I managed.

"I'll do that and more. I'll send you her number and e-mail address too."

As the phone cradled I recalled the coincidence that first brought us together back in college. Similar long odds rolled in our favor again.

"I don't believe in coincidence." I offered to the handset after I hung up.

I thought of contacting Sasha immediately. Too intrusive? I turned and put it out of my mind.

Two days later a short e-mail from Sasha appeared acknowledging that our mutual friend had forwarded my greeting. Smile widened she'd taken the initiative to reach out.

Sasha and I exchanged another e-mail or two. A brief talk on the phone reintroduced her melodious voice. I held the receiver tightly to my ear. Time melted. Memories – and warm feelings -- resurfaced, feelings that had lain dormant half my life.

"Your co-worker invited me down for lunch before that meeting he's planning. Let's see, that's ten days away. Do you know where he works?"

"Oh, that's right in my building." She informed.

"How about you join us for lunch? Make it a three-some?"

"I'd be delighted!"

"Great!"

Alexa suggested before we hung up. "Why don't we exchange e-mails and catch up on the years?"

A day later I sent her my e-mail summarizing my work in the US and overseas, touching on my youthful desire to make a difference in the world. In a few small ways I had kept that dream alive, trying to work toward sustainable development, church matters, and world peace. I mentioned my volunteer activities with children. But as I wrote the equivalent of my abbreviated life history I realized I'd strayed from the altruistic dreams that buoyed me as a younger man. I'd given up on my dream of helping those in the greatest need and settled for a sedate middle-class life.

In the e-mail, I described my family, my wife's new office and our three wonderful boys.

I covered the less than flattering highlights, too. Here is one passage from the "let's get reacquainted," e-mail:

"… Sad to say but it is true; no 'Taj Mahal' relationships developed despite my romantic persuasions.

"You remember the story of the Taj Mahal? Prince Khurram, later Mughal emperor, so loved his second wife Arjumand Banu Begam that he built a great white palace in commemoration of their love. That palace is now called the Taj Mahal. Before we digress, let's balance the story. The Mughals were part of a conquering movement that swept through India. They inflicted trauma on the indigenous peoples. They weren't all lily flowers and roses! And the emperor only built the structure *after* his beloved's passing. Just like a man! In any event, the Taj Mahal remains a glorious symbol of love.

"Always the dreamer… I wanted a Taj Mahal relationship! Young girls can have their knights in shining armor, romantic hero savior, whatever. I wanted to be so in love that a grand and beautiful palace was an appropriate display of our shared affections. Well, it didn't happen that way for me. I don't know if not having a Taj Mahal relationship puts me in the minority or majority. My informal and quite unscientific survey of friends suggests couples that much in love are about as rare as the Taj Mahal. There is only one!"

Strange thing to include in a catching up e-mail, but for some reason it bubbled to the surface and seemed important to share.

I hit the "send" key a week before our planned lunch meeting and remained eager to read her summary.

None arrived.

A day before our lunch Alexandra's co-worker had a change of plans. Instead of a threesome, it would just be Alexa and me.

Eric & Kay

"A whirl of pleasurable sensations is connected with the
perception of the organ of touch. The desire for such experience is
the cause of the state of erotic excitement in both man and
woman. In the woman, it manifests itself as a diffuse desire for
contact with the man, while for the latter, it is desire of the
pleasure of touching, especially the thighs and center of the body.
Karma Sutra

Welcome Eric and Kay into the fray—our exploration of love and truth.

Eric and Kay's message is about space, the space that grows between couples. Sometimes the space is absence that makes the heart grow finder. Other times enough space emerges for a cute blonde or brunette to squeeze in. In their case the space grew to so much you could park a moving van in it.

We met through recreational sports. Their son played on a youth recreation teams I coached. Eric was a doctor, and his on-call hours made for a harried life.

"Our wedding night was right out of a fairy tale," Eric confided one day in his place. "Fairy tales pan away when the story gets to the happily ever after part before the lights go out. So any wedding night could be right out of a fairy tale!"

Eric went on, "On the night of our blessed union, Kay pointed out how big a day it was and how we'd need to get up early to catch our flight. She asked to skip the sex part. I gave in to her wishes. Mind you, we'd remained celibate through our courting.

"I told her, 'Hey, we turned in early for this! We've waited for this night! Let's make it special.

"But no dice. I gave in. I assumed we'd be in the Bahamas tomorrow night and our intimacy would unfold.

"Not!" He rose, paced for thirty seconds. Eventually Eric sat but couldn't remain still.

"I hope few couples undergo the frustration we experienced when it came to my wife's unwillingness to engage in sex. Damn, it was rough! It made a huge hole in our marriage."

Eric lowered his head and spoke just above a whisper "We came back from our week on the islands in the same celibate state."

I lighted the mood "Hey, I thought my wife was the only conscientious objector of the sexual revolution!"

"We fooled around," Eric said defending his virility, "but no intercourse on the weeklong honeymoon. You know, years later it didn't change much. She seemed *deathly afraid* of my semen." With deep furrowed brow, Eric humorously reiterated "deathly afraid."

Serious toned, he added, "Not for romantic effort on my part."

I knew both Eric and Kay well. After Eric told his story, I later confirmed with Kay. She added, "Looking back, it's obvious we should have had a major heart to heart right then. I suppose… I suppose we did." She gave a weak laugh, "Eric wouldn't have let the urgency of his feelings be put on hold indefinitely. But I cannot recall any specific conversation."

"So you confronted this issue. Smart."

Eric confided they didn't find resolution. "We talked about it. But it never seemed to improve. Kay always said it got better, but I had a hard time seeing it. Yeah, it got better from *abstinence*! But she never got passionate. Hell, I wondered if she was gay."

Eric rose and went to the fridge. "Want a drink?"

"Umm, yeah, got any Vanilla Pepsi, something like that?"

Eric's look turned derisive. He reached into the back of the fridge, rummaged around, and took out a soda. Then he took out a small bottle from inside the door condiment compartment. He took two olives, replaced the bottle and flipped the door closed with the back of his foot.

"I meant a drink." Eric echoed. He proceeded to fix a martini.

"Ah, no the sugar water is enough for me. Actually, just water, ice water, please."

"Suit yourself."

I entered the fray as Eric concocted his 007 imitation. I poured myself a large glass of ice water.

"Snack?" Eric asked.

"No thanks."

"Years later…" Eric fingered the olives into a buoyant swirl; "I think I figured out Kay years later. She acted like she was saving herself for someone else. I swear to God that is what it felt like." Eric set down his drink, shook his head and wrung his hands. "She never admitted what was so scary about becoming intimate with her husband."

Afterward Kay confirmed, "It was a concern. We worked on it. I didn't see my lack of passion or desire as not reciprocating love. Eric may have. I definitely loved him. As for sex, we talked about it, worked on it, but it was a major problem for him. I loved him and I'm sure he knew that. I just didn't need or want sex. Cuddling, just being close was good enough for me."

Eric went on, "I went into the relationship realizing this would be one of our challenges. Kay's mom and dad pointed out that she didn't experience much love growing up. On the surface her mom and dad were friendly folks, but Kay later told me they fought all the time. The lack of physical expression of joy and love in her upbringing manifested itself in her adult life.

"I accepted the challenge of drawing her out of her emotional shell. I just didn't appreciate the stubbornness, the tenacity, with which a hermit crab can resist!"

I eased the tension, "Women can be stubborn! And they have the right to change their minds. Marry-- yes. Sex-- no." I laughed knowingly of the conflict that sets off in the male of the species.

"Took me years to sort out her hesitancy. The best I can describe it, she treated me like I wouldn't respect her in the morning if she gave in to sex without a struggle. Don't know that's true, but that's what I concluded our last year. I supposed as a young girl she formed an image of what a woman was, and was not, supposed to do."

Eric took a few sips amidst a prolonged pause, "She never allowed herself the freedom to be a complete woman."

Feeling the incessant barb of rejection that lingers long after the damage is done, he continued, "I presumed early in our relationship that her 'pre-marriage' image of herself would evolve, that this 'pre-marriage' concept, the celibate woman, would be replaced with a caring and intimate woman. She would mature beyond the chaste little girl image. Right? She'd mature to equal footing on the emotional, the intimate side."

I inquired of Kay separately to get her side. She said, "Sex was good when we had it. It was satisfying for both of us. I say that with all sincerity. When we had sex, we both…"

Kay hesitated so I added, "Felt the thunder."

Kay and I had a good relationship, but we seldom talked of orgasm except in a joking way.

Kay confirmed with a nod and repeated, "Felt the thunder. We just didn't have intercourse for extended periods of time."

"Extended like a week at a time?"

Kay nodded affirmatively, "Like weeks at a time. Like months at a time. Extended like fifteen months at the extreme."

"*Fifteen months*!" I was startled beyond containment. Unwittingly surprised, I lost my friendly interviewer façade by a reality so separate, so removed from the ideal.

"Fifteen months. Eric reminded me on more than one occasion. And he was right." Kay added, "We sought mental and physical counseling during that dry spell."

"Well dear, if you both liked it, fifteen months without shared intimacy seems like self-inflicted exile rather than a 'dry spell.' How did it affect him?"

Kay looked absent, ignoring or unhearing, and sighed.

"You guys were together during this dry spell? You weren't separated by work, living in different cities?"

"No, we were together." She waved her hand in a 'what can I say?' posture. "Then I went away for three months."

Kay's tone changed, scrutiny on the items she wouldn't include on the highlight reel of her marriage has run its course. I did the math as we sat in silence. They must have been without intercourse for eighteen months, at least. Damn dry. Across the Sahara and back parched dry.

"When we got back together," Kay said, "we put that behind us and started doing better."

Eric continued on dissolution of their marriage. "A turning point occurred one night when we had company over." His mannerism changed as he recounted that night four years ago and he became joyfully animated.

"That night we had dinner for two other couples. Afterward we played some board game." Eric excitedly added "An old girlfriend of Kay's came to town with her husband. These friends happened to know another couple in town. So Kay's friends invited their friends."

Eric's energy remained jubilant as he told the story and his jumpstart had me confused. "So there were how many people at the house?"

"Six. Six folks. Me and Kay, Kay's friends, and their friends."

"Got it."

"Somebody brought a game board. I can't recall what game it was, but it required us to split into three teams."

I could imagine them sitting around the dining room table, clearing dishes, and then regrouping to play a game. I used to play board games, awkward at first, but fun to gather friends together and the interaction offered excellent entertainment. It had been years since Celeste and I played a game.

Eric went on, "Kay paired up with her old friend. And Kay's friend's husband paired up with his old high school buddy. That left our guest's wife and me." Eric sat up straight and enthusiastically filled the room with his story.

"The game pitted three teams against each other. Two teams of old friends who knew each other for years against this young lady and me, strangers until tonight." Eric rocked his chair with the energy of a Kindergartener.

"Success required familiarity with your teammate. But this attractive young wife and I smoked our spouses!" Eric laughed.

He stood up sending his chair skidding backwards, waved his hands like a baseball umpire signaling "safe" and reiterated, "We smoked 'em!" Eric wiggled his hips and shook his arms amusingly as if he were doing a triumphant Chicken Dance.

"It was a riot! We could read each other's minds! We got almost every question right, we were on a roll. She was a few years younger, vivacious, we hit if off instantly. Bang! We connected and we rocked! The old friends grasped for air and grappled in vain as they tried to work together. Kay and her old girlfriend stepped on each other's toes. The two husbands were befuddled."

Eric smiled as he relived the evening.

"When the game was over, we laughed and teased our spouses. That girl and I pranced around and high-fived. We rubbed our victory in because it was such a surprise. The others knew each other, and in a game like that, we weren't even supposed to be competitive much less win. But *we* connected; we rose to the occasion with spontaneity and spunk.

"Spunk, that girl had spunk! We played with an enthusiasm that the others lacked. It was great.

"At the end of the evening, after our company left, I was struck at how alive I had been with the other woman. It was strange, considering my wife and I never seemed to have much fun together. I forgot what letting loose and being carefree was like."

Later, I asked Kay about the evening long ago. She confirmed it happened that way. The only discrepancy; Kay didn't think she and her partner did all that badly.

Kay added, "About a year later, we heard from Shelly, my friend that was there that night. The other couple we shared an evening with had split up. Their marriage hadn't lasted two years.

"Apparently, the wife who hit it off so smashingly with Eric had an affair with a co-worker. She was a live wire for sure! But it was sad in a way to think that couple hadn't stayed together for more than two years."

Her comment was tinged with residual judgment as if she considered divorce synonymous with failure. One failure could be worse than another— as if years of marriage were a tangible asset.

"Kay, I reserve judgment. I don't pretend to know what to feel or think about people that split after two years, two days, or twenty-five years. Cut bait and run in the short run or hang in there for the long haul? It isn't for me to say what others should do.

"Most married folks expect their relationship to last until death do us part. But we've created a throwaway society that reflects on our relationships. About the only definitive statement I'd ever heard about divorce; 'having kids make it all the more complex.'"

Haltingly, she reached over and touched my leg just above the knee signaling an end of the line. Her face melted into a sullen stare.

I redirected "OK. Let me take this another direction for a minute or two."

She brightened.

"Nuclear hot. Did you ever have someone you loved in a way you'd describe as all consuming, a love or lover that was nuclear hot?"

"My, that isn't a connection I'd make—nuclear and lover."

"Well I mean…"

"Victoria Secrets model hot? Playboy bunny hot for men? I know men are all about that kind of thing, young a beautiful. You first."

"Oh yeah. Once there was a girl who I lit up around… alpha, beta, gamma particles, the works."

"What came of it?"

"Not what I'd hoped."

"You missed a golden opportunity. You should have listened to her. You should have followed her lead and let it happen, unfold into the passion you felt."

"I tried but…"

"Then you should have taken it physical."

"Kay you surprise me."

"Yeah, I know." Kay agreed playfully. "Sometimes I surprise myself." She said with a glance that looked almost like a wink.

She drew closer and said, "Brian, you and I are a lot alike. We carried a moral dilemma through our teenage years and on into adulthood. We felt desire, we felt passion, but we redirected it. We didn't succumb to the physical urges."

"For the most part," I agreed. "No one night stands for me."

"Not everyone lives like we did, like we live."

"Agree. But isn't the moral approach somehow superior? Shouldn't a guy and girl try and forge a meaningful relationship." I rubbed my chin. Stubble scraped fingertips then pinched my nostrils closed to better digest her perplexing words.

Kay got quiet. Sadness again hunched her figure and darkened her face. Gone was the joviality of exploration and discovery. She was here but her mind shifted miles away, drifting somewhere back into an earlier time, a different world, struggling with a realization she had never confronted before.

"Brian, you should have taken her. You should have fucked her."

My neck snapped back in surprise.

"Brian, if you'd had sex with a woman you felt that much passion for I'm not sure what would have happened in the long run, but you would have matured. She would have saved you... from yourself."

"From myself?" I asked.

"You and I... we formed this little image of the perfect man and the perfect woman. We set out to find that perfect companion right away. We didn't dabble in distractions because we wanted serious relationships. We didn't fancy just having fun, dating as a lark. Emotionally we were too serious. We should have focused less on finding the right mate, and just having fun. I'm not saying we should have cavorted in one-night stands, but we should have left marital obligations completely out of the picture."

"Be kids… grown-up kids!" I surmised.

"Exactly."

"Experiencing the opposite sex, especially someone you felt was 'nuclear hot' without strings attached or expectations would have made you a more well-rounded person."

I smiled the guy smile… just given the keys and a hall pass to the ladies dorm.

Kay's demeanor ruffled and she said briskly, "I'm *not* talking sex! Well, not necessarily, I mean not just sex. But open heartedly playing the field for the sheer joy of being young and alive."

I confirmed her spirit, "Kids again."

"I see another flaw we share."

"We both wanted the perfect spouse, the perfect lover, the perfect companion, nuclear or otherwise."

I nodded.

"But did we work on ourselves to become better? We didn't do all we could to make *ourselves* the perfect spouse, lover, and companion. We held out hope for that in our partner," Kay said.

She went on, "Don't get me wrong, we improved ourselves, we tried, we were good honest people of high integrity...

"We wanted the best... but by and by we didn't give back *our* best."

She abruptly looked up, raised her left hand, and poked me hard in the bicep.

"You should have listened to her!" Kay bellowed. "A woman you're so passionate about could have been your guiding light, your savior. She would have taught you something... something you needed to know. You would have learned to love, to release your passion, to marvel at the union."

Kay stopped. Before I could answer I saw her eyes turn red. She sniffled and wiped her eyes with the back of her hand and glanced around for a tissue.

"Say you're right…"

"He would have taught you so much if you'd have opened up," she concluded.

"He?"

A tear in her eye punctuated her distant shift.

"Who was 'he', Kay? Who was your *nuclear* guy?"

I inflected nuclear as she had, as if I was a jealous man disparaging her previous flame.

She smiled. A brief laugh emerged pinning the corners of her mouth, offsetting her soul searching. She sniffled again, wiped her eyes one at a time and then let out an "Ohh."

She stepped towards me and gave me a big hug. The strong hug continued. After a tender moment I moved her back.

"It was Eric. It was always Eric for me."

Eric continued, "It wasn't long after the news of the other couples split up that Kay and I packed it in. We left way too much space between us. She never got over her hang-up about touch and intimacy. In the end, we had become roommates sharing the same house. Neither of us wanted that. And separation made sense."

Disclosure had lifted Eric's weight. "I used to feel embarrassed to say a lack of intimacy was a major stumbling block in my first marriage. It was like a slap at my manhood. Now I realize how much our relationship suffered because of the lack of intimacy.

"This isn't just my little head doing the talking!" Eric commanded as if a forceful voice could inflict reason where passion was denied, "Since the end of my marriage to Kay, I've had complete relationships. I'm married again and my new wife and I get along in all aspects. It is not perfect, but it is a *shared* relationship. As for Kay and me, I don't know if it was me or if it was her; I guess it was a function of us. We couldn't get over that big hurdle."

The acid that dissolved the delicate bond of their marriage was the sour residue in from a lack of intimacy. Two of the leading issues attributed to troubled marriages are money and sex. Eric had money, but he wasn't unique on the second failing.

Eric added, "It wasn't just sex. Ladies seem to get confused when guys want sex. The sexual drive isn't an expression of rational desires or expectations. Sex drive doesn't fit into rational discussions. That's the thing, see, you cannot discuss sexual impulse in a rational conversation and do it justice. It is like talking about music. Talk all you like—it isn't anything like music. Feelings run deep and talking without action doesn't solve anything. It helps, conversation puts it in perspective, but a young couple has got to get it on. Get it on regularly. Hell," Eric emphasized, "that attraction is part of what brings couples together. To put up an impenetrable wall is to deny the attraction, to deny your love."

I chimed in, "I can relate to being shut out. Sexual drive is something that is urgent. And it is important in its own right. But it shouldn't retain the most coveted, the most important place in the relationship. However, in the absence of sex, it becomes *very* important and *very* urgent! It becomes overwhelming to the man who lives without and in want. It becomes so overblown that the whole relationship revolves around the desire for sex. That's not healthy."

Eric continued, "In the absence of sex, it becomes the overriding impulse, the single purpose, and the one ambition of a married guy who rightly thought he entered the relationship expecting passionate intercourse."

"Sex should be only one of many facets of a healthy relationship," I injected. "It should be a natural outgrowth of healthy touch and passion. Living without… sex becomes the driver and every other need walks or gets in the trunk!"

Eric continued thoughtfully, "Engaging in sex allows the importance and urgency of passion to reestablish itself at a reasonable level. Engaging in intercourse allows the couple to make sex a part of their intimacy, part of their actions they share to express their love. Abstinence of sex becomes a massive roadblock that defies all rational effort to describe or improve.

"I didn't realize how the lack of shared interest and expression of intimacy slowly dissolved my attraction for Kay."

I added my own experiences. "Massage was a big part of my life before I met Celeste. I took a massage class and gave shoulder and body rubs to friends. I didn't think twice of reaching up and giving a neck or shoulder rub to anyone. Massage was a natural expression of touch and healing, caring. And I became very good at it.

"Physical contact was a point of contention for us too." I admitted. "I was devastated when I discovered I'd married a woman that seemed to care so little for touch. I enjoyed giving massages and benefited from both giving and receiving massages. But it was made all too clear that part of me would atrophy in my marriage. We exchanged massages, I gave she received. It wasn't a communal interaction shared by people who appreciated the value. It was more a means to relieve her immediate stress and not a bonding experience."

Eric wound up his sermon, "Well, I've said way too much about sex. But let me conclude with something about feelings. What really killed my heart were all the rejections. All my efforts to share and communicate through touch were flung back in my face. It hurt me. It really hurt. It wasn't just sex she dismissed. It was *our* passion she dismissed."

Eric added in a bitter whisper, "It was me she dismissed."

After a quiet pause, "Touch is a central part of a marriage, a healthy and necessary part of bonding. The intimate touch is the only truly unique part of the marriage relationship. And my wife was foreign to it. Kay rejected me nightly.

"Rejection became the reality I came home to. Whoopee! I wanted sex but I knew the answer was no. I'd try, but the answer was a cold shoulder. Rejection became a reflection of our condition. I didn't realize it at first. I mean… I lived it… God how I lived and suffered with it at the time! But I didn't know what the future held. Didn't realize it would *always* be that way. I didn't know it was harming me."

Eric's demeanor bordered on melancholy, but he continued. "I felt rejected. Night after night, year after year, I was rejected. She rolled away nearly every night. I tried for six years but it persisted… a forever rejection."

"Stopped trying the last year?"

Eric nodded, "Gave up."

Eric took to silence like a warm blanket. He drew in his shoulders. "I didn't admit it to myself… how much it hurt. I hid it from my heart because… I mean what does that say about a man who is constantly rejected by his wife? His *own* wife! The worst part was I couldn't do anything with that feeling. I felt rejected, but couldn't… deal with it. I mean what could I do?" Eric said in a pleading voice, agonizing as if he had just rolled out of bed frustrated by another 'no' in an endless nightmare of 'nos.'

"Kay and I talked about it, she *saw* how frustrated I was, and she must have known how distressed I was." Eric leaned over with his arms crossed in front of him rubbing his shoulders.

Then he sat up calmly, "I wanted to share the healing balm of touch with my wife, to move on the passion I felt. But to be rejected on such a regular basis…" Eric stood and shook his head from side to side as he looked down at the floor. He took the last swig from the martini he'd nursed and popped the olives in his mouth one after the other.

"That is when I started having these." Eric whirled the now empty glass in his hand freeing any residual clinging to the bottom. He lifted it to his lips and drained an empty glass.

He walked to the kitchen sink, washed it out, and gently placed the glass beside the sink. His ritual bore all the markings of years of practice, a carefully conducted lonely ceremony.

Eric stood in front of the sink and spoke to the window in front of him. "When I realized how much pain the rejections had caused, and I had no recourse, I started drinking. Rejected all those years… it soured me."

Eric spun around facing me. He rested his butt and hands the edge of the sink, "Lasted about four to six months, my drinking. Never heavy. Didn't get drunk. Just a way for to acknowledge my sorrow."

Eric retrieved his glass and filled it half full with water and headed for the freezer. He loaded the rest with ice and joined me laughing, "Didn't help a damn bit! All in all I went through a couple bottles of olives and enough vermouth, gin, and vodka to bathe them. It didn't help. I wasn't about to drown myself in vodka…" he swirled the ice tumbling in the glass, "over a frigid woman."

He took a big healthy guzzle. I mimicked him.

"Kay wanted better 'communication.' She went on about that. Oh God, how she went on about that! Communication. Fucking communication! To me, touch is communication. But her frigidity was part her mind-set of avoiding the 'one-night stand'."

"Excuse me. One-night stand?" I asked. "What one-night stand?"

Eric answered, "Kay treated me like she was trying to avoid sex. Like she was still single and I was a guy she wanted more from than a one-night stand. It was like she never got the fact that we were married and she could release her sexual desires. She never got in touch with passion, never explored that side of her being, never allowed herself to be creative in bed."

I rubbed my lips with my left thumb and two fingers, then said, "So she treated you like a date she wanted more from than a one night stand?"

"She brushed me off for years. Years, before I finally said 'fuck it' and left."

"I never imagined that the root of a married woman's challenge with intimacy might be something as debilitating as vestiges of childhood mores. If a woman was hung up on her past image of the 'right thing to do' when she was married, how could she resolve it?"

"We'll, I'm here to tell you we all grow at different rates, but if someone is still hung up like that after five years, brother don't make it seven!"

"There were times, lots of time I felt I married the wrong woman."

Eric looked at me and interjected, "And I *always* thought you and Celeste had the perfect marriage. Well, not perfect, but damn close to ideal. You two always seemed so happy, so right for each other."

"*Not!*

"I put up with my share of rejections too. So many, I was sure Celeste was *supposed* to marry someone else. I honestly felt that. I concluded she was saving herself physically and emotionally for someone else."

I hadn't ever admitted that before, and I hadn't thought of it in years, but it all came rolling out into the conversation.

"She warmed up like our marriage had been arranged. It was like she was bequeathed to someone else, that's how I felt. Yeah, that's it, given to another. She put forth just enough to keep us together, the vestiges of civility. I asked her if that were true. Hell, I even asked if she was gay. And if so… she could bring her girlfriend over for a threesome!"

Eric's mood lifted, "Did that sense of humor ever get you in good with the ladies?"

"No," I laughed, "I kept trying! When all you've got is a sinking curve ball…"

Eric recapped, "Didn't land a three way, surprising!"

"No, but now that you mention it, I'll put it on my To Do list!"

Like Eric and Kay, Celeste and I talked about it but never completely got over our challenges. Maybe some folks just cannot live in the moment, tap and share passion together. Maybe some are so removed, so remote from passion it isn't part of their being.

Eric looked up, "Touch and sex were not the only problem we had, but they created a void, a large gap between us."

After my chat with Eric and Kay I realized marriages that make it are either a union between people that absolutely need each other and their need remains strong. Or they both see the marriage as sacred. Now that's a concept almost foreign in our disposable society.

Sacred.

Both the husband and the wife must see the relationship as sacred. Otherwise the few changes for the better and the many changes for the worst drag it asunder.

Lunch

June-12

A field of butterflies nested in my stomach on my drive down. I arrived at her office a little early just before anticipation overwhelmed.

Sasha came down and met me in the atrium-like lobby about fifteen 'till. It had been nearly a quarter-century since we'd seen each other, and she might have ballooned out, taken a turn for the worse.

I heard, "Well hello!" and turned.

She was radiant, as beautiful as I remembered her. Her longer-than-shoulder-length dark hair glistened in the sunlight that streamed into the large open foyer. I was awestruck. Her beauty of spirit and body endured. We hugged. The greeting was natural and fluid -- two old friends together again.

"I wasn't sure I would recognize you after all these years."

She raised a quizzical eyebrow.

Smiling, I reassured " You look marvelous, like you stepped out of time still in your early twenties."

"Cafeteria ok, or would you rather go out?"

"Cafeteria is fine. Is it good?"

"Very nice." She said leading down the wide stairs to the serving area.

We beat the crowd. Only one or two others were getting food in the self-serve arrangement.

"Pleasant variety!" I cheered.

There were five short food service lines -- salads at one station, pasta at another, sandwiches on this side, full course meals on the other, drinks at the fifth. With an afternoon meeting looming, I opted for salad.

Sasha got in the pasta line and pouted, "I don't eat very well."

I glanced up at her as I finished building a mound of greens. She stood with her back towards me. Her sage-green pants suit tailored trim in the waist accented her marvelous figure. Strong shoulders tapered to a narrow waist and the lower half of her pantsuit hung from her hips flatteringly. Her hourglass figure remained the shape that captivates. Poor diet? I held my tongue.

At the drink counter, Sasha pointed out, "This is shade grown coffee, my favorite. It is one of many lifestyle-awareness, energy-saving, and ecologically friendly features promoted here."

With pride Sasha added, "Shade-grown coffee is easier on the environment than regularly grown coffee." She helped herself to a large polystyrene cup.

"How's that? I've seen coffee fields. I don't remember any shade."

"I'm not sure." Her confidence waned but believing the Department of Health's willingness to tout it, she brushed off doubt.

"Sweet tea for me. It does absolutely nothing for the environment, far as I know, but it tastes delightful and keeps me awake!"

We made our way to the checkout line. Buying a lady lunch is socially acceptable and on all our dates I paid. But things were different. She was a professional with the government and I was a contractor. We went Dutch.

"Inside or outside?" She asked carefully wheeling her tray surveying seating choices.

"Outside! Too nice to be in!"

An elevated veranda offered a pleasant view of a man-made lake just outside the cafeteria.

Sasha chose a table that sat four-- close to another group of people, but far enough away for privacy. I sat with my back to the building and she took a seat opposite.

"I see your picture in the grocery store."

"What?"

I let the quiet linger a few seconds to see her response.

"Oh, Clairol!" She shook her head reliving a moment of youthful glory before rejoining me in the present. "Thanks for remembering… and noticing!" She said with sincere delight.

"They still haven't found anyone prettier for that shade of hair color. Don't think they ever will."

She took the complement graciously.

This day she wore single pearl earrings accented by a pearl necklace, slightly longer than choker length. The pearls graced her like a dignitary whose calm inner beauty was but a polished reflection of the gems. The necklace fell gracefully beneath the nape of her neck accentuating the slight indentation where neck meets torso. I was drawn to touch her, dance my fingers in the gentle indentation, and run the back of my hand across the pearls, but refrained.

We spoke about what had transpired since we last saw each other.

She was married in 1988 and I a few months later.

We talked about my kids and how they were the center of my life and how much I enjoy coaching sports. Sasha told me of her involvement with modeling was short and sweet. It had landed her a few products when she was younger.

"I'm a member of a museum support group, Museum of Fine Arts."

"Really? Cool. Didn't we visit the museum on a date?"

Alexa replied unsure, shaking her head a hesitant no.

I winched my face to squeeze a recollection of the place, "I remember going as a student… boy it was a long time ago."

"Oh, you need to go again! It underwent a vast expansion that improved the surrounding grounds as well. It's a real treasure!"

Her emphasis convinced me. It would be a prize to walk the halls with her.

"You know… my mom had some artwork on display there a few years ago."

"Really? Probably not. This is the North Carolina fine art museum." She said with a hint of indignation and a quick headshake.

"Oh probably yes!" I smiled, "Mom turned into quite the photographer after dad retired. The museum showcased photographs from each county across the fine state. Two of mom's photos made the grade." A smile seemed appropriate but I held family pride in check.

We seamlessly switched gears and talked relationships. She didn't mention the name of her former husband. I didn't ask. It had been years since her divorce. We didn't dwell, but I inferred traces of lingering tension, residuals left from arguments and lives turned and twisted in ways unplanned.

"My wife Celeste brought forth three wonderful boys whom we enjoy and try to raise right. She just opened her own office this spring. It's a challenge to operate on a single income until her new venture generates revenue.

We talked careers. After tiring of her first job out of college, Sasha settled in with the government. After her divorce, she'd moved to Atlanta but stayed with the Department of Health. She moved back to Raleigh when she'd had enough big city.

"Now I live in Raleigh with my dog." She cited the name of an exotic sounding breed.

"I've got a beagle. Name is Wee Captain." I felt like Charlie Brown at a dog show, plain in comparison, but I loved him. "Wee Captain is great with the kids. Heck of a watch dog. Hard headed."

"I have a male roommate, a guy who works full time and attends night school. He lives in the apartment downstairs."

Her words seared my mind. A tinge of jealousy like a rusty blade gnawed its way through my conscience in a gouging plunge.

Wow! What was that? My balance swayed in jeopardy. I swallowed and quietly blinked back intense jealously to reform composure.

She said lightly with a casual laugh, "My dog is great, but my roommate is pretty lame! He doesn't help out around the house. He doesn't do any yard work. And doesn't offer much protection either!"

My head raced, I can do yard work. I'm great protection! The intensity and insinuation of these ideas dumbfounded. I stirred. My heart and mind sprang to life as if a dormant vein carried ideas and energy I hadn't felt in…

Mercifully, the conversation shifted. I told her about my career, my world-hopping adventures and how I wound up in Virginia. I complimented Lynchburg's small urban environment and how the quality of life suited me.

Throughout our lunch I remained transfixed by her beauty, especially her carefree eyes. I remembered how I'd tried to read her emotion through those eyes years ago. Their sparkle made me smile, almost giddy with youth and vitality.

About an hour into our joyous reunion the sun shifted from behind the building glaring straight into her eyes. Sasha reached into her purse and retrieved her sunglasses. I had been enchanted soaking in her face as it radiated the day's beauty. With the sunglasses barring me from gazing into her eyes, I felt loss, like a prisoner at the end of his hour on the open grounds.

Glancing at the edge of the glasses I looked hard to find a wrinkle. "Has twenty-three years done nothing but enhance your beauty?"

She shared an unreserved smile and we laughed as the conversation unfolded. When she laughed her teeth gleamed white and all was well in my heart.

God! All I want in life is to make her smile and laugh. What a blessing to see her smile!

Her hair was soft and luxurious – attractive enough to earn the endorsement on the hair color product long ago. Sasha's hair used to be jet black, or so I thought. Now it had highlights of deep auburn making it even more captivating. The outdoor sunlight displayed subtleties ranging from deep chestnut to black. I wanted to run my hands through it, bring it near, and breathe it in deeply. Would gray be a natural highlight? I'd welcome and revel in the gray as freely.

A strange realization hit me-- the same time Sasha had gained her freedom from her ex, I'd had a vision and written a poem about an auburn haired woman who rose to accept the challenge life brought. In this brief vision, I couldn't see the woman's face. In this instant across the table I knew it a premonition, a hidden vision of my Sasha emerging from her marriage.

I've never seen anyone I would describe as more comely than Sasha. Nature gains momentum as it approaches the ideal. As charm and beauty reach their highest state, they form an attraction more powerful than magnetism or gravity.

Watch a guy while he watches an attractive gal. The fellow's head will turn-- whole attention drawn. If other people notice him absorbing beauty, they'll pick up on the attraction. The result: a lady turns one head, then other heads. She stops traffic. What starts as one person eyeing beauty becomes an expanding experience.

Alexandra was that kind of traffic-stopping woman. She drew my heart, my mind, and my soul, and I couldn't get them back. Whenever I thought about her, I entered the "event horizon" and was drawn further in. I was a goner. STOB.

Well, on with the story. She put her sunglasses on, remember? The rest of her was still a delight to behold. I noticed her cheekbones appeared flatter than I remembered. I wondered if I'd forgotten how her cheeks fell.

We talked about work and my goal of expanding my consulting business with the government. She talked about her work and its community outreach projects.

Sitting on the veranda at lunch, I'd forgotten how beautiful she had been, and still was. I'd forgotten the central figure in my mind she had been, how all else was irrelevant. I'd blotted it out of my mind, but it came back in a torrential rush.

She was again... my Taj Mahal princess. She was definitely my heart's desire. She was the one I'd always wanted as a woman, a lover, and a wife.

Time flew.

"Twenty minutes until 2:00," She said.

We gathered our trays. As we walked in, Sasha offered, "I hope it doesn't rain. I plan on attending an outdoor event at the art museum tonight."

I eagerly thought, I wish I could go with you! Instead, I caught myself, "I hope for good weather."

"Where is your meeting and who will be there?"

I offered the name, best I could pronounce, and mentioned a room number on the fifth floor.

"Yes of course, right down the hall from my office. I know the gentleman. Very nice and knowledgeable." She said as she escorted me through the building.

The elevator door closed. Quiet and isolated-- the two of us alone. She didn't let silence set in, as the door closed asked me about the meeting.

"It won't be well attended." I said.

"Really?" She came back genuinely surprise.

"No. Most people from industry will take advantage of the conference phone linkup and just call in."

Sasha took a slight startled step away.

"I could have just called in for the meeting. The only reason I drove down was to see you. I thought you knew."

Dull ding and jolt announced our floor. We walked to the conference room.

"I'll have to stay with you if nobody else is in attendance-- security rules."

"Fine by me!"

My mind raced ahead. I hoped nobody would be there to extend our time together. Just my luck the meeting convener was no slouch. He was already in the room.

Alexa greeted him formally and introduced me as "an old college friend."

Old College Friend.

Stung. But that's what we were. Old College Friends.

Our time together was now fleeing. I became anxious to keep her as long as possible. I led her outside the conference room into the short hall where we were alone.

We exchanged business cards, then spontaneously hugged goodbye.

It was a long, deep, sensuous, hug. We lingered in the embrace, heartfelt and sincere. The tenderness educed more feelings than old college friends. We held each other, maybe ten seconds, maybe a lifetime.

Sasha walked away toward the doorway that led to the larger pedestrian hall.

She turned and held my card.

I said, "I'll call."

"OK." She turned.

I watched her gracefully walk away. The door closed. She was gone.

I looked down at her business card perched between my fingers. I brought it close to my nose and gently drew in the last of her essence.

Oh… the meeting? Right… my other reason to be there. The meeting went fine. I kept my head completely on business. I saw a number of ways to help and offered insights that were well received. Then it was time to head home.

> It was autumn
> Time for brisk nights-- and flight.
>
> Standing beside the pond at night,
> A twist of hand and neck let down her hair.
> A breeze picked up and wisps arose
> Not randomly--but as if by destiny.
>
> The moon broke free from low hanging clouds
> Enough to reflect a tinge of auburn in the air
> And illuminate a thousand dreams-- yet realized.

Drive Home – Desire Returns

June-12

"I try to walk away and I stumble" -- Macy Gray

I was flying! Whee! Hormones surge in youthful torrents. Feelings sequestered for decades engulfed me as manicured lawns and little farmhouses zipped by. Restless squirming consumed me. I fidgeted with the energy of a busload of kids heading to summer camp The wheels turned and the miles raced by, I was a kid again-- a kid head over heels in love.

Long ago when wishing was still of use…

My mind recollected all the good times we had and the awkwardness of youthful dating. My gentlemanly offer of a ride floated by and love swelled my heart two sizes too big. Sasha… again across from me… in reach to touch and hold, to love! Life doesn't get better than this! My heart knew it and twisted my body. Bobbing and swirling in amorous waves as the odometer ticked, I twisted again and again, almost standing in the seat unable to find a comfortable driving position.

Sasha had said she was divorced and had no children. Had she wanted kids? Didn't most women want kids? What a wonderful set of genes she possessed -- sad she didn't pass them on to the next generation. Worse than sad. Sasha not having kids was like the very seed of creation wasted and the impetus of evolution waylaid.

"We could have had kids!" I blurted shocking myself with brute honesty. "My kids could have been 'our' kids." I stammered.

My feelings for Sasha amplified. Lunch sprang an unexpected emotional reserve. My heart beat stronger and my body pulsed with renewed enthusiasm.

Squirming interrupted my posture again.

Soberly I check my elated state. "This woman isn't mine." I informed the windshield.

She wasn't my girlfriend, and she wasn't my wife. The whole episode shocked me; thinking of another woman as more than a friend just wasn't me. Definitely not me!

A case of SOTB warmly washed over me, a most agreeable case and I embraced it whole-heartedly!

I wondered about her divorce. Had they fought; had they grown apart? I shouted, "How in the world could any guy lucky enough to marry you let anything interfere? What fool could waste that opportunity? Idiot!"

Sasha was still alone four years after the divorce. Why?

Thoughts of love hounded me from all sides. I was ecstatic, deluged with endorphins, serotonin, or whatever the emotional brain emits when on fire. Sasha fit every shape and contour of my heart, as if it were created for her—created for her.

Confusion intermingled euphoria.

> "When the presence of the object provoking our passion is denied, our heart is in pain, our spirit fettered and our mind troubled. A great effort is needed to behave according to the dictates of society." Karma Sutra

I recalled how I'd cut off two relationships after Alexa and I parted. I cut them short because Sasha left a void no other woman could fill. I'd preferred the absent shadow of my Taj Mahal Princess over wonderful, caring, and giving women.

Entering a hard curve too fast, I redressed the task at hand and steered clear of trouble.

I'd given up on two relationships because of her… the same could occur again.

'Tis a strange curse this affliction, Sasha On The Brain. What a most joyous and devouring ailment. Only a large dose of Sasha could cure it. My body jerked as if to leap out of the speeding car headed north, away from my love.

Seat gymnastics finally made sense. My heart knew my brain steered north. Heart wanted to go south. I was driving the wrong way! Body squirmed to free itself of the seatbelt and hasten back to Sasha. Not again, not this time, my heart demanded. Don't let her get away my heart pounded. Don't put an end to these feelings! My body did everything it could to overcome my rational mind's intent of heading home.

Desire broiled. Was this really me-- a married man with three boys? Was this really me feeling in love and alive?

More alive than I'd been in two decades. "If this is me where the hell have I been?" I demanded of the steering wheel.

Arriving home that evening was… a unique moment. In all my married and bequeathed years, for sixteen years, I had never thought of another woman in any way except friendship.

Celeste and I had a heart-to-heart talk that night. I doubted our future. I wondered if we could stay together, should stay together. I did more than wonder. I said quietly, "I think we're over."

The honest and serious discussion drew Celeste to my side. We got into a discussion about past girlfriends and boyfriends. I told her how much I had felt for Sasha years ago but kept current feelings quiet.

Celeste brushed it off. "You had a long day, a long drive." She laughed. "One lunch? Relax and take a shower!"

"Maybe your right." I stood accepting her calming wisdom, "it was a long drive, both ways. Might not have a good perspective. Maybe this was just a blip, a hiccup of a mid-life crisis."

After the shower I didn't let it rest. Steeped in engineering and problem solving, I reached out for contact. I telephoned some friends, Tony and Phyllis. Tony and Phyllis lived in Chicago and had been married for seven years, a great couple from our perspective looking in. We'd grown trustworthy close, despite a half continent's separation.

Tony and Phyllis got on extensions and we had a three-way conversation. "Do you recall feeling love for someone other than your spouse? Did you love someone equal or more than the person you married… any unrequited love stories?" I asked.

Tough questions to pose to both the husband and wife at the same time! With a brief pause each identified at least one person in their past that they had very deep feelings for. Feelings that were certainly equal, or exceeded the feelings they held for their beloved spouse. But in both cases, the love was not returned to the degree of advancing the relationship.

I turned the question around, "Figure there were people that loved you more than you loved them in return? Think someone saw us as that specials someone they longed for but we blew them off? Have we been on both sides of unrequited love?"

Both Tony and Phyllis answered yes.

Yes again!

Since that eye-opening conservation, I've postulated a hypothesis. In each person's life, at least one of the relationships that got away means the world to us. My theory is that many folks harbor feelings and memories of "one that got away" and the one we really wanted to try and make it work. But we couldn't find a way to make the relationship that seemed the brightest, the best fit, with the most joyous possibilities mature into marriage.

There was something universal in my small sample group. Folks retain a little ache in their heart, a stretch mark, a smidgen of emotional scar tissue that surrounds the memory of the one that got away.

It usually isn't debilitating to most folks. It's just how the cards play.

But for the moment I was drawn like a plummeting anchor, I'd get to the bottom of this straight away. It wasn't just a matter of heart; it became a quest for knowledge.

> "I believe that fate has brought us here
> And we should be together
> But we're not
> I play it off but I'm dreamin' of you

I'll keep it cool but I'm fiendin.

I try and say goodbye and I choke
I try to walk away and I stumble
Though, I try to hide it, it's clear
My world crumbles when you are not near."
     -- Macy Gray

Measuring Up

"Ain't I rough enough? Ain't I tough enough?" -- The Rolling Stones

I don't know where I fell short of Sasha's expectations. There must have been something that kept me back in the orchestra of those playing for Sasha's heart, out of the precious First Chair.

Ladies, what are you looking for in a man? Come on, girls! Spill the beans! This is one Bean who needs to know.

In my head, I figure there are many categories in which a man might have to measure against to win a cherished share of a lady's heart. Sasha must have had her own image of the ideal mate. Among these might be:

- ✓ The Alpha Male --Aggressive, domineering, competitive
- ✓ The Hunk Factor -- Muscular thoroughbred
- ✓ Rich - Deep pockets, or a profession that would support a wealthy lifestyle
- ✓ Sensitive, Healing, Gentle - Kind man with a big heart
- ✓ Athletic – Fit and excels at the physical challenge life is likely to throw at him
- ✓ Brave - Hero type, unafraid of the trials and tribulations
- ✓ Smart - Brainy and likely to get a good paying job
- ✓ Fun - Funny and fun, able to share a good time
- ✓ A Worthy Chase - Fulfill the desire for mystery and adventure in finding "Mr. Right"

In my head, here is how I stacked up to this wish list:

ALPHA MALE... Aggressive and domineering? Nope, not me. She would have been right to reject me on that count.

Lot of guys fill that bill. We've all met guys hell-bent on subjugating the world, and the girls they meet. To the alpha male, so full of himself he ignores the will of others, the end justified the means-- and the end is domination.

The Alpha Male takes without asking. He forces and redefines the future according to his whim. The Alpha Male ignores the desires of his mates and exerts dominance. A sobering thought for women attracted to the dominant male; you are three times more likely to acquire a sexually transmitted disease from a demanding violent prone partner.

Ladies, never mistake self-control for a lack of interest! Just because a guy contains his lower instincts, it doesn't mean he isn't virile. Just because a guy doesn't act like he is on fire doesn't mean he can't torch the sheets when given a green light!

"Virtue is of two kinds, inclination towards certain actions and detachment from others." Kama Sutra

I wanted a relationship of equals. Humanity isn't about continuing the dominance of women, but rather unfolding a new reality based on equality. That reality has to start in the heart, between hearts, and grow in relationships. If she were looking for the Alpha Male—count me out.

HUNK, STUD? Never has a sober woman mistaken me for a hunk.

When I think of a stud, I think of a guy 6'-4" or so, full of bulging muscle. As a high school freshman I was the tiniest kid on the football team. Though I was in excellent shape, I didn't fill out my frame until the end of college.

Strong and wiry. One day my family was on vacation at a resort catering to athletic tourists. There was an impressive rock-climbing wall forty feet high. On the face of the wall were small protrusions, toe and handholds, to mimic the climbing face of a cliff.

The wall had four grades of difficulty. The climbing track furthest to the left had hand and toe grabs spaced close together, offering the easiest path up. At the top, a bell hung for the successful climber to announce triumph.

The hardest path was on the right. This climb included an overhang jutting out six feet off the face of the wall. The climber would have to work up to the precipice and lunge away from the wall to grab the bottom of the protrusion. Once suspended away from the wall, strong fingers scale the last few feet to ring the bell.

I watched the first day, few climbers managed to ring a bell on the easiest path. None made it more than two thirds up on the middle paths. None dared the overhang.

I asked my oldest boy, "What do you think?"

Neither had climbed a rock wall before, but we eagerly got the attendants attention. My son tried first and did very well, considering his small size hampered his reach on a course designed for adults. He didn't make it all the way up the easiest climb but we encouraged him and made him feel good for trying.

My turn. I zipped up the easiest face like it was nothing and rang the bell faster than smoke rises. No sweat. The resort worker holding the safety line congratulated "Awesome dude! Don't waste your time on the next paths," he said looking at the beginning of a line at the attraction. "Why don't you try the hardest section?"

I scaled down and reattached the safety line on the hard climb. No fear. I scaled like a scalded monkey and reached the outcropping that jutted out, hung from my fingers as I slowly worked my way until I was flush with the last face. Then I power lifted up and rang the bell. Ding!

After I came down I told the attendant, "Easier than it looks! Bet a lot of people try and succeed at the hardest climb?"

He shook his head no. The young resort worker holding the belay rope was impressed, "Easy? You made it look easy!"

"Get to climb much?" I enquired.

"I get here early lots and climb before work begins. But I've never completed the hard climb. You missed your calling, man. You should have been a US Ranger!"

I tried the climb two or three more times before we ended our vacation. Every time the event was the same-- no challenge.

But a hunk? An overly muscular body? Not that it showed.

RICH? Millionaire or millionaire to be?

While dating Sasha I was enrolled in engineering, a curriculum offering a chance at steady employment with income slightly above national average. The only engineers that get out of the profession get rich. If she wanted rich, hunt elsewhere.

Wow! I'm 0 for 3! But let's plod on and see where this goes for the Bean.

SENSITIVE? Attentive to her needs? Hey! Here is one I pass muster. That would be 1 out of 4, for those keeping score. Hope Sasha saw this side of me.

I empathize with people. And generally, I can deduce their feelings in a way that helps them get in better touch with themselves and the world around them. Surely she couldn't miss that, right?

COMPETITIVE & ATHLETIC? Display capability on the fields of play? Despite my lack of outward bulk, I was a very good athlete ingrained with a competitive streak. Sasha must have seen I was in shape. OK, I'm giving myself at point here. That's 2 out of 5. Batting 400!

As a kid I played basketball, football, and baseball regularly, and I played to win. Any sport I tried, I competed intensely. But I had been small as a kid and realized I didn't have a future competing as a professional athlete so my competitive attitude evolved. I saw sports as healthy, joyous exercise. As I grew up sports were for joy, exercise and recreation.

Epitomizing my new low-key altruistic approach to sports, I enrolled in soccer for PE at State. Why soccer? Did I mention it was co-ed?

Like most Americans in my generation, I hadn't tried soccer before but the co-ed part feature invited. The possibilities seemed infinitely more interesting than the highly completive, male only, sports I'd been weaned on.

Last class of the semester was the "tournament." The class was divided into two teams, and the winning team would be "crowned" which, of course, carried no significance except whatever gloating might occur on the walk between the soccer field and the field house where showers awaited. Showers, in case you were wondering, were not co-ed.

Both teams played hard. I was around midfield when our defense cleared a ball high and long toward our opponent's goal. I outraced the defender nearest me and headed the ball toward the goal. My header surprised the next defender and I blew past and skillfully gathered the ball. Speed and dribbling agility allowed me to get past the final defender and then it was just goalkeeper left to beat. I don't miss that kind of opportunity. GOAL! Later in the game, I scored another of our team's goals.

As the game ended, the score was tied 3-3, and we went into a penalty kick situation. My team asked me to play keeper and also to take one of the five shots we were awarded.

Insisting it was a team game, I offered to do one or the other. I'd distinguished myself as goal keeper during the season, so that was the quick team consensus.

It was still tied after four kicks. One last kick for each team and my teammates implored me to take our final shot, but I glanced at the scheduled shooter and gave him a reassuring smile. His missed his attempt wide. The other team kicked, I made a diving save and the game ended in a tie.

What a parade we put on that afternoon! Everyone from both teams felt like champs. When you're in college you feel all grown up, but in reality you're just a kid. The kid in each of us showed that day.

BRAVE?... Caring enough to get involved at my own expense? What about brave? Another category I did well. Another point for the Bean!

I've got a good balance between risk taking and self-preservation. For starters, I was the youngest member of the 82nd Airborne Sport Parachute Team.

My dad's last station of duty before he retired was Fort Bragg, NC. Bragg is home of the 82nd Division and other significant Regular Army and Special Forces units. On Post there were three sport parachute teams for soldiers to sharpen their skills. The clubs also provided girlfriends, spouses of either sex, and in my case, an adventurous dependent the chance to experience the thrill of skydiving.

It was spring. Dad lamented, "I'm sorry we arrived on post too late to sign up for football. Going to go out for baseball?"

We both knew we'd likely be moving before the end of baseball season. Why start?

"I know sports means a lot to you, and staying busy is good…"

"I saw a flier at the PX about a sport parachute club."

Dad was delighted. "Do it! I'll let you borrow the car."

Cool. Adventure and the car! Dad had an Oldsmobile Cutlass with a 350 cc four barrel. It was a rocking car with tight suspension and a top-flight stereo. Yeah, I drive the car pop!

I signed up--club's first high school member.

There were a dozen students, some airborne qualified. Airborne guys joined to increase their jump experience and get into free fall. The majority of regular army jumps are static line, which means a special rope attaches between the jumper and aircraft. This yanks the harness in a way that the parachute automatically opens. The club offers free-fall using a ripcord rather than the military static line. The freefalling skydiver experiences a longer plummet before opening his parachute.

For novices who had not yet jumped, ten static line jumps were required before attempting freefall. This safety precaution, probationary period, made newbies show competence and lack of panic.

Three students didn't have any jump time. Novices included yours truly and two women, girlfriends or spouses of class members.

Five days of ground school taught the basics. The school was conducted in the evenings and it went well. We had no accidents. All students caught on quickly.

The first day to jump came early Saturday. We packed up and headed for the landing zone where two Hueys buzzed the air like queen bees hunting a new hive. These are the Vietnam era workhorse helicopters, also known as UH-1H's. Two birds ran that day, doubling the airlift capacity and speeding things up nicely.

The club had a good thing going. We hitched rides for nearly free, actual compensation was a case of beer for the pilots. The pilots were National Guard or Army Reserve. They flew on the government's dime maintaining hours to stay flight qualified. While these guys alternately practiced landings and punching holes in the sky to maintain their flight status we rode as airborne vagabonds.

I got assigned to the second chopper run. The first run took only experienced jumpers. Our Jumpmaster, the guy in charge of us and our jump, watched the first group's descent reading the wind to help keep the novices in his stick safe.

Each jumper packs his or her own main chute in sport parachuting. That was a big part of the ground school training. But during practice packing, we never went through the last stage of attaching the static line.

Before I put my parachute on my back I looked at the bright yellow chord. It was bundled tight with two small rubber bands and dangled awkwardly a couple of feet. The loose arrangement seemed disorderly considering everything else was taunt and secure.

Where to stow the loose static line? I didn't want the line getting stepped on or caught as I boarded the helicopter, so I tucked it under one of the bungee cords that secured the parachute to the harness strapping.

As we got prepared for our flight, one of the experienced jumpers, a sergeant, helped me get my harness and parachute on. For a lightweight kid, the parachute added a substantial increase in total mass. Damn thing was heavy! I leaned forward to maintain balance and kept my legs spread to maintain stability.

The sergeant worked on the leg straps, "Are the family jewels out of the way?"

"Excuse me?"

Like everyone else, I was wearing a jumpsuit over my jeans. This created a cluttered situation at the groin. The sergeant needed to ratchet the parachute's thick harness leg straps to secure the chute, and he was being careful not to yank the strap while my testicles were in the way. It took another second to figure out his colorful question. I smiled and confirmed he was clear to tighten the leg straps.

Once a parachute was secured on each jumper's back, the Jumpmaster initiated the last ground check. The Jumpmaster pulled his boot through the sandy Carolina soil and made an outline of the floor plan of our ride. A Huey has a big engine compartment occupying the center back passenger area. The open area around the engine area forms a U shape. The pilot and copilot's seats are at the bottom of this U. The purpose of the sketch in the sand and final preflight check was to make sure we knew where we'd ride on the chopper. The Jumpmaster assigned everyone a position inside the aircraft.

"Three inside the right door, three on the left, the rest in the center.

"Whitlash, you've got the back position on the right door. You'll be first out."

Cool, baby!

"Stand up! Get in your position!" Commanded the Jumpmaster.

We moved like top heavy cranes ready to fall over into our assigned positions forming up in the U shape he'd described. The Jumpmaster did a final inspection of each jumber. Important job. To his credit, our Jumpmaster was very thorough.

He worked around the whole group standing in the "U" before getting to me. His voice bellowed out in a detached voice as he pulled and pushed my gear like a village crier reporting a death to one and all, "TOTAL MALFUNCTION FAILURE!"

The sound of his voice trailed off. The echo returned muffled as it made its way back from the tree line a good distance away. "Total Malfunction Failure" he repeated in a quiet, exasperated voice.

I knew what this meant. Everybody knew what this meant. Heck, I bet folks that haven't had ground school know what this means!

A total malfunction meant the chute, *my* parachute, would not open. Zero chance of success. Total chance of failure. No chute to slow me down my descent. The only thing I would have to keep me from becoming an unsightly stain on the ground would be my reserve chute.

A competent person packed reserve chutes. This they told us in ground school. The Army allowed only certified master riggers to pack reserves. And the master riggers have to jump with randomly assigned reserves, so they do a good job and made sure their co-workers stay on the ball.

And if I panicked and didn't pull my reserve chute what would happen then? There was an emergency circuit made up of an altimeter with a pressure switch and a small blast cap. In theory, if a jumper descended below 1000 feet at a velocity that suggested he was in peril, the altimeter and pressure switch would send an electrical signal to the blast cap. The detonation of the blast cap would blow out the retaining ring holding the reserve shut. The reserve, in theory and design, would billow out and give me one more chance to cheat the devil.

Landing's rough if neither chute opened or they tangle providing minimal drag. OK, let's be honest. The landing would be brutal. The end of an unchecked freefall is forceful enough to cause the unfortunate skydiver a noticeable rebounding bounce. Even in sand. Probably three bounces off asphalt. In such cases, the onlookers are the only ones that do the feeling.

Well, I am a trusting guy. But I didn't plan on using my reserve that day. I didn't want to rely on the master rigger. I didn't want to rely on the safety system either.

What had I done that got the Jumpmaster riled? He spun me around so the other jumpers could learn. His quick maneuver nearly cost me my balance. I regained posture with my parachute facing the rest of the jump team still standing in their helicopter loading positions.

When I'd tucked the end of my static line, I'd threaded it beneath a bungee cord. This held it out of harm's way. But the bungee cord would have prevented the static line from transferring enough force to the thin twine that held the chute closed. The twine would have stayed intact. The static line would have remained attached to my parachute and not broken free. And I would have dangled at the end of the line hung precariously close to the chopper's rear propeller.

Ah, now that *was* something that was mentioned in ground school. My trainers had warned me about tail propellers. Someone mentioned the helmets we wore and the rear propeller in the same sentence. I'd naively asked, "Would the propeller ding my helmet?"

The instructor said drily, "It would put one heck of a dent in your helmet." No one said anything. The quiet was homage as they reflected a grizzly first-hand experience.

A helicopter's tail rotor is a blade about four or five feet long. The blade spins so fast you cannot see it. Think blender. But instead of a three-inch blade at the bottom of your Cousinart, imagine a five-foot blender. Dent my helmet? That rotor would spit me down, back, up, and forward all in the same millisecond. Any morsel of me that survived the first chop and stayed around the rotor would, for good measure, be pureed. If I had gotten caught in that propeller, the larger pieces of my former self would have landed within a mile or two. But most of little old me would have become a fine mist, a mist that would have lazily trailed the helicopter before settling. A mist caught in turbulent winds, remnants and memories of me would have swirled and moved about on the currents set about by the blade that did me in.

Would it leave a dent? From man to mist in a moment. The helmet offered protection, but only from bumps in and around the passenger compartment, not dancing with the tail rotor.

Well, no worries. The thought of a total malfunction didn't faze me at all. Just fix it, let's roll.

The Jumpmaster straightened out my static line laying the wadded section on top of my parachute with a thump. Done deal. Now we waited for our bird.

Winds at ground level were 12-15 miles an hour. Tops for novices. We were fortunate the weather was accommodating. Any higher wind speed would delay or scrub the jump. In a few minutes the wind would soon introduce itself in a way I had never experienced.

Ever ride on a helicopter? Kind of loud. OK, more than kind of loud. Think *deafening*! In a Huey, passengers sit beside the aluminum cover that separates the engine from the payload area. You can talk and hear when the bird is idling on the ground. But when it rotates up to flight speed, well… you can still talk.

Once the chopper rises off the ground and starts moving through the air the wind noise adds to the racket. From that point on, you can't hear someone unless they shout directly at you from just three feet away. And in that case, you can understand them only if you look intensely at their face and read lips!

Another memorable thing about riding in a helicopter is the seating accommodations. There aren't any. The only blokes who actually ride in seats are the pilot and copilot. Jumpers kneel in the payload area squatting on harsh aluminum floor plates. The metal plates are great for loading and unloading cargo but bare metal floors are rough on knees, especially when you're weighted down with a chute.

The flight up was fantastic. As our purpose was to jump, doors remained open. We had an unrestricted view of the ground and sky and an introduction to wind like never before. The spring air was clear with blue skies and scattered clouds. Sky was breathtaking, especially once you become an intimate part of it riding in a helicopter sans doors.

Despite how beautiful the sky, the ground absorbed my attention from the ascending platform. Looking immediately down and to my right was an inch of aluminum floor, then the sharp edge of the door support slot, and a few feet below that the tubular landing skid. Below that nothing but air separated us from the ground dropping steadily away. Comforting Mother Earth never seemed quite so remote.

The large expanse of open area constituting the drop zone stretched welcomingly, offering a large cleared are for a safe landing. The drop zone's soil was Carolina's sandy loam that dates back to when this area was submerged by ocean some odd million years ago. Clumps and hearty stands of blonde-brown grass still in winter's slumber held tight to the sand.

A deep green pine canopy covered ground that wasn't cleared. Treetops looked like tufts of sap green cotton balls. From our increasing elevation, the pine needles blurred into a soft envelop hiding supporting limbs.

Air temperature immediately dropped with speed and altitude. For all the noise and cooler temperatures, no crosswind cut through the chopper, but you could hear and feel the effect of the cold air. My jumpsuit fluttered on my right shoulder intermittently clinging to my arm and then flagging wildly as it responded to air rushing by the open door.

Each jumper was in his own little world, packed like sardines, but alone because of the deafening noise.

Resting there on my knees and toes, I enjoyed the ride, but it must not have shown. I looked toward the center of the chopper. The Jumpmaster made eye contact. He slowly raised the tips of his two index fingers to either side of this mouth. When he was sure I was following, he raised his fingers up a fraction of an inch and smiled. *"Smile!"* he was pantomiming. I smiled back. Yeah, this was fun. It doesn't get any better than being with a group of enthusiastic die-hards doing what they love to do. And it doesn't get any better than experiencing a beautiful spring day doing something awesome for the first time. It *was* great!

Glancing to my right, I could clearly see the jump zone and our vehicles parked in neat rows. A large white circle painted on the ground displayed our landing target. It was big circle, but you had to know where to look to see it. Once your eyes picked out the thin white line, it became an obvious beacon.

Not far from the target, the road we drove to get to the drop zone looked like a grey line. A few cars scurried along the paved two-lanes oblivious to overhead observers.

Looking to the sky, the open parachutes of the earlier flight were in the air, some at our altitude and some below. Our helicopter was a safe distance away so we didn't cause any turbulence or disrupt their canopies. Most of the jumpers used the US Army issued T-10 parachutes; a few die-hards used their own personal "squares." These squares displayed vibrant colors, adding a flying circus feel to the scene contrasting sharply from the otherwise olive drab exercise.

While staring at the horizon, the earth's greens became hazy blues farther left and right. Sky and land merged. It seemed like a hint of the earth's curvature could be seen, but I guessed that was an optical illusion.

We made our way to our jump height of 3,300 feet. The Jumpmaster took out two confectionery paper streamers and tossed them out the left door. He pitched one purple and one red streamer. The pilot reduced our forward speed to nil and rotated the bird to give us a better view of the falling streamers. As they unrolled, each streamer formed a colorful vertical line lazily dropping to earth. The streamers shimmered twisting in corkscrew fashion as they fell.

The bright purple and red colors stood out against the khaki sand and dormant grass below. Man that was beautiful. The streamers were about as dissimilar in their environment as a bunch of human beings clad in green jumpsuits and perched in a helicopter -- ready, willing, and about to jump from our safe haven and join them.

The Jumpmaster determined wind direction and vectored the pilot. Despite the noise that challenged communication, the pilot, co-pilot, and Jumpmaster used radio headsets. They could talk and hear above the din.

The pilot tilted the main rotor so it dug into the air and the bird started running forward. We were completing the ride part of this adventure. In a minute, returning on the desired line set by the Jumpmaster it would be time to get some wings.

There are three commands that precede a parachute jump. "Jump Run", "Get Ready" and the final "Go." "Jump Run" informs jumpers they're on their final approach. As novices, we'd exit the bird singularly, all on static line. I steeled myself to be first out and set a good example.

I watched the Jumpmaster intently and *"Jump Run!"* rang out. Excitement went up a notch and anticipation ran rampant.

In a minute the second command was issued. *"Get Ready!"* That was my queue. "Get Ready" was the command for jumpers to prepare to exit the craft. As first jumper, "Get Ready" was my command to stand up in a low crouch. I shifted weight and groaned quietly. Straightening legs was work after the long stint kneeling. I had to be careful not to tilt to the right while gaining my feet otherwise there would be a sudden and unplanned exit!

I leaned forward on my buddy in front of me trying not to send *both* of us out as I rose. I was glad I was young. Someone in their thirties or forties would have a tough time with this part of the jump because the knees and other muscles would sorely regret the exposure to the floor and extended crouch.

I stood hunched in a three-quarter stance. The height of the cabin didn't allow a fully upright position. I looked at my Jumpmaster. Raising my right hand, I secured the steel slide rail on the outside of the airframe that the door runs on. My legs were slightly spread so I could make a little jump to the right when the time came.

Another important ground school lesson reasserted itself. "When you jump, don't forget to let go of the rail. Otherwise you might leave your fingers behind!"

Glad my instructors mentioned that.

In time of trial or duress, understatement is a fantastic way to bring a laugh and release tension. It does more than that. It unites. It binds the participants by acknowledging the risk they share. It binds by reminding we need one another. We need each other to watch and take care of each other. It binds by confirming we are all survivors in the challenges we face. Understatement and humor buttress confidence. There may be a chance for peril, but we will be fine. Or maybe not. Either way it will make a good story on the 11 o'clock news. Men who used understatement and knew the bonding effect and comic relief of this style of communication surrounded me. I felt right at home.

I stood perched in a stable position beside the open doorway behind my crouched compatriots. I locked my eyes on the Jumpmaster's lips.

The command came "*Go!*"

The "Go" signal is shouted and reinforced by a hand signal, a thumb up. Receiving that signal triggered a higher state of alertness and mental activity. In that split-second I realized what I was about to do.

It hadn't hit me. I had gone through the week of ground school without imagining what jumping would be like. I signed up because it was available, convenient, a challenge, and seemed like fun. I didn't have a passion for this sport like the guys around me. These guys seemed to live for the thrill. But there I was, ready to jump. But all the while I never once pondered the moment I'd face.

Later, after we landed, the Jumpmaster described, "After I gave the 'Go' command your pupils dilated to the size of saucers! You hesitated a split-second, and then you just hopped out."

That split second of dilated thought stretched longer in my head. Mind ran at hyper speed. But I didn't hesitate more than a second. I just did it. Hop!

What a rush!

Zero gravity is a trip. I felt the acceleration. At first the feeling is total suspension and no movement, then the bottom drops out. In my heightened mental condition I felt a primal rush. I instinctively kicked backward like there should be something there behind me and below me. But only open sky greeted my foot's lunge.

Instantly, I connected that primal rush to being born. Some early memory of helplessly sliding just appeared in my mind and it was like being born again, whisked from a safe crouched environment into the unknown. Except this time, my umbilical cord wasn't connected from navel to mother, but to a chopper flying suspended in the air beside me.

I assumed the spread-eagle position as taught. All the rush and recollection of being born happened within the first 10-15 feet of my fall. That's about two seconds.

Then I heard a faint sound and felt the gentlest tug above me. Noise faded instantly. The wind stilled, a hollow whistle ran through the risers above me. I looked up and there, unfolding very quickly, was my green T-10 nylon lifeline. The chute deployed magnificently.

I let out a joyous yelp! The chopper was long gone. No more helicopter sounds, no more rushing wind noise. All was quiet and serene. I reached up and found my control risers and worked them left and then right to get a feeling for directional control.

The view was spectacular. I could see two open parachutes far below, cradling jumpers who had made the earlier jump. The wide open azure sky was framed by my risers right and left, the edge of the open chute above, and the earth's horizon in front. Awesome. I looked down for the large circle denoting the drop target.

But I wasn't interested in landing just yet. During the first minute of my descent, I enjoyed the ride. I drifted unaware of which way the wind was blowing and worked my risers just for effect. A perfectly placed landing on the bull's eye wasn't my intention. My goal was the large flat area anywhere within the outermost circle. Soon, I realized even that too was an ambitious goal. I didn't need experience to tell coming close to the target was impossible. I was drifting away from the drop zone, getting further downwind with every passing moment. There was no way I could turn and run into the wind. I was downrange and coasting even farther.

The T-10 parachute is designed to carry a fully loaded 170-pound combat infantryman carrying sixty additional pounds of gear-- into harm's way. And it will deliver this soldier in a manner that ensures he lands at a speed no greater than if he jumped unrestrained from a height of 18 feet. Eighteen feet is a long way to jump and land, but we were taught in ground school how to roll to distribute the landing impact.

The problem was, I didn't weigh 170 pounds, and I didn't have sixty pounds of gear. And by being the first to jump out of the helicopter, I was closest to one end of the drop zone. Given the wind direction that was a big problem. I drifted. And drifted. At perhaps 2,000 feet above the ground, it was obvious I would not be landing in the cleared drop zone that day. But where? I began looking for hazards that might make this less than a Kodak moment.

The pine trees so benign from high above no longer looked cozy or inviting. I could see not-so-welcoming branches. Trees and descending skydivers are natural enemies.

A substantial part of our ground-school training had included landing technique, beginning with jumping off two-foot-high platforms and working our way higher. The normal landing calls for legs together at the knees and ankles, with knees slightly bent to absorb impact. Right before landing the jumper releases the risers to minimize turning and looks straight at the horizon. Then, when boots touch the ground, the skydiver rolls to distribute the shock across the body.

Landing in trees was quite different. In that eventuality, we were supposed to cross our legs to keep them together and avoid being painfully violated by a molesting branch. The Jumpmaster said a crossed position might keep a vertical branch from being shoved up my ass. As the upward reach of pines became more obvious, I searched for options.

I was down to perhaps 200 feet when the road appeared. Any driver that might come along wouldn't see me descending. Scrub forest owned this side of the road. Power lines ran parallel to far side of the road.

I had four choices. Land on the road and risk becoming a hood ornament. Hit the trees either side of the road and take my chances of becoming a eunuch. Find the power line... a very bad idea. The fourth, and far more preferable, option was to use what control I had in the last few moments and find a clearing.

Miraculously, I saw one! The trees in that spot were saplings, just getting started in their push towards the sun, and there was room enough between them to squeeze in. I angled over, and then it was time to release the risers, get my legs and boots right, and stare at the horizon.

I touched down in the little clearing, missing power lines by enough the deflating canopy didn't contact them. My landing and roll worked, to the credit of my instructors. I gathered my parachute and my first jump was in the books.

I started hoofing it back through the sparse underbrush toward the drop zone.

My wayward decent drifting toward South Carolina was noticed by alert ground crew and family. The ground team scrambled a few volunteers in a large white van to find me. My older brother and sister offered to join them but were denied. Only trained ground crew would be first at the scene. A road, tree, or power line might leave me in a shape family should not see.

I made it a hundred yards on foot before the van arrived bounding roughly through the underbrush. When we got back to the drop zone, parents, family, and my newfound jumping buddies congratulated. The ground crew chief piped, "You looked like a green puff of cotton floating away, away, away!"

We all laughed.

The Jumpmaster joined us and apologized profusely. "I owe you a case of beer for the release spot."

"Thanks but I'm not old enough to drink! Don't worry about it."

He'd learned something about wind, and I had a most excellent adventure -- even though I missed the target by about a mile.

On the ground, I was informed one of my classmates, a woman student without previous jump experience, didn't carry through with her jump. She was slated as the number two jumper in our stick, first out on the left. But she froze and didn't take the bunny hop into thin air. No wings for her.

Sport parachute jumping is strictly a volunteer sport. Regular Army jumps are different. There is a sergeant with a size 11-jump boot parked near the door on US Army airborne training jumps, and part of his job is to help reluctant sparrows find the courage to leave the nest.

But in sport parachuting, it's all up to the jumper. In the case of the lady who froze rode the bird back down accompanied by the Jumpmaster. She may have jumped later that day or another day, I don't know. If she didn't she missed a great experience.

Brave enough? Hey, I'm scoring on this topic! Maybe I can make up points!

Another event proved my valor before I met Sasha. It happened on an autumn Saturday afternoon my freshman year and it included a taste of football.

North Carolina State plays its home games at Carter Finley Stadium, close to I-40, a few miles west of campus. At State, freshmen were not allowed to have cars unless they lived off campus. I lived in a dorm, so the student shuttle bus would have to do. Unfortunately, I forgot to sign me and my buddies up for the bus.

No problem. Clay, Gary and I had our tickets to the game, and as three young men, we decided to walk.

The trek of several miles to the game was fun, and so was the game. Halfway through the third quarter, the return walk pressed on us and we opted to leave early. We had almost reached the entrance to campus when Clay said, "Hey, I want to stop for some french fries."

"You're kidding, right?"

Gary and I searched our pockets and had only one dime between us. Flat broke, was synonymous with college student. We shrugged our shoulders and ducked into an Arby's fast food restaurant to sit with Clay and watch him eat. Clay ate leisurely, oddly insisting on finishing his fries there rather than taking them with us. Gary and I were amused by his seemingly selfish act, but we were tired from the walk and appreciated the break.

We left the restaurant and walked on the sidewalk past the adjacent business, an automotive service station. The station had two service bays enclosed by clear-glass rolling doors. A man stood inside the closed garage behind the trunk of a car. Upon seeing us he waved vigorously. It wasn't a one hand wave, but a clownish two hand gesture spread widely over his head. We waved back and smiled.

About three steps later the frantic gesture sank in, Gary voiced a concern, "Hey, maybe that guy needs help!"

Gary's words drove home the realization-- the wave was the ubiquitous emergency signal.

We turned. The man was no longer visible. We rushed across the adjoining concrete apron to the station. Reaching the outside of the closed roll-up door, we saw him passed out prone on the floor.

The service bay door seemed locked. I stood up and gave a little push against Gary creating space between us. I reared back, leaned slightly to my left, cocked my right leg, and gave a sidekick with my right foot that would have made Chuck Norris proud against the lower pane. The glass gave way with a crash and created a large enough opening for me to squeeze through.

The air was filled with car exhaust fumes. Sure enough, the unconscious fellow lay stone still behind an idling car asphyxiated from carbon dioxide and carbon monoxide. I stepped over the man and shouted to him. No response.

He was a big fellow, probably about 240 pounds well over six feet, sprawled lifeless on the concrete floor. I grabbed him and spun him on the floor so his feet were under the rear axle of the car and his head near the door. Meanwhile, Gary and Clay assumed the dangerous work of clearing the shards of glass out of the window opening with their bare hands.

I faced the door and straddled the guy, putting my hands under his armpits and heaved. Just as I moved his head into the opening, the last of the glass shards came free.

"Watch it! You just about cut his head off!" Clay said franticly.

"No time to wait. If we don't get this guy into fresh air quickly he'll die."

Take note, all you hunk-loving gals, there was something to be said for being a little under-sized. I fit through the opening, but the huskier victim would not. His shoulders wouldn't clear the windowpane. I held him there with his head projecting through the opening as mind raced and assessed options. He definitely wasn't going to fit.

I knew the man was in trouble. More than that, I knew I was in trouble, for I had been in there too long. Carbon monoxide is a silent killer. A little voice-- the spirit of a coalmine canary-- chirped inside my head telling me that if we didn't get out soon, the big man wouldn't be the only one on the floor.

Carefully, I pulled his head back into the garage and laid him back down on the cool cement floor. I turned my attention to the door. Where was the lock? How did the door go up? Why hadn't he opened the door? I looked up to see if there was some kind of electric opening mechanism, but saw nothing. Time was running out. I sensed that if we didn't get out real soon we wouldn't get out.

After a moment of calming silence bordering on prayer, I grabbed the base of the door and yanked up with the strength of desperation. The sound of rolling cams in their slots echoed through the garage. Freed, the door rolled up with ease.

I reduced my effort and the door continued to slide up out of the way. We lifted the guy out and carried him into the apron-- one of us on his legs, one supporting his head, one carrying his chest—instinctively hauling him far enough away to ensure he was in fresh air. The unconscious man wore a medical alert bracelet but in our hurried state its symbolism was lost and undecipherable.

The gas station attendant hadn't moved or made a sound since his frantic hand signal. I stood, repositioned myself, and straddled his torso. Small groups of onlookers gathered on the sidewalk between the apron and the street. A man at the left front corner of the service apron talked on a pay phone as he watched the drama.

I leaned down over our departing, or departed, mechanic and got in his face. Like a drill sergeant I was nose-to-nose, about six inches apart. I shouted at him in a gruff voice, "Don't die on me!" The intensity of my command was complete and moved my soul. No response.

Then I got closer, noses touching "Nobody dies on me!" I said intimately. My skin crawled with spiritual determination.

That didn't get a response, so I moved from my straddled position to beside his head -- the ideal position to give him CPR. I looked at his pale face, eyes closed, gray-white lips inches away.

Up to that point in my life, I'd never trained on mouth-to-mouth resuscitation. I'd heard of it, might have seen it in a movie or TV episode, but I hadn't been in a position to use it. As kids we used to joke CPR would be a great way to sneak a kiss out of a female lifeguard, but I hadn't used it for trickery or to save a life.

And to be honest, kissing was a sought-after activity in which I didn't have much experience. Darn rare, highlighted by that one embarrassing time when my mom had a lady friend over.

My mom had invited a thirty something divorcee over to the house as a guest. I was walking through the house when the lady arrived at the front door. Mom introduced us in the tight little entry foyer, and I tried to shake hands, proper etiquette. Yet a lack of space in the foyer, a lack of decorum, or because of a teenage lack of coordination -- I had a most unfortunate social faux pas. Within the same tight space, and for her own reasons, our newly arrived guest simultaneously leaned forward too. Instead of shaking hands we kissed on the lips.

Zing! Hello! It surprised everyone. *Whoops*!

Mom took a startled step back. Guess we all did. Neither the guest nor I knew exactly what to do.

But she knew we were a *friendly* family!

Then we shook and I excused myself and assumed as fast as a walk would take me. Man, how did that happen? "I'm glad my Mom's friend was female." I said to myself as I walked down the hall. Nice lipstick. I can still remember how red those lips looked, although the kiss was far too rushed to enjoy.

So here and now, I knelt on the pavement of a Chevron service station. A different face, a more needy face, stared back. A face with lips paled with death quite unlike those I'd met in the foyer a year before. My very first *planned* kiss as a college student would be with the dead or dying.

I bent down and puckered up. I closed his nose and lifted his neck. With lips within millimeters he gasped. Quiet at first, but the spark of life was within him. Our unconscious man breathed.

Gary and Clay were reassured by his breath and quickly adjusted him on the service apron, treating him as among the living, and comforted him as he came to. I stood up and glanced toward the street. The man on the phone was still talking. A few onlookers kept silent but attentive vigil from a safe distance.

Relieved that the service bay wouldn't be the attendant's or my sarcophagus, I made my way to the idling car and turned off the ignition. The bay was neat and orderly. I went into the small adjacent front office. The cash register was wide open and the drawer full. Stacked neatly were ones, fives, tens, and twenties. Coins too.

This isn't a situation you see often. Washington, Lincoln, Hamilton and Jackson rested in their stalls, staring mutely at the ceiling. Too impoverished to buy french fries, the thought never entered my mind to help myself. I thought of closing the drawer but opted to turn and leave the office as I found it. Hawaii-Five-O and Colombo had instilled enough knowledge not to disturb the scene.

I came back outside and joined Clay and Gary beside the guy. He was doing better, according to his color and sitting posture.

Clay said, "I was getting worried. You were in there a long time."

I didn't respond. Young men are invincible. Don't remind them otherwise.

A policeman had arrived and had parked his cruiser, summoned by the guy on the phone. The two walked towards us.

"I saw the whole thing and told him everything," the man who'd called in the report stammered.

The caller was agitated, like the cop would misunderstand the situation. It never dawned on me that a man sprawled on the ground and the cash drawer open might have painted us as robbers.

The cop gave each of us two-handed burly grasps as he shook our hands enthusiastically, "You men should get a commendation! Many other people would have walked by."

I shook my head and said casually but sincerely, "Not on my watch."

The policeman almost wept at that and shook my hand again between his big paws pumping wildly.

As we left the scene, we felt really good about ourselves. Hell, we were ecstatic! What a team! If I had been more organized, we would have ridden on the bus and missed the moment. If Clay hadn't been hungry and insisted on stopping, we wouldn't have been in the right place at the right time to see the mechanic's mute plea for help. If Gary hadn't commented that the guy might need help, we might have just thought it a weird prank. If I hadn't gone in and gotten the guy, he would have surely died.

As we recounted how it all fit together, there was the shadow of a larger, more all-knowing and benevolent hand at work. We glimpsed it, but we didn't see it clearly.

We didn't even see the smaller shadow cast at our feet as we walked forward -- the shadow of a bird perched on a wire above the sidewalk. As we walked underneath, the bird pooped on Clay's shoulder, putting us messily back in our place. We laughed hysterically as tension dissipated by this humbling conclusion.

And that was pretty much the end of that story. We never got a call from the police department, despite the officer's comment about a commendation.

Brave enough? Since then there have been other incidents when I've thrown self-preservation to the wind to help others. I was the first on the scene risking life and limb for a stranger who'd driven a hazardous waste truck into a ditch. Another time I arrived just after a convenience store had been robbed and went after the robber on foot. Each of these might have shown a would-be girlfriend that I had enough bravery to measure up.

So I *should* have passed the bravery test. If Sasha cared to find out. If bravery was one of her criteria.

SMART ENOUGH? "Smarter than your average bear," as Yogi used to say. But not a full flegged rocket scientist despite the two semesters of co-operative work experience at NASA. Smart enough to get through engineering school and later get a graduate degree. But not smart enough to figure Alexa out!

FUNNY? I always had a great sense of humor. I hope Sasha saw and appreciated that side of me. I was a class clown growing up, the kind the kids love and teachers have "mixed feelings" about. If "funny" was on the list, I ought to have scored well.

FUN TO BE WITH? I may have under-performed in this category. See, I wanted her so much yet was stymied. Maybe my wanting to be more than friends got in the way of our just being ourselves.

A guy isn't charming if he's stepping on his tongue and lunging at a restraining chain. Alexa saddled me with "just friends" early on. Painted into that corner, I wasn't carefree as I worked to elevate from just friends.

And *fun* is important. If someone just isn't fun, to a young person, that equates to dull and *that* is *not* attractive.

ADVENTUROUS? Willing to spend time outside the box? Yeah, I get that point too.

Attraction is a quirky thing. Someone too straight laced is boring. Someone too wild should be avoided to preserve mental and physical health.

Many people struck me as being too "square." But what does "square" mean in a society that includes kids with rooster-spiked hair? What is square when folks pierce their face with so much metal they resemble a snow tire? What does square mean when there is a drug culture that includes kids and adults melting their brains with crystal meth? Where do you draw the line around square when half of the American marriages fail?

I wasn't a conformist, and I didn't want a completely square woman. I wanted someone who could experiment around the edges of socially accepted norms, who wasn't locked in to what she could and could not do. A woman merely living a legacy of tradition passed down from previous generations was unappealing.

On the other hand, I didn't want to live on the edge all the time. I didn't want a girlfriend so rough that by repeated admissions she was on a first name basis with the staff at the hospital emergency room. I wanted adventurous and healthy. That is how I lived, and I figured our lives would be most happy if I could find that in a girlfriend and spouse.

You'll find a detailed disclosure of my heart and feelings in this book, but I am the father of three impressionable kids and I coach. So, lest I lead anyone astray, let's just gloss over the part about being adventurous, living outside the norms of the straight and narrow. I never got arrested for being drunk and disorderly. No misdemeanors or felonies. But I experimented… and became experienced. As Jimmy Hendrix said "Not necessarily stoned, but beautiful."

Experimenting on the periphery of socially acceptable norms yielded awakening experiences, but love is the greatest anti-drug. We'll leave it at that.

AUDACIOUS ENOUGH? Audacity-- one part brave, one part over-confident, one part non-conformist. Another winning point for me. Sasha, didn't you notice?

Growing up an Army brat exposed me to the Army's people, life, and expectations. I figured I could succeed at it and all the equipment was pretty neat-- tanks, helicopters, guns and such. The mission of protecting America and her interests abroad was appealing, too, because it seemed noble and significant to a young impressionable man. But I had three questions in my mind: Did I want to be in the business of killing? Did I trust the chain of command? And were national "interests" legitimate or the trappings of empire? These questions were important to answer before I committed, so I signed up for ROTC to get a better perspective.

Freshmen reported to the ROTC office before the first day of class to gather gear -- olive drab fatigues, hat, socks, canvas belt, and boots. A sergeant who'd had his share of tougher assignments manned the supply room. Many of the regular army soldiers who ran the tranquil ROTC detachment were on their terminal assignments, their last tour of duty.

As I reported in, I encountered a classmate from my junior year in high school in Fayetteville. Another Army brat, his dad had also been assigned to Fort Bragg. We made small talk as we headed for the supply room.

The sergeant bellowed, "New boots or used boots?"

My friend said flat out, "New boots."

I wasn't sure. There was something ever so subtle in the sergeant's voice making it sound like a trick question. I answered "Old boots" figuring I'd save the taxpayer a few dollars. If they were good enough for someone else, they'd be good enough for me.

As the sergeant turned to collect our footwear, I could have sworn he nodded approvingly at me. It was the slightest motion, a nod made only by his eyebrows.

ROTC classes were attended once or twice a week, depending on how students arranged their schedules. We wore fatigues, boots and all, to class. We learned to muster in lines, call roll, and report our attendance in a very organized military fashion.

Activities included PE and marching, so we did lots of walking and running in our boots. Ever break in a new pair of boots? Many kids limped. Ever slip into a pair of boots someone else earned calluses from? I never had any problems with sore feet!

My audacity was displayed when the mid-October autumn colors changed. It was on our first small unit tactics drill held in an isolated and wooded area of campus.

N.C. State is an urban campus, positioned between two major thoroughfares through Raleigh. But along the southeastern side of campus, near Western Boulevard, there were some athletic fields and a line of small, tree-covered hills. This would be today's training area.

Our drill started on the open fields. We were assigned an upperclassman, an ROTC lieutenant, as a squad leader. After a few minutes of instruction, he led us up into the higher ground, mottled orange-brown clay soil, fallen pine needles, and decayed leaves abounded. Visibility this time of year was pretty good because some leaves had yielded to natures calling. Still, branches, and occasional thick underbrush limited view and impeded progress.

A few minutes into the hills we stopped. The squad leader asked us questions about the best places to deploy troops and position certain kinds of weapons. We were clueless about positioning weapons, but his questions started us thinking like officers to consider terrain a factor.

On the move again, we marched along the crest of the hills, parallel to the athletic fields below. I fell behind looking at terrain for the obstacles and military advantages it offered. I wound up at the tail end of our little band of green-clad kids. After a few minutes, our squad leader stopped in a small clearing where he waited four our squad to reassemble around him. I closed the distance but hesitated before leaving the thicker wooded area.

A thin line of bushes formed an L shape along the clearing edge. I was at the edge of the woods that defined one corner of the open area while the rest of the squad was in the open.

Within a step of the clearing I glimpsed something out of place to my right. Peering out of shadows thrown by the overhead canopy, I saw two eyes and a face masked in camouflage paint hiding among the bushes! My mouth opened slightly and I started to raise my hand. I looked at my squad leader but his expression was that of a man patiently waiting for a bus.

Just then there was a loud "Hoo-ha!" from my right, and two figures emerged from the row of bushes that formed the lower part of the foliage "L." My squad had been led directly into an ambush!

My squad jumped in total surprise as two attackers with faces painted for added concealment poked forward in camouflaged battle dress. Both assailants held in their hands the ubiquitous symbol of the US Army, the lightweight M-16 rifle. Of course, live ammunition had been omitted but the two ambushers had my squad squarely in their aim. Some of my squad had even been looking in the general direction of the crotch of the "L" from where they emerged. But they hadn't seen the assault coming.

I hadn't entered the clearing yet, so the two attackers didn't see me. Just off my shoulder another member of the ambush team was standing up. As he gained his feet, I instinctively whipped my hand toward him and took a half step in his direction. I intended to hold him back from entering the clearing so he couldn't bring his rifle to bear on my squad mates. As he heaved forward the edge of my hand inadvertently caught him in the throat, just below his voice box. He never saw it coming.

His surprise and lack of air suspended the neural link between brain and feet even as his momentum kept him moving forward. Surprised and gasping, he fell hard to the ground, his weapon careening in front of him.

The first two attackers heard the brief one-sided mêlée and turned toward me. A look of disbelief replaced their triumphant grins as they saw their fallen comrade. Their attack had been perfect, their stealth nearly flawless. They were prepared upperclassmen that knew the drill. It was their show and we were fledgling underclassmen, unarmed prey.

The ambush leader's face began to drop as it dawned on him that he had sprung the surprise a moment too early. There had been a straggler.

It got worse. Immediately to my right there another attacker was getting to his feet. I'd stopped about a step past his prone hiding place. He was hidden in high grass and brush. My squad walked right over him.

Unfortunately for this fourth attacker, his superb concealment was a mixed blessing. While his choice of cover offered a perfect hiding spot, extracting himself from the thicket took a few extra seconds, and now he was late for the party. He faced my squad as he rose to a half-standing position and attempted to step clear of his hiding place, raising his rifle as he gained his stance. He was so consumed with getting upright he hadn't seen me on his left, I reached out and took a firm two-handed hold on the weapon.

The M-16 has a steel sight at the front of the stock where stock meets barrel and this affording me a secure hold. I gripped his weapon firmly and yanked.

Still rising and moving forward, his right index finger was wrapped inside the protective trigger guard. As I drew the weapon it lunged away from him and the trigger guard gouged his finger. The stock of the gun smacked his right wrist, knocking his hand loose. The M-16 was now in my hands and I turned it toward to two remaining attackers as the fourth ambusher clutched his injured hand and dropped to his knees.

My eyes were fixed on the original attackers as I stepped into full view with M-16 pointed their way.

The leader's face dropped saying: "This isn't happening." He and his partner still held their M-16s on my squad members.

I stood about 20 feet from my mock enemy. With my eyes locked and barrel pointed their way, I said in monotone, "Drop your weapons."

Meanwhile one of my squad mates zipped over and recovered the loose M-16 on the ground. He immediately trained it on the two attackers, "Drop it or we'll blow your fucking heads off!"

With that, I slid the butt of the rifle to my shoulder. The barrel never left the target. As I raised the weapon, my finger instinctively felt for and unlatched the safety. The M-16's safety made two soft clanks as it moved from safe to fire mode. The quiet metallic click chimed noisier than I would have guessed and carried a weighty message. The metallic sound was the proverbial pin dropping that all ears understood. The situation felt grave.

The ambush leader replied shaky and startled, "But the guns aren't loaded."

"Good. Then you've got no reason to hold them." I said flatly.

Then I changed my voice from plural to singular and said: "Now, drop your weapon!"

The single-case sentence sent a subtle message to both men. Neither attacker had taken time to look at the other. They didn't know if their teammate had lowered his weapon or not. Each may have though the other already dropped their weapon.

I immediately told my squad members, "Collect their weapons and see what you can do for these other guys." Three squad members stepped forward to aid the two injured attackers.

The upperclassman attacker who went down first was on his back. The other was squatting on one knee with his other foot drawn beneath him, holding his injured hand. As my third squad member stepped closer to help the attacker on his knee, I waved him off by jerking the muzzle. I didn't want him crossing between my weapon and the remaining ambushers.

It may have been the initiative shown by my squad member that dove for the M-16 on the ground. It may have been the prompt way my teammates moved when I ordered them. It may have been the hopeless situation in which they found themselves. Whatever it was, the two remaining attackers lowered their weapons and prepared to relinquish them to my advancing teammates.

Just then one of our ROTC instructors, a commissioned captain, bellowed out. "What is going on here?" It was a command voice I'd learned from my old man, sure to get attention from afar and very effective at close distance. The captain was out of sight just below the crest of the hill but closing fast.

The extra shouting about "dropping weapons" wasn't part of the script he expected.

The captain approached and joined my squad leader in the clearing. He saw two guys in woodland camouflage fatigues on the ground, with several olive drab clad underclassmen helping them. The first upperclassman I had disarmed with a quick strike remained on his back, his knees in the air. He was fine, breathing well, but was in no hurry to get up. The other upperclassman seemed only mildly injured but still out of action. Most surprisingly, the captain saw freshmen with M-16s. And by the looks of it, another underclassman was about to take the weapons from the last ambushers!

"I said, what's going on here?" the captain demanded. His voice inflected a sense of command, mixed with uncertainty tinged from exertion caused by hoofing it up the hill double time.

Silence met his inquiry. Who was supposed to answer and summarize the recent events the underclassmen, our squad leader, or an ambusher? Everyone remained still, like a bunch of eight-year-olds caught in an awkward moment by a teacher. Clearly he knew what was supposed to happen, he was the teacher after all who helped plan the exercise. But his eyes and ears told him events had taken an unexpected turn.

One of the girls in my squad standing in the clearing beside the captain said, "I'll tell you what happened." Her voice came out singsong, as if she were tattling to her friends about some big news. "Cadet Brian Whitlash kicked these boys' ass!"

Many squad members started laughing quietly and a smile crossed our squad leader's face. This guy who had knowingly led us into the ambush was OK with the outcome. He looked tickled that we'd overcome the odds stacked against us.

The ambush team leader, on the other hand, took it personally. He had been in charge of the first pretend ambush in the NC State ROTC that had failed in favor of the prey.

The captain and I needed no introduction, and not because I had scored third best in the physical fitness test. He knew me personally because he always found something about me that needing correcting. It started our first week of drills because of a green tee shirt under my fatigues.

I knew we were supposed to wear white tee shirts under fatigues. House rules. But as a college student, I didn't have too many pairs of pants, shirts, underwear, socks, or white tee shirts in my freshman "ensemble." And as college students living in an all guy dorm, laundry wasn't the center of our lives. Sure there was a Laundromat somewhere in the dorm, I'd even visited it from time to time, but it stayed surprisingly clean from disuse. It was the only area of the dorm that didn't need custodial cleaning and few used it. I kept clothes clean enough to my standards, but on that particular training day I didn't have a white tee shirt. So I substituted a green tee shirt, one my dad had worn in Vietnam. I figured an olive drab tee shirt made a hell of a lot more sense than a white tee shirt anyway.

The captain didn't agree. I was the only cadet without a white tee shirt the day of our first run in, and he firmly corrected me, "I cannot believe you, Whitlash!"

It seemed to be like that a lot between us—something small to me was the world to him.

When we met again on the hill after the ambush, and he saw me standing with an M-16 that I hadn't been issued, the captain shook his head: "Is that true private?"

I hedged, "Well, not exactly, sir." The Captain and I had settled into the human equivalent of oil and water-- we didn't mix well. And neither one of us knew how to improve the mix. Some leaders pick on one or two people to drive out to form greater cohesion among the faithful. Captain acted like he would love to drive me out. So naturally he became the authority figure I didn't mind tweaking.

"I guess it could have looked like that from over there. We were ambushed, but when one of them stepped forward, he caught a low hanging branch that knocked the wind out of him. It may have looked like I decked him."

I turned on my right heel and pointed to the upperclassman kneeling holding his hurt wrist. His index finger looked swollen and connected to his hand at an unhealthy angle. One of my attentive squad mates had wrapped a handkerchief around his hand and finger. There was blood on it and my squad mate gently secured his finger.

"And this guy was the best camouflaged of the bunch," I continued. "He must have been lying down when we marched by because nobody saw him. Heck I still can't figure out how we walked by without *stepping* on him!

"But he must have tripped on a root or rock or something because as he stood up to attack he lost his balance. We just came forward to collect the weapons and help."

All eyes became suspicious scanning the surroundings for protruding roots that might lend credibility.

The guy on his knees meekly glanced up. What I was doing registered in his eyes. I looked over to the ambush leader and his number two man and added "And these two guys just scared the crap out of everybody. If they had live ammunition, there wouldn't be..."

The captain interrupted. "Is that right?" he asked facing the ambush leader, before turning to our squad leader. Apparently he trusted these two upperclassmen to give him a straight answer. Something didn't jive between what he heard from down on the practice fields, what he saw when he arrived, and my story.

The ambush leader decided to go with my story.

"Like cadet said, everyone probably saw something different. I was looking at the squad we ambushed. I didn't really see what happened over there."

The captain wasn't anybody's favorite officer and the trend of benign deception continued. Our upperclassman squad leader immediately echoed that description.

The captain wasn't convinced, but realized he wasn't in a position to get to the bottom of it. "Well, I'll get back with you later." He strode over the crest of the hill to check the results of another training ambush.

After a few moments, our squad leader looked at his watch and said comically, "I guess that's all for today." A smirk danced across his face before he regained command composure.

Early to pack it in we thought but nobody complained. Some of my squad fell in behind the squad leader and started down the hill. The two injured upperclassmen walked without assistance.

As the two healthy ambushers approached, my squad mate handed all weapons back to the leader. He said, "Thanks," and closed positions with me.

Some of my squad walked quietly. Some joked reveling in the surprise. As we got ready to clear the hill and enter the open field, the ambush leader came beside me and drew breath like he was about to say something. Instead, I said in a voice loud enough to carry to all my squad mates, "What happened on the hill stays on the hill."

The light chatter ceased.

It was funny in retrospect, but intense while it happened. I didn't see any of the ambush team after that day. Underclassmen and upperclassmen in ROTC were in different instructional classes, so that wasn't a surprise. Neither of the guys that relinquished their weapons suffered injuries that warranted a trip to the infirmary. The cut on the one cadet's finger was superficial and didn't require stitches.

I saw the captain many more times. He corrected me on one or two other uniform infractions that year, but he never again asked me what happened on the hill.

Apparently somebody talked. "I'll tell you what happened ... Cadet Whitlash kicked these boys' *ass*!" got around.

I didn't get congratulated outright, mind you. But my esteem went up a notch. Nobody had trouble pronouncing my name anymore. After that day, "Whitlash" came out of everyone's mouth like they were cousins.

It was the crusty old supply sergeant who confirmed that someone had let slip my accomplishment. He came up to me one day, handed me a little U-fold flier and said, "You ought to read this. Let me know if you're interested." He then turned smartly on his heel and was gone.

I opened the flier. It announced a special training exercise put on by the US Rangers. The Rangers were planning to hold a "pre-rangers" training program for people who were likely to be interested and able to qualify. I read the flier and gave serious thought of attending. But I had a conflict. I had already committed to the co-operative extension program and agreed to take an assignment at NASA.

I didn't last much longer in the ROTC. The experience helped clear up my questions. Are officer and men trustworthy? Yes.

The question of "national interests" still haunted me. I left unconvinced national leaders have sufficient wisdom to know when to ask young men to kill for in the name of democracy and America. I'd take my talent and passion elsewhere.

Audacious? How many guys could have done that? I had strength and speed, just enough disrespect for order, and sense of humor to ruin their ambush party! I knew the weapons weren't loaded. Guess that's why I made so much troublesome fun out of the incident.

There is one other audacious episode worth adding. A couple of years later, I did construction management work in Israel. One of the challenges my employer had was maintaining relationships in the community -- especially when it came to collecting rent. The institution owned properties, some of which were leased apartment buildings. Some properties were located in areas that had run down over the years.

Wars between the Arab states and Israel were the kind of thing that fouls urban planners. Wars had ravaged the area leaving legacy gashes in sanity and buildings. The blight they bring to humanity was still obvious.

Propaganda had stirred hatred before the war. Both sides proved quite effective at defining "other" and "enemy." Arab nations had particularly tight control over state-run media. Syrian, Jordanian, and Egyptian newspapers ranted and raved about the upcoming conflict. One disturbing theme in the Arab press was that everyone in Israel would be driven into the sea by the attacking Arab armies. Some inflaming articles went further to say Arabs found in Israel upon the entrance of their brethren would be treated as traitors and driven into the sea as well.

There is brotherly love for you!

Some local folk took these messages to heart. Feeling unwelcome and believing the propaganda, a few hundred thousand Arabs pulled up stakes. Allah would secure victory they were told. Believing in success and the threat they'd be seen as traitors and run into the sea by "liberating Arab armies" these folks packed hastily and left. Thus began the Palestinian Refugee crisis. Mind you, those that left expected to return after the short war and regain their homes.

Didn't work out that way. Homes and neighborhoods remained abandoned for a while, then became squatters' paradises.

Whole neighborhood of the city went through drastic changes. Worn rough over the decades, potholed streets and burned out cars accented the area. Some buildings stood roofless but until claims of immanent domain could be made, the property remained legally in the hands of the vacant titleholders. The building's stark, ghostly exterior walls, beckoned mischief and bred less than ideal behaviors among the remaining inhabitants and vagrants alike. The worst areas were destitute; most folks skirted them to avoid the blight. Local coworkers advised against driving through these areas at night.

My office was on the edge of one decayed neighborhood. One day I saw a group of men hang a large Arabic banner on a wall adjacent to our office. A lot of agitation for our quiet zone. There were many more young men with beards and some had AKs. Well, there goes the neighborhood I said to a coworker before strolling out to confirm trouble.

Not knowing what was going on I strode out into the middle of it all, "Whoa, whoa, whoa! What do these banners say? You can't hang banners that defame Arab or Jewish sentiment near our property! And no death to America bull shit either."

A man slashed in, racing toward me. He was the director of a Lebanese motion picture film crew. Joyfully, what we had beside our officer was movie that had found the perfect location mimicking a bombed out neighborhood. They were using the dilapidated buildings as a background.

"We'll only be here for a day or so." He said in perfect English.

"Buddy that's great, but you've got to understand we live here and we're caretakers in a long line of folks building a better world. Can someone translate those banners? If they're inflammatory…"

"No, no, no…" The director conceded the temporary stoppage and searched for a translator. Our native workers arrived and confirmed the film crew's appeal; the banners didn't agitate. We stood back and let the show go on. Later we congratulated the crew for their ingenuity of finding the perfect setting. The producer said sadly, "Sites like this aren't all that hard to find."

Notwithstanding dilapidation all around us, part of my job was to ensure the properties we owned didn't follow suit. We regularly made improvements to some buildings regardless of how time and fortunes eroded the surrounding structures.

The property manager came to the Works Office, a British term for engineering and maintenance, looking for assistance in visiting these properties.

"Whitlash, I'm looking for volunteers. Seems you are on my short list."

"Let me see that list!"

"Never mind!" he playfully snatched the note away.

"Luck runs deep in my family what can I say!"

The property manager and I were buddies. He was an attorney from Arizona, and we used to play Pictionary and go on various hiking and snorkeling adventures. We had a great friendship and if he was going into what could be harm's way, I wanted to be with him.

"So, who put my name down as a volunteer for your harebrained mission?"

"You come highly recommended by the many people who turned me down!"

"Flatter all you want, mister"

The property manager and I made up an inspection team. Turned out that some of our properties were not on any list I had, so we never had looked in on them. Neither of us spoke more than a few Arabic words, although I did learn a useful phrase as we walked out the door from a local worker, "Shoot him first, he's the boss!" I got a kick out of it; he didn't think it funny. Some people!

We headed outside. Parked at the curb was the attorney's jalopy.

"Let's take one of the office vans. You can't possibly expect to be treated with respect if you show up driving you piece of petrified…"

"My boy, it isn't respect we're looking for. Blend, blend in! That is the name of the game."

"We'll blend all right!"

He drove an old station wagon with exterior parts from three manufacturers, made on two different continents. An unrecognizable fender, possibly from a train yard, completed the oh-so-ghetto look.

"Besides, no one will steal it," he said fiddling with a key and the accelerator until the hood vibrated as the engine caught. "I'm the only one that knows how to start it!"

"What a surprise! Knows, or would want to? Your junk car looks like the kind of vehicle a terrorist would use to practice car bombing. Mind you, they wouldn't be seen driving up in it to a real job site, only practice!"

We went on property errands intermittently for a couple of months. Intact buildings stood garnished with strands of spiraled concertina wire protecting the perimeter. It doesn't add to the skyline and it only took a pair of wire clippers to breach an unguarded fence but it's a start. Careful scrutiny along the razor wire showed signs of separation here and there, but we went in anyway. We parked amidst lots strewn with rubble and ignored a nagging doubt about securing a quick getaway in his rag.

As we walked to the front door I turned and offered, "Your rust mobile looks like its home!"

"Actually, it looks rather inviting, don't you think, relative sanctuary?" he replied.

"It will look even better if we aren't running for our lives as we come out. It takes you forever to start it!"

We discussed the plan at each building, start at the top and work our way down, talking to each tenant to ensure they're being treated respectfully and maintenance is satisfactory. We took a deep gulp of air to boost courage and opened the door. The building was laid out like a typical apartment, a central hallway flanked by tenants' doors. The property manager said as we started up the stairwell, "Let me get in front and knock. If they shoot, they'll get me. I'm not married."

Speaking for all married men, I responded, "No, I *am* married. Let *me* go first!" and bolted up the stairs.

One day a week we'd enter our buildings in very good shape standing unscathed amid fields of ruins. Fortunately, the people living inside always proved they didn't reflect the harsh exterior. Each time a door opened the initial suspicion dissolved within a minute and we were invited into their homes and treated graciously. We were a good team to send in -- unassuming, kind, gentle ... and expendable!

We never knew what would befall us on our visits, but we accepted our task with joviality and camaraderie. He would knock sometimes. I would knock if I bound up the stairs and got there first. When the door opened, we never met anything harsher than questioning stares before the tenants displayed their renowned Arab hospitality. Despite the harsh conditions these folks lived in, their hearts still had kindness to extend to strangers. And I was surprised to learn how many of these good people had kids living in America.

It said something for our faith in our fellow man; trust in God and audacity to willingly go into those dilapidated neighborhoods amid such social tension. I should have scored high if she cared about audacity.

OPEN HEARTED? Caring enough to reach out and help? I would have given anybody a helping hand the evening I met Sasha; she didn't have to be gorgeous. It just made my decision to give her a ride easier!

While dating Sasha I did volunteer work that reflected the Open Hearted category. So there you go, another point for the Bean!

Before the breakup of AT & T, one of Ma Bell's pet activities was "Beep Ball." Beep Ball is an interesting variant of softball designed for the visually impaired. Like the title of the game implies, the game uses an oversized softball that beeps. A battery-powered device inside the ball constantly emits a warbling tone enabling sightless players to find it. Players with some vision wear swimming goggles painted black to eliminate their sight advantage.

Instead of baseball's standard three bases and home plate, "Beep Ball" uses two construction cones rigged with buzzers and toggle switches as bases. Cones are placed in lieu of first and third bases. As soon as a ball is hit, a sighted base coach flips one of the base toggles alerting the batter which way to run. The object of the game is for the batter to make it to the alerted cone and switch it off. Meantime, fielders hone on the balls beeping sound. If the batter makes it to the cone first, he scores a run. If the fielder grabs the ball and shows it in his or her hands before the base's toggle is turned off, the player is out.

A wide range of visually impaired men and women filled out our team, ages fifteen to forty. Ryan was my age and his was a tragic story. He'd been sitting in a car at a shopping mall when a stranger walked up beside the car and fired a pistol through the passenger window. The bullet severed both optic nerves as it careened through his skull. Police confirmed it a completely random act of violence. Ryan was a great athlete up until that horrible incident. Now, one of the few outlets for his youthful energy was Beep Ball.

I visited Ryan's home. He rented a room in a house a few blocks away. I said, "Hey, we don't live very far apart, maybe we can get together. Let me write down my number. Give me a call."

Big hearted but clueless.

I stood beside him in the modest living room scribbling my number. Ryan found his way to the kitchen and took a small Braille writing device in hand, "No, let me write it down."

James was another Beep Baller. James was the pride of his teammates because, though totally blind, he rode a bike. James rode on a quiet street free of through traffic. We had adventurous people on the team. Fortunately, we had openhearted people, too.

My first lesson was gleaned the first practice. It was a pleasant spring day. The Park and Recreation folks who scheduled the quiet and isolated field really looked out for us. In fact, there wasn't a better field in the whole city. The field displayed a luxurious stand of grass, and a chain-link fence defined the play area. Mature oak and maple trees displayed with grandeur new growth shading the third and first base lines. Dugouts had long wooden benches free of age or splinters.

Standing behind the dugout the first day I wondered how I would contribute and teach. I shouldered pretend responsibility of new assistant coach and waited for the team to arrive. My mind rumbled through years of playing experience searching in vain for a technical starting point.

I'd been early, one solitary player sat on the bench, but the sound of a car approaching and doors closing announced another arrival. A lanky boy accompanied by his mother emerged and walked ever so tentatively toward the field. They moved carefully, taking a great deal of time traversing the thirty feet separating their car and the bench. With mom and son holding arms, she shared quiet encouraging conversation each step.

Trepidation froze the boy's face. He relied exclusively on mother's love for confidence and direction.

The seated player heard them approach and recognized his teammate's voice. He thumped the wooden bench with the palm of his hand beckoning "Here Bennie! Let's get started." My eyes watered with his show of sensitivity, friendship, and direction. I stopped wondering about my role and told myself quietly, "Stop wondering how to teach and start learning!"

A few games into the season I passed the head coach's unwritten initiation of regular attendance and genuine interest. He let me pitch.

Pitching Beep Ball is not for the faint of heart! The sighted coach pitches from dangerously close to full-grown batters! Danger close—these men rip a ball all the way to the fence with a powerful jolt. Yet we stood about as far away as you'd lob a whiffle ball to a toddler.

Quite often the only way to escape a bone-crushing line shot is to dive. God must have been with me because each time line drives came hurtling back, I successfully dove out of harm's way.

The true art of Beep Ball occurs between pitcher and batter.

The key is to loft pitches so unsighted players can hit them. Shout "Ball!" or "Swing!" the moment the batter should begin his swing. The pitcher must arc the ball and announce swing at just the right time so the batter's normal swing makes contact.

The batters and I got in sync so well that each hit the first or second pitch. A rarefied connection grew. Confidence and team spirit shot to the stars. They felt so good about cracking the ball and I was delighted "to see" for them. That's what it was-- I saw for them. I watched the ball as if I was batting and in a symbiotic way I did see for them. We went on an unstoppable role, batter after batter hit like they were seeing through my eyes. I was honored to share the field with them.

As the season wound down, the coaches, parents, and siblings were invited to take the field and play. One volunteer was a bright lady that worked for the phone company. She was athletic and jovial, had long curly, red hair and was cute in a freckly kind of way.

One inning I was pitching to the blind team and the coaches and family team held the field. Sighted fielders, including our spunky red-haired engineer, wore blacked-out swim goggles. What she and all the other goggled fielders didn't see was a red Irish setter stroll onto the field.

I turned when I saw the dog, wondering how it got in through the back fence, but paid it no mind. It was only a passing distraction, like a cloud. A minute later, someone hit a hard grounder that rolled into left centerfield and the redheaded fielder went after it. When she got close to the beep, or thought she was close, she dropped down on all fours.

She yelped "Where's the ball!" as she groped in vain she hopped and bobbed on hands and knees scooting one way, then another. All the while the wailing ball called attention. Motionless it remained hidden from her frantic search. The tension of the play subsided when the batter made it to base, but the redheaded fielder remained comically dedicated to her task.

Wouldn't you know it; all the excitement caught more than our attention. Our K-9 visitor's attention was peaked. The big Irish setter loped over to the engineer down on all fours. Jus then her squirming lead her to inadvertently present her rump to the dog. Grateful of a now stationary target he mounted her haunches and began humping with wild enthusiasm.

Sighted participants howled! Even the dog had a smile on its face! His tongue fell sideways, swinging in the breeze, as he went through his courses. We had a time explaining *that* to the blind players, especially the one young teen on the team.

When the red headed coach got back into the dugout I reminded her, "Volunteer work gives back in so many joyous, unusual, and unexpected ways!" A swell of laughter enveloped us a second time. Her face changed colors enough to hide freckles.

I still enjoy giving to the community through coaching, though I keep a better watch for stray dogs!

THE CHASE? "The Chase" is a very important category in which I scored poorly. Don't get me wrong -- I chased her. It was just that she didn't need to even try to get me interested.

Chase is pretty important to some young ladies. As soon as I saw Sasha I was whipped. I knew from the first day I saw her; that I wanted us to be close. But what fun is there in that for her? She didn't have to work womanly charms on me. I was an easy catch from the get-go. Like fishing when the fish offers no resistance. Too easy.

Not even the circumstance of our first meeting included a chase. She just looked at me and I was hers. At a young age, when getting there is half the fun, a guy who isn't a challenge to rein in appears less "interesting." I was hooked and gaffed the first evening. A guy already captured by a woman's beauty is too easy a mark to take seriously.

"Once contact has been made, the woman's state of mind
must be studied, her feelings examined, ascertaining whether she
is sure of herself and her resolution is firm, whether she has

amorous relations with anyone else or lives with him as his
concubine." Karma Sutra

We saw each other many times over the course of that semester.
We'd go to dinner, a performing arts dance, anything I could find that
might interest the two of us. Very early on, she made it clear she had a
boyfriend back home. I respected her situation and feelings. I let her
know "I wouldn't step on what you've got going. But I want to be there if
and when it dissolves."

For fifteen months we shared loving evenings, if not mutually "in
love." We supported and nurtured each other with quiet conversation and
encouragement. Time and again our dates were kindhearted and sincere.
I hoped each minute together brought her closer to "in love" locked in a
holding pattern doing all the chasing.

One evening we took a little stroll on her campus upon returning
from an afternoon outing. We stopped by a picturesque pond, so
romantic, a perfect place for her to open her heart. There was a bench,
maybe a kiss? It seemed worth a try to draw her out of her solitude. No
dice.

The summer came. I rotated back to Huntsville, Alabama, for my
second semester of co-operative education work at NASA. While I
commiserating from SOTB that summer, I met an old friend I'd known in
high school. Joyce was only the second person I'd run across again from
our widespread travels. We struck up a boyfriend-girlfriend relationship
that summer. But SOTB reigned supreme. My heart and intentions
remained true.

When the fall semester began and Sasha and I returned to Raleigh
we quickly got back together and dated. I inquired early if things had
changed back home. I wanted to know where I stood. She was warmer
but still reserved.

The one-sided nature of our dates wore thin. I always call her, never
the reverse. But I hung on. We went to the State Fair. We went to a real
nice restaurant-- hard for a struggling college student to pay for, but I'd
pay for anything to be with her.

Later that fall something shifted for the better. Sasha accepted my invitation and joined me for an Elton John concert. We invited friends to join us for a pre-concert party in the dorm recreation room. The party went well, though we went overboard accommodating the girls' taste for Pina Coladas.

Despite my first hangover the next day from the rum, I felt my luck had changed. The semester was winding down and Christmas break loomed. With Carpe Diem as my motto, I took a chance and invited Sasha to my dorm room for dinner. My roommate would be gone and we could have a quiet night. I made spaghetti sauce from scratch and the evening was pleasant.

Mistletoe above the door positioned to remove reluctance. As we were leaving my room, I stopped beneath it and said, "Mistletoe. It's a tradition."

"Oh, you are going to kiss me?" Sasha said hesitantly.

We embraced and kissed. I pressed my lips and she didn't resist. Hoping she'd return the favor, I stayed close a few moments, but she remained coy and didn't return the kiss. None of that lifting her leg you see in Hollywood as the lady leans in for a second kiss. But she didn't slap me either, which was nice! We left it at just the one kiss, for now.

I drove her back to her dorm that night and I was optimistic my waiting game was not futile. Eleven months and one kiss, but that kiss had just happened, so things were looking up, right?

The end of the fall semester was on us. We shared a tender phone conversation; she said was flying home for Christmas break. I offered to drive her to the airport, sensing another choreographed romantic moment. At the airport, I yearned to draw her close into what I hoped would be the start of a lifelong embrace. There must be some way to get through to this girl, to press the relationship forward!

As our goodbye was upon us, I could see she was torn. Her eyes were tender and open, but not without reservation. She wanted to reach out but hesitated, feeling something else as well. I desperately wanted to kiss her again, but youthful timidity and uncertainty ruled. That "something else" won out that day. We parted at the glass doors as she headed toward luggage check. I remained outside and waved as the electric door closed. As she turned I unthinkingly placed my hand upon the pane and watched her back disappear into the reflections and shadows. Hand to glass, it was a lonesome pose that would separate us again many years later.

A golden opportunity for two youngsters' passionate goodbye kiss failed to materialize. Had any man worked as hard for one kiss? I deeply regretted the lost moment at the airport, but I didn't lose optimism. Spring was just around the corner.

The lone kiss and the melancholy drive home from the airport were moments I revisited again and again. It was *way* beyond unbearable… ending each date without a kiss, without a hug, with her seeing me as what… her older brother? Is that what I was to her?

January marked our one-year anniversary. Hurrah! My co-operative work experience took a different turn. I didn't return to NASA because I wanted to stay in Raleigh and be with her. I got my last co-operative extension assignment locally, in Cary.

My buddy Clay and I rented an apartment. We were moving up in the world and showing independence. Sasha and I often got together. Sometimes she'd come over, other times we'd go out on the town. We dated many times that winter, sadly, no romantic interludes. "Sad" doesn't approach the heartache of blocked passion, the endless yearning, of a Bean eager to embrace his reluctant Princess.

About the first of spring we rendezvoused on a pleasantly warm Saturday for tennis. I'd suggested tennis and she readily agreed, saying Meredith College had courts directly behind her dorm. The weather was immaculate as winter's grip receded. A bright blue sky and warm sun invigorated, making the cool air enjoyable. The campus grounds were manicured and idyllic as she led me to the courts. A nearby mature tree spread its branches masking much of the western sky. I was in heaven. Alive and young, this day could be the turning point, just as I had imagined each of our previous dates.

Few others ventured out that afternoon; we had the courts to ourselves. She wore white tennis attire, complete with the little skirt.

Women look so powerful and petite in those outfits, so self-confident and so attractive. I have no idea what I wore, except heart on sleeve. Her strong legs and adorable body were captivating.

But the day turned dreadfully black.

As we gathered our equipment after our match, Sasha offhandedly remarked that the college had sponsored their annual spring party the previous weekend. It was a dance with the age-old Sadie Hawkins tradition that the young ladies invite their dates. Sasha had gone. She didn't go alone. She invited someone. It hadn't been me.

My world crashed. The high chain link fence masked with green wind-block fabric enveloped me and spun. Dizzy, I lowered the head of my tennis racket to the ground and braced my sway. The world I wanted to create vanished.

Sasha's inviting another local guy to a dance finally opened my mind to the sad reality of my unrequited love. Though we were done playing tennis, she had just pounded a heartbreaking ace past me. Game, set, and match!

Torn? She may have been torn back at the airport… but it wasn't between her old boyfriend back home and me.

On the way home I dropped my trusty wooden Wilson tennis racket into a Goodwill collection bin. I needed to disassociate from the day's events. The racket was a good one, Jack Kramer series. A trusted friend, we'd been together for years. I opened the narrow donation bin built like a mail drop box. The large wooden frame that prevented warping didn't want to fit in the narrow opening.

The racket resisted abandonment as if it asked, "Are you sure? Are you sure you don't want me anymore?" Its little plea made me slow down. I told it: "You're a good racket, strings intact, handle a bit worn, but someone with a love for the game will pick you up." With patience the racket glided down and out of sight.

My balls seemed superfluous, too. Mighty bad feeling for a guy.

I dropped two tubes of balls behind the racket. I could hear the "falump" as they found the bottom, bounced, and rolled to quiet rest. The hinged bin top clamored shut sealing the deal.

I haven't played tennis since.

She had broken with the guy back home enough to invite a local guy to the dance, but it hadn't been me. I'd lost my waiting game. We didn't have a present or a future. So, what the hell was I doing loving someone who didn't care enough to even ask me to the dance?

My window of opportunity was closed. I sensed that I never really had a window of opportunity. It may have been a window, but it wasn't the operable kind-- more like the plate glass in a store for display only. She was on one side and me the other. She let me "look." I'd lived for fifteen months with undying hope.

Loser or helpless romantic, is there a difference? Grief about the lost opportunity consumed me. Thoughts of Alexa didn't go away quickly. SOTB took about a year and a half to get fully over. Clearing my head took work. Bereavement is bereavement, whether you lose your lover to death or someone else.

> "If, notwithstanding a great deal of effort and time, he fails
> to reach his aim, he must realize that the enterprise is fruitless and
> that the liaison must be broken off." Karma Sutra

Sasha and I saw each other one more time. A couple years later she was walking on NC State's East Campus with a big, curly haired guy. They seemed close, more than "just friends." Maybe they were holding hands, I don't recall.

I walked with Gayle. Gayle and I were just friends-- fortunately, by equal and mutual desire. But we walked close, talking about spiritual and religious subjects.

Gayle and I crossed paths with Sasha and the blonde moose and exchanged pleasantries. Sasha was quite energetic and delighted to see me, and I her. Her voice was joyous and her eyes sparkled when she addressed me.

It was an easy and unstrained moment between old friends. I didn't register jealousy and refused to let desires surface.

As we parted ways, my gaze lingered on Sasha. Gayle asked with a knowing edge that only women pick up on. "Who was that girl?"

"Who? Was someone just here?"

Gayle smile grew to cover her face and she darted her head knowing she'd discovered a secret.

"Come on! I saw you look at her!"

"Long time ago Gayle, that girl and I were almost something."

93 out of 100 = 'A' for Effort

"Uncontrolled eroticism leads to failure." Karma Sutra

Know any urban legends? A few people are credited deeds remarkable enough to enshrine them in oral history. People like Joe, a student at Virginia Tech, whose claim to fame strikes a chord somewhere between revolting, amazing, and awful.

Awful as in '"full of awe," as in "inspiring," or awful as in "hideous?" You be the judge.

Goal setting is an important part of becoming an adult. If you want to accomplish something, you've got to have a goal or two because self-motivation is at the core of accomplishment. And, lest we forget, some girls like a driven man! We accept some goals without acknowledge them; we just keep working toward them like a sapling rises toward the sun without question. But Joe was very vocal about his sophomore goal-- having sex with 100 girls in one semester. Go Hokie!

An unattainable goal for the mortal man? The physical feat was not unbelievable-- most college guys could physically accomplish the mission. It was the emotional, the psychological baggage, that would have stopped the average guy from contemplating such an undertaking.

Not Joe. He set off with vigor towards his century mark and temporarily took many women away from more rewarding relationships. He embarked on his quest for sex. The pursuit of his goal undoubtedly affected his long-term ability to create lasting relationships, but consequences didn't stop Joe.

To be fair, there were redeeming perspectives to his venture. He learned a lot about sex that semester and honed his approach toward single girls. Pick up lines were tried and proven on the academic grounds.

Donnie was one of Joe's friends, and when Joe confided his plan, Donnie was struck at the impudence. Yet he marveled at the simplicity, and left Joe to his own destiny.

Donnie saw Joe sparingly as the semester got underway. The pursuit of his goal consumed all of Joe's free time. Like any died-in-the-wool workaholic, Joe was married to his work.

About a month into the semester Donnie caught up with Joe in one of the cafeterias. As they completed their selections and gathered food, Donnie invited Joe to sit with him and talk about what was going on. Willing at first, Joe then excused himself upon spying two girls sitting beside each other and another girl dining alone.

Wasting not a second Joe took his tray to the single girl. After a very brief time, Joe got up carrying his tray. Strikeout.

Undaunted, Joe strode over toward the two girls eating together and sat down. This arrangement didn't end abruptly. When Donnie left, Joe was still chatting with the two. Did the encounter notch Joe's count? By one? By two? We'll never know, individual women blurred in the hunt for 100. Donnie realized Joe didn't have time for mingling with guys. Success does require sacrifice!

On another occasion midway through the semester, Donnie caught up with Joe early one morning. They met in a dorm hall that Joe didn't live in. Joe was closing a door to a room that definitely didn't belong to him. As they saw each other in the hall, Joe said, "The girl in there is so drunk and just waking up. If you want to have sex with her, go on in. She probably couldn't tell you and me apart!"

Donnie passed on the opportunity.

But a passerby, a complete stranger walking the hall, overheard the offer, accepted the ruse and rose to the occasion. Despite an unmistakable difference in physical stature between last night's guy and this morning's guy, the girl never let on that she knew or cared!

Awash in the stress of exams two days before the end of Joe's time limit, Donnie saw him again and asked if he'd fulfilled his goal.

"No." Joe sounding dejected. "I only had sex with ninety-three."

"Ninety-three!" Donnie flabbergasted. Donnie's hard work in engineering flashed before his eyes as he compared his scholastic journey to this man who'd become foreign, just an acquaintance.

In the end, pursuit of his ill-conceived goal preoccupied Joe's world. He dropped out of school a semester later.

As an urban legend, Joe defines one side of the male spectrum -- the Alpha male staking his territory. And what of the 93 young ladies whose hopes and dreams of love and meaningful relationships were toyed with so casually? Notches on his belt, the women that strayed near were just a means to an end.

Crystal Stiletto

Beauty, courage, bloom, radiance, perspicuity, gentleness,
and wiles are the qualities that make women attractive." Karma
Sutra

You've heard of Cinderella and her glass ballroom shoes. Her fabled romantic interlude captures young hearts and minds the world over. Cinderella is one of the first stories that introduces the mystique of "happily ever after" between Cindy and the good Prince Charming. That concept enchants long after the child's book is shelved.

Let me introduce to you the Princess and her crystal stilettos.

Remember Prince Charming and Cinderella at the ball -- dancing and whirling, talking and holding hands? Needless to say, the Prince was smitten with Cinderella.

What? A couple of twirls around the dance floor and he loses his noodle? Only in Fairytale land? Let me tell you, that's exactly how it goes for princes in the real world.

Upon Cinderella's hasty departure, there was no time for a lingering goodbye, no parting pleasantries. But she dropped a shoe. Oh how convenient! Of course, she couldn't leave her cell phone number. As she was living like a slave, she had major reservations about giving the Prince her address. Maybe something magical would happen if she left a shoe behind.

Make no mistake this was no accident. Cinderella didn't commit a misstep the whole night, even with all that whirling and twirling, lifting and dancing. But she somehow managed to lose a shoe while departing? Sounds like a calling card to me!

And call, he did. The good Prince traveled both town and country with one of Cinderella's glass shoe. He hunted for the wearer with sincerity because he *knew* that shoe fit the foot of his beloved. Aren't we glad Cinderella had an uncommon shoe size and that there wasn't some other unaware young lady that just happened to fit the shoe before the Prince got to Cinderella?

Our storybook Prince had it easy. He had a known entity, the shoe. His challenge was to find her again. He was sure the shoe fit the woman he loved. There might be false matches, sure, but he could start with a solid short list.

Odd, isn't it that Cinderella's smell, her laugh, her voice, face, or name weren't part of the distinguishing characteristics the Prince used to locate her? Maybe he had a poor memory, like most guys, and couldn't recall her name. Couldn't he have just hosted another ball and smoked her out that way? Grand boy that he was, he took the personal approach. Fortunately the story ended with them living happily ever after. Whew!

Now blow the fairy dust away and think about the conundrum in terms of a real man. Guys in the real world have it doubly tough. First, we don't start out with a glass slipper that we are *certain* fits the woman we love. That fact alone makes it much harder. That fact alone turns many would-be princesses into settling for the beer-belly guys that fill the world. Not *knowing* we have an accurate template means we're not sure of anything. We aren't sure we have a clue what we're looking for. We might find a girl that fits well but inadvertently discount her because our measurement scale is wrong. Or we measure up another and date her, maybe even marry her, only to realize much later that it was a bad fit. So the uncertainty of the shoe is a problem that causes many guys to drop their "ideal woman" profile and settle for warm, friendly, and here!

Because real men aren't given a shoe to match, we have to *create* the "shoe." Out go eighty percent of the remaining would-be princes! Why? Too hard. But some persevere. How do these stalwart romantics toil to create the shoe?

Instead of fitting a glass slipper we fortuitously stumble upon, diehard romantics forge a crystal stiletto from our mind and matter stitched and drawn with faith. Our crystal stiletto is made from the rarest sinew of our hearts, clay from the dust we were created from, and the sand from the endless shores of time. Fired with passion and forged under tremendous pressure to yield the finest crystal.

Once a fellow fashions his shoe, he has to *find* someone who fits his crystal stiletto. Prospects of this daunting challenge extinguish all but the hardiest of would-be princes. Like salmon swimming upstream, few manage to hold onto their dreams through this ordeal. The rest settle for cute, or convenient, or available. Only those with deep romantic impulse struggle on, fools though they are.

Sadly, it turns out there can be additional complications for the few remaining princes like the bears swatting the salmon right at the edge of the breeding ground as they desperately hurtle through the last few obstacles. *I'm making it! I'm making it to the Promised Land. I'm there!* Then whap! Caught in bears' teeth, romantics are thinned once again.

This last complication stems from reluctant princesses. The stiletto may be perfect craft, the prince diligent enough to find his heart's desire, the princess duly sought and found, and the fit nearly perfect. But maybe the princess feels like wearing tennis shoes, sandals, or blue suede shoes instead of the prince's offering.

To a dutiful prince, however, the odds of success are irrelevant. We must have the best shoe we can fashion, and put up with the lousy odds. So how and why are these crystal stilettos formed from the mental ether and our temporal environs?

Most guys start out unsure of what they are looking for in a girlfriend, a fiancée, a lover, and a wife. Moreover, as a prince gains knowledge and experience, the measurements, configuration, and style of shoe he forges may change. Some guys opt to craft a cross-country trainer; others may try to fill horse-riding boots. But *hopeless* romantics like me aim for the elegant -- a crystal stiletto with a moderate rise, open toe and a sexy strap.

We forge our crystal princess-location device with as much sincerity and honesty as we can muster because it really matters. To a young romantic man it is the most important, most hallowed, mission he'll undertake.

At some level of consciousness, we churn our own code and whittle down possible dates and mates. Our attractions, our likes and dislikes, are very real to us, and it is part of feeling attracted, falling in love, and eventually passing on our genes.

In the days immediately after my lunch meeting with Alexa, I wondered what she wanted in a guy and delved into my own recollections of what characteristics were important to me. I made a table that represented the crystal stiletto I used in my twenties. I'm not advocating the wisdom of the criteria I lay out, only reporting it as recollected. The criteria would certainly differ now that I am wiser.

In true engineering fashion, I assigned a weight to the categories calling some Wants and others Musts. What is a Want versus a Must? A Want differentiates. A Want is something that was important and would help choose. But a Want was not important enough to discount a would-be princess from the court.

A Must was live-or-die. Must categories were things so important a girl *had* to have to consider as a girlfriend, fiancée, or spouse. Think about your own criteria. What was a Want and what qualified as a Must? How pretty did she have to be? How charming and good-looking did a guy have to be? How wildly did your heart have to flutter to move from friend into being romantic?

Let's delve into the categories. The first attracting Must was a woman's sense of spiritual purpose and depth of character. Surprised? You thought it would be T and A?

Patience.

Spirituality was a Must. This category reflected how inquisitive of life, of love, and of nature. A possible spouse needed a spiritual identity. I rejected a number of girlfriends because they didn't have any spiritual direction or yearning to grasp life's deeper aspects. Rightly or wrongly, I felt a lasting relationship needed a shared interest in spiritual matters.

Religious denomination didn't matter. Being aware of how unique the gift life is, and wanting to make a contribution to our ever-advancing civilization mattered. A woman without any penchant for figuring out where she fit into creation was too shallow to take seriously. I was attracted to those who were joyous and nurtured a sense of purpose and place in our little corner of the universe.

OK, now that I've weighed in on the spiritual side, let me show you the *other* side of the Bean. Beauty was important factor too and physical shape was one defining aspect of beauty.

"Eroticism is the touchstone of virtue." Without sexuality, the body would not be born and life would not propagate. There would be no society and no continuation of virtue. Karma Sutra

Consider a girl's figure. To me, that was a "Must." It may not be important in the grand scheme of life, but if a girl didn't have an attractive figure, I wasn't inclined to be more than friends. A girl's figure has two components. The first is the shape of her body seen from the front and from behind. The old saying that the ideal figure for a woman is 36-24-36 comes to mind. Numbers didn't matter but proportions do. Taken together, her figure had to vaguely resemble an hourglass.

There are many nuances to the hourglass. For some guys 36-24-36 may be ideal. To me a girl's figure must taper in at the waist. An hourglass is not a cylinder without difference between top, middle and bottom. And an hourglass is not a football shape wider at the middle than the top and bottom. Although an attractive figure was a Must, this didn't exclude many girls because most young ladies have figures that fall within the broad category of "hourglass."

The second part of a lady's figure is seen profile. A woman's profile ought to cast a shadow in front of her just below the shoulder, about mid-chest. OK, I'll be blunter. Guys like boobs.

Nutrient production for newborn babes is the primary purpose of mammary glands. But face it, the average American woman has two kids. And *if* a woman breastfeeds before switching to formula, the duration of suckling is very short. So *most* of the time, breasts are for "display purposes only." And what a nice display they make!

What constitutes a nice pair? Guys are never given a choice like; "Here are a half-dozen equally attractive women lined up, from no tits to a full house. Choose your favorite." Life doesn't unfold that way. *Bummer.* When it comes to boobs, most guys would look like shy malnourished Oliver Twist; "Please sir I want some more?" At least a mouthful, please!

The more the merrier I thought because breasts were a mystery to young men. They were something girls had and guys wanted to hold and enjoy. Guys are first attracted to girls while they're wearing layers of clothing. The telltale sign that there is something worthy to behold is cleavage-- the billboard to heaven! Men's eyes follow cleavage. It doesn't matter how often a man sees cleavage his eyes wander tirelessly. A guy could have cataracts, glaucoma, anything short of total blindness and never tire of seeing cleavage. A girl sporting cleavage and casting a bit of a bulge from the profile has a pair well worth appreciating.

Make no mistake about it when a guy meets girl he'll notice chest regardless of how loose fitting her clothes. Men gather key information on this vital subject regardless of circumstance. No matter how well hidden, if a guy meets a girl strapped into a life jacket on a raft or boat he'll discern a thing or two about chest size using advance geometric skills only guys possess despite the floatation shielding. *That* is why guys are good at math! We routinely use those parts of our brains to assess girls' curves. We notice something *that* important. The color of her eyes might be overlooked. Whether a girl is an all-out bitch might slip our attention. If it is raining or sunny, a guy's apt to miss that too. But no self-respecting American male would miss a hint of bulge mid-chest! Hey, we're just looking out for our offspring's suckling opportunities!

As a youngster I didn't know how women's breast sizes were calculated. It was a divine mystery; a step or two down from the Holy Trinity. But I knew the scale ran from A on up to D, DD and maybe even beyond that to udder sizes. I didn't know how small an A was, but when it came to chest size, I wasn't looking for the kind of grades medical school students would rack up. To me a C was nice; maybe C+ would be fantastic. I figured there were diminishing returns above C, so a D was about as attractive as a B. Sure it's shallow, this physical aspect of a woman wasn't important in the big scheme of things, but the presence of cleavage was erotic and inviting. As a single guy, I figured I could find someone to fall in love with who was somewhat sweet and kind *and* had a nice rack!

Shallow? Lost interest in the Bean? For the record, boobs were just a Want, not a Must. Breast size was immaterial once hearts bond.

One of the most important crystal stiletto categories was how a lady looked. Physical beauty is skin deep, and measured in the eye of the beholder but the attractiveness of facial features was a Must. A girl had to be attractive enough to me so I would see her as attractive. Had I become fond of an unattractive woman, and if that fondness turned into love, so be it. Most folks who fall in love look with adoring eyes. Seeing someone as beautiful is as much a reflection of your love for them as it is that person's actual physical beauty.

The final Must was an overall composite feeling of attraction, infatuation, and love that exemplified my overall feelings. The final Must required the girl to reciprocate my love.

Now, on with the results.

I penciled the names of women I dated, from Sasha up until my wife, Celeste. My little love matrix, displayed an interesting realization. O all the women I thought of as friends or more there were only two that didn't get a red mark from lacking a Must categories. Celeste and Allison. I wouldn't have guessed that before completing the matrix exercise. Allison was an attractive blond I met in that PE soccer class. Celeste and I had married.

I looked over the matrix to make sense of why life came out the way it did. Summing up the columns arrived at the "winner." The high score was the gold nugget that panned out the best.

Guess who the stiletto fit? Alexandra. Sure. I knew she was my princess, even before the matrix. I *was* a romantic soul after all! I *knew* the answer before the data was in.

The second highest score went to Celeste. Not bad. Not bad at all.

This crystal stiletto exercise helped me recognize the filters I imagined and placed in front of myself as I sorted what was important and why I discounted the possibility of furthering some relationships.

Some of the sweetest women got scratched for all the wrong reasons—but they were my reasons.

Am I shallow? Am I no better than the drooling guys that chase tail to no end? Am I in Joe's league, dousing nearly 100 babes in a semester with his seed with no more compassion that a trolling shark? Is it despicable that two of my Musts were face and body? What a heel I was, to let face and body play such a predominate role. You judge. But do me a favor. Decide what floats your boat. Figure out how a man or woman has score to stay in your game. Forage through your memory and rank those current and old "friends" and flames of yours. See what you come up with. Create and share your crystal stiletto if you dare.

And what of my Cinderella', my Taj Mahal princess? Poor Alexandra got a red mark. Her failing Must score was on reciprocal feelings. She didn't care enough to allow our romance to flourish. That was the one thing that kept this Prince Charming from rescuing his princess from her evil stepsisters. The shoe fit, but she didn't care for the fitter! Alexa's failing mark was reciprocity. I was the salmon that made it up stream to the sanctuary of the quiet estuary shared by my princess. Finding bear molars at the last jump would have been a more satisfying destiny than living with her cold rebuff!

Just as the sun's heat makes butter melt, so, when love melts reason, affection is formed. With increasing affection comes consideration. When consideration grows, confidence appears, and when confidence is full, passion develops. When passion reaches its highest level, it is known as infatuation. Karma Sutra

From the crystal stiletto exercise I learned two things. My heart wanted Sasha. My heart beat for her like my blind beep ball friend thumped his palm on the bench, "Come here, sit. Be with me! You might not see me as the man of your dreams at first but trust me, we make a good team!" Once my eyes beheld her they had seen all the beauty they could ever hope to see. My emotional brain knew I wanted to be with her and hopefully marry her. Every fiber in my being wanted us to forge a deep and lasting relationship.

Thinking as a detached researcher, I shared my matrix in a first draft with Celeste that evening. A glance around the kitchen confirmed there were no sharp knives on the kitchen table or dinner ware within short reach.

"I'm second?

"Excuse me? Oh, no." I walked away suddenly realizing the lack of brilliance in the move. I flipped my hand. "It was noting, just a tabulation of… hindsight. No relevance today."

"So, I guess that means you leaving me?"

I looked back, her hands empty of projectiles, "Honey, that was how I felt years ago. I'd have different criteria now and you'd come out on top!"

Cheer ebbed too soon to convince. Further comment would muddy the fiasco. The tread of stairs beneath my feet punctuated our lack of communication skills on the deepest matters of heart.

Celeste called from below, "There is no way you can spread love neatly into columns and rows. Love's more than a composite score index!"

"Absolutely!"

I declared to the blank hallway at the top of the stairs, "Hard to put into words this thing called love, the attraction that draws…"

"Well you put a whole lot of effort into this chart!"

I turned to see her standing at the bottom of the stair, her hand on one rail and mine on the opposite. "There's passion, attraction, desire. But love… my love is a response to the light reflected by a woman's soul. From those few women I was attracted to, I saw their life force, spirit I guess, as a shining orb. I was drawn to their life, light, and the love I hoped they'd be able to share. Yeah, attraction might be quantifiable as Musts and Wants, but the willingness to act on it and commit—that came about because I responded to the shining orb of their spirit—of your spirit. The crystal stiletto categories were just mile markers along the way, tangible trappings, neither journey nor destination. When I got close to you, I felt the warmth of your spirit and responded. That's the attraction that bonds and can evolve into lasting love."

As sleep took hold later that evening I wondered if anything could anything change the long odds laid out in the crystal stiletto and rapidly elevate a person from someone you might date just once or twice into a more significant relationship.

Learn from Mary.

And Along Came Mary

"Happiness both given and received is mutual enjoyment.
For this shared happiness and pleasure, a man is willing to give
himself entirely. For a man as for a woman, the total gift of self is
a source of wonderful happiness and luck. Sexual intercourse is
not merely a pleasure of the senses: more important is the
sacrifice of oneself, the gift of self. To understand the mystery of
sexual intercourse, to know and make use of what is fitting is the
essential difference between man and beast." Karma Sutra

God bless Mary!
Wherein lays the root of joy? Is it fate, good fortune, or just
people making the best of the opportunities that present themselves?

Definitely the latter. For the freedom and discovery of seeking and
doing yields far sweeter fruits than any that dismount destiny's charger.

The Crystal Stiletto presented a stoic approach to sorting factors and
forces that drive us toward some potential mates and hold us back from
others. This chapter is a counterpoint. This is the story of Mary and Mary
torpedoes systematic.

I met Mary while in the cooperative work exchange program shortly
after Alexandra dumped me "game, set, match!" Work morphed from
large to small, from NASA to independent contractor with office in in
Cary, NC. Throughout the winter I installed equipment in the field. First
of spring, about when my tennis game came to an end, outdoor work
gave way to indoor assembly work. The new assignment kept me around
the shop where I introduced myself to the office's secretary-assistant-
receptionist. Her name was Mary and her youthful vigor refreshed.

Mary and I met as I walked out of the owner's office through a tiny
hall past a bulky copy machine. The do-it-all front office help
approached the tight passage from the opposite ends and tried to squeeze
through. We both turned our hips at the constricting copier and pressed

into each other. Hello! We nearly became intimately acquainted between the collator and the green start button.

She spilled the invoices.

"Sorry," I offered, catching the folders as they tumbled awry.

"Do you always dance like that?" She quipped.

I made a quick on-the-fly assessment. My heart was still with Sasha, but *that* hadn't done me much good for fifteen months. A vivacious yes would refresh.

At quitting time, safely separated by a filing cabinet, I queried, "How would you like to go out? Not dancing right away of course."

She smiled and laughed. "Yes, I was hoping you'd ask."

Yes. What a beautiful word! You can't quite print that large enough. YES! Even though Alexandra had said yes to nearly every date I'd asked her on, Mary's yes glinted with promise that made optimism ignore my abysmal track record.

At the end of our first or second date she invited me to her house. Mary lived in a rented house near campus with a few girlfriends. I didn't think about being invited to her house—put two and two together. Seemed like a brief stopover part of the evening's events.

"My roommates are out," she said as she dropped the keys on a table and headed to the kitchen. The keys careened across the smooth surface before skidding to a halt. "Make yourself at home."

Open invitation to snoop.

I listened, scanning for sounds of inhabitants and took in the atmosphere as I made my way inside. The home was sparsely furnished. It wasn't a matter of Zen, Feng Shui, or artistic spatial awareness. It was a result of the abject poverty of youth we shared.

Keys parked. No hurry to jaunt back out the door… roommates gone. Imagine that! Clever girl, that Mary!

A rustle away from the kitchen caught my attention. Alone? Feet approached light and quick from the carpeted living room.

Alone except for her roommate's dog. The yellow lab lumbered and greeted me fondly. I joined him in the living room.

Mary returned with refrigerator standby Kool-Aid. The two of us sat at either ends on the large living room couch, comfortable and big enough for three. The dog demanded attention I happily rendered. He parked himself at my knees and sensed a loving being genuinely open to his company.

"This dog has good taste in boyfriends!" I joked.

The dog nuzzled closer pressing his head into my lap. I ran my hands soothingly over his head and face carefully massaging his ears. He nosed his head closer.

I thought aloud, "Wouldn't it be nice if people were like dogs? When you want some love and attention, you could just put your head in someone's lap?"

Well, this isn't a book about pick-up lines, but *that* works!

Mary zipped across the couch like it was a water slide. The broad couch instantly became a rather small love seat. We began to kiss. She slid on my lap. Thank God for Mary!

I mean that. Thank God for Mary.

In fifteen months dating Sasha, checking my sexual desire in deference to the woman's consent kept me without contact. But here we have a green light. Big green light. Mary showed some initiative and reciprocity. In fifteen months, Alexandra had never opened her heart and displayed compunction for intimacy.

With Mary no discussion of other boyfriends got in the way. She wasn't holding back for a boy back home. She didn't paint me into a "just friends box" without exit. No words or heavy pondering intruded. No tickets to the opera or fancy restaurants needed. No need for imported French wine. Kool Aid would suffice.

We got along rather well that semester. Our physical contact and romance remained strong.

"The final aim of sexual pleasure is spiritual." Karma Sutra

But something was missing. That something missing in this relationship was *me*. I couldn't warm completely to Mary. We were very close for two people who knew little about each other, but as time went on, Mary sensed I was holding back and we talked about it.

Mary came back into my life two years later. She called, was friendly, and asked if I was dating. I confirmed the news a man never wants to admit. Mary expressed interest in getting back together. By then Clay and I had joined forces with others and rented a house in downtown Raleigh. Mary came over to the house in hopes of giving us another try. But I never sensed a deep spiritual connection with Mary, and my love didn't reflect the joy of her heart. We didn't rekindle the relationship. As adults we wished each other well and ended it.

Mary torpedoes the systematic approach to assessing relationships. Mary's reciprocity and willingness to be more than just friends launched her to the top of my world. Our romantic and urgently shared expression of desire made stoic comparisons irrelevant. She vaulted to number one, if but temporarily. Acknowledging *some* attraction gave our relationship a chance to prove itself. We *got* physically close, and then sorted out if we were in fact compatible, attracted, passionate, etc. It didn't make for a lasting relationship, but at least it made for a relationship! And that was more than I could say for all the time I dated Sasha.

Rusty & Barbara

What if, once upon a time, a guy offered a girl a ride and she accepted and later those two became a couple? How nice and simple. Well, sort of. Meet Rusty and Barbara.

On my quest to understand life and love, I pried into my neighbor's life. I asked Rusty how he met his wife Barbara.

"I was a teenage boy, just sixteen. We lived in the little town of Big Island. Flush with driving license and my dad's set of wheels, I went for a Friday night ride. But for that we came down to the big town of Lynchburg.

"Just cruising. Driving without a clear-cut mission in pop's convertible. Out for a spin, radio on and top down. Nowhere in particular to be, no timetable or errands to run, just driving."

In Rusty's cruising youth the automobile was in its heyday. Cars had a ton of chrome and ragtops abounded. Drive-in movies were popular because people didn't want to leave their precious wheels while they socialized! It was just too electric to stay in the car rather than get out and sit in a theater.

"I cruised down to the favorite strip where all the teenagers hung out when they had time. You know most of us worked on the farm or in town, so free time was scarce. Passed the White Castle, past the A & W stand, I headed for the Sonic drive-in. No particular need for food or beverage, mind you but we loved to see and be seen in our cars!" Rusty's joy bubbled and he laughed and the frivolity. "At Sonic, we could get out, horse around, and enjoy our buddies that might stop by without the formality of a sit down meal.

"That's the way it was. Nobody called ahead. We'd rendezvous. Made it exciting to be somewhere and see who'd show."

The car, that big bold symbol of independence figuring so centrally in young American's rights of passage, became the preferred place to grab a quick bite. I added, "Of course there were girls at Sonic. Some might be looking for a ride perhaps?"

"Of course!" Rusty continued. "Being of sound mind and youthful male vigor, I noticed three unattended young ladies. Naturally I offered them a ride. All three accepted. One got in the front, the other two hopped into the back. And off we went.

"I was looking for a good time and so were the girls."

All safe, all clean, an all American Friday night.

"We drove around awhile," Rusty recalled. "Got to know the girls in a cursory way, their names and where they lived. Conversely, the girls checked me out. Then I drove back to Sonic. And that was the end of our first date."

The night they met Rusty was scantly sixteen and his future bride only twelve. She was the youngest of the three girls.

"Barb and I kept in touch. When Barbara came of age, we got back together and married young."

"Congrats, you're still together as you approached retirement age!"

Rusty nodded yes, "Barb changed jobs a few times. I've worked for the same employer nearly my whole life."

"Why Barbara? Why of the three girls you took did you focus on Barbara?"

"Easy! She got in the front seat!"

I laughed, "Shit! That was easy to sort out. Was it a simple twist of fate, or a knowing young lady who entered the car that night?"

You offered, she accepted. That is the way love is... for some.

"It all sounds so easy."

Rusty corrected, "There's more.

"I was drafted into the Army. Vietnam was just getting started. I caught the ramp up but received domestic orders instead of an all paid twelve-month excursion to Southeast Asia. Good for me. I couldn't take the humidity, and didn't care much for the business.

"Barb and I stayed in touch-- at first. But the longer I was away, communication ceased.

"Two years later I came home. First thing I did was dropped in on her folks and discovered the gory details. Barb fell in love, or enough in lust to get herself a swollen belly. She'd moved off to the beach, Ocean City, with her man and gave birth to a healthy daughter before picking up stakes and moving to Baltimore. Barb's mom always liked me and confided that Barb wasn't happy—'miserable' was her exact word. Her husband drank a lot, found too many excuses to stay away, and they lived in a dumpy place. Mom didn't care much for Barb's choice or how her adult life got off to a bumpy start. She hoped against all hope that things could be different for her precious daughter and grandchild.

"Well, I called Barbara. Took me a few calls, but I managed to get her. I drove to Baltimore. Little old me all the way past DC. Back in the day it was long haul. But the Army had changed me that way. Distance wasn't anything to limit a guy after being in the service.

"Brother that first visit was dizzy! Talk about awkward! There she was, my high school sweetheart in a dump. Now don't get me wrong, I couldn't provide better, but as I stood at the door and peaked inside, I didn't see nothing but a lamp and an old ratty sofa.

"Barb was kind, but nervous. She hesitated on inviting me in. Claimed she didn't want to wake her sleeping girl in the tiny row house. We retreated to the stoop and sat and talked outside the front screen door surrounded by a neighborhood that repeated Barb's story of fallen dreams. Row after row, the blight of the homes appeared indistinguishable from the crushed spirits of the folks that inhabited them."

As he recounted the wrinkled lines on his face vanished and he was young again, just out of his enlistment. I could see a sparkle in his eyes and his cheeks took on the shine of a man on a mission.

"I told her, 'Come on. Pack your bags and get your girl. You're coming with me.'"

Rusty hesitated with a distant look and a smile that lit his whole being. "Barbara thought about it, but not for long. She returned with me that evening and went home."

Rusty added, "As soon as legally possible we married. I got some technical school training and we made a life for ourselves."

Clarifying, he added, "We made a great life for ourselves. Barbara made a bad choice, but we all do dumb things."

Follow-up with Alexa

June-14

"I know some day you'll make a beautiful sun in somebody
else's world but why, why, why, can't it be… mine!" Pearl Jam

Resurgence of feelings for Alexandra and exploration of unrequited love with friends got me exploring virtue, faithfulness, and the strength and value of my marriage. I felt compelled to hasten to my Princess for answers and another taste of the vigor for life I felt in her presence.

Thoughts revolved around four subjects. First were feelings for Alexa. I wanted her to know how I felt. It wasn't to finally have the relationship she effortlessly parried years ago. That was too much to ask for in this lifetime! I wanted her to know because it mattered. It mattered to me. Maybe it mattered to her.

Maybe it mattered to her more than she knew. Alexa had not remarried. Did she wonder if there was anyone out there that could love her unconditionally? She might not want my love, no surprise eh, but if one fluttering butterfly approaches the nectar of her heart, there must be other genuine suitors worthy of time on the dance floor of life.

The second group of thoughts revolved around my wife and family situation. Celeste and I had not gotten along well over the last few years, though we had a pretty good marriage. Over time we had been increasingly less communicative. To say the least I didn't unconditionally responding with love to the orb of her spirit any longer. If what we still had was love, it had mutated.

Early in our marriage, when we felt at odds, we didn't get to the root of problems. Mediocre communication and recovery skills plagued us. Sometimes we couldn't come to grips with what ailed us and we'd go to bed frustrated. Without resolving our feelings, we couldn't lock in the gains to prevent regression. Lately my wife had taken up sleeping in the guestroom for weeks at a time.

Busy lives were another source of dissention. Three kids and a two-parent working family, plus MBA night school meant long days and late returns. We had precious little time for us. Given the poor recovery practices we developed before kids, things didn't get better after we became parents.

We seldom took time for ourselves. Our priorities had become work, kids, and household, then us. God was in there somewhere, but it was hard to tell where. Things that had once been at the top had been squeezed to the point there was little room for us.

The third subject that kept running through my head after my business lunch-date with Alexa was the notion of unrequited love. Granted, I had a tiny sample pool, but a relationship hypothesis had emerged. Intrigued that many people had loved someone that they couldn't marry, the whole subject caused me to wonder how people fell in love and the quest for happiness.

Alexandra had said during our lunch "We all make compromises."

I hadn't thought of compromise in the context of marriage. There was give and take before "I do" and there was a lot of give and take after "I do." But I hadn't thought of acquiescence, settling for less than what I wanted, as compromise. Give and take was an organic repositioning, a shift of wills. It wasn't winning versus loosing, but redefining win-win.

If unrequited love is universal what does that say? Does that mean we all gave up on the one we truly loved and compromised for someone else? What if most folks, by the luck of the draw, the long odds, the bears at the end of the salmon run, marry someone other than the person they really love? What if compromise ran that deep? What if most folks felt that they settled for second best, or third, or twentieth place? More importantly to me, what the hell was I going to do now that I felt that way?

The last group of thoughts I kicked around after my emotional lunch meeting was "why." Why hadn't we worked out as a couple? The other three questions didn't lend themselves to a quick answer. But I could, just might, get an answer on the fourth subject. Alexa was the one path that could resolve this nagging question.

I fired off a quick e-mail to Alexa saying how much I enjoyed our lunch meeting. I told her I expected to be back in Raleigh next week and would like to get together. I knew she liked the museum, so I suggested we meet there for lunch. Safe and neutral site. I intertwined some business related questions to tone down the personal request.

Alexa replied right away. It was a kind note that confirmed our extremely pleasant lunch but she made it clear that my desire to meet at the museum or elsewhere was dead in the water. Her reply stated she didn't "date" married men but "thanks for the invite." She provided me a contact for my work related questions but made it clear she couldn't be of more assistance.

Wow.

"Thanks for the invite." What the hell was that?

I was perplexed. Lunch had been so warm and heartfelt-- her joyous eyes, the hug a momentary visit to heaven.

A day or so later I got a cold call from a telemarketer. After declining the sell, I politely ended our conversation with a marvelous phrase "Thanks for the invite!"

I felt a shudder.

Had Alexandra said, "Thanks for the invite" instead of *You rude and pompous son-of-a-bitch? How dare you meet me for lunch, chat me up, and then pry yourself into my life. You're a married man. Act like one.*

On the other hand, there are many ways of interpreting "Thanks for the invite."

The weekend came. It was Father's Day weekend.

Father's Day

June-15

O Son of Dust! "The wise are they that speak not unless they obtain a hearing, even as the cup-bearer, who proffereth not his cup till he findeth a seeker, and the lover who crieth not out from the depths of his heart until he gazeth upon the beauty of his beloved. Wherefore sow the seeds of wisdom and knowledge in the pure soil of the heart, and keep them hidden, till the hyacinths of divine wisdom springs from the heart and not from mire and clay." Baha'u'llah, Hidden Words

Such wisdom seldom befalls me. I am not the wise bearer who proffered not his cup until he finds a seeker. I was committed to letting Alexa know how beautiful she was to me.

Ever look at an e-mail? Notice one small subject line-- one teeny tiny subject line. Designed for, and fitting a single topic. Complex content is hard to digest. Include more than one theme and the audience isn't conditioned to respond.

What I had to say didn't fit e-mail. I wanted to share my heart. What I had to say needed to be shared in person, preferably while strolling outside. But that option had been blocked.

"Thanks for the invite" left me blunted but still committed to the foray.

Misgivings about the medium aside, I charged.

It was June, Father's Day. I woke very early and booted up the computer:

Dear Sasha,

Thank you for your reply. E-mail is an inappropriate medium. A phone would be no better. I'm at a loss for choices.

You were, and always will be, my Taj Mahal princess. My Taj Mahal princess.

I hope there's joy in this realization.

Your integrity about not dating a married man conveys well your morality. Integrity is not foreign to me either. Recall, the first time we met you told me you were dating "a guy back home." At that moment I accepted the role of patient suitor so not to come between you and your boyfriend. Relationships spanning between cities, between home and college, seldom last. But I would not step in while you had feelings.

Instead I opted to stay close to you. Nurturing friendship, I tagged along at the edges of your time and attention. All the while my feelings grew. My hope was that you would care for me when you broke with your old boyfriend.

On more than one occasion you reminded me you saw me as just a friend. A far cry from how I intended the relationship to blossom. But I remained close. Now, when I watch a movie like Star Wars and see a Jedi Knight stabbed clean through the heart with a light saber, I have empathy. I know what it feels like. Stings a bit. I feel like saying, "Hey pal, hang in there. That'll take a while to heal!"

For fourteen years of marriage I never contemplated a date outside my marriage. My integrity, too, was flawless. On day two of the fifteenth year, I saw you again.

You are my Taj Mahal princess.

I learned something from our lunch. I now recognize *my* likeness. I'm like a "shade-grown coffee bean." I opted to stay in the shadows and abide my manners hoping I would move from "friend" to "boyfriend." Like shade-grown coffee, I did not present myself strong and demanding like espresso. I didn't robustly exhort my self-worth or press my attributes like the popular Colombian roast. Quiet, gentle, patient, holistic and healing. That was my tact through life. Shade-grown coffee.

It does me good to know that my humble plant kingdom counterpart is your chosen drink. It *is* part of your life. It is your preferred desire. It enters the Princess by her own volition. Small is the measure of solace I find in this.

Shade-grown coffee. It enters the princess by her own volition. Honors I never merited.

I may soon be raising my three boys by myself. This is a fate that I often deal with. No news there. My wife calls for a divorce about every two years. Like clockwork. Tick tock-- time bomb!

Each time the demand for separation occurred, part of me knew she was right. But talk... we always talked ourselves out of it. But whether with two parents or separately I will father these boys into fine young men. And I hope you'll clarify for me this uncertainty:

Was there anything I could have done to move up to the "A" list and become close to you? What were your feelings for me?

My life didn't work like I *thought* I wanted it. I never determined if my love for you was real because we never got to that level of relationship.

But life is about learning, and passing knowledge to the next generation, knowledge gained from success and mistakes. I want my boys to grow up, fall in love, marry, and live life to the fullest-- self-actualization augmented by the right person. They'll suffer their own emotional scar tissue, but like any parent I hope for the best and brightest future for them. I need to pass on lessons of love and how to deal without love.

I felt devastated from one-way love that leaves no physical trace, just an emotional hole. And in that hole a little pebble tumbles. And as it tumbles, it makes a sound. And the rattle gains a voice. And the voice wonders if we would have been a really great couple. Alexa, I didn't ever get a chance to see how you performed *off* the princess pedestal! Alas, I never became more than a "friend" to you.

Anyway, I told my wife the gist of all this last night fully expecting to perpetrate the bi-annual discussion about dissolution. I have no mending argument left.

I conveyed all I could remember about each girl I felt something for from childhood through adulthood. There was only one I loved more than my wife. Guess whom?

As my wife and I discussed lost loves and how we felt for them, I called some good friends. These conversations confirmed people often have at least one person they felt more for than they felt for their spouse. It appears that each person in my small sample loved someone that did not reciprocate.

I then turned the questions around. Was there someone who loved us far more than we loved them? Yes! There was at least one person we could identify in each person's life. So, all of us loved someone more than they loved us. Each had someone love us more than we felt for him or her in return.

Rather insightful for a shade-grown coffee bean, don't you think?

So, excuse this poor medium of conveyance. Your latest reply didn't give much hope of a face-to-face. I hope sharing my feelings is healing or enlightening to you in some way. And I do really wish for your feedback so I might learn.

I wish I could have held you close as I shared this.

On Friday I'll be back in town. I intend to visit the contracting officer at your facility. I hope to set up a meeting with the officer if I ever get more than his voice mail.

Friday afternoon from about 1:30 to 2:30 I'll stroll the NC Fine Art Museum. Please join me. Not on a date if that is objectionable to you, but rather on a search for beauty, a reflection of love.

Alexa, of this I am sure. We come to this world for three reasons. The first is to know and love God. The second is to help carry forward an ever-advancing civilization. And the third is love. This constitutes the purpose of life. Our lives have more meaning and joy when we engage in activities aligned with these purposes. And I've never felt more love for someone than I do for you.

The museum may house some sculpture or other artwork that measures up to the beauty I see inside you. There may be an exhibit that suitably conveys my feelings for my Taj Mahal princess. I hope you join me there.

your college friend

There. I said it. I said I loved her and wanted to talk.

BDA

Mid June

Exposure to world events expands vocabulary. Take BDA for example. Twenty years ago, few Americans knew what BDA stands for. Think Gulf War I and the Return to Gulf War Part Two. BDA stands for Bomb Damage Assessment. BDA is an inexact science assessing the effect of exploding ordnance. BDA's are often performed a long way from the blast making it an educated guess at best.

Let's use the concept to assess the effects of my follow-up e-mail to Alexa. The first thing to do in BDA is identify the target. Did I hit the target with my Father's Day e-mail to Alexa? An e-mail has one subject so that could be considered the target. My subject line said "The Bean and His Princess." I guess I nailed that.

But what about my objectives? Had I hit the mark? I wanted to ask Alexa for feedback on why we hadn't made it as a couple and open up dialogue. When I sent that e-mail I was plumb sure it was succinct, expressed my feelings, and asked her a few simple questions. When I went back and read it, I just about *died*!

What had I said? The words were jumbled and thoughts gobbled. It wasn't clear. Where were the questions? I couldn't find my own damn questions! My God! How could anyone read and respond to that e-mail?

My heart sank. How would she feel getting that? Would she think I was crazy, an Internet stalker? I expected she'd reply quickly but upon reading it again I had my doubts anyone could reply to that discombobulated display of heartstrings.

My main objective was to tell Alexa how much I loved her. Somewhere within the wandering pages that point got across, but what the hell had I said to get that point across? "I love you" is a three-word sentence. It doesn't take three pages to say that. "I love you. You are beautiful. I wish you the best in your relationships." Hell, that's an e-mail. That is surgical strike e-mail!

My last objective of contacting Alexa was to rejuvenate our friendship if there was mutual interest. I insinuated we meet at the museum. I told her specific times. I hoped she would be there.

A Noose by Any Other Name Still Chafes

Mid June

I expected my Taj Mahal e-mail would garner a quick response. We had a great comforting relationship once. Sharing *should* be easy between friends, and we'd been at least that if not more. Lately we'd exchanged phone calls and e-mails before lunch where we'd talked fluidly for two hours. Her welcoming and joyous eyes… the meaningful hug. She'd respond. Any day now… any day now.

But how? Alexa had my business card listing home, work, and cell phone numbers. I had sent her e-mail from both my work and home.

I told Celeste, "Expect a call from Alexandra. I contacted her to clarify why we didn't make it way back when."

Turning to confront she raised an eyebrow, but remained quiet and the conversation abated.

For a few days I anxiously checked my messages and caller ID at home. No messages. Over dinner one night the stress got to me. Sitting in the kitchen nook for dinner with my family my heart was 160 miles away. The table's conversations left me on the periphery. A ghost, a specter of my former self, my mind took on a historic pall: *"Here is the family I once had. My wife and sons are all gathered around our kitchen table eating supper just like we used to do… when I loved them… just like we did when I was a central part of the family."*

I choked back a precursor tear.

The boys were in their own worlds and didn't notice, but Celeste asked, "What's wrong?"

"Oh, nothing… a lot of pressure." I lowered my head.

Later that night away from the kids I told her "I'm edgy about a call from Alexa."

Celeste stiffened, "You're not waiting on a call from a person that you used to be friends with. You're expecting a call from someone you still care for."

I closed my eyes and nodded, "Yeah.

"Look, I'm really confused why I still care for Alexa and why it's important to know, to hear from here about why we didn't make it way back when.

"You still care for her?

"Whose turn is it to sleep in the guest room?"

What had dad said about getting lost in women? Where's a lensatic compass when you need it?

As the days passed my life wasn't complete unless I soaked in the sweet memory of Sasha. I dwelt on my princess while driving, and all other times I wasn't fully occupied by my job or family duties. Good thoughts, but far from productive. The stain of SOTB bled into my every waking moment despite my halfhearted decision to not drag myself down wishing for the impossible.

The drive home led me into another kind of ambush that I saw coming but was helpless to avoid. No cunning efforts could save me from the effects of the big yellow "Deer Crossing" sign two miles from home. If I'd been a good dad and restrained SOTB, the wildlife sign slammed me into wishing.

"Paint it 'Dear Crossing, Old Flame Ahead!'" I mused.

It made for an awkward reentry into my home life. I braced for the worst considering what a phone call between Old College Friend and current wife might ignite. I turned into the drive expecting clothes thrown on the front lawn.

Was I still welcome in my own home? Part of my heart wanted to be coming home to Alexandra. The fatherly part of me wanted to make sure my wife wasn't in tears and if we could restore what we once hoped and worked for. And the dad in me certainly loved his kids above all and wanted them to be untouched from any of this.

As I walked through the door separating the garage and family room, kids descended for hugs. "Dad!" they'd scream as they leapt into my arms. And there was my wife. When our eyes met disappointment crossed my face.

Later that night… "I guess you can finally see what I'm talking about." Celeste led as her voice raised an octave. "You never understood being in love versus loving someone."

"I love you, you're my wife."

"You aren't in love with me!"

"Ok. I hear you, but how do you know? How would you, could you? Of course I love you."

"But you're not in love with me. Not anymore. There's a difference…"

"I love you, you're the mother of my three boys."

"Exactly."

"Yes, of course. Glad we've got it settled."

"You love me as the mother of your, our, three boys. Simply be in love with me!"

"Oh, we still don't see this eye to eye?"

"Do you lose sleep over my feelings?"

I clenched my face and shook out a silent no.

"Well there's the difference! I bet you're losing sleep over Alexa who you haven't seen in two decades. You care what she feels, but you don't lose sleep…"

"OK, got it. Your right. I love you. Goodnight."

That night I tossed and turned over Sasha. Celeste's feelings were not central to my concerns, hadn't been in years. Her troubles didn't keep me up. I tallied our display of commitment: Flowers about once a quarter; check. A spectacular diamond ring big enough to draw her attention from unmarried women; check! But feelings, her feelings, were not paramount. We were a team, but we were an autonomous team.

The next day was about the same, triggered by the road sign. My internal script on coming home went something like this:

Two miles from home—"Sasha on the Brain! I'm swimming in love!"

On the driveway-- "Good, no clothes on the front yard!"
Open the door hoping-- "Alexa! … No Celeste."
Deep sigh.

My life turned to mush. The firm parts of my love and my life went squishy and unstable. The pillars of my world crumbled; quaking in desire's wake as unrequited love pressed against the world I'd built.

Emotional limbo consumed me, drifting without word from Alexa. But I realized there was a story in the whole mess. I forwarded e-mails to and from Alexa to my home computer so I could make sense of the correspondence.

I drafted up a rough copy of the book and gave it to Celeste. There wasn't much in it at first. But it contained the e-mail I had sent Alexa, notes about unrequited love and such. I dropped the copy on our kitchen table. Celeste thumbed it momentarily but opting not to read it. I put the draft away, but I left the e-mails on our joint e-mail account at home.

Did you know you could create a noose from an e-mail?

A Dream Lost and Found

Denise is one trick card. Full of Southern Bell spunk, she became plant manager at a small facility in South Carolina. She is the only woman to hold such high position within her company.

The company spent the late 80s and early 90s weeding out the old-boy mentality. Sexually related jokes became taboo. Long gone were the Rigid Tool calendars and other sexist trappings that once were staples of the American workplace. It took the newly appointed Denise to put the transformation on its head.

It was at her second executive meeting. Plant managers and corporate staff gathered and reviewed performance. In business jargon, "shorts" is a term for shipments that don't meet customer length or quantity expectations. To "short" a customer is to send less that ordered quantity. Denise knew a counterpart plant manager had an upsurge in shorts so she came prepared. Denise got to the podium and started her presentation with a slide of a Jessica Simpson as Daisy Dukes in cutoff shorts and snug checkered halter top.

"Here's a little something for that spike in your shorts!" She lit up the room.

Coffee stains still linger on the carpet from the choking laughter.

Denise's' contribution to our "how not to love in the 21st Century" journal deals with reuniting. Imagine two people very much in love but who later grew apart. What if they reunite? How might that turn out?

Denise and I talk about everything without fear of miss interpretation. I shared my passion for Alexa rattling off how appealing Alexa was.

Denise discounted my story outright. "Alexa couldn't have been the most attractive person."

The hair on the back of my neck stood up and I braced myself for a good fight.

"I'm here to tell you with absolute certainty, God never made anyone more perfect than my Marvin."

"Your daft woman, Alexa had perfect skin and eyes to die for…"

"She wasn't half the lover Marvin was…"

"Oh, what the hell kind of name is Marvin anyway?"

She retreated defensively, "Strong, mature…"

I pressed my point as she recovered, "Sasha had a gentle personality that never riled. So much charm…"

The gauntlet was thrown and the joust was on. Pace and volume escaladed. We sparred, expounding the fairness, beauty, joyfulness, and other lovable characteristics of the object of our desire. I fought for Alexa; she countered on behalf of Marvin. We upped the anti recalling attribute after attribute indicating our old lover was the fairest in the land.

The conversation abated in a standoff. Towering above the dregs of mere mortals, we'd both built extraordinarily pedestals for the object of our adoration. We called a truce and Denise proceeded to tell me about Marvin.

"The love of my live was Marvin. Was, as in past tense. Twice actually.

"Marvin was a godsend. We ran up on each other at a most opportune time. We were both young and free. We became boyfriend and girlfriend. And honey we were hot!" Denise teased repeating, "Hot! Hot!" in southern twang to the point she had me laughing.

"We couldn't get enough of each other. My my! Gives me goose bumps just thinking of it! We were passionate baby! He got in my drawers regularly and I'm not talking my dresser drawer neither!"

"A little lower, perhaps?"

"Darn tootin! We developed a love that was as deep and sincere as any shared between two very young…."

"But something changed?"

"Something changed. The whole thing fizzled. Poof." Denise reenacted a dandelion blown to the wind as her eyes drifted away.

I goaded, "You lick all the red off his Tootsie-pop?"

She smiled before clarifying sourly, "Air leaking out a balloon, we lost it over time, and the relationship went flat. Guess we didn't stand up to the challenges the world brought. I can't recall one event that burst our bubble it just petered. Petered away, the relationship bearing marks of total bliss fell apart. Before marriage, before kids, like many young romances, this relationship based on so much attraction and passion flamed out."

"Wow! I'm sorry." I consoled. "Alexa and I hadn't gotten to the hot passionate relationship stuff and I always assumed-- if we had we surely would have succeeded. How could any relationship between two so much in love not work?"

Denise went on, "Wouldn't you know it, some years later I was at this party and guess who's there? Not hard to imagine, we're both from around here, and never left this little town, but I was still surprised. More than surprised." Her eyes flirted with a coy rise, "I felt a twang in my gut, lower actually! It wrenched at me-- hope and anticipation."

"Oh Lord! So you're telling me your laundry load increased for washing sheets!"

"We hit it off ok at the party, but I wasn't totally sure we'd see each other steady or anything."

"What did you do? Didn't he try and get your number, or a follow-up date?"

"No. I didn't need to leave my business card," she giggled freely. "I'm in the phone book, boy!"

She laughed with great release and I shook my head smiling.

"That evening Marvin showed up at my door."

"No! Unannounced and unwelcome?"

"Unannounced." Denise smiled broadly. "We rekindled our romance immediately. The L word was back in my life. Bedroom doings, them under the covers things, yep, the whole works. Baby we were hot and heavy!" Denise laughed again at her youthful vigor and added, "We didn't leave the house for a month unless it was essential for food or work! We were back in each other's arms and the world seemed perfect."

"Then what? You're not married to the guy now."

"I started getting inklings that things were not right. Woman's intuition you know! Inconsistencies appeared in Marvin's story. At first, I wasn't listening closely because I was overjoyed with the whole reunion thingy. But his heart betrayed him and I sensed something in Marvin's past, maybe something in his present that I needed to know about."

"Out on a short parole?"

"Worse! Turns out he had a wife! Oh my God! And his wife was going into her last month of pregnancy! What a terrible blow. The man I idolized and loved turned out to be a man that ran away from his wife when she needed him most!"

"Ouch! I'm sorry! It must have hurt."

"Distraught, wished I'd never seen him. The image of Marvin had been perfect. We'd had such a marvelous time together years ago. And we'd just finished an amazing month together. But Marvin proved less than the ideal man."

"Denise, there's a silver lining here. Seeing Marvin again may have been a blessing in disguise."

She pulled her head back glancing with piercing eyes.

"At least you got to take Marvin off the 'perfect pedestal.' The return visit that ended so badly made you realize there was no going back to Marvin in the future. After you got married, there was no more fantasy of Marvin. When your marriage hits rough spots, if it floundered, Marvin has already been dethroned."

She confirmed with a slight head movement. "Yeah, definitely no thinking about that man again. Marvin's pedestal had been kicked out. Maybe that helped me focus and make the absolute best of marriage."

Harbingers of Trouble

Mid June

"Even when his desire has a particular object, the wise man
forgoes becoming attached. Even in the case of affection, the texts
warn against realizing an attachment. The sages deem that virtue,
interest, and pleasure must be coordinated." Karma Sutra

"What is the meaning of showing me second in your heart?
What should our future be if there's one you love more?"
Celeste found much to dislike in my Crystal Stiletto matrix. Her
memory astounded and her eagerness to discuss knew no end.

"Loved more. OK? I'm saying the crystal stiletto was my way of
reflecting twenty-three years after the fact. The matrix showed how I felt
as a single guy."

"Well, if it's single you want…"

"It wasn't the full picture, just a synopsis, one way to codify how I
saw things a long time ago. A way to understand why things turned out
the way they did.

"This is the reason guys don't share their feelings. We're wrong if
we do. Self-help book and afternoon TV shrinks say there are no such
thing as 'wrong feelings' but I disagree. Current discussion proves
otherwise. Any feelings a guy has are 'wrong feelings.' Sorry I shared!"

Guys' feelings are always downplayed. Maybe it is best to ignore
them for the family's good. If guy's feelings don't matter, than guys need
to go back to the old ways and bottle their feelings.

"When you used to ask me how I feel, I tried to communicate my
feelings until I figured out what you were really looking for."

"Oh, and what's that?"

"You know."

"Know what?"

"Expressing my feelings, my needs and desires led nowhere. I learned to play your game. Comfort you and kept us married. But look where that led. It made it harder to acknowledge my real feelings and impossible to share them.

"Don't you see? Alexandra shut me up when all I wanted was to share the love I felt for her. And look—I got the same from you."

"You've been stoic most of our marriage. Now you've got lots of love to share. But there's this little problem. You want to share it with someone else!"

"I cannot go back to living quietly, ignoring my feelings. My feelings run to deep, always have. Her 'just friends' isn't good enough."

"Maybe my 'just husband' isn't good enough. That's what you're saying!"

"No, I'm saying it really hurt me years ago to be ignored by the woman I loved. Any now that we're all grown, I hope for a mature accounting."

Celeste's war paint didn't soften.

Sharing feelings had quickly pushed us onto thin ice. Consolations didn't pull us closer to the bank.

"And how exactly do you feel now?"

"I don't know. I honestly don't know. I regret she and I didn't make it as a couple. I regret not being the man she wanted. I especially regret if there was something I could have done to…"

"About me! About us! What do you feel about me?" She turned avoiding an answer.

Celeste and I had had fourteen good years. I was blessed with the wonderful opportunity of living with someone I cared a great deal about. And God blessed us with three healthy boys. We had a lot of happiness through the years. But as Celeste regularly reminded we were not "in love."

I squarely faced our relationship for the first time in years and felt profound sadness-- a sadness that percolated through the whole body leaving its mark. It started in the heart and quickly spread to the head. Hints of despondency shadowed my every move and stress staked out my forehead building a small furrow of tents where once smooth skin reigned. Creases set up permanent residence at the corners of my eyes.

Weighing possible futures I surrendered, "Feels like the joy of our relationship is a thing of the past."

Dogfights and Dr. Seuss
Mid June

Plans to return to Raleigh unfolded. The meeting with the contracting office was set for Friday, the twentieth. Directions to the museum were secured. Good to go.

Like a lone traveler caught in a raging storm far from home, I was increasingly stranded and separated. Newfound affections headed me away from my wife and family. Alexa's lack of reply left me cold. Her recluse cast a shadow cloaking the confounding gulf separating us obscuring any trail or clue how to close the distance and cross the divide.

Stranded and isolated. I found some reassurance when I reverted to my old cherished pastime, sports. Playing basketball one evening with my boys, the ball hit the rim but didn't go. "The only way to succeed is to recover the rebound, and with determination, go to the goal again. Time and again, tenacity is the blueprint of success. Persistence is the key to accomplishment. Success requires resolve." I inspired the kids and retained a measure of wisdom. I wouldn't give up on Alexa or my questions despite her unresponsiveness. Drive to the backboard, baby!

Next day I rang Alexa, her voice-mail kicked in announcing she'd be in the office all week until Friday at noon. I smiled at the early departure on Friday and reiterated my plans and encouraged her to contact me. A call to her home found residential message.

Plans, men and their plans! Females bent on figuring out the male of the species will enjoy this little story. Manly enough to keep the other half entertained, it shows the ways of men as they face uncertainty.

When I was a kid, I thought beauty was something young and unscathed. Like the perfectly smooth skin of Sasha's face and the twinkle in her eyes. I learned later that's a young man's illusion. The beauty of life is how we go on, make plans and go on, regardless of the odds, despite the troubles and wounds we've already received. The beauty of life is how well we do with the scars, because of the scars. Those that try in spite of the odds are beautiful and the real heroes.

You're beautiful and a hero because you rise over troubling circumstances. We develop greatness in a large part because of the trouble we face. We aren't beautiful as adults because our faces are unscarred or our hearts unblemished from failed love, but because we've survived and remain joyous. In the face of adversity, or unrelenting silence, we press on. We rise above difficulties and carry on, not just to persevere, to elevate. We rise up and love again, overcome obstacles and contribute to the human experience. Not giving up on life, on learning, on teaching and sharing, makes us champs. To the backboard, baby!

Got any heroes in your family tree, the old fashioned heroes? Got any knights in shining armor that lived honorably and died young? Was it living honorably or dying young that earned distinction? Honorable living doesn't lend itself to flashy comparison. But checking out of the gene pool early in an ostentatious way puts one in contention for hero.

Heroes that die young get pruned out of the family tree often before they bring forth fruit. Given their early demise, and interrelated nature of our species, we can all claim such chivalrous heroes as our own. The story of a life snuffed out ever too soon tells an important part of the fabric of life, it tells of men and their plans. Consider this young man, whose experience illuminates the ways of all men.

He was young, still a boy really, a young man who came of age during war. The Great War was on, and he was separated by the Atlantic from the fateful struggle. Like many whose ideals and ambitions were world embracing, he considered himself kindred with those fighting in Europe in 1916. Though his nation had not yet committed, he threw his lot in and became a pilot in the Allied Expeditionary Force.

When he got to France the First World War was a quagmire, bogged down and full of grizzly horrors at ground level. But our young hero would have none of the trench warfare and chemical weapons that took so many young lives and caused lifelong suffering. As a pilot he was quickly assigned to a fighter squadron.

In World War One the magic number was five. Survive five air combat missions and your probability of living through future missions was much better. Getting through the first five was the trick. "Survive five and stay alive. You might become an ace instead of a plot of ground." Read the banner hastily tacked above the briefing tent door.

Green pilots comprised the majority of dogfight casualties because young pilots usually make fatal mistakes that lead to their quick exit from the sky and duty roster. The novice might hesitate when he should plunge in, or plunge in when he should show patience. He might press an attack a moment too long. Seasoned pilots, trained by at least five previous confrontations, had a distinct advantage of seeing the game played for keeps.

New pilots put their hopes in their own skills, luck, fate, and good mechanics. And they prayed they'd make it through their first five dogfights. Then they figured they might just avoid the long solemn journey home in a crate or burial in a foreign field.

Our young relation survived unscathed his first five sorties and was on his way to becoming an ace. He met that milestone and more. In a few months he'd seen a lifetime of trauma. The proximity of the dogfights left little to the imagination.

Early planes were small and woefully underpowered. Biplanes cruised at speeds that modern planes would stall and crash. The planes were made of wood, wire, and fabric. Armament included very short-range machine guns made unreliable by the variations in ammunition. When bullets did find their mark fabric would tear and engines and gas lines once punctured would spew fumes prone to igniting.

The slow speeds of the planes and short distance of the guns meant dogfights were up close and personal. The pilots would motor past each other about the same speed as opposing cars on modern interstates. You could see the pilot you engaged, and he in turn could see you. And when a fellow took a hit, you could see that too. When a gas leak caught fire the results of an in-flight fire were pronounced for miles mimicking a meteor about to make its mark.

Another day's flight done. Another novice pilot so sure of his abilities earlier in the day wouldn't join them for the debriefing.

As the returning pilots entered their squadron quarters the uncertainty of an overdue return became confirmed. The squadron leader completed the duty of sorting through Philippe's personal belongings. Without welcoming the arriving pilots, the squadron leader's detached sneer hid all feelings, "Not a thing. Not a single thing in here that cannot go home. Poor fellow didn't even have time to acquire one single bad habit or wayward trinket." He flipped carefully scanning envelopes as he completed his sanitation search, "And here, letters from only to one woman, scant else. Send it all back as is." A shudder worked its way down his shoulders to his hands as he closing the small footlocker. The ratchet clasp snapped closing the final word on Philippe's short career.

His bunk would be assigned another before it had a chance to properly air out.

The grass pasture used for the squadron base made the airfield smell like the farms most of the boys hailed from. Comforts were sparse, lives simple, but the pilots and ground crew knew it beat the hellish conditions infantry suffered. On a quiet walk around the base with his closest friend stride for stride our relative confided his greatest fear. "It's fire. Fire is the one thing I worry about."

The men knew the ritual. They remain silent after a death if they had no direct firsthand knowledge of the circumstances. But they'd find the strength to speak if they'd seen the end to teach, to share.

"I saw Philippe go down." Our great uncle confided.

The men took about two-dozen paces in silence, a step for every day they'd known Philippe.

Neither looked above sod level as if the ground held some mystery they shouldn't miss. "Promising young man." His quiet friend encouraged.

Bravely our relative added, "Went down in flames. Watched as he struggled to land. Blaze spread. But he had a chance!"

The men stopped and looked into the cool white sky as another of their squadron turned on final approach and bounced down the converted cow pasture. Winter was setting in and late fall rains had given way to a field that had a firmer frozen surface. Tires bounced and the two men continued to stroll.

"He had a chance?" His friend distanced himself by refusing to acknowledge the deceased's name.

"He landed in a farmer's field behind our lines. But he must have broken his leg, maybe his back in the landing. He couldn't escape the flames. Couldn't get out."

The two young men walked with reverence so as not to desecrate the spirit of their comrade.

"Saw him struggle. He was alive after his forced landing but he couldn't get out of the crumpled cockpit."

The men stopped and released agitated air from their lungs and it condensed in the dreary air before disappearing forever without a trace.

"Withered in agony and succumbed to flame." His friend surmised.

Our great uncle nodded, "There's only one thing I fear in this big world. Burning to death trapped my cockpit wakes me up at night in a cold sweat. It's what rattles me—burning to death. I'm not going that way."

A fire on a plane in the air was horrifying. Punctured fuel lines and engines quickly leaked trails of oil and gas that spread along the canvas and into the cockpit. Once ignited, the flames would dance toward the pilot. Flames swaying in front of the cockpit wouldn't be content to say there. As canvas and wood caught fire, the spread of flames would lap back and dance around the pilot's leather helmet. If he swatted that flame with his gloved hand, his actions hasten the spread inside the cockpit. The white-hot heat and black smoke made visibility nil when the pilot needed all his concentration to land. Gasping for air, flames would scald the inside of his mouth as choking smoke fill lungs. Landing was difficult in the best circumstances and nearly impossible consumed in conflagration.

The two pilots resumed their foot patrol, quietly walking the perimeter of the landing field as three others lifted off.

"I'll jump."

"You'll jump?"

"Right here and now, I'm coming up with a plan. If my plane ever catches fire, and it looks like it'll spread, I'll take my chances. I'll jump."

Pilots didn't have parachutes back then.

"Just bale out of the cockpit? Think it will remain steady long enough? There's no water in our area of operation."

"We always scout for terrain, looking for hey fields and freshly plowed fields because the lift characteristics are different, the thermals."

"Sure."

"I make a metal map every time I go out. I remember the plowed fields, the river and every farm so I don't get disoriented and can find my way home."

"Sure, we all do."

"Well, I'm paying special attention to possible ditching zones just in case."

"In case of what?"

"Fire. I'll return to a freshly plowed field and a haystack and make a dive from low altitude. I won't burn! I sure won't burn." He shook involuntarily before forcing soldierly control.

Surviving the first five sorties and becoming an ace wasn't insurance. A fellow was still prone to have his ticket punched on any given flight and one day our not so young relative got the worst of it.

The sortie started as a non-combat training exercise for seven green pilots and three experienced. Fifteen minutes into the exercise clouds hid an opportunistic and prepared adversary that swooped down and raked his flight. Overwhelmed, many broke ranks and fled. Too many departed to make a stand this day. Three Allied pilots engaged the enemy to distract and fiend long enough for the novice pilots to escape. Our great uncle was one that bought time for others.

His stalling action worked. He downed one plan in the initial fray putting a dose of caution back into the attackers.

Moments later his plane shuddering as machine gun rounds slapped his canvas airframe. He gritted his teeth instinctively turning sharply to avoid additional damage.

"Jesus that was close!"

His mind raced pushing the yoke increasing airspeed and turning for all she was worth to slip out of the expected incoming trajectory. He assessed how loud the impacts had been momentarily reliving the encounter to figure out if the damage serious.

The sky cleared of Allied as one then another compatriot broke contact. Assessing the situation, he realized the jig was up.

"Time to bolt!" He oriented himself to make the speediest exit.

A thought of self-anointed praise for handling the dogfight so well formed in his mind but was cut short when blazing machine gun bullets rocked his unsuspecting plane. The impact pushed the plane forward and sideways piercing the fuselage behind and in front of him. He jolted in his seat from the jarring and adrenaline. The sound caught up a fraction of a second afterwards from eight o'clock signaling enemy on his left rear quarter. Instinctively he turned toward the noise and bullets to reduce his enemy's chances of locking on his tail.

Fortune and technology spared bodily harm. The cyclical rate of the machine gun wasn't high enough to pepper the entire plane. The air speeds involved and the relatively slow rate of fire left gaps between holes. Graciously the cockpit had been among the gaps.

He flew his stricken aircraft keeping a watchful eye. Glancing back he realized the adversary had disengaged. The rounds that had struck his plane were a parting shot before the enemy gave up. The fight was over as quickly as it had started. Combat-- days of preparation and boredom punctuated by 90 seconds of wet your pants terror.

Our great uncle took a deep breath and turned for home.

He checked himself, ensuring he hadn't taken a hit not noticed in the fray. "A OK" he reassured.

The low-slung cockpit seat prevented him from seeing the extent of holes so he didn't know how bad his plane might be. But he'd felt the plane shudder under impact. "The bullets struck something solid and didn't pass harmlessly through." He glanced at the scant instrumentation looking for more information. RPM looked steady. "Oil pressure… maybe dropping" he cautioned.

"Two miles closer to home," he thought. "Come on baby!"

A terrible racket cascaded within the harmonics of the loudly rumbling engine. He squinted as if it would improve hearing. Metal on metal. The engine began missing.

His plane's growing listlessness kept his intention. "Come on baby, we're in this thing together. Get me home and I'll take care of you." The tips of his propeller became noticeable as the engine slowed dangerously. It kept running, barely. Coughing and sputtering he limped home. "Two more miles, hang… hang in there!"

Attention riveted on the airworthiness of his craft. He released anxiety by assessing what was working, "Enough power to maintain steady flight." His mind refreshed the day's ground survey.

By the time he saw the smoke he knew it was trouble. He lifted himself as high in the seat as he could without losing control and looked over the cowling. A wisp of smoke appeared then was gone. He tried again to lift up but it didn't help. He put the plane in a gentle turn so he could see behind him. Heartbreak-- the aircraft was leaving a trail of black smoke visible for miles.

"Damn. The smoke must have slipped beneath his lower wing following the fuselage!" He hadn't seen the problem for minutes. "No wonder the enemy broke off so quickly. Damn!"

He rose to survey forward. The conflagration was apparent and grew severe. The first visible sign of fire lapped upward then was gone. Extinguished? He didn't think so, only momentarily following an unseen route.

With foreboding patience he assessed the fire's spread aloud, "Visible, trailing smoke for miles, it's probably engulfing the lower half of the engine compartment… oil's on fire!

It'll spread. Probably consume the nose any minute."

He faced the scenario that doomed others. Theoretical became real. Work the plane down risking engulfment in flames? Or try the exit strategy? Land on an unprepared surface and risk being broken in two and not get out?

"Ride her down or jump?"

He opted for the latter.

He did the best he could on his leap. With the plane low and slow he made a dedicated run over a plowed field. With the plane barely above stall speed and no more than 60 feet above the ground he unharnessed himself and stood. He shook with nerves a degree below total panic. Hard to rise… movement awkward… and slower than he hoped… but it had to be done carefully.

The plane was about 30 feet off the ground when he launched himself tumbling sideways as he came down.

One hundred years ago the rural countryside of France had many freshly plowed fields. But alas there weren't many piles of hay to break a fall. Picket fences were even fewer.

That's how it ended for this one branch of our family tree. He came to rest instantly, head impaled upon a picket fence.

I'm sorry. Sad ending.

But is it really sad? He had choices—fly home and probably crash, or work the stricken craft and hope he didn't break his legs in the crash, or try his luck with a jump.

Don't focus on the outcome; chances weren't good either way! Rather celebrate the lesson he exemplifies. He faced a tough situation, came up with a plan, and executed best he could despite the rotten chances.

That is the hero part of the story. He's a hero because he believed and he acted. What made him a hero wasn't the fact that fate helped him survive the first flights, or that he became an ace. He heroically faced his torment armed with hope, with faith, and a plan. That's it. That's all a man can hope for when the shits flinging all directions off the fan. Men, when given a mighty long shot, devise plans however ill conceived. The real test of their character and courage is if they execute their plan or if they just give up.

No distinction between bravery and fool hearted. Faced with overwhelming odds, is it the brave or totally stupid to proceed with a plan? He was going to die either way. But following his plan made it his way.

Modern life seldom presents life and death struggles. Yet I faced my burning cockpit. I faced my troubles though my arms got weary and my sneakers did leak.

Marriage was going down in flames. At the end of my flight, a grueling divorce waited. Would I jump or ride it down sucking 500-degree flames that cauterized the esophagus on contact and then turn the body into a crude unsightly concoction of charred organic goop?

I got my mind level and slow, and I was ready to leap. My second pass over Raleigh was upon me. Jump or ride it out? Alexa hadn't called back and she hadn't acknowledged e-mails. No sign of freshly plowed ground in sight. Would there be hay at the art museum? Or was there a fine picket fence?

I found both. A parking spot instead of a field made the journey's end survivable, but I found myself impaled on the equivalent of a picket fence stuck through my heart. Unless Alexa showed, I couldn't move forward toward my reluctant princess, my ever so uncommunicative Taj Mahal Princess. I couldn't move back to what seemed more and more like a stillborn relationship. This fence wouldn't kill, just leave me stuck and twisting.

But I would act! I felt good about that. I sought out life! I'd taken life and fate into my own hands and leaped to find the answers.

If Alexa doesn't show with forceps in hand, does anyone else have a pair of pliers big enough to get this plank-sized splinter out of my heart?

The Museum

June-20

"**S**ure"
That's the kind of clear answer you get from a bachelor.

I contacted Gary a couple of days before my trip to the Museum hoping to spend the night with him. Gary lives in Chapel Hill, close to Alexa and the art gallery. Logistics fell into place. Trusting his feedback, I sent a copy of the Taj Mahal e-mail.

"That is a quite a load! Did Alexandra realize how you felt?"

"Can't be sure, she plays her emotions like a world-class poker player. But, no, it shouldn't be a surprise, more of a reminder."

He got quiet on the phone then suggested, "You probably confused her. Maybe a little threatened by so direct a revelation?" His voice was conciliatory as he welcomed me to spend the night.

I arrived at his place before Thursday evening's rush hour released its masses and strolled his neighborhood. It was a new development where vinyl siding takes on so many hues and textures you almost believe it's real. A year ago the land was forty acres of field and woods. Now a few dozen starter homes sat empty of life except persistent gnats and one angry migrating bird squawking in wonderment of what happened to the field and oak trees he used to visit.

As I walked I thought about the e-mail and Alexa's lack of response.

Screwed the pooch? I wondered aloud kicking a loose stone along the deserted neighborhood street. Had my e-mail made me a social outcast? Did I skip a chapter of the human handbook growing up that directs wise men never to act on heart alone, never reveal their true hopes, desires and love?

Homes waited for their dual income owners to return. The stillness smacked like ostracization. The mundane neighborhood took on a sinister, Twilight Zone feeling. Might Alexa, my Taj Mahal princess, like the absent owners of these houses, turn her back and not be there for me?

Gary got home and we talked, small at first, graciously saving my miscarriage for later. Gary related, "I had a crush on this girl from work. I say that now, but calling it a crush does injustice to my feelings.

"Anyway, she was interested in me but more interested in some other guy. Guys? We had our heart to heart and we left it like adults on friendly terms. But romance was clearly off limits.

"Two years later a mutual friend asked if I was still interested in her. I said, 'Sure.' We spent a fun weekend with a couple of friends. By the end of that weekend, enough had transpired to convince us that the attraction was real. Yet we weren't interested in growing our friendship into anything else. We shared an attraction, but other aspects of our lives weighed against us. Our attraction wasn't strong enough to overcome the obstacles. Great experience. I saw how old friends who wanted to be more than friends might, if given the chance, choose instead to stay just friends. Thing was, we made that choice. *We* made the choice through interaction and communication, not remote indifference."

"Nice that you shared and explored the opportunity."

Gary nodded affirmatively, "Mutual closure was surprisingly beneficial. We got wind in our sails, got on with our lives without missing a beat, and carry no emotional baggage."

We drove to Chapel Hill for dinner. The college town wasn't crowded that summer evening. Restaurants, bars, shops and streets were underutilized. The cosmopolitan street felt intimate to those in attendance. Folks appreciated of each other for being there because with a few less it wouldn't feel right.

We spied two young ladies with books open. Studying in a public place was a clear sign that schoolwork wasn't their exclusive priority. I launched into conversations with the medical school co-eds. Gary was surprised at the fluidity with which the girls shared where they were from, what motivated them to get in school, their career hopes and dreams.

"I'm amazed how easily you got these girls to open up," he said shyly after we left.

"Everybody has a story. Most folks share if you pose the right questions with genuine interest. Don't more women respond to honesty and friendliness? The blonde especially could tell I was being kind, and her friend relaxed as the conversation got deeper. I gave them a break from their routine, a chance to reaffirm what the heck they are doing here, that's all. The fact that we're two guy strangers, well that just made it more…"

"Mysterious?" Gary added.

"I was thinking along the lines of 'reassuring.' Two guys could chat them up without expecting anything or leading them on. That reassured them that they are attractive and in control."

Gary and I perched ourselves in a quiet pub and continued our conversation. He lamented, "Most of my relationships twisted unrequited."

I struggled, "Remember Red Skelton? One of his shows describes a chunk of our turmoil."

"Red Skelton?"

"You know, the clown? Red Skelton was America's clown. His television show was the tail end of Vaudeville; TV mimicked earlier entertainment with variety shows. His show included dancing, singing, and comedy. Red featured standup comedy and part of his act was pantomime. He shot the show in front of live cameras to catch the unrehearsed audience response. Folks would howl at his goofy Freeloader the Hobo, Seagull, and the like."

Gary recalled, "Ah, the days of real laughter and not sound tracks!"

"One night Red came on stage, stood there humbly with hat in hand, and told the audience he was upset. He stopped his live show and spoke directly to the audience and via the live camera to America. His solemn monolog wasn't an act. It was uncomfortable as heck because he was out of character. He said he was miffed because last week's audience hadn't laughed at one of his jokes. The lack of response disturbed him. Then Skelton retold the joke. The audience gave him a forced laugh, but he got his response. The audience gave him encouragement and he bowed graciously with a broad smile. He offered thanks not as a comedian, but from a man, a humble solitary man-- and then went on with his show."

Gary looked genuinely lost.

"Anyway, as a kid I wondered how in the world a successful comedian, who'd done standup his whole life, would be peeved about a lack of audience response? Why would that upset him?"

Gary offered, "Feedback… response... he needed to know he was connecting?"

"Exactly! I learned that day we all need feedback. So going back to get response… to connect isn't bad. We *all* need it. Red loved comedy and his audience. I loved Sasha. Not that much to ask!"

"With all my painful experience on the subject of unrequited love, I see the merit of connecting. At least one person in the world understands you."

Gary paused, rolled the beer in his hands, "Ever try and get her drunk?"

"What's that?"

"When you dated, ever get her drunk?"

"Ha! No. Wasn't my style, man."

"Might have been an effective primer, 101 proof crow bar."

"I never wanted to take something, start something that she wasn't in full agreement with. I wanted her to warm to me, you know?

"Getting her drunk wasn't the kind of love I had in mind. Expanding, lasting, fulfilling love. That's the relationship I wanted. I wanted a girl that wanted me. Not someone that needed coercing."

"Wish now you did?"

I laughed. Weighing the merit caused my head to swing side-to-side, "All I needed was the tiniest encouragement, a glimpse that she was trying to open her heart, you know?"

"Might have torn down a barrier or two." Gary mimicked ripping a crow bar.

"Need something stronger that Crown Royal for her barriers. More like C-4!"

Gary hauled us back to the current situation, "What was the deal with the Bean, Shade-Grown-Bean?"

I filled him in on our lunch get together and how I adopted the nickname "Shade-grown Coffee Bean."

Stupefied he said, "Shit! You gave yourself a nickname? You're fucking screwed, man!"

"That's only half of it and I need you for the other half.

"Oh no! It's too late for C-4 now pal…"

"I want to track down some shade-grown coffee and give it to Alexa. I made up a little card and plan to drop the card and coffee to her at work. Playing that imagery for a little humor might ensure she shows at the museum."

Gary shook his head seriously and confirmed, "You're fucking toast!"

The absurdity of my plan and the long odds sank in. But it was my plan. "As bad a plan as it might be, it's what I've hatched. Unless we audible to something better there are only two options: give up and be a failure-- live without trying, or forge ahead and live knowing I tried."

I imparted a modicum of emotional wisdom as we wrapped up our light meal, "Look at your spoon. What do you see?"

He inspecting the back of the spoon like a surgeon might an instrument of dubious sanitation, "Yesterday's French Onion soup!"

"Picked this place for the ambiance, huh, not cleanliness?"

"Scenery isn't bad." Gary flicked the end of the spoon sideways referring to two young ladies sitting catty corner from us and finishing their meal. The waitress had just deposited their bill on the table as Gary drew my eyes to them.

"Right you are. Now peer again at your spoon."

"I see me in the reflection."

"Turn it over, so you're staring at the concave side."

The young ladies seated nearby inconspicuously inspected their flatware.

"I see myself," Gary answered.

Broadening the conversation to include the two women, I said loudly in their direction, "Sure of that?"

They both looked up and smiled, realizing they were caught listening in.

The one woman added, "I see myself upside down."

"Sure?"

Gary and the other girl raised a hand and realized the image was also reversed.

Gary announced his discovery first.

"Right! Upside down and reversed. Your eyeball's retina is the same general shape so you initially see everything upside down and reversed. All visual images hitting our brain are distorted likewise. We spend the first few months of infancy coming to grips with that. From then on, the mind makes immediate corrections of everything we see."

"I've heard that." The second girl confirmed.

"Amazing we can catch a football running away from an incoming spiral pass. With a single glance over our shoulder, we snare a ball flying in from above.

"The mind has to reverse and turn everything upside down. What approaches us high and to our left is presented to the brain as an object low and to the right. Our brain instantly adjusts what our eyes tell us so we can interact in the real world."

Introductions were in order-- one young lady from Michigan another from Oklahoma. Both were on campus for Resident Advisor orientation training. They were graduate school students who would collect a meager sum of money mentoring undergraduate kids lodging in their dorms.

From one sense to the next I added, "Ever snore? No you two. You're too young and pretty to snore! But a parent, an uncle?"

"Yeah, I've got an uncle that shakes the rafters!" admitted our new mid-western friend with a laugh. Both girls leaned closer.

"Ever notice people that snore seldom wake themselves? They sleep right through it. Even if they raise a racket like a chainsaw, "People tune out noise without a second thought. But consider a parent listening to a newborn child. Most times the parent immediately hears their offspring's cry for momma's milk, or a change of diaper. Believe me, a responsive parent wakes up even as the cry forms. Before the airwaves vibrate with a newborn's call, a sensitive parent tunes into the rising distress and the intent of a cry. I know. I've cared for three.

"Point is, our mind twists everything we see, and we listen to only a small part of what we hear. But we tune our senses to let important things get through. And some of these important things trigger feelings? Feelings based largely on what we see and hear.

"So why do we care so much about feelings?"

The group went quiet.

"If we ignore most everything external to us, and turn things around with our mind anyway, why care about feelings? Feelings are just interpretations of filtered sensory inputs. Why care?"

The student from Michigan launched first, "Because they're *our* feelings?" Her voiced unsure, rational mind tagged on doubt but her intuition spoke loud and clear.

Gary added, "Feelings give us a sense of soundness, connection to the world around us."

"Right," Oklahoma added. "They connect us. Confirm within us what's important. Of all that we take in, what we feel is the part which resounds."

"Resounds!" I added.

Michigan reiterated, "What we feel is the part which resounds. Deep. I like it!"

I added, "Feelings complete the circuit. They make us whole. Good feelings connect and feel warm. Emotional pain stings of disconnection, they tell us we're moving away from life, from love."

Proud of my little ad-hoc group's openness and ability to wax profound I concluded, "The deepest feeling is love. Love reigns supreme. We can feel love bleed through the moment, straight on through the day, in and out of weeks, and far beyond months. Years later, the impression still lingers. Love tinges our being like nothing else. Love reaching through decades, even transcending temporal life!"

Compelled to leave on the next leg of my quest, I said, "Ladies, if you don't mind, it would be my honor to pick up your bill. I remember what being a student is like."

"Why, thank you!" Michigan drew out. She twisted her words accentuated "thank you" making it more invitation than courtesy. I smiled and gracefully lifted the bill.

"Just remember when your undergrad students rave against NC State, you met one kind gentleman who went there."

Gary lingered a moment and chimed aggravating the rivalry between his UNC Alma matter and NC State. I glanced back and waved a quick goodbye as I headed toward the register.

Gary caught up with wide eyes, "Catch the way she sounded? Like she was appreciative in a way that… maybe the evening didn't need to end so abruptly?"

"I caught it as an invitation. Maybe our interpretation is a function of hearing loss from too many rock concerts! Besides were on a mission! I've got a plan! There is only one woman in my sights, no time for distractions regardless how cute and available."

"Too bad, I favored the one from Michigan."

"Yeah, and I'd sooner take the Sooner. But we're dialed in. Lock on target. Execute."

"Dialed in on a woman that isn't Celeste. Look Brian, you know I love and support you and Celeste. We've joked a lot over the years, but I've never seen you chart a course that put your marriage in jeopardy."

"You're a trustworthy navigator. I haven't ever strayed nor took to wanting to. But when it comes to Sasha… right about now my wife is just a shadow across my sights, throwing my aim just a smear."

"I can't believe it." He shuddered.

"I can't either."

Gary and I strolled through town, checking out a number of coffee shops. He pointed out the absurdity of my effort to acquire shade-grown coffee and present it to her, but he reluctantly went along as quiet accomplice and a great friend.

"So, help me get something straight. Is this an effort, some kind of engineering failure mode analysis? You know, like finding out what you did wrong in the past? Or is it a quest to resuscitate a dormant love?"

"I don't know where it will lead, but I've got to see her."

"If you don't, you won't know emotional rest for years. I mean, she's simmered for what, twenty-three years and you can't get her out of your mind?"

"This is real important to me, and I thank you for your help."

"This is going to dog you, man. Your plan better work! If she doesn't show and share her heart you'll probably fret over her for the rest of your life."

Gary stopped us outside the first coffee shop, "OK bud, you're on! Go sniff out some of your brethren beans."

I slapped his back and went shopping.

There were four coffee shops in the pedestrian shopping area. We struck out at the first three. Finally, through blind perseverance, a keen sense of smell, and a bright storefront sign, we entered a Starbucks that had my princess' environmentally friendly coffee. A loud "Bingo!" prompting the clerk to close the distance and immediately attend his boisterous customers. Starbucks sold it in bags and the attendant would gladly grind it free. "I take a bag but leave it in tact." I cringing at the thought of my namesake crushed by unappreciative hands. Let her grind 'em. Maybe she'd keep a bean or two as a memento-- a keepsake.

Joy spread across my face. "I hope one of those beans she hangs onto is me!"

"Are you going by her house tonight to drop it off?"

"Intriguing possibility… hadn't thought of it. I haven't been invited. No, I'll give her the gift at work first thing in the morning. She knows I'm coming, so if she's planning on meeting me she will, if she isn't…"

Gary concurred, "Better to give her the chance to show at the museum. You go ninety percent of the way and let her come ten, is that it?"

I nodded.

"You're still toast!"

——————————— · ———————————

Friday arrived, the day for the museum, a day for my contractor's meeting, a day a hidden part of me had waited twenty-three years. I gathered her coffee and personal note and made my way to her office building. I told the security guard and desk clerk to call her down but the clerk said they routinely deliver courier packages. I left the heartfelt gift for Alexandra at the same reception desk we'd met at less than two weeks before and headed to my meeting.

Afterwards I rode the calm breeze afforded by excellent planning, time to linger. I visited an upscale store with a wonderful flower section. I waxed emotional muttering to myself, "I shouldn't go by her house uninvited. No. Give her a chance to show. Go ninety percent and let her go ten."

With flowers picked from the many festive assortments that begged to be part of the mission, a woman approached down the aisle. She made her way near then halted a few feet in front and exchanged glances. Quickly she looked down and walked past. I could feel her sense my conundrum.

A small mirror at shoulder height confirmed my eyes were red.

"God I'm toast!" I said aloud not giving a damn who heard.

I took a deep breath and put the flowers back. *She'll show. She'll show!*

Twenty minutes later eyes adjusted to the subdued lighting as I glanced in vein at the guest book's signatures. The place was bigger and nicer like she said. I quickly surveyed my options and the best chances to see her. Scanned the layout, spied a gift shop, and all other optimal recon spots. Damn, no ideal place to see the various floors and entrance. My wandering mannerism spurred the receptionist, "Do you need some help?"

I chuckled, "Does it show? I'm expecting someone, a young lady."

"It is a big place, but if you're persistent…"

"Oh, that I am, ma'am. That I am!"

She smiled. A male coworker standing to her right and clearly interested in the receptionist smiled giving away his heart.

The receptionist flashed a hint of a smile in return knowing full well the man beside her wanted her. She could feel his shy smile even though she wasn't looking at him. She knew what his face portrayed.

Ok, this can work. People around here are helplessly tumbling toward love. This will definitely work!

I added, "If you see an unaccompanied beautiful woman looking about as dazed, well, she won't look dazed, probably just radiant, make sure she glances at the guest and she knows I'm here. I'd hate to miss her!"

The art museum was large enough to warrant an extended visit and small enough to see in two hours if you were on a mission. Curators wince at the meager allotment. Taking in all the exhibits might require a full day for the contemplative but I breezed through quickly keeping a wary eye for Alexa. I'd hoped to see O'Keefe's work and impressionistic pieces but they'd been moved, temporarily stored to make room for a tribute to the Wright Brothers.

The search for a floor-length mirror was futile. I'd fantasized our Red Carpet reunion with a romantic twist. A full-length floor mirror with a six-inch wide gilded wooden frame that had resided in a Roman senator's home or some such thing would be on display. We'd stroll together seeing the wall mounted exhibits. Then I'd walk her in front of the mirror. Peering at her reflection, I'd introduce her to my Taj Mahal Princess.

But there was no mirror. And there was no Alexa.

Time dragged past our appointed hour.

She didn't show. Surprised?

"Jesus… I need to be with her." I fumed quietly as I retreated to the museum's restaurant. Nice restaurant with delightful food and attentive wait staff. A single red rosebud garnished my table. *How fucking nice.* The flower offered solace but a single Bean at a table is one lonely Bean.

Lonely. It was a new feeling. I couldn't recall feeling lonely at a meal in decades. Youthful enthusiasm made me blind to such melancholy. In that moment shared by the red rose, I remembered waiting tables as a college kid and serving a middle-aged woman that dined alone. Her comment as I served her shrimp cocktail; "I drove all the way across town for this!" In youthful ignorance I assumed she was partial to our appetizer. That's all she ordered before she left.

Tables turned. Today I sat alone astride my adult years. I'd driven hours… for this.

I finished the meal. Dessert extended my welcome at the well-positioned table with a strategic view of the main entrance.

I stopped willing things to be different and watched patrons arrive. Just be in the moment. Be the moment. Small groups and families came to take in the beauty and history. A large class of middle-school kids arrived. Handicapped kids and their summer aides came in just before 2:00. These children would get more from the visit than I.

On my way out the cheerful receptionist touted the museum's holdings one more time, "Did you have a good time? Take in the Greek artifacts?"

For the first time in my life cheer in another human being's voice brought a remarkably sour feeling in my throat. I swallowed to remove bitterness before spreading it to the unsuspecting.

She continued as I halted staring at the glimmer of light spilling from the front doors; "We get many complements on our solid gold mask and…"

I nodded politely without eye contact, "Yeah. The Eurydice and Orpheus piece. I got it."

Time progressed aggravatingly slowly on my somber trip home. I listened to CDs and heard the melody and lyrics. On my last ride home from Raleigh I'd been so high with amorous delight I didn't notice anything except my love for Sasha. Now music was a welcome companion. No squirming body. My heart offered no quarrel against a northerly tack.

I chastised her ex-husband, "Fool! You fucking idiot! How dare you spoil the chance to love her! Squander the marriage? For God's sake fellow, you couldn't have possibly *cheated* on her? And I know you couldn't have raised your fist or voice to her.

"Bliss might not survive for eleven years, but fella' you ought to know what you've got!"

If the cold does not seek the flame, can either fulfill its destiny?

Does the wave crash into the beach? Does it return? Does it have a choice?

What is choice when you're a wave responding to the forces around you? And what is choice when all you are is a man in love?

Sasha's absence drove the spear of the picket fence deep. Did she feel *anything* for me?

Like a male mosquito separated by a windowpane from its heart's desire, the insect flutters his little wings and hopes with all his might while it's hearts desire, it's little winged mate opposite the glass, turns away uninterested. So close but yet so far. It never had a chance.

What *was* it about Sasha? What *is* it about Sasha? I have to know.

Deep sigh.

Long drive home.

Man Asks for Directions

June-24

After my lonely visit to the museum, I was in the checkout line at the grocery store when I overheard a young girl of eight or nine giving encouragement to a guy she wanted to date her mom. The little girl asked as they stood between tabloids and racks of candy and gum, "Why haven't you asked my mom out?

The man turned quickly knocking candy bars to the floor. He bent down to address her eye to eye and surveyed the mess. "Would your mom mind if I got her flowers?" He replied sheepishly so the mother couldn't hear.

"Well," she said raising the anti of the conversation by placing one of the errant sweets on the moving belt that the man was paying for, "Mom would mind if she *did not* get flowers."

Flowers?

Flowers. Flowers for Alexa!

I'd considered the possibility in Raleigh. Flowers could amend if my e-mail had disturbed. Flowers might be the leverage needed to pry a reluctant heart.

My own wisdom on the subject was shallow so I reached out for advice.

The next day I had lunch with Kevin and Jerry, two friends from work.

"Can you guys keep a secret?"

They uneasily exchanged reluctant glances.

"Hey, I promise the subject isn't national security or anything to do with people at work."

They sat back relaxed.

I unfolded my saga about Alexa, my conversation with my wife, and the insights into people who felt they loved someone equal or more than their spouses. Surprised by the depth of the subject, both admirably followed suit and shared their own relationship history.

Then I asked, "Should I send Alexa flowers?

Responses varied.

Jerry replied, "I'm once divorced and twice married so I disqualify my ability to give advice. I'll remain silent."

Kevin, once married and no divorce, was quicker with guidance. "Forget Alexa and send the flowers to your wife!"

"Forgetting Alexa is out of the question. But I see your point; sending flowers to Alexa may not be smart right now."

Flowers. How many guys have used this as a way to open a rusty, untrusting, unresponsive heart? They'd come in handy before and after marriage. Sending flowers helped keep my wife happy and feeling loved. It wasn't a monthly occurrence, but she received them regularly.

I called Alexa's office to see if she was in. Instead of her beautiful voice her answering machine announced she'd be out all week. Kevin's wisdom became palatable. No reason to send flowers to someone that's probably not there.

Out of the office this week? Had she not shown up the previous Friday at the museum due to existing plans? If she was out a half day Friday and then this week maybe… she *couldn't* come to the museum!

Instead, I sent flowers to my wife. I knew I had shaken her heart with the crystal stiletto matrix and our discussions. I wanted her to feel special. Best I could.

Flower Power

July-7

Restraint had as much chance stopping me as a levy has holding a cresting tide. I held out about a week.

Sending flowers with a note is not as easy as wiring and letting the florist pen a card. But a Raleigh florist heard the need in my voice and agreed to take the order and coordinate the delivery with my card mailed to the agent:

DEAR ALEXA

I'm OK.
You OK?

Talk?

You choose.

Love Brian.

Being an idiot I couldn't leave it at that:

Dear Alexandra,

Thanks for doing lunch the other day.

A flood of emotion overwhelmed me. I shared. Sorry if I startled you.

You are like the sun to me. I feel alive and in love in your presence.

I watched a TV nature documentary the other night. It was about some remote islands where crashing surf pounds the sand, coral, and rocks. Pretty but harsh environment. The narrator said; "Powerful and tumultuous forces are at work shaping and transforming life."

I've recently felt similarly powerful forces sweep through me. For this I am grateful. I would not have realized the strength of these forces had we not seen each other.

I came away from our lunch with a rediscovery of feelings. I dove back into the pounding surf of feelings and thrashed gasping for air, stumbling over the how-and-why of yesteryear and more. I am a stronger person because of that swim.

Here is what I figure: life defied all odds just to come into being. I don't know how it all began. I don't know where it will all go. The sea of life crashes. We frolic the best we can.

Alexa, I don't want to lose you as a friend. I don't want to say or do something that isolates us. But I don't want to place artificial chains around my neck or blinders on my eyes to hold me back from feeling or prevent me from seeing the beauty in you.

And I do want to talk to you and see you again under whatever terms and conditions you feel appropriate.

My intentions? My intentions are life, and love, and joy, and happiness, and responsibility, and contributing as much as possible to the world of creation.

Love,

Your college friend

A grain of sand caught in the swirl of pounding surf. What in heaven's name do you *do* with feelings so primal, so sincere, when you're sure you're doing the right thing by listening to your heart?

"Just as fire burns the dead, so anxiety burns the living and reduces them to ashes." Karma Sutra

Alexa's Reply

July-14

"Love Stinks…" J Giles

With flowers sent, interest in a reply peaked. No immediate acknowledgement or "Thank You" surfaced. No message on the phones, no e-mail, no letters in the mail, and no reciprocal flowers. Girls *never* do that!

I awoke each day one hundred percent certain a response was coming. At home I checked the caller ID log. Two calls came through from her area code, but the rest of the number disappointed.

I checked work and home e-mail accounts scanning names as the inbox filled. The download process firmly renewed disappointment.

I called the flower people and waited patiently as the store owner scurried, "Oh yes, I remember! You sent the note to accompany the flowers. One moment and I'll check." Delay ended with the same kind voice, "Yes sir, I confirm delivery. Was there a problem with the service? Did you not get what you expected?"

Days crawled without word. Just one meeting face to face was all I needed.

On Monday a week since I sent flowers to Alexa I was at work. My computer chimed the arrival of new mail. I opened the message without looking at the sender:

"Brian, Sorry it's taken me a while to respond."

I held my breath, anxious and excited.

"The confidentiality letter attached looks like it will meet the criteria…"

Confidentiality criteria... what? Shit! It's work. Breathe.

"Mission Control we have a problem."

Alexa's response was a replica of her response to my three-page e-mail. Let's review, just for the daft, shall we?

It was her idea to exchange a catch up e-mail but she hadn't followed through. Strike One.

I'd sent her a three-page love letter tangled up in an e-mail. Stupid medium, but a love letter none the less. No reply. Strike Two.

The museum, Strike Three. But wait... I got a reprieve on that one because she *could* have been out of town. Count that a foul tip.

But flowers, the tried and true delivery of flowers? What of her response to flowers? Surely *flowers* would precipitate a woman's reply! Strike *fucking* three.

I dreamed about Sasha that night. I was in a building constructed of curved walls. Maybe it was a cylindrical lighthouse or the foyer of some antebellum mansion. A long, curving stairway rose to an upper floor. In the dream, my dad, Celeste, and I were present. Sasha and her dog completed the dream.

There was a platform, an open landing, on the curved stairway about where the second floor should be. On the landing was a bed, which Sasha shared with her dog. She laid face down, presumably sleeping. She wore modest nighttime attire uncovered by sheets or other bedding. I ascended the curving stairs to a level above Sasha and talked in hushed tones to Celeste and my dad.

All the while Sasha remained quiet and motionless-- comatose in her deep sleep. I didn't know what to think of Alexa lying face down in her bed, oblivious of those who passed beside her on the steps, those of us able to walk, talk, and interact.

The next scene in the dream instantly transformed to a grassy yard. Sasha sat on the bed, which - in the strange way dreams progress – was outside. Her feet were flat on the ground. Her dog accompanied her motionlessly. Both sat staring ahead. A road flanked the left side of the yard, and traffic whizzed by. Sasha, devoid of emotion, focused down the road. The thought crossed my mind; *if I had a motorcycle I could drive by and catch her attention!*

I awoke and pondered the dream. Dejectedly, I surveyed my empty heart and figured it would stay that way.

Lewis and the Standing Eight Count

"It's all so confusing, this brutal abusing. They blacken your eyes, and then apologize." Pat Benatar

Ever hit anyone? Ever been hit? There is something primal about fisticuffs. Common civility gets jarred when your head snaps back or to the side. You trade one type of focus for another. If you didn't see it coming fear cannot be your first response unless of course you've been hit by the same person before. In that case one punch signals the start of a cascade of derision and bodily harm you may be right to fear.

Come stroll with me. I promise it's safe.

Let's go below ground level and walk the underside of the civic arena. It's a side few see. Forget the concession area, walk with me in the confession area.

Friday Fight Night. For some that happens infrequently. Professional boxers schedule fights with ample training time between bouts to recover from ferocious blows. For amateurs, bouts are more frequent but wisely scheduled. In the case of domestic brawlers, any night could be Fight Night.

Let's walk.

Dull halls painted flat grey below the audience trace avenues for service, utilities, and support staff. We get a different sense of the pending spectacle compared to seated guests above. Through this main hallway and to our right... there through the open door... see the fighter taping up? He's the one sitting on the table, head's down in a reflective pause before the storm. A guy's mind thinks about life, maybe his wife or girlfriend, training tips too. He should be thinking about his adversary, or even better, calming his mind thinking absolutely nothing. Better not be scared. Lord he'll get torn up if he's eat up with fright.

There are differences between ancient gladiators and modern prizefighters, but as you watch man in quiet contemplation before the challenge, well, the last 2000 years kind of just disappear. Similar fight, similar show, common personal challenge.

Keep walking. Hear the crowd above? The ten-inch reinforced concrete floor separating the arena muffles sounds. Noise descends reverberating like rumbling bowels of a giant beast. The boisterous crowd's impersonal and remote, like it's in a different world.

Turn left here at the ramp; we'll go up. Through these double doors and we'll re-enter the world of spectators.

Got it? Push hard, the doors are heavy. Heavy doors keep the noise down. Homes don't have these heavy doors... it's not as easy to keep the neighbors from knowing about domestic disturbances.

Step through and stop. Bright and loud. Linger a moment. Don't rush it; take it all in.

Every millennium, every century, every generation, some form of violent entertainment finds its way in front of willing spectators. Call it sport. Call it brutality. Call it entertainment. This sanctioned display of force sadly mimics a lot of folks' personal lives. That's why it draws such a raucous crowd. The brutal exhibition shadows people's lives like a secret admitted only by attendance.

Hey! Quick, open the door! Here comes one of the ring girls. "Hi!"

Did she flash a smile? She's the gal that struts between each three-minute round with a tall placard announcing the next round. She often makes an appearance between fights just to keep the crowd suitably riled in an erotic way. What a job!

Don't know if the ancient Romans used scantily clad vixens to excite. Hell, this lot doesn't need stoking. But she is sweet, isn't she? Eye candy for sure. Go ahead, turn your head and gape as she goes by. If you don't stare and swoon, she'd probably be fired. I'm sure some schmuck gauges the extent of the crowd's reaction to the ring girl. Not enough shouts and gawking, not enough heads turning, and she's written out of the program. So give the girl a whoop and help her get a paycheck.

And just look at her as she makes her way down the hall. How long does a woman *look* like that? Most never do. At best she's got another fifteen-year-stint of flesh defying gravity.

Did you see her outfit or was it too small? That, my friend, was a day-glow yellow two-piece bikini inspired by the beaches of St. Tropez. The yellow triangular bra cups are shaped that way for a reason. They resemble yield signs affixed to a very curvy terrain. The yellow yield color sends a subliminal message to the howling masses of men cautioning: This woman is for viewing only.

Come. Let's head up the ramp.

See the fans above us at the edge of the stands propped against the thin steel pipe railings? Hope the rails are strong enough to keep them from tumbling. Most of these fans aren't drunk, but when the punching gets fierce they'd lose their balance for sure if it weren't for that little bit of metal sanity.

Let's go to the ring. Don't worry about the two security guards ahead. We're allowed. No worries. Look like you belong, ok?

That's it. Good job. We're a few paces from the corner of the ring. Take a 360. Blinding lights! Man, I can never get used to how impossible it is to feel genuine when bathed in blinding light. It separates humanity—those on display from those doing the cheering. Squint; see if you can make out the audience. Hard to see faces past the first row or two, but real soon all eyes will soon be fixed on the carnage center stage. Fixed and horrified, enthused and elated. Necks stretched with malice. Many will shout advice. But believe me, the boxer can't hear. Shouting congeals into a whirlwind of noise. It's weird. He'll be in front of thousands but unable to hear or see anyone.

Quiet. Time for the announcer.

"Ladies and Gentlemen!"

Always draws a thunderous applause. Just like "Play Ball" before a baseball game.

"Welcome to tonight's marital madness!"

Bedlam! The announcer waits for pandemonium to abate.

"In this corner, wearing the royal blue trunks with white and yellow piping, standing 5'-9", weighing 188 pounds, our Lewis, the Hunkster!"

Cheers and jeers, about half and half. They cheer and they boo -- some folks get so excited they cheer and boo at the same time!

"In this corner, wearing white trunks with soon-to-be red splotches, standing 5'6", weighing 126 pounds, is Lewis's third wife, Victim Number 3."

What do you think? I mean about the crowd's reaction? More cheers than jeers? Most pull for the lady; we naturally pull for the lady. She's the underdog giving up that much weight.

Before we go back underneath and get away from this madness gaze ringside and stare at the front row. See the middle-aged lady with the young man and young lady flanking? That would be Lewis's first wife, a.k.a. Victim Number 1. And over near the corner, the lady with the little boy beside her is Victim Number 2. You know whom they're pulling for.

Let's get out of here and go back where it's quieter. I hate a mismatch like this. She hasn't got a prayer unless she holds a third degree black belt or Lewis has a bad case of the flu. Otherwise, forget about it! You can't give up that much weight to a seasoned fighter and have a chance. It will be a slaughter. He'll tear her to pieces if she's dumb enough to keep getting up. Hope the referee does his job and stops the fight before she needs an ambulance… or worse.

What's that? What's that you say? If it's so unfair, stop the fight?

Sorry friend, not mine to do. I love to help, you know me. Get involved and do what I can, but this is way past me, pal. When she put that ring on, she stepped *into* the ring. If she didn't know it, shame on her. She is, after all his third victim -- I mean, wife.

Blind to the signs? All the time she caressed his curly blond hair, gazing endlessly as his gorgeous blue eyes while they courted, she should have seen this coming. Love's blind. That doesn't change until black eyes appear.

On the surface Lewis is every girl's dream -- the curly blond hair framing his darling face, the body sculpted full of muscle. If he poses you'd swear it is the famous "David" stature. He used to compete as a bodybuilder. Still has the form, still pumps iron religiously.

There are two drawbacks to marrying a guy with that much passion for his own physique. It takes a lot of time away from the relationship. Second, you hope they don't turn their honed muscles against their women and kids.

Lewis the Hunkster has two broken heart tattoos, one on each butt cheek. After his last knockdown victory he dropped his drawers and mooned the crowd, spinning around to make sure everyone got a good look.

I've experience boxing so I qualify as a color commentator. My time in the ring came in college as a PE elective. For a non-violent fellow who had successfully curbed his competitiveness and aggressiveness, boxing was an about face. I hadn't been in many fights growing up and my lack of experience hitting and being hit made me wonder if I could take it. Boxing would prove if my gentle heart could stand up to aggravated physical contact.

Boxing is best performed between people of approximately the same size, hence the weight classes. NC State tried to organize kids by weight. As the lightest kid in the class I would fight kids in seven weight classes—Super flyweight to Lightweight! I love a challenge!

Each boxer fought four bouts during the semester. Each bout consisted of three rounds, and each round was three minutes long. Far fewer rounds than paying customers would expect on the card at Atlantic City or Vegas, but our fights weren't designed to sustain a crowd's appetite. Ours wetted the whistle and proved mettle.

Our training ring was more appropriately called a square. No elevated springy taut canvas cordoned off our boxing area. Our boxing "ring" was fashioned from white tape squared on red mats that covered the wrestling room floor. The mat gave some spring to your legs, and some protection in case of falls.

The equipment issued didn't include boxing shoes either. High-laced shoes were prohibitively expensive. Motion was a little precarious-- dancing in sock feet on the mat. State did issue open-style head guards and gloves. Head guards were made of the same material as the gloves, hard padding wrapped in a tough red leather shell.

Gloves varied in size and weight. Some were made for larger hands and generally were heavier. The smaller and lighter gloves made a boxer more maneuverable. It gets quite tiring holding your hands up and punching, and all the guys clamored for the smallest, lightest gloves to gain an advantage. Heavier gloves wear the puncher out faster. Keep that in mind during your next domestic dispute. Hey, I'm in your corner.

Actually, most family disturbances don't go three rounds. Husband beaters and wife beaters never experience how tired your arms get when boxing. Sport boxers learn real fast that adrenaline coursing in your veins and heaving punches wears down stamina at a pace similar to wrestling.

I didn't lose any of my bouts that semester. After four fights, I was 4-0. The coach said, "Son you have boxing instincts!" A retired golden gloves champion, he'd seen his share of boxers and was dutifully impressed. After a match he became animated recounting the things I did right. "Did you see that!" he'd shout to the class, "He ducked and punched wham wham!" He shadow boxed how I'd out boxed my opponent for the class to see, "That's the way to do it! Great job Whitlash! You're a natural!"

I didn't tell him my proficiency in moving, ducking and landing punches came from a strong desire for self-preservation! My success was based on the fact that I didn't want to hurt anyone, but wanted even less to get hurt. I was good, but it was because I had a gentle heart.

I got an "A" in that class, based on excellent physical condition and not losing a fight.

At the end of the semester, the coach invited each student to attend a tournament. The tournament would allow us to go up against kids from other classes.

Fights started at 8:00—early for a college student's Saturday. The room was filled with guys of all sizes. All wore the standard PE outfit -- badly tailored and poorly fitting red shorts, white socks, grey tee shirts with red lettering informing one and all that this was "Property of NC State."

My fight time arrived, and they paired me with a kid from my class. Bummer. I'd already beaten this guy. He was an aggressive kid with long blond hair. He was a ruffian, not a young man in serious pursuit of higher education. He was one of those kids on a short ticket, a student who wouldn't make it to graduation. In our previous fight, I'd ducked, danced, dodged and then landed effective punches to win the match. He'd been aggressive as hell, a better brawler, but I was the better boxer.

When the bell sounded, my longhaired adversary charged and never let up. Same strategy he used the first fight, but this time I couldn't shake him. He had obviously talked to someone about strategy. Two guys in the room coached him through the match from his corner. I fought alone against a man determined to make me fight his type of contest. Like a tick on a hound, he wouldn't allow any separation. He wanted me toe-to-toe exchanging punch for punch. His brawling style and heavier weight was a huge disadvantage for me if I committed to it. I had to box, not commit to a slugfest. But I couldn't dodge and break free like our earlier bout. Time and again we went toe-to-toe frantically exchanging punches. I'd manage to break free and he'd immediately close the distance.

The bell announced the end of the first round. I walked to my corner shaking my head knowing I had to find a way to fight my style. His in-your-face approach left no room to maneuver. I wasn't sure if I was winning or losing, but I figured the judges would give him the nod, as he had been the aggressor in an otherwise even match.

Boxing is a sport in which it's hard to tell how the fight's progressing. No clock or no scoreboard displays standing. Three ringside judges score it. They count punches thrown and punches landed, how hard the punches, and if a boxer is injured. Boxers get a score from ten to seven each round. The winner of the round always gets a ten. If the round was closely fought, the loser rates a nine. A distinct advantage held pretty much throughout the round would yield a score of ten for the winner and eight for the opponent. And if a boxer takes a dive, hits the mat on a knockdown, he'd get a seven. Of course, if someone is knocked out or disqualified by the referee for whatever reason, the fight is over and the winner's pronounced regardless of the score. Assuming both combatants are standing after the final bell, the judges tally scores and determine a winner.

By my reckoning, the score was ten for him and nine for me.

The second round started with the crisp bell. There is nothing like a boxing bell to get you going. It calls you up and out. A line of alarm clocks ought to recreate that urgent sound. Anyway, we both advanced and before I got halfway into the ring he recklessly charged. He set the tone and I did my best to box against a brawler. We'd fight his fight for ten seconds. Just when he settled into a pattern and assumed we'd continue trading jabs and punches, I'd duck out. Two steps back and three to the side. He'd close and we'd slug it out some more. Three steps back and one to the side.

Break contact. That was my response, the only way I could turn this pounding into boxing. I established a pattern of engaging and then exiting. He closed and we'd be at it again. The Bean was set on changing reality to meet my abilities but I was coming up short.

The bell sounded ending round two, a carbon copy of the first. Judges would give him the otherwise even round based on aggressiveness. I issued the same advice to turn the tide as I walked to my corner.

Round three, same bell, same bull-headed opponent. But I'd learned his methods, and in a fight, if you don't get whipped outright, well... he who adapts usually wins. I instinctively used his reckless aggression to my advantage. About halfway through the final round I started away in the same pattern of breaking contact. But this time I feigned withdrawal. As he lunged forward to close the distance, I came hard catching him with a pounding right.

Bam! He went down!

I stood over him looking down at the cocky young man sprawled. A lot of guys would sneer, spit, or try to intimidate their fallen opponent, but I checked the animal impulse, regained composure, and I walked to a neutral corner. The referee stepped forward and took up position in front of the fallen student.

As the kid got to his feet the referee began a standing eight count --
a mandatory procedure to ensure that a boxer who hits the mat or shows
an inability to protect himself is OK before continuing the fight. The
referee held his gloves in front of him, wiped the punching surface off
against his shirt and began counting. At eight the referee checked the
dazed boxer's eyes, asked him if he was OK, and wanted to continue
fighting. My opponent nodded yes. We finished the round. He'd lost a
step and gained a newfound appreciation for boxing versus brawling.
The final round ended without further incident.

I was pumped. It was a single elimination tournament and I was on
top. If I was right about the first two rounds, the judges' cards would
have him with twenty points and me eighteen. In this last round, I easily
picked up three points with a ten to seven decision. By my swag, I'd
boxed myself into the next round and my tournament would continue.

As the judges tallied their scores, I overheard one say, "I'm
changing my score on that knockdown. I think it was a slip." Another
judge said, "OK, yeah I'll call it a slip."

A slip? A slip? What the hell! I heard my coach, the third judge,
voice his approval of reassessing the knockdown.

I told the judges, "Hey I connected and knocked him down. That
was a clean knockdown. Look at him he's still shaken. I would have
planted him again before it was over if this wasn't PE!"

The other kid said nothing as we cleared the ring and removed our
gloves. My opponent went to the wall, with his back against the painted
masonry blocks, slid down to a lifeless seated position. The judges
stayed put in their chairs and, in their infinite wisdom, made their minds.
I'd done my job; they'd do theirs.

When the winner's name was announced it wasn't mine. A chorus of
cat calls and boos went up from the boxers. A guy beside me said: "Yo,
man. You got robbed!" Others added more colorful commentaries in my
favor.

I told the third judge, my PE coach quietly after the announcement,
"Ah, you knew I knocked him down!"

It was over. The decision was made and that was that. No big deal. Just in the heat of the battle, when you know you won...

I stayed around as a spectator paying particular attention to the fighters I would have faced. The morning progressed and unwound the clock. Between bouts I walked to the kid I'd decked. He remained sitting with his back pressed against the cool concrete block wall. His head looked to be stiffly bolted to the wall. The left side of his face was still bright red some forty-five minutes after our fight. I squatted down and looked past his outstretched legs into his glazed eyes. I shook his foot consolingly, "You OK? Nobody came to the tournament to get hurt. I didn't mean to hurt you."

His eyes were glassy. He fixed his gaze like a drunk, not exactly sure which image to focus on, then nodded briefly acknowledging the fact that he was OK and that he appreciated my concern. His simple nod jarred his head and he grimaced as he placed his head back against the cool wall.

Subsequent bouts generated a few cuts and nosebleeds, but only one kid hit the mat that day-- the opponent I nailed squarely with a hard right. He was the only guy to get planted.

My weight division's second bracket fight was announced. Names were called and one kid from another PE class popped up. But the kid I'd put down didn't respond. He was awake, but he couldn't get to his feet. The referee sensed something wrong and came over. By the time the coach got there, his two buddies helped him plant his wobbly legs. My adversary slowly left the room flanked by his two friends.

The second round fight was called off. The guy I decked was deemed unfit to fight, too hurt and dazed to protect himself. I turned to the coach and said, "Hey! Let me fight! I'm ready to go!"

The next contender was already in the ring. "My fight didn't end with a slip guys, but a well-landed punch!" I lobbied. However the coach said no.

I was stunned. The kid I should have fought in the second round was announced the winner and he shoved both hands in the air triumphantly hopping about the ring.

Shit. Yeah, buddy, you won by a residual TKO from my right hand. I'd seen enough and left.

All in all, boxing lived up to what I expected-- a great opportunity to explore something I would never have otherwise experienced. Hitting and being hit is quite primal and I'm glad I tried it in a safe environment under watchful eyes.

Lewis on the other hand engaged in fights nobody could win far beyond the guidance of knowledgeable officials. A referee didn't oversee his rages. No one was there to put an end to the violence... until the police arrived and court time ended each episode.

What motivates a wife beater?

Lewis moved in with me temporarily when he separated from his second wife. "Let's have a movie feast, manly movies." He said his first weekend in the house. "I'll go to Blockbuster and get titles like *Conan the Barbarian...*" Lewis reeled off three or four movies that featured muscular men, violence, and lawlessness. Movies set in times and places that the rule of law predated modern justice. As the week passed he released his pent up urges and calmed down.

Months came and went and we shared many insights into life, relationships, and love. I offered listening support and drew him into conversations. I asked Lewis to elaborate about his penchant for abuse, and his silent answer might scare the hell out of you.

The truly frightening part was he couldn't approach the subject. He never came to grips with his violence, never approached root cause. Veiled in mystery and shrouded by silence, whatever impetus, whatever insecurity, whatever character flaw drove him to violence was off limits to his rational mind. He could not, or would not, address it.

Still, there were clues. For example, Lewis said he avoided listening to music on the radio because most of the songs were about "addictive love." I asked him to elaborate.

"Shouldn't listen to that stuff. Most songs are about someone who can't live without the love of another. Most songs are about adolescent love. They praise folks whose lives are shallow and meaningless without their lover. That isn't love, it isn't healthy love."

He elaborated, "Most songs use love as a theme and are either tragic or describe unstable yearnings toward unsustainable love. Pop lyrics usually don't linger on the kind of love and maturity that withstands the tests of time. Most harp on the peaks and valleys."

"Huh, you're right. I've listened to music all my teenage and adult life and never realized the shallowness and emotionally misguiding nature of most songs that get on the radio."

"Music takes you for an emotional rollercoaster floundering in teenage delusion rather than promoting healthy love." Lewis preached. "You'd be wise to limit such an influence in your life."

Lewis moved out and went to another city after the divorce. I lost touch, only to hear that he married another woman with two kids. Sometime after that, they did the canvas shuffle and she came out on the short end of the scorecard.

There are guys out there who look good on the outside, but inside they are shit. Sorry, ladies. Maybe you know some. To be fair, there are ladies out there of similar constitution; people with a hang-up they never confront, never learn from, and never overcome. Yeah, they are out there... about six billion of 'em.

Color

Look around. Notice any colors? Feel for a moment if sitting in the presence of color affects your mood. Color paints our lives cheerful or somber. I know about as much about color and color therapy as I do about love, but let's pretend.

Few colors pop into my head when I think of Celeste. Gee, I'm sorry about that!

When I asked her best friend to name Celeste's most lovable characteristic she unhesitatingly said, "It's Celeste's wit!"

I was dumbfounded. Celeste hardly ever displayed humor around me. She seldom laughed aloud during comedies. And a belly laugh? No way! In all our many years of marriage, an unrestrained joyous laugh remained rare. For her friend to say Celeste's most lovable trait was her humor made me realize I didn't have a clue how others saw my wife.

In the absence of true understanding, the one color I attribute to my wife is light blue-gray, the color of a shaded cloud. Not a white cloud that says, "All is fine, expect clear weather ahead." Not a dark gray cloud that says, "Storm imminent, batten down the hatches." Celeste is a pewter cloud requiring finesse to read, a color requiring careful interpretation.

My first color is also a sky color. Imagine the peach-pink-orange-purple glow of sunlight reflecting late afternoon clouds, when the sun begins setting and the sky lights a fervent display of possibilities. This peach-purple color is a promising color, a joyous color. It says: *"Hey, I don't know how you feel, if your job was hectic, if you are strung out or in an emotional valley, but look here! Today is beautiful! Be joyous. This evening's possibilities are breathtaking! Enjoy this fleeting moment of life!"*

That is exactly the kind of joyous uplifting pastel color that depicts me. Look for it in a sky near you.

Alexandra, on the other hand, is vibrant yellow. Not the yellow lines on a road -- those are too orange. Not like the yellow sun that overpowers. Sasha's yellow can be found in some flowers. Think of the brightest yellow flower you can imagine. And if you look closely, really inspect it, there's more than yellow. Deep within the surface a hint of crimson veins appear intermingled so delicately giving the yellow a rich luster. A deep passionate part makes itself known only through loving intimate examination.

My other color is deep green. Why do *I* get two colors and everyone else just one? Author's prerogative.

Imagine peering at the edge of a forest forming a wall of green on a late summer day. Look at the shadows between the trees. Shade appears darker. Now gaze at the shadows within the shadows. You'll see branches and trunks and leaves lurking. Deeper green still. Now let your eyes take in the space between the spaces. See where the shadows disappear into darkness? Your eyes see holes in the forest. Dark inviting places. They look black but your mind tells you green. There has to be green in there. If only there were light, you're sure it would be green, not black. Eyes say black, mind says green. A green just this side of totally dark. Got it. Found me!

Sasha's vibrant yellow. If I am dark green without my yellow... maybe that is why I feel so... blue.

Bon Voyage Cappy

July-19

As stressful as the month started, it got worse. When things look their worst, there is always room for greater loss. Wee Captain had kidney failure.

Wee Captain, our beagle, was faithful and stubborn. We treated him like our first son. He'd always trot out and bark a greeting opposite the driver's door as my car came down the driveway. With joyous eyes and an unmistakable beagle bark, tail wagging his whole body, he'd welcome. Stepping out the car door each day I met his large joyous brown eyes and swaying body and the sight of him brought out the best in me as I transitioned from work to home.

As the years went by we added to our family. Cappy graciously gave up his only child status and accepted the role of pet when human sons swelled the family. He was good with the kids and boisterously protected the yard.

Rapid onset of lethargy prompted a call to the vet. The day before his appointment was the first day Cappy didn't greet my arrival. I searched for my boy.

He lay in one of his favorite spots under a small tree. His choice location gave him a clear view of the front yard, optimal for security. As a guard beagle, he was second to none. But he wasn't sitting at attention and he didn't get up. Too weak to stand, I picked him up and loved him.

That night, I had a soccer league meeting and returned home about 9:00 p.m. Midsummer, so the night sky was just getting dark. As I drove up Celeste stood beside a bush. She looked attentive like she expected kids to return home from an evening's romp. But it wasn't the kids on her mind, it was Cappy. He'd parked himself in tall ground cover providing a niche.

I got a blanket and a bowl of milk and sat with him. He finished most of his milk as we shared a cozy vigil. We talked about our lives together. OK, I talked, he listened. I recalled how I first met him when he was ten weeks old and Celeste brought him home. He'd been joyous and showed wariness of humans. A bundle of puppy love, he grew to love us and we played like I was a kid. I thanked him profusely for being good with the kids as he'd gotten older. He nodded as if to say, *what had I expected? After all, we're brothers!*

We quietly pondering the falling dusk, night smells, stars, and beyond.

The next day Cappy made my day by just being alive. We drove quietly to the veterinarian. He had lost five pounds since his last checkup. Clearly in pain, his body had a quake and he shook uncontrollably in the lobby. He shuddered as if bravely facing his fate.

The vet drew a blood sample and asked me to leave him. Results in an hour. She'd call.

I was at home when the call came in. Terminal kidney failure. The vet said his future was in pain and any respite would be temporary.

Cappy's condition pushed me over the top. Emotionally troubled for months, Captain's condition was the final emotional straw. I walked into the living room overwhelmed.

I returned to the kitchen and concluded to Celeste, "There's no good choice for Captain. We should put him down."

The time to say a last goodbye was upon us. I told Celeste "It will be best for my boys to be together one last time for a final goodbye. Bring the camera-- easier to erase the digital images if we cannot bear looking at them rather than rely on memories."

I cut a funeral warp from a large swath of cloth and headed to the vet in two vehicles.

When we got to the vet's office, I took Cappy out of the kennel cage and carried his shaking body outside where we gathered the kids in a little grassy area. Celeste and I encouraged each of the boys to pet Cappy, love him, and say goodbye. My littlest boy, just two-years old, didn't understand what was going on. The five and eight-year old took it all in. They were thankful for another chance to love Cappy. Celeste told them this was the last time they'd see their four-legged older brother. Their gentle minds were unable to fully mesh with the unfolding reality.

A heartfelt and tearful goodbye enveloped as the finality of the moment settled.

I sent Celeste home with the boys and I took Cappy back into the vet's office and held him as shots were administered. He didn't go to sleep with the first shot—the vet said low body fluid levels prevented proper circulation. Cappy was a little conscious and awake when the second injection stopped his heart. I held him and kissed him goodbye.

"See you in the next world." More tears.

"Goodbye, Cappy! We'll keep you in our hearts!"

Captain made the return trip home in a white shroud. Celeste cut flowers from the garden and laid them atop his bundle.

I prepared a hole.

Captain would have approved of the location. His burial place was under trees near our driveway. From his final resting-place, he viewed our driveway and the road. The UPS man might have lost a barker, but Cappy could spiritually keep an eye on traffic.

I dug deep alternating pick and shovel. Tears and earth flew as the hole crept lower. I wished all my feelings were just for Captain, but passions for Sasha intermingled.

I thought of her needs. Without children and without a husband, all she had was her dog. Who would share the joys of life with my beloved Sasha? How would she take it when her dog dies? Will she need a heart to share the grief? And who will cry for Sasha when she dies? My sadness waxed between memories of Captain and reflections of Sasha. I dug with fury.

I said as I plied the earth, "Take me with you, Cappy. What am I going to do?"

The hole excavated large enough for my shrouded dog and tattered marriage.

Celeste arrived beside me then quickly backed away in the same shuttle step Sasha had veered in the elevator. "My gosh!" Celeste wondered aghast, "Who or what is such a large hole meant for?"

She turned and scurried to the house.

Take me with you Cappy!

Hole completed, we gathered the kids. Some of my children's friends joined us and we commenced a burial ceremony for my first son, my four-legged son. Two of Captain's dog friends attended reverently remaining quiet and calm, they sniffed the burial package, and sat beside their human handlers. Some said prayers, others offered praise of his good points.

Cappy was put to rest with his little head toward the street so he could remain our watchdog. Celeste laid the flowers, the kids put in some dog biscuits. We gave the neighborhood dogs their own biscuits to eat. Then it was time to cover it all with dirt. The kids helped with their hands, me with a shovel.

His death was a clear and present sign to make the most of life. Losing is a part of life. I know I lost Sasha-- hell, I know I never had her. Letting go was beyond my ability because it meant closing a chapter of my heart. Until the day I buried Cappy I never grieved at the loss of the woman who, when I stood about two feet from her, made me feel as though I was within arm's reach of my dreams.

Sacred Tombstone

July-22

I waved a silent salute to Cappy's resting spot on my way to work and back again for about a week. Then I forgot. I caught my lapse and acknowledging his grave again, but daily salutations became rare. The sacredness of his tombstone diminished.

I asked Kay, "Have you ever heard of the sacred tombstone principle?"

She shook her head.

"Kay, imagine a burial ground. A group of people hold it sacred. It is an integral part of their lives, the final place for loved ones. They know it will be the ultimate destination of their bodies. This isn't a remote or lonely place, but right in the village, a site that connects the whole circle of life.

"The burial ground remains sacred because it contains their bodies. But the notion of hallowed ground exists because they're in tune with a reality that transcends material. Decaying flesh doesn't make it hallowed. It is hallowed because of memories testifying joy, love, and family. The burial ground is sacred because of love shared with ancestors and the promise it signifies of perpetuating the tribe, the village, people."

"OK, I see it, a community cemetery. There is the church, well-marked graves."

I pictured a Native American burial ground, but a contemporary cemetery works if it isn't forlorn and isolated from the people, if it remains connected to the living.

"Over the passage of time and changing circumstances, the community thins. They lose touch with their living relatives. Relationships become secondary. They lose touch with those that have gone before, and the connection to those that will come. They lose touch with the sacred nature of the burial ground. Not all at once, mind you, but over time. They forget."

Kay took up the idea, "Or they just get too busy."

"Too busy… folks move away. Calamity strikes. Or they just lose touch with the notion of sacred altogether."

Kay stilled.

"What's a field of dead when nothing is sacred?" I asked, driving home the point. "What would happen to the burial ground?"

"It would be forgotten, get… overgrown."

"Humans have lived pretty much on every square mile of the earth from time to time. Maybe this ground we were standing on was once sacred to someone.

"Family burial plots come to mind-- a mute reminder of what was. Residing quietly beneath large oak trees, ground outlasts remembrance, and sanctity dwindles. The lot gets covered in tall grass, weeds, and then saplings emerge."

"As the sacredness diminishes, so too goes the care, the love, the attention." Kay reflected.

The light in her eyes shone bright as she saw the link between keeping something sacred and close to the heart.

"It doesn't have to be war, famine, or the dying out of a population. Forgetting and not caring will do the same thing," she added.

"Right. Same is true among the living," I said, pausing to be sure Kay made the transition.

"Consider our friendship. How long has it been since we talked? I mean, really talked?"

"Two-and-a-half years, I guess?"

"Maybe more, since we *really* talked. I mean, since we shared something deep. Until my yearning for Sasha, we hadn't gotten into anything deep for years. Our friendship had become, well… some things and some people get squeezed out of your life. They get marginalized until they're history. We didn't see each other and our friendship got put on hold. Put on ice."

Kay asked, "But did we lose anything sacred?"

"We'd lost all the joyful wonderment, the explorations into the matters of life and everything else we used to talk about. When you and Eric were together, we made plenty of time to interact. Then we put our relationships on standby. The last 'See ya!' between friends that looks like a momentary pause winds up lasting years.

"You can put some friendships into suspended animation and pick up pretty much where you left off," I said, acknowledging the kind of connection we had. "Other relationships are lost after a long hiatus."

We looked at each other for a moment before I added, "Kay, for years we treated each other about as significant as an old picture album on the shelf. We didn't call. We didn't share. Guess we didn't need to. But we didn't lose anything sacred, because we didn't further jeopardize our relationship in the absence of contact."

I drew close to my final destination, the final turn of the screw.

"But what about a marriage? Can a marriage lose its sacred status?"

"Sacred is a very good word for a marriage," Kay voiced her statement signaling a full stop.

I added, "I think *that*'s at the heart of most separations, most divorces. I think losing touch with sacred is the first real trouble. It applies to most marriages whether they stay together or split."

Kay followed, "A marriage remains sacred as long as you keep it sacred… as long as you hold it in high regard. You can't forget it, can't let weeds build up. For God's sake, he can't bulldoze over it and set up a new foundation, a new house right on top!"

A tinge of remorse colored her exasperated voice.

I returned to our initial jumping-off point. "You can't lose sight of the tombstones, the sacred tombstones!"

We both remained quiet. The obvious direction of the discussion at this point was no longer aimed at ancient civilizations, or a lost burial plot, or friendships that had become dusty with disuse. Now it was time to take stock in our current friendship. We'd been good friends once, but now we weren't sure if we could broach the subject of our own failed marriages, how we'd lost touch with the hallowed in our own lives.

It was Kay who broke the silence, "Did you lose the sacredness of your marriage? Did you lose the sacredness of your marriage *recently*?"

"No," I replied. "I lost the sacredness of my marriage a long time ago."

"You're kidding, right?" Kay was stunned. "You and Celeste always seemed to be the perfect couple!"

I glanced hard, "We were a great couple for many years. The thing about other couples is you pretty much only see the problems once the relationship is gravely fractured.

"I've known many people who eventually got separated and divorced. And while some couples seemed to have one kind of problem or another, those who ended their relationship didn't seem worse off than those who remained married. No telling what's going on from the outside."

"I disagree" Kay said, "I can spot trouble long before it dissolves a marriage."

"That's where we differ. I can't tell the normal difficulties from the terminal traumas in others' lives. Worse, I might not even be able to tell them in my *own* life!

"But back to sacred. Celeste and I had a sacred relationship and we treated it as such. At first, it didn't require any work to maintain that stature. Our marriage was sacred, done deal, maintaining that status was… natural.

"The inviolability of our relationship was a plateau. It wasn't something that could degrade. It couldn't be reduced. When it started to erode I didn't notice. I didn't apply any more effort to keep it sacred. I mean, how would you redirect the loss of sacredness?"

"Well, by not sending that *damn* e-mail for one!" Kay shot.

"The *damn* e-mail? Ahh, the Taj Mahal e-mail, the best love letter I've ever written."

I playfully winced and feigned being stabbed. "Touché Kay! The real problem existed long before Alexa's reappearance. The real problem wasn't seeing 'my old college friend.' My predicament was clear-- I had grown to the point that I cared less for my wife than someone I had strong feelings for years ago. How did that happen? That was the real problem, not the resurfacing of an old flame. Where did the sacredness go in the first place and how do you get it back? Can you?"

Kay remained quiet so I echoed, "Can you?

"Is it really just taking someone for granted? Think we can take someone for granted long enough that we don't see that we love them? We get to the point we treat our spouse like a friend? Maybe even treat them like a friend that we've disregarded. Just another old *lost* friend, another dusty book on the shelf, someone we've said 'see you later' to a long time ago?"

Kay looked thoughtful, "In Eric's and my case, I think he lost the sacred feeling. Pretty sure that's how it went. I never put in these terms before, but I see he lost touch with how sacred *we* were as a couple. He stopped investing in our relationship. Stopped doing the weeding and pruning... "

Kay then confided in a sullen whisper, "Maybe we both did."

I laughed "I know that dejected feeling, the realization of failure in a relationship. Damn, I know that feeling!"

Only then, ever so slowly, did it dawn on me that my real failure wasn't way off in the past. It wasn't in Raleigh; my real failure lay at my doorstep with Celeste.

I comforted Kay, "Well, I lost sacred too. This notion of keeping a cherished relationship sacred is fresh. I lost touch-- forgot that keeping a marriage paramount is critical to our joy, happiness, and the survival of the relationship.

"If a marriage isn't sacred, we're not sacred, maybe that is the reality of married folk. If we don't hold our marriage sacred, individually we aren't sacred either."

Kay offered, "Maybe it's the reverse."

I nodded, "In our case, just about everything else took precedence. As the years went by it was jobs, kids, caring for the household. I didn't cheat on her; I never hit her. Our love diffused into a comfortably numb friendship. And neither of us reversed the trend.

"When we started… when Celeste and I met … we weren't a wild and passionate couple. There was attraction for sure, but greater than that, our relationship was built on a gentle friendship. Our marriage emerged from a soothing love and companionship that could withstand the tests of time.

"But this same gentle love was easy to mistake for strong friendship. The disjointing took place slowly. Each passing month and year didn't feel much difference. It wasn't like we were wildly passionate and then it stopped. That, I would have noticed.

"No, from one day to the next, from one week to the next, we did less and less together. We didn't share as a couple. We took care of business. Near the end she often pointed out that I seldom planned vacations and fun things for us to do."

I quietly confirmed, "She was right.

"Lately, she planned our rare dinners away from the kids. If we took a vacation, she brought up the idea. Sure I planned outings but generally she made more effort."

Kay paled at a reflection shockingly close to her own.

I added, "Over time, I wondered if we'd fallen *out* of love. Then… then I wondered if we'd ever *been* in love. So, yeah, when Alexa came along I was pretty darn sure I always loved Alexa more. I was undeniably more head over heals in love with Alexandra. And by then my love for my wife was…"

Kay interjected, "Alexa more? You loved this girl from college more than Celeste?"

"Um, yeah. That is what my heart said emphatically. That is what the e-mail was all about!"

Kay looked stupefied.

"Kay, you know I loved my wife. I think it's fair to say I still love her. When Celeste and I met, I knew we had a lasting bond, a stable love. I was sure we could live, work, and walk hand in hand for the rest of our lives. And I felt good about that. But when I saw Alexa again this summer it reminded me of how I felt about her."

"A different feeling, a different love?" Kay plumbed.

"Absolutely different! With Alexa, I felt a passionate consuming love, totally enveloping. With Celeste it was a responsible love with less passion. We made a good couple sharing compatible ways of life with similar expectations and needs. But she remained aloof, passionless. Alexa was a totally different attraction. It wasn't about compatibility and walking hand in hand. There was no walking-- I floated. With Alexa… my heart moved with a new beat. She was the sunshine of my life!"

Kay saw clearly, "Your Taj Mahal princess!"

"Exactly!" I took a deep breath and added a final sentence: "I felt with all my heart and soul we were created for each other."

I lowered my head, "Silly to feel that way about a relationship so long ago, from a youthful age so impressionable. Most painful of all, it hurt to feel that way about a woman who stoically didn't reciprocate as an adult."

Silence formed an eddying stillness that chilled. A thousand hopes and dreams gathered like pooled water reflecting the vanished joy of two wayward travelers. We remained comfortable in quiet awareness of lost love and abandoned promise.

Finally Kay injected words into our tranquility, "I'm sorry, Brian. I didn't pick that up before. I assumed… "

She grew quiet, not wanting to desecrate, "You assumed what?" I asked sharply spurred by her condescending tone.

"I assumed you wanted a fling. I thought the e-mail to Alexandra was you being… a *man*! Chasing tail! You know-- a roll in the hay with your old flame. I didn't know you had such strong feelings for this other woman!"

I bristled defensively before snorting, "I cannot imagine my contact with Alexa could be interpreted as anything but the most sincere admission of love!"

A wisp of rage unfurled; "It wasn't about a quick one-night stand! Alexandra wasn't a skirt I blew up just to see what I could find!"

I shot, "Didn't you think a man could have feelings beyond his dick?"

With a deep breath I let frustration pass and Kay remained still.

Eyes locked and conveyed the last of my bewilderment, "Damn Kay! If I just wanted pussy, don't you think I could have gotten some with a whole lot less trouble?"

I notched my chin and head lower and rolled my eyes in a playful gaze, "Kay, you know me."

Kay weighted the value of our association. Our friendship spanned more than a decade and she warmed as insight cheered the edges of her lips into a tiny smile.

"You're right. All I've ever seen from you is gentle love, good humor and patience. A regular Prince Charming if you draped a cape and could waltz!"

Her smile grew and we laughed. Kay relaxed, gracing me with more than the benefit of the doubt.

I added quietly "Kay, my love is the real thing, no holds barred." With a smirk I admitted the physical, "I would love to tongue Sasha to the edge of ecstasy and follow in with my seed time and again to the end of our days. Yeah I would love to have sex with her, unrestrained sex, passionate lovers wrestling as one. I was crazy about her, still am. But the sexual desire grew from genuine love. Sex was not the prime reason for reaching out."

"This Alexa," Kay said, "did she care for you, does she care for you?"

I gave her a sideways sour look as I shrugged my shoulders in an unknowing way and lifted my hands in surrender.

"So that was the end of your marriage," Kay summarized. "Not from an affair of the body, but a love of the heart?"

Compelled to refine her point, "No, Kay. Not just my heart. Alexandra was a love of my whole *heart* and *being*! Helpless to resist, I couldn't ignore my whole heart and being, could I?

"But no, she wasn't the end of my marriage. Alexa wasn't a marriage wrecker; she was a gentle and graceful doe, foraging peacefully on tall grass beneath a stand of large oaks.

"Celeste and I were like inattentive bulldozer and backhoe operators carelessly churning tracks over thick weeds and saplings that had once been sacred ground."

Marriage Abandoned

On the well-traveled highway of two-by-two, some folks zoom past "Caution: Loose Gravel Ahead" and reach "Road Ends" careening. They give up on their relationship; they give up on their spouse, and the part of them that believed in love. Some run back to the single world hoping to rediscover life.

Take Ray. Ray was a happily married man, but he lost his handle on "sacred" with such dexterity it makes you wonder if he ever saw marriage that way.

Ray's story begins in the large home behind our house. He was a neighbor for two years before his job took him to Asia. Traveling extensively as a salesman, he spent much of his adult life outside the US. He lived for a time in Singapore, Micronesia, and a host of other places.

He had a loving wife and two kids along with his respectable job. The family traveled to far-flung destinations in the name of free trade and global markets. They liked the adventure and challenges of each locale.

As time went on, Ray tired of the husband and father role. He took "walks." At first these were solo ventures, innocent walks. He'd tell his wife, "I'm going for a walk."

Trouble was, these quiet strolls morphed into social encounters. Ray strayed, and soon much of his "walking time" didn't involve shuffling his feet -- or remaining upright.

Ray lived in a locality that catered to Japanese tourists. Typical tourists were middle aged and older with children accompanying. The cultural understanding of "vacation" differs from the typical American family's notion.

Remember the movies starring Chevy Chase, the "Vacation" series? In one movie Chevy fantasizes about having an affair with Christie Brinkley. It is comedy in American because we relate to guys that look and flirt. Rare for a family vacation to include adultery, wouldn't you say? Hooking up with someone other than your spouse is not a culturally shared expectation in America. American men might look. Banging strangers graciously pro bono or in exchange for money? No, that's not part of the holiday itinerary of typical Americans.

"Very few men would engage in this sort of behavior." I theorized.

"Well, maybe," he replied. "I really don't know what most men would do. But it worked for me.

"The Asian husbands I encountered do more than think about an extramarital fling during R&R. These men have a number of intriguing infidelity options open to them and quite a few open their wallets. The traveling dads make time for intimate fun with the natives while the kids and mom do the beach and shop."

Ray elaborated on the local entertainment, "Let's start with the 'Soak-'n-Pokes.'"

"Soak-'n-Poke?" I laughed.

Ray chuckled confirming the street name for these establishments. "In fact, one had a small sign with those very words announcing the services it offered.

"None kept the true nature of their activities hard to determine lest they lose customers. Dog-eat-dog out there!" Ray quipped.

"These are spas that mix saunas, hot tubs, and hot chicks. It is a pay-as-you-go service rather than a single fee at the door. These are great at relieving all kinds of stress and pressure that builds up in a married guy."

I shook my head but smiled.

Ray continued: "The next type of holistic stress management for traveling pops is massage. Parlors offer full body massages and the women are quite good at many massage techniques. Let's just say the girls narrow their attention to certain areas of the body for an additional fee. Crude western society could learn from our Asian brothers instead of judging!"

"Near my house there was a boulevard, one block off the beach, lined with small strip malls. In the little shopping center a store sold ice cream, another tee shirts and flip-flops, and a bar sporting a flickering martini glass rocking back and forth. The biggest tenant lures its clientele with a neon profile of a guy sitting in a hot tub with bubbles rising along with the head of a girl bobbing up and down. Yeah, it draws!"

"Did a lot of expatriates engage in this kind of thing? Did many married Americans stray from their marriages in the Soak'n Pokes?"

"Some of the single Americans warmed to it. A few with access to the hospital had a ritual where they acquired penicillin and conducted their own hygiene for their favorite damsels." He shrugged and leaned back as he admitted, "Most married men kept their distance."

"You were more… "

"Open minded! I started taking in the extracurricular massage parlors and the saunas that offered more services than your local YMCA."

"What got you started?"

"I changed on vacation. I sopped in Oahu traveling alone on my way home. On a whim I turned a two-hour layover into a long weekend visit with my best friend from years gone by. Hadn't seen him and his wife in ten years."

"How'd it go?"

"Miserable! They'd changed, gone vegetarian! Didn't laugh at the same jokes, didn't spend time on the same things. We had nothing in common.

"At the airport on my way back home I mulled how they'd changed for the worse. I picked a deserted gate adjacent to the maddening crowd packed for my departure. The attendant in my empty section paged a delinquent passenger one last time and closed the gate. I watched the quiet spectacle of the attendant close the ticket counter, the plane door close, and the gate roll back. Next thing you know this guy runs full speed, a New Zealander, to the gate. The rolling gateway that connects to the plane is clearly visible through the window. It's moving from the plane as he looked out the window. He gave a little wave like the pilot might wait.

"I chuckled like *that* was going to do any good!

"The attendant reemerged from the gate, called his name, and explained calmly he missed his flight.

"Thing is, the guy never got riled. Didn't fuss, didn't show anger at the attendant or himself.

"The attendant was stiff in anticipation of a rampage, but seeing none ventured a suggestion that he book another flight. He calmly walked with her to a computer terminal and gently asked her for her assistance which she graciously extended.

"No worries mate! I was amazed.

"That is one way to handle adversity! I watched as they calmly worked the problem. He didn't chastise himself but turned immediately to the one person who could help. Brilliant. Tardy but brilliant!"

I added, "If you missed your flight…"

"If I missed my flight I'd have been angry at myself fuming wretchedly at whatever had made me late. And I would have squarely vented at the nearest airline employee."

Ray breathed deeply, "That's when it hit me. I live full of worries. Things get to me. I blow up way beyond proportion. I get mad at myself, mad at my kids, mad at anything and anybody in my path, especially family. This New Zealander was different. The Kiwi was the man I *used* to be.

"Brian, the friends I'd visited hadn't changed. I had. I'd become curt, cynical, and demeaning."

"I walked to my crowded gate stunned at my debased condition. A beautiful young lady sporting a watermelon pink top caught my eye. It was a tube top, except it had the thinnest spaghetti straps up and over the shoulders. Embroidered across the front were the faded yellow-white letters MANGO. I propped myself against the exterior glass in plain view of my new favorite fruit and looked at her long blond hair. She was beautiful, fully tanned from vacation with a relaxed face that didn't turn away even though I gawked. Her vibrant young breasts were the size of tender mangos and I wanted her, despite the guy standing beside her.

The attendant announced boarding. Mango and the fellow she traveled with took their place. I watched her walk in front of me.

Beautiful long legs stepped through a shadow into the sun. I held my gaze as sunlight streaming through the window illumined her tiny terry cloth shorts. The shorts couldn't have been cut any shorter and still have a crotch. I gazed at her from behind wanting her. Forget the guy holding your tickets, woman, I want you!"

She stood with her back toward me and her bright blond hair held my attention. Her man distractedly focused on the tickets and itinerary fidgeting in doubt that he'd got in the correct line. She turned to her right so I could read the curved M and she stared her own impulsive gaze back at me. She wanted out of her current situation too! Hawaii or man hadn't lived up to pre-vacation expectations. We looked at each other realizing we're both returning from vacation, but neither traveled with anyone we loved. She had her slug of a man and I was stuck with me. We connected for just those few minutes, but long enough to give desperation a homestead in my heart. I was through being a dull married man who put up with mango flavored Jell-O pudding. I want the real thing, damn it!"

"Did you see her on the plane? Ever see her again?"

"Nope. But you asked why I strayed."

"Yes I did."

"The opportunity had always been there. For a guy to stray that has walked the straight and narrow his whole life, something inside has to break. At the airport my compass set to whirling. I realized I'd become a social ogre. The relaxed New Zealander who could take disruption without worry, and Mrs. Mango made me realize I was playing a role. I was disgusted with compromises I'd made. In a warped way, breaking and giving into lust was my way of... I don't know... acknowledging the fall, cementing the demise."

"So that's when you started to go to these liberated YMCAs?"

"Memberships at health clubs stateside would be *way* up if they offered personal attention."

It isn't uncommon for social patterns and trends in one area to migrate to other parts of the world. Disco flourished in one hemisphere and then another. Karaoke bars were social magnets in Japan long before they showed up on US shores.

Maybe Ray was right. Maybe a time would come when clubs and bars would open in the US to offer extramarital activities.

"Or maybe not," I countered.

"Why?"

I felt I had to defend the traditional monogamy framing American society. Why not, because the Native Americans didn't do it? Because Puritans didn't openly live that way? Because laws don't allow it? Fear of AIDS?

I ventured out on a limb and tested. "Americans for all our debauchery on TV and the movies are tied to a narrower moral code that treats men and women more equally. We hold each other to the same standards."

I added, "I wonder if the Japanese men use these girls as an outgrowth of their World War Two exploits with 'comfort women.' The Imperial Army had the absolute worst record in modern warfare of killing civilians and subjugating the woman they spared as sex slaves."

I surprised myself by the connection, feeling no animosity toward the Japanese. But prostitution always smelled of exploitation, especially as it revolves around underage girls.

Ray remained silent; he had lived in Asia and the Pacific Islands a long time and was far more knowledgeable.

I elucidated, "Hell, soldiers raped women in the cities, country, and villages they occupied and then they'd stab them in the heart when they were done. Those raped once and killed quickly were the lucky ones, because the women -- and I mean young girls, too -- confiscated after their first rapes became comfort women, sex slaves who had to service 50 to 100 men a day until they died. Shit, Ray, the World War Two Japanese Army fucked them to death. Remember the Korean women seeking restitution a few years back? They were the rare survivors of such atrocity."

"Are you done?" Ray calmly asked. He took no offense at my litany. "I'm sure you're right, but the tragedy is not unique. Gentleness and compassion are seldom the defining characteristics of marauding armies.

"This modern trade isn't solely a Japanese thing, I've seen it elsewhere that catered to tourists from other countries. Look, the reality of the world is…" Ray serenely gathered his thoughts. "Sexual mores and promiscuity take on very different flavors in different parts of the world and it is kind of hard to get your hands around the issue unless you really study all aspects of a culture. I can't speak to what happened by pillaging armies more than a half century ago. But contemporary lessons are easy to grasp. First, most young kids grow up in abject poverty. Second, people tend to have more sexual drive than sense resulting in a large and ever-growing population that outpaces jobs. The cycle of growth and poverty gets pumped faster and faster.

"Poverty is the only reality a third of humanity ever tastes. A third of humanity-- that is two billion people Brian! Prostitution offers a way out of poverty for many youngsters. Yeah, I've heard about the young age of comfort women, and many of the girls that get into prostitution in Asia start in their early teens. Are they forced to work? Is survival a motivation? They use the one asset they can barter, their own flesh. Girls in the sex trade grow up quick. They're done with this career by the time they're twenty."

These young girls intern as whores like young American girls take part time waitressing jobs. Do possible suitors judge them or limit their possible futures by the job they hold as kids? I don't know or really care. I sense there cultures are OK with it. It's the way they live."

Ray remained calm explaining something his long walks gave him time to reflect upon.

"In the case of Japanese culture, many traditional married women consider sex an act performed for procreation. Period. Interacting for sexual pleasure or casual sex beyond procreation isn't forbidden, but it 'isn't what good girls do.' So the men go on vacation looking for relief. I don't know how many married couples still abide by this traditional culture, but I from what I've seen many older ones do.

"You got an MBA-- put it in business terms. Supply and demand. Wives don't supply enough to meet husbands' demand, so there is spillover-- pent-up demand *is* met on vacation. What do they call that…

competitive or alternative products and services? Excess demand creates a market that flourishes near resorts. A whole infrastructure of establishments, willing women, and local ordinances condone the activities and increase supply. Free markets at work my boy!"

I added "Oh yeah, I see. The great thing with their approach to vacation solves a recurring problem in America. Those husbands will take a real interest planning family vacations!"

Ray continued, "I lived in a lot of places throughout Asia and the Pacific. Factories and service companies thrive but pay squat. Companies bring in migrant workers-- like magnets, the prospect for jobs and money offer a chance at a better life. Waves of poor flock in droves destitute and motivated."

Ray remained tranquil in his social studies lecture, not at all bothered about economic deprivation that generates sex slaves and child prostitution. He treated it without judgment like the nasty stain on walls left over by a flood. The high water mark leaves a solemn reminder; it lingers and becomes part of the scene quietly accepted as a sign of the past and present, and a hint of what the future might bring.

"When the jobs done these temporary working peasants leave as poor as when they came. Jobs offer a dry bed, food, and a chance to contribute. And that offers a chance to sustain life and breed the next generation of workers."

Ray turned directly to me and said. "Heck, you and I are really not much better off. How much money do you save at the end of each year? In the end, our jobs pretty much cover our day-to-day cost of living. And that's the case for nearly all of humanity. The lucky folks have jobs that cover living expenses. Damn rare, damn rare indeed, for someone to come out way ahead. If one of those factory workers stash away greenbacks, the savings go a *long* way back home."

I remained silent as Ray's economics sank in.

"In America, the cost of living is *so much* higher than most of these places you wouldn't believe it. If someone in those conditions saved $1,000 over a few years that's huge."

"So these young girls, these 'working girls' did a lot better than their peers?" I inquired.

"Oh hell yes!" Ray responded emphatically. "I'm not sure how much the 'house' kept from the fees the girls generated, but tips went to the girls. The girls got paid a better wage outright than factory workers. The tips were icing on the cake. Icing. Shit, those girls did great financially."

I followed up "So, if the economy tanks in the US to the point…"

Ray cut me off. "When a young girl sees getting into the business of 'personal service' is her best financial option she'll be attracted. I'm not saying a girl will necessarily get into that line of work, but attracted. And if she does join the business, keeps off the drugs and saves dough, working in one of these brothels can turn the last few years of childhood into enough money to get a good start in adulthood."

"Damn, Ray, you're talking about exchanging our daughters' vivacious childhoods and sexual appeal for… cash. Trading their *innocence*…"

"And I'm telling you that is the way of the world, at least a big part of the Third World."

"Oh, man, I don't know! I'm motivated by the notion that we're creating a better world -- more just and more merciful. I want a better brighter future for everyone, where men and women are equal and we strive for an ever-advancing civilization," I retorted.

Ray somberly reply, "Yeah, me too."

He was being serious and the contradiction stunned.

"I want that in my head," he laughed, "but my dick wants young, exciting flesh! Here baby, more icing!" Ray laughed maliciously.

"Sometimes the big head wins, sometimes the little head wins. And innocence is something we all trade for experience at an opportune time."

"Well, innocence should be something an adult or a mature individual relinquishes. But yeah, most guys want that. Most guys, I'll grant you nearly every guy, relishes the sexual encounter. Every guy wants that excitement at some level. But Ray, what about social restraint, decency, and laws to protect minors? Just because you want candy 24/7 doesn't mean you gorge yourself on lollipops. Buddy, we'd lock you behind bars in Virginia for that! The warden would assign a maniacal murderer who suffered molestations as a child to keep you company in your cell!"

"Let's walk," Ray suggested with a smirk. "I do some of my best work when I'm walking!"

We headed outside. The delicate screen door slapped closed and we stood for a moment before choosing direction.

Ray started again: "What is the divorce rate in America?

"Fifty percent?" He answered his own question, and I nodded, confirming hearsay.

Ray took a long breath. "Many traditional cultures in Asia position the wife as servant to her husband. Her first role is servitude. That doesn't mean the women are slaves, they can have jobs outside the family, individual will, rights, voting and all that, but first and foremost the social expectation is servitude to their man. Women grow up with this reality and the men do too. It's their culture. It's a shared expectation."

Ray shrugged not judging or condoning.

Then he added, "Ever wonder why there is an infatuation with Asian girls, Asian women in America?"

"I didn't know there was such a thing."

Ray educated, "It isn't big breasts I'll tell you that! It is because of ingrained servitude. It isn't derogatory to say servitude. That attitude provides a framework, a bastion of power that leads to more security, happiness, and less divorce.

"Brian, I agree the equality-based model is integrated into modern American. Our dominant moral compass aligns with equality between men and women. And we've achieved more equality than existed decades ago. Why, I bet twenty or thirty years ago, wives were subservient by today's standards. Now a more balanced equality is the norm. If you expect it, you live it without questioning.

"Equality based culture is the single most profound and underreported revolution going on throughout the world. Overall that's a good thing.

"But in male-dominated cultures," he went on, "women have little standing in society outside of marriage. They're coerced to be submissive. A woman's needs, a wife's needs, are deferred.

Drawing the parallel to a wider experience, I injected, "This servant expectation probably aligns comfortably with our ancestors' lives, our grandparents, and maybe even our parents. Look at American census records from a century ago. You won't find many occupations listed for the women outside the household. Not until the Second World War did American women take to the workplace in large numbers. Their role was very important inside the marriage, but historically they had little social standing outside of marriage. Trendsetters broke the mold. So anything approaching equality cannot be more than a generation in its making in the US.

"Consider other cultures especially the excessively male dominated. Movement to equality is the major conflict within male-oriented societies. It's the crux of the social challenge in the Middle East. The power structures in male-dominated cultures are stressful and bubble to unrest and violence because some men don't want to relinquish control. Their expectations were set in their youth. They grew up expecting women to be second-rate citizens. No voice outside the home. But women see different models and deep down inside *know* they are equal. Modern equality clashes against old-world expectations. The sweeping action of change creates friction-- social tension."

Ray nodded, "I think men who arise as terrorists are fighting against this transformation. These young men and their older leaders wage a war of control. They want to protect their standing, control their 'higher male station,' ensure male domination over woman. They say they want traditional values, but cloaked within it is female enslavement. They strike at America and their own regional authorities, but what they are really doing is striking at the threat to their continued domination. They may pretend to fight for the Koran but they're looking out for number one. They want dominance, power, and control.

"These angry men want to preserve the bastion of male authority regardless of grandiose claims. Yet they wage a losing battle, my friend. You can't put women back in the bottle. Barbara Eden taught us that!"

Revolutionaries pick palatable subjects like religious freedom, nationalism, or some other chord that resonates with enough of their peers to instigate trouble and form militias. Guys orchestrating militias are scam artists looking for personal power and control. The grand cause is only a ruse to get a larger group to act and unknowingly instigate their private agenda.

Ray surmised, "The battle for women's rights isn't won, and 'I Dream of Jeanie' isn't even on reruns, but men and women are created spiritually equal and societies will adapt one way or another.

A grin crossed his face as he redirected, "But back to women, yeah, I've tried submissive women and I've tried assertive women. To be honest, I like both. Best of all I like *access* to both! Preferably at the same time!"

Ray let out a laugh disguising what was joke, fantasy, recollection, or ambition.

He added seriously, "I think the Japanese men do, too. They're bored at home. They go out looking for variety. That is all, really, a touch of variety.

"Guys like young women!" Ray shouted as if it were an extraordinary discovery. "We *like* young flesh because it makes *us* feel young again! Guys want to be passionate forever. A trip to the Soak'n'Poke renews vitality. Afterward the men go back to their wives. And the wives perform their wifely roles and the husbands play husband roles. During the vacation wives are off duty, off sexual duty, and that lingers a while after they get home. Wives don't want to act a nineteen year-old when they are 39, 49, or 59. And they're ok with some young tart grounding their husband's impulse.

"The wives retain their cultural bias against sex. Poppa knows he can find a willing teenager to dance exuberantly upon his cock. For a fee the girl pretends their intercourse is a big deal. Sure, he knows it is an act, but it is pretense with purpose! The girl's display of eagerness and excitement serves a purpose. He blows his wad once, or twice, or three times with starlets during the family vacation, and then he is good to go. His wife looks good again as a middle-aged woman and the husband knows in his heart that he 'still has it.' The husband erases the nagging image that he's getting old."

Ray summarized, "So the end result is the Japanese marriage is more secure. The divorce rate is lower. Husbands bang, wives shop, and kids do the beach. Everyone gets what he or she came for!

"Send Chevy Chase on an 'Asian Vacation' and watch that old comedian come back to life! He won't just flirt, I promise you!"

"Ray, I hear what you say, but your feet are planted on extremes, equality and exploitation. How can you reconcile?

"Maybe it works for some older Japanese, and I see the merit of allowing teens to be teens and older adults to be older adults. Heck, it even makes sense for a woman, a wife and mother, who doesn't want to do the wild thing to allow a mistress the honors. But there are costs. There are costs…"

I'd hope we'd swing it back to the costs and explore the downside to the extramarital promiscuity.

But Ray took a new direction.

"Remember when Mitterrand died?"

"Francois Mitterrand, president of France for fourteen years? Died in the mid-nineties, didn't he?"

"Right on the money, you get the memory prize," Ray joked. "Remember his funeral?"

"I… I remember a blurb on TV. There was an outdoor ceremony, a casket. I remember his wife standing there and …"

Ray cut me off excitedly.

"Exactly! We saw the same footage. Who was there with his wife? Remember? Who was there in tears holding the widow's hand?" Ray gave me a few seconds to fill in the gap.

"A beautiful young woman…"

Ray leapt forward before I could coax the full memory. "His mistress! There, right there at the funeral, his wife and mistress held hands beside the casket. They mourned together!"

"Wouldn't happen in America," I conceded solemnly, "because the wife wouldn't be there. She'd be locked up on manslaughter charges!"

We both laughed and Ray proclaimed, "That's my point! Old man Mitterrand had a young thing on the side, quite dazzling. He had his squeeze and his wife accepted the reality. Well, at least in public she accepted the young skirt. It was healing for everyone to see the two women holding hands at the funeral. They each brought the president joy and shared life and love with him. Seemed quite humane all in all."

"Quite humane! What you're saying," I countered, "is that short-term affairs are accepted in Asia, or at least some societies in Asia, and a long-term affair didn't bring about divorce in France. But... in America, people's expectations are different. Here we expect sexual loyalty. Infidelity is a charge that can bring about an immediate divorce in Virginia. No one-year waiting required. Period."

Ray sadly shook his head, "Conformity, more likely. Despite American's liberated minds, women seethe if their man gets some on the side. A man would act the same if his wife did the horizontal bop with another."

I asked, "Think Mitterrand's wife raged at home but kept up appearances for the camera? Life could have been hell for the couple behind closed doors. Or was it quiet acquiescence surrendering the things of youth?"

"I don't know," Ray admitted. "All I know is what I see on the TV news-- a sound bite here and fifteen seconds of film there. I'm no scholar; I like to form my opinions with minimal information. Suits my life style!"

I barbed, "Before we leave this subject, what if your wife fooled around on you, Ray?"

"Don't know. I figure I might have been pretty forgiving actually, open minded on that. Now, if she had a girlfriend..." Ray's voice cracked with glee.

"OK, Ray, OK!" I laughed along.

Silence shared our walk for a mile.

Ray redirected, "Look at it this way. Making love with your wife after a few years is like… taking a trail ride."

I smiled at his analogy. "A trail ride, huh? You're being generous aren't you?"

"Yeah, you're right-- more like a few weeks after you're married! We both laughed heartily.

"Get your cowboy hat on partner! Saddle up your ol' nag."

His hand jutted it in front of him portraying holding reigns. I laughed again. The image sank in, saddle lofted and girth secured with a biting yank, mount and stirrups toed. Giddy up!

Ray lowered his voice, depicting a dragging ordeal bereft of vigor, not at all the spirit you'd want on an amorous adventure. "Guaranteed a walk, you're guaranteed a walk. She'll carry you, low energy with her head down as if it's a tremendous burden.

"Might get a jog, a rough clumsy jog, which makes it hard to stay in the saddle. If you are *good* you might coax a momentary canter. But there will be no galloping here, no brisk wind in the face excitement, no wild running. A safe, antiseptic ride. Damn lame if you ask me, dame lame.

"And you know in your heart…" he sighed, "You know in your heart what your steed wants… what's on her mind. You can feel it in her lack of responsiveness. She wants to get back to the barn to graze and rest!"

Ray straightened up and swung his left hand in front of him, slapping away a memory, a ghost of experience, lingering emotional misery. His demeanor livened again as he spun the other half of the comparison.

"But take a ride on a rented mount! Different story! Instead of a trail ride where you ride a reluctant mare, now *you're* the stallion, and your partner is the jockey! And it isn't a jaunt around the barn. This ride isn't about safety, about sticking to the well-worn path, this is Churchill

Downs and you are in the race of your life! This is excitement, adrenalin, uncertainty, and risk. There is showmanship, bright colors…"

"And that mud and sweat from previous rides, let's not forget." I mused.

Ray trampled on, "This jockey is serious about her play! She rides for pride and money! She's motivated to deliver a winning performance and you respond. Together, her with whip and spurs, and you chomping at the bit grinding through the turns, together you enter the home stretch and ride for all you're worth!"

Ray's portrait had me imagining pounding hoofs and sand churning shoulder high—flailing and huffing-- committed to the moment. I was there mentally grinding the turns.

He took a breath and a smile crossed his face as he concluded, "This is one race that you want to run hard, give it all you've got, but don't rush the finish line!"

Then he relaxed. He'd made his point vividly. No need to argue the difference between married sex and what he'd experienced through adultery.

I could have spoken up for the mares of the world, the wives, working women. I could have championed moms who clean and cook, and conduct their lives juggling responsibilities ranging from house payments to grocery shopping to commuting and punching the clock for forty hours plus overtime. Little resemblance between the free-form girls Ray paid for services and a woman in a healthy lasting relationship. I could have challenged Ray to make him see it was absurd to compare the giddiness of a teenage harlot to the emotional responsiveness of a grown woman. And I would have, if it would make a difference.

But Ray already chose his path. He realized the dichotomy. That realization was a big part why he'd chosen ripe mangos.

I steered toward a different path. Assuming there were many awkward moments and loneliness associated with buying sex, "Was sex really better with hookers?" I was sure to get a no that would vindicate my position.

"Not always," he admitted, "there were bitches, some hard as an anvil, others strung out on drugs. But there were times…" His smile returned, "Look these women are professionals. They make it their living and they learn from each other. These girls finely craft their skills and abilities. Like any activity, sex is something you have to practice to get great at. Some of it comes naturally but to really hone one's abilities takes honest feedback, coaching, and plenty of practice."

Ray continued, "Prostitutes have all three prerequisites to become great– youthfulness with natural desire, practice, and coaching from their peers. Girls of the night form an ad hoc support group to help each other cope with the emotional baggage, and they serve as mentors to develop the tricks of the trade. They benchmark each other. Sadly, most people who don't make a living at having sex never get better at this vital aspect of a relationship. They don't talk, learn, and benchmark."

As testimony to the talent level and dedication shown by the working girls, Ray offered his account of a single session. He took a fancy to a young girl who turned more than one afternoon into the stuff of porn movies.

"One day when my wife and kids were away, my Korean 'girlfriend' came over and made love, or more accurately exchanged sex for money-- major clarification-- in our living room. We huffed and puffed through our fracas. As I came she took my oozing wang in her mouth, relishing her newfound libation and drained all the fluid. But she didn't stop. Man she didn't *stop*!

"She resuscitated my waning woody into a willing appendage slowly drawing new life. Now *that* is uncompromising commitment to prostitutional excellence! She worked me back to a full erection without delay and we proceeded to have sex again."

I admitted, "I want one! Do they make that in a wife version? Of course, I want her to get an education and pursue a career, help cook, do her share around the house and a great mom, too!" We both laughed.

Plan backfired, so much for downplaying sex with the paid nymphs. With this kind of experience hooking him, he took girls home with him on varying durations of "home study."

Ray's recount isn't included here to make guys wail at what they're missing. This story defines what life and sex *could* be like. A guy wouldn't need this kind of treatment *all* the time, but it sure made for a hell of an afternoon and a memorable and lasting moment in Ray's life. And if married couples shared something like this sexual encounter with amenable regularity, guys probably wouldn't start "walking" in the first place.

"Seriously, Ray, men want a wife full of sexual vitality, but marriage is more than sexual gratification."

"Learn that the hard way did you?" Ray beamed and we both shared a knowing nod.

"What I mean is the best definition I've heard for marriage is it is a 'fortress for spiritual wellbeing.'"

I let that sink in before driving home the point, "What's a fortress?"

"I imagine remote castle. A strong structure designed to keep trouble out, keep inhabitants safe." He kicked a loose stone setting it to roll and added, "Yeah, keep them safe, healthy, free, not slaves or casualties to those that would do harm."

"So what is wellbeing?"

"Opposite of illness, trouble, sickness."

"Maybe even more," I alluded. "Think very healthy, happy, and self-actualized, freedom… think about the life, liberty, the pursuit of happiness kind of wellbeing.

"It doesn't say 'Marriage is the vehicle for sexual satisfaction.'

"Doesn't say 'Marriage is a guaranteed chariot of bliss.'

"Doesn't even say 'Marriage is a means to financial security.'

"Marriage is the fortress of wellbeing."

Ray challenged, "You said 'spiritual wellbeing' first time."

"OK, let's try!"

Ray immediately offered, "Spiritual. Beyond physical, beyond bodily, transcendent."

He recapped, "A fortress for spiritual wellbeing… A stronghold for transcendent self-actualization."

We mulled the phrase over in our heads, reveling in the truth of the statement. As we walked, the possibility that this was what marriage was all about kept us occupied. We didn't utter a word for thirty minutes. As we turned to go back, my thoughts alighted on Ray's kids. He'd walked away from them. He didn't see his kids more than once a year, if that. I presumed he hadn't intended his "walks" to lead to this absolute separation from his children.

"What about your kids, Ray?"

He thought for a brief moment, "Ah, raising kids is way overblown. Raising kids is a pastime for the boring! No offense, mind you!"

"No really, don't be shy. Tell me what's on your mind!"

He delighted I hadn't taken his jab personally.

"Look back in time. What was America like, say 100 years ago?"

Before I had a chance to answer, Ray was off again. "I'll tell ya'. From the inception of the country well into the twentieth century, America had no concept of 'childhood.' Poverty was the norm, and children were… capital. There may have been some well-heeled folks whose kids lived sedate play-filled lives devoid of manual labor. But the ninety-nine percent of Americans our ancestors came from lived very hard lives, and their kids directly contributed to the family's survival.

"Your description couldn't have been more remote from my kids' lives."

Sensing my surprise, Ray kept on, "The first child labor law was signed by Woodrow Wilson about 1916 however the Supreme Court struck it down! Country had been around for one hundred and forty years by then, yet our concept of children had't evolved. Only then did society grapple with the notion that kids should have an easier life, and education should play a larger role. It wasn't until twenty years later under FDR that child labor laws began to take hold. Until that time, kids were pretty much property. Property Brian. Wasn't until World War Two, probably just after the war, that people started to look at childhood as something sacred, to be cherished and enjoyed. Until then, being young was just being a little person who'd work for very little…"

"Damn, I didn't know our sense of family, of modern parenting was so new."

"Fact is kids can do a whole lot more if they need to. So yeah, I walked away from fatherhood, but I know kids are tougher and more capable than we give them credit."

"Which is better? A world that abandons kids and uses kids as workers, or a world that gives kids a chance to play? I mean, isn't there a social benefit to avoiding exploitation? And the kinds of jobs kids used to do before widespread industrialization don't exist."

"What do you mean, which is *better*?" he replied twistingly.

"Well… which is better for the human spirit, the human condition?"

"Hey," Ray replied, "I'm not advocating a return to child usury, I'm just pointing out that our morals have changed drastically in a couple of generations. And I'm saying that they're apt to change drastically again. I for one do not feel like a deadbeat dad by walking away from my kids, because kids are a hell of a lot more resourceful than modern American society believes."

I took another angle, "Well, what about the emotional impact of the separation? Forget the notion that kids worked, and could still work at much younger ages. Didn't you love your kids and want to be part of their lives?"

"Yes and no." Ray's answered curtly.

"Which was it?"

"Both. You asked two questions. Yes, I loved my kids. No, I didn't particularly want to be part of their lives. And definitely not if being part of their lives meant staying married to my nag mare. He waved his hand like a horse's tail shoos flies."

Waxing materially I wondered, "How much does divorces cost America? What's the cost of divorce on a grand scale? If fifty percent of marriages end in divorce, that means a second home is needed for half the families. Demand for housing rises. Up goes the price of housing, more urban sprawl, more utility bills, more expenditure on furniture, less savings, and less taxable income for schools and other socially advancing causes. What can't we afford as a nation because single parents spend money on what they could otherwise share?

"So we've gone from what… horseback riding… riding hookers to justifying abandonment. What's next?"

Detachedly I added, "Seems like America's gone full circle on the kids."

"Say again?" Ray asked.

"Well, a hundred years ago we saw them as expendable assets, nice to have around, but expendable in a pinch. And now they are again dispensable, not cherished."

"It isn't a circle, more like an unfolding spiral. It may look like we're back were we started but we aren't. We're farther down the road. The divorce rate would have been much higher a century ago if women had the economic independence they have today. People stuck together because they had to.

"I bet there were brothels in every damn city and town a hundred years ago. It was just increased disposable income, economic stability, and good old-fashioned materialism that distracted men for a couple of decades. Now that we've got six channels of ESPN , now that we've got surround sound TVs and all manner of contrivances, I think there will be a general disenchantment with materialism."

Ray went on, anticipating my thoughts and roundly negating any optimistic take on such a turn of events.

"And we ain't goin' to no maharaja spiritual dimension kind of way! And we ain't going toward world peace Shangri-La. We's a'goin' more and more slimy. We're a lookin' for love in all the wrong places.

"That's my take on the twists and turns. From materialism to pussyism."

Before I countered Ray tagged on, "You asked 'what's next?' That, my friend is what I think is next. I think it is 'hell in a hand basket.' It may challenge everything you hold dear Brian, but I see a turn for the worse coming. Unless… unless *you* make a difference."

It gave me a shudder, but I saw it coming. The social transformation I'd hoped for and worked for seemed stagnant, on hold, or worse, sliding backward. Few championed social improvement beyond the comfort of their lives. Not enough visionaries and the tide ebbs toward decadence and chaos. Digression results from the masses stumbling after illusions.

Faced with a larger threat I conceded the point looking for ground to make a stand and turn the tide.

"What do you mean if I make a difference? Social change for the better in America is stagnant. We integrated our schools and shopping centers but now what?

"We enabled older folk affordable longer lives but now what?

"We're run amok in debt and can't see our way out of deficit spending and war. Fools shake their fingers shouting 'enemy!' Ray, do you realize we spend as much on defense as the rest of the whole word combined? All the while we grow deeper in debt.

Ray added, "Hard to redirect our focus away from the military industrial complex. That's another twist of the spiral toward pussism!"

"When I first heard Eisenhower talk about the military industrial complex, I didn't think that was too hard to overcome, because a complex is a big thing. An alert democracy can see something as big as a 'complex' so we could root it out. Now I realize 'complex' is shrewd and camouflaged. It is a mental complex that debilitates America. A phobia shrouds us, sensational news media, religious leaders and political leaders instill fear and offer smoke and mirrors. They often don't lead toward a better world. They revile in the sensational. We can't see real problems because we're unknowingly chasing the goal of defending an empire. An empire none of us knowingly built or wants. It wasn't part of the American dream, but baby we're toting the bill and have the military to defend it! "

Ray, if you're expecting people to make a difference, I'm telling you Americans are hoodwinked. We can't extricate ourselves form the morass without leadership. We're mired struggling to solve the worlds' problems spending at a pace we can't afford. A nation in debt is a weak country. We're about as bad as Bolivia and Peru when it comes to our balance sheet."

"Brian, you and all your dreamer friends that believe in world peace have got to wake up! Make a stand damn it! Make a difference while America still has a chance. Pussism isn't pretty. It's the end of the world you hoped for. It culminates in the world I settled for. Don't look to guys like me for advice. I'm lost!"

I took the challenge, "OK. Start small, start in the family. Let's say that we've always loved our kids. But when poverty requires work, they work. And when economic stability ensues, kids have extended childhoods, but marriages flounder because couples can make it as singles."

Ray added as if he read my mind, "I kept my marriage together-- by being anesthetized. That's no way to live. I'm not saying you're necessarily a dyed in-the-wool looser for staying with your wife and devoting so much time to your kids…"

I offered jokingly, "So now that I've wasted my life sticking with one woman, and missed the tremendous opportunity to scatter seed in a plethora of young women… and I've spent way too much time nurturing my kids through sports, homework, and such. Tell me; is there any hope for a guy like me? Anywhere for a guy like me to live without hanging my head in shame?"

 Ray made a priestly cross with his hand, "You are forgiven! Don't get me wrong! My promised land started out like yours but I reset my aspirations. Shallow? You bet. Immediate gratification with nary a concern for consequence became my world. After my marriage I didn't want talks about laundry detergent, or what's for supper. I didn't want conversations about who did, or didn't do their share of housework. 'You never take me out anymore, why don't you look at me like you used to… blah, blah, blah.' I didn't even want long walks on the beach or old-fashioned romance.

"I wanted to get to the punch line. No dating. No spending countless nights wondering 'does she like me?' No charades. No wondering if she will, and if she will when. No waiting for Mr. Right to get the hell out of her life so there is room for me. No lost time hoping in vain that she'll see me as the right guy. What a fucking waste! Yeah, dating to me was a fucking waste of time. Life is short my friend. So I opened my wallet and paid my way to shallow bliss. I spread more seed in more warm, moist places than you ever will, and I know those places were well protected, so the seeds never took root. I gave up on depth and got into being the crashing wave on the shore of life, pounding against rock and gliding through the crevasse I found along the way."

"Hey," I jovially shot back, "I thought you were a stallion being ridden hard and put up wet."

"Yeah, well, the ride was at the beach then, through the drenched sand and I was both! Waves and horses-- that's my story and my life!"

We quieted down, totally at a loss. Ray didn't jump into the void. He seemed to be standing on the precipice with me. What had become of our idealized selves, our romantic characters, and our loving souls?

When I looked to Ray for assurance, he gave a goofy look and shrugged.

"Jesus, Ray… when I was in college I felt at one with the universe. I was young and healthy, took yoga, studied religion and spiritual paths, along with my technical studies. I even went through massage classes so I could give comfort and peace to others. What happened to *that* guy?"

The E-mail

July-23

The sprit of an opening soda can flung fine mist into the air. Celeste took a sip and entered our home office. The comfortable mesh chair spun, she plopped down, and slid toward the keyboard. With a few clicks she read through old e-mails. The rest of the soda went untouched.

I got a call at work on my cell phone.

"Are you in your office?" She immediately jumps; "I was going through the old e-mail account…"

The Taj Mahal e-mail finally got a response. We talked for an hour.

She had plenty of steam in reserve and my scalding continued through evening; "It wasn't so much that you contacted Alexandra – you told me about that. I just can't believe you called that other woman your 'Taj Mahal princess!' I'm destroyed that you wrote a love letter to someone else!"

Nightfall found us still at it. Oh if there were somewhere to play hide and seek now! "I cannot believe you announced our marriage was on the rocks. Maybe it is, but to tell a total stranger! I can't believe you shared our problems with a total stranger! I haven't shared our difficulties with my best friends and you announce to this woman. You shit, this is my life too! 'Tick-tock like clockwork' you're telling her you're available and you're blaming all our problems on me."

"Oh come on! Which is it? Is it a love letter or is it declaration of your deficiencies? It's not that long. I mean… it can't be everything, err, I mean it can't be all the things you claim in just three pages.

"Read it again." I calmed, "I'm not blaming you for our problems just stating the facts. We're not doing well. Every year, July or August, you get into it with me like you're reliving a period of your life when you were dumped. Every year in late summer you tell me we're through. OK. I see it. I'm a believer."

"We're having problems, but is this any way to address them?"

"I acknowledged the facts and my feelings."

Waves crashing against the shore can be messy when it's the start of hurricane season.

After the heated conversations subsided for the second time we accounted no bruises, no cuts, and zero punches thrown. Late evening proved to be as good a time to ague as right after work. Like the rising of a drowning victim, the magic number was three. The deepest pain surfaced in the third round.

Celeste started, "You know what really upsets me most?"

I shook my head baffled, "I really don't know." Learning from the earlier stalemate I opted for another strategy. I listened.

"It was that you sent her the love letter. You called her your fucking Taj Mahal princess!"

"It was the best love letter I ever wrote."

"That is my point! It was good, it was great! We've been married fourteen years. How many love letters have you sent me?"

My mouth widened but she reminded me it was for breathing and not talking. She answered for me. "None! Nothing. Zip. Nada! Don't I deserve any appreciation? Am I no more that something you want to scrape off the side of your shoe?

"How many love letters have you sent me?"

"I'm sure…"

"None! Not one, damn it!

"Oh, but how thoughtful of you. Turn to your old flame, a woman you haven't seen for two decades. For her you have nothing but love. Three pages of sweetness." She sobbed.

"There were questions too," I countered. "Like why didn't we make it as a couple? The e-mail wasn't just about getting us back together…"

"Really? Where were the questions? Point them out, because I fucking missed them!"

"There were questions, it rambled. I'm sorry you're hurt, I didn't intend that. But passion was bottled up in my heart and I did the best I could. I had to share, to move ahead, I had to let her know. I didn't mean to hurt…"

"You didn't intend me to be hurt? You didn't intend me to ever see the damn e-mail!"

"Not true. The e-mail was in the draft I showed you, remember? Remember the Crystal Stiletto?"

She didn't tarry from the task of skewering "The best love letter you wrote. Wonderful. Written to another woman. Wonderful! Life's a bitch, isn't it? My husband finally expresses his emotions and they're all directed to another woman! Cheery day for me!"

"I can see you're upset…"

"Well, if you want to fuck her so much, why don't you drive down to Raleigh right now and see if you can bunk in with her? I'm sure the little love note made her more receptive. She's probably waiting for you."

I was packing as we spoke, but not for a night with Alexandra. The process of packing compounded the finality of the conversation.

I was on the verge of a weekend vacation to the North Carolina beach. It was time for the Back Row's annual golf game, the Back Row Open. The only trip I took apart from family. The Back Row kept our tradition of reuniting in the Tar Heel state to renew friendship. This year we planned a family affair at Emerald Island, on the Outer Banks. Despite efforts to include family in these annual gatherings, Celeste found an excuse not to go. Other spouses attended some, but never Celeste. This year, even before reading the e-mail she'd graciously backed out. But earlier she had said the boys would go. .

Second thoughts emerged. "You're not taking the boys anywhere, especially across state lines!"

"What! I've never done anything to…"

"Just pack heavy and leave tonight. The boys stay in Virginia."

"I'd hoped to make a fun weekend for the kids at the beach."

"Oh yeah, I'm sure this will be one fun weekend for you and your old college friends, but my boys are staying here!"

"Our boys."

I stewed in my juices for another hour remaining the attentive listener, sharing enough to give her what she wanted and absorbing her frustration and hurt.

Celeste issued traveling orders-- return with a plan.

Next morning I dropped the two youngest off at the day care center. The phone rang at the desk as I signed them in. The staff member said, "Yes, they just got here. Would you like to speak to Brian? No? The kids? OK, have a great day!" and she hung up.

Porn Star Saint

July-24

E-mails and long distance phone calls kept the Back Row in touch. Supplementing the remote dialogue with an annual golf outing kept us close.

The B Cameron Langston Bridge and tinges of salt air and warm breezes confirmed arrival at Emerald Island. The southern-most Outer Bank, Emerald Island is five square miles of vacationland. Not much wider than the main road, this narrow gauntlet of dune is home to about 3,000 and vacation destination for upwards of 50,000 on a busy summer day. Vehicles proudly sport OBX or SOBX oval bumper stickers so if you were to wake up really drunk on the beach you'd know where you were once you regain focus and can lift your head bumper high.

The weekend started according to plan – less, of course, my family. Married folk lodged as families. Single guys rented a shared house and partied pretty much unchanged from when we all shared that status.

Two of the single guys plus me piled in Gary's car and headed to dinner. I took the rear seat. Condos and single family dwellings each like circus performers high on stilts whizzed by as we cruised Atlantic Beach heading for a dinner rendezvous in Morehead City with the rest of the gang.

The car hadn't gone a mile before Paul asked, "So where is the family? Thought you'd have Celeste and the kids."

I launched us into the deep end where shark fins glide aand the smell of divorce lawyers pervade. Alimony and custody battles may await my return where I'd be chum; "Celeste and I aren't getting along. Pretty sure we're headed for separation."

It stayed quiet for a few seconds before Paul offered genuine sympathy.

His acknowledgment was a floodgate opening. A wave of compassion and support flowed from the guys. I was just one of the guys again, nothing to hide.

I looked down to my right placing my hand on the seat. The leather was cool, smooth, and pleasant to the touch and I ran my fingers along a reassuring seam. I looked around and saw my old buddies. After all the years we still cared for each other and took comfort riding with the single blokes.

News of my domestic problems didn't dampen supper. The mood was light with a suitable amount of mandatory raunch. The waitress' voluptuous curves gave us more reason to wax juvenile, and the presence of wives only tempered the volume.

I shared a discussion on the long fishing pier with one couple. Stretching past the breakers, the wooden pier was active as gulls clamored overhead and fishermen cast along the sides without reward. The undercurrent in a conversation about separation rocked the married couple.

The next night Clay and his wife turned a quick after-meal goodbye into a lengthy but welcomed heart-to-heart. We stood in the summer night air talking under the glow of sodium and mercury vapor lights. The three of us braved hordes of flying insects in the name of friendship and love.

The night before the golf outing we gathered at the bachelors' rental. It was a modest home set high on its stilts out of harm's way from but the worst storm surges. Beer, chips and the like, were in ample supply but the fridge was otherwise bare. That evening none of the kids were invited, and all the wives stayed away. One wife suggested a curfew and brought a chuckle as families went their own ways and the men stayed behind. No one ventured a guess about duration. Back Row members had mischievous bark, but not a worrisome bite and the wife took reassurance we'd stay out of trouble.

During the late night session we reminisced. It didn't take long before the issue of my current 'challenge' bubbled to the surface. A quick poll was conducted, "Who remembered Alexandra?"

Only Gary and Clay put the name and face together. All the guys had been at the Elton John concert when Sasha brought her college friends, but other than that one night, my Princess was a personality long forgotten.

Lucky bastards!

Dave recalled, "I remember the day! You climbed the side of your dorm!"

Mental gears whirled as others chimed in.

Gary added, "That's right! You climbed up the outside of the brick dorm three or four stories! Then you scaled over to the window before tiring. Remember? I was below and offered to catch you!"

I clinched my fingers recalling the peril and exhaustion. "What can I say, Gary, you're always there for me!

"I climbed the dorm as a lark, jazzed by the evening's possibilities. The dorm's mortar gaps and a narrow offset ledge beneath the third floor windows gave sufficient finger and toe holds." I laughed at the stupidity, "I was drained after climbing the dorm's façade. When I got to the windowsill I couldn't get a toehold and my fingers were spent. Thank God Dave and Paul saw me clinging on the windowsill and hauled me in!"

Hysteria let loose at the youthful display of foolishness.

Paul asked, "What were you thinking, man? What were you on?"

"It was going to be a big night with Sasha and seven of her friends!"

Gary added, "And it was there. The building I mean. Like a mountain needing climbing."

"Remember the party with the girls?" Paul asked. "What was the deal?"

"I remember shuttling two carloads of Meredith girls…"

"I mean the drinks. Who insisted on the Pina Coladas?"

"Alexa and one of her friends. I bought the mixers, drink and a blender to accommodate."

"I'd have chosen beer and Jack Daniels." Paul said in manly disgust of fancy booze.

Recalling my first hang over, I added, "First and last time I drank rum! Whew!"

Mark fast-forwarded to the concert. "What happened to Brian at the concert? You disappeared."

"Yeah. One of the girls, I think the one Bob was sweet on…"

Bob chirped alive and on topic. "What? I was sweet on one? Just one…"

"She spilled her drink."

Paul vexed, "Rum will do that. Pina Coladas…"

"No she spilled Sprite in Reynolds Coliseum before the show. Fantastic seats, at the front of balcony beside the left side of the stage." Gary offered.

Music connoisseur Mark recalled, "Excellent show, excellent seats!" "No reverberation that usually kills indoor shows."

"So anyway, Alexa and I sat at the end of the aisle. As host and closest to the end of the row I slipped away to get napkins and a new drink for the girl."

"Now I remember her!" Bob's mind raced, "We went out a couple of times. Gee, what… ?"

Mark redirected, "So what happened, Brian, what took so long?"

"He got into a fight!" shouted Clay.

Dave laughed, "You're shitting me!"

Paul chimed "Man, I can't believe Brian would ever get into a fight. Peace, love, and brotherhood Brian?"

"A misunderstanding." I pushing my hands forward creating space between unseen foes. I looked at Clay and our eyes came alive as we returned to that distant folly.

"Nearest place to get a napkin was a concession stand. Damn long line! I couldn't get close enough to grab the paper napkins. I remember a couple of security guards and a slew of people, but everyone was polite and patient. I waited and bought her a drink and grabbed gobs of those nice white napkins they used to use, not the rough brown stuff that goes for napkins these days. I shoved a few in my pocket and held the rest.

"I went after you." Clay nodded. "Alexa said something about how long it was taking and I ducked down to help."

I smiled appreciatively at his search and rescue.

Clay led, "That's when I saw you get into it on the ramp!"

"A fight?" Dave questioned.

I offered in defense, "Yep. It was a fight. But a short fight! So short I get to keep the 'nice guy' saintly wreath!"

"I walked up the ramp and passed these two big goons loitering in the passageway. They were uncouth drunk bastards. The bigger guy was going on about a girl, 'Did 'ya see that good looking two-bit sitting at the end of the row? I'll take that bitch home and give her my own show! See how she sings with a mouthful…' My mind put the pieced together as we walked past. He added where she was sitting calling out our section, our row. The jerk was talking about Sasha!"

"That's why you stopped!" Clay exclaimed realizing a piece of that night's mystery.

"I gave Clay the sprite and exchanged the napkins from my hands. Told him I'd be up in a minute."

"Gee, if I knew what was about to happen I would have stayed!"

"I know.

"I stepped back to the goons and politely redirected the foul mouthed asshole from his disdainful expectations. Told him 'I like your taste in women! But she's my girlfriend! Turn your wealth of male charm on another. I'm sure someone else will take up your audition offer…'"

"In your dreams!" the second guy chirped.

"I hadn't expected confrontation but Reynolds was my house as a State student, and I felt the need to set a polite tone.

The first guy bellowed, "Fuck you! Your girl my ass!" They laughed like that was something novel and particularly funny. The two closed ranks hemming me in just as Clay disappeared beyond the top of the ramp.

Deep within my belly something started to roil inside. Magma worked its way up from my core starting at my diaphragm hardening as it rose. Blood boiled. It was the quiet desperation of nine months of dating Alexandra, getting eager joyous eyes and verbal acceptance corked by an immovable 'just friends' label. Untapped love instantly turned into an unstoppable energy, a molten fire. This asshole's pressure transformed my unquenchable passion for Alexa into a menacing torrent.

Standing chest to chest I checked my rage, "Look, I commend you on your taste but she's taken. OK? Just want you to know before you stumble up there and make an ass out of yourself. She may be sitting alone, but she's definitely not alone. She's mine!"

The guy bulged out his barrel chest. His thrust pushed me back nearer the concrete wall. His friend followed sealing view and exit up the ramp.

"'She isn't going to want anything to do with you when I'm done pounding your face!'"

Dave broke the tension, "Damn! Getting your head busted for napkins and a soda?"

"What'd you do?" Mark demanded.

"Two on one with the feistier guy right in my face and wall behind me, options were limited. I glanced down the ramp remembering the cop. He looked attentively our way. I thought, 'Shit, they're going to throw all three of us out if we fight! I'm not getting thrown out because of this looser.'

"I looked the guy in the eye, 'Get out of my face!' He didn't budge. Another glance down the ramp confirmed the policeman had seen enough. He was slowly moving our way. I wanted to end this without eviction. But the boiling rage spoke for itself.

I told misguided Romeo, 'Look, the first mistake you made was bad talking a girl you don't know. The second mistake you made was threatening me. Chill out. Enjoy the show."

The guy flared out his chest once more and forearmed me back against the wall.

I glared at him patronizingly as if fighting was beneath both of us and I tried to squeeze through them and head up the ramp before anything serious started. The guy thrust his left arm angrily blocking the exit.

Hair on the back of my head stood up. I looked as his friend assessing how complete their trap. Cop or no cop, right or wrong, this was turning nasty.

The back row guys were amazed all this happened while they sat blissfully entertaining the girls. While they killed time between the warm up act and Elton John I was about to get my face rearranged.

Clay added, "Man you were crazy mixing it up with that guy. The guy had the broadest shoulder's I've ever seen like a Marine Corps recruiting poster!"

"I kept my eyes on his face. Coldly, he took on the look of a man who wasn't there, no expression at all. Color vanished from his cheeks. A glaze came over his eyes and a distant spirit that relished punching and torturing descended. Eyes dark and hard, pupils fixed, he savored what was in front of him like a gourmet chef addresses raw ingredients before filleting.

"A spark animated his still face as three tiny crow-feet lines formed beside his left eye. The right side of his mouth and cheek grotesquely retracted. He rolled his shoulder back and withdrew his arm for a powerful windmill punch.

His fist drove forward. I remained still, eyes wide, conveying a sure target."

Clay chimed in. "That's when I got back to the top of the ramp." Clay put his two hands together approximating the mad man's fist. "I saw this Thor sized sledge hammer of a fist lunging toward Brian's head. Man, I knew you were dead!" Clay laughed nervously.

"I stood still until the last moment and then ducked down and to the right. His thumb skimmed my head. A terrific thud announced his fist met concrete. The blow bloodied knuckles and broke a few wrist bones!" I smiled recalling the near miss and thump.

Clay added, "I couldn't see you. Your head was gone. I thought he'd knocked it off!"

"Fortunately not, but in his demented state he recoiled and weighed his options-- swing with his left, or try again with what remained of his right? His head was slightly bent down and forward as he plotted his next move.

"That's when that magma churning inside leapt out. It leapt out of my gut, traveled at the speed of fury through my right arm and balled my fist. From a completely passive position, my right shot upward and I caught the guy square on the nose!"

I held my fist showing the Back Row the small indention separating middle and ring finger knuckles. "Caught the base of his nose, the columella, right here." I rubbed the narrow hollow between knuckles for show and tell. "It was a perfect fit, my knuckles found the soft fleshy base of his nose. His nose retreated into his head. His neck never pulled his head back to lessen the blow as punch accordioned septum.

"For an instant his eyes remained clear. Then demonic possession lifted. He stood there focused on something from long ago. Maybe he saw his fourth grade teacher rapping his knuckles with a ruler for bullying the kid with a hearing aid, or recalled his granddad telling him not to torment the family dog, possibly he relived his mom whipping him for relentlessly teasing his younger sister. Whatever it was you could see he had an epiphany! The 'Golden Rule' finally got through."

Eyes watered and reddened. A single drop of blood appeared shyly beneath his right nostril joined by a more energetic stream from the left.

"One punch. Wham!" Clay cheered. "Man, you don't know how happy I was. I couldn't see your head from behind his friend. All I saw was this hand zip up and nail the guy! I ran toward you figuring the other guy was going to join in!"

I nodded at Clay's willingness.

"That's when the cop arrived with a hint of self-chastisement for not getting there sooner. He didn't see my unlicensed rhinoplasty. From his angle all he saw was the guy's first punch. He grabbed the jackass' right arm and looked at the wall expecting to see my head smeared from the brutal swing.

"As the cop spun him around he was relieved to see my face intact and surprised to see the big guy's blood darting over his lips and launch itself toward the floor."

I immediately offered, "Just a little… misunderstanding. No problem officer. What we had here was a difference of opinion about who had the rights to a particular seat beside a pretty young lady."

I launched my hand into my right pocket securing my ticket stub. I waved the ticket victoriously in the air confirming my place with my Princess, "But we've settled that, right boys? Have a great show!" I pressed napkins to his leaking nose with my left hand.

"He raised his hand clumsily taking the absorbent cloth. I stepped quickly through the two thugs toward Clay and away from whatever justice the law may impose.

"The other guy momentarily blocked my departure. He quietly relented, 'Sorry man. He really isn't that bad. He just has this thing for blonds, pretty blonds.'"

I nearly bit my tongue in half, "Blonds? Blonds you say? Well, blonds, brunettes, whatever. A man still has to be respectful!'

"Clay was beside me and we both headed to the top of the ramp. I offered Clay the last of the napkins as unwanted evidence needing disposing."

The guys shook heads. Paul offered in rough English brogue, "Aye, tis rum that makes a swashbuckling pirate out of a kind and gentle lad. That's why me pirates love it so!"

We laughed and Bob added, "Damn Brian, next time just get the fucking napkins and come straight back! Do we need to put fucking breadcrumbs down?"

We all laughed.

When I got back to my seat, lovely Alexa said, "Where were you? What took so long?"

"Her beautiful eyes and gentle body language conveyed she missed me. But her cold tone said she was pissed. I sat and leaned over eagerly to tell her what happened as bright stage pots flared and dry ice fog clouded the air. Reynolds erupted as Elton started with the *Funeral for a*

Friend. Everyone stood and the Coliseum rocked with 10,000 cheering fans and solid walls of sound."

Paul asked, "So you didn't tell her?

"Then? Couldn't. Too loud."

"I mean later? Ever tell her after the show?"

I shook my head doubtfully "Shuttling the girls back home that night… don't think so."

Gary added, "Could have helped. Girls like guys that come to their rescue."

I shrugged offering a parting thought, "I didn't tell her. What would I say? Sweetheart, I got in a fight for you… except it wasn't exactly you… turns there was this gorgeous blond on the other side of the same isle…"

The guys laughed and we moved the conversation into the present.

The subject of recent news, fallen idols and "failed" marriages arose. Most of us didn't follow the gossip columns so the events were news.

"What's wrong with men?" I interjected. "Those guys must be playing with a half deck. What the hell did they find that lured them away from those women?"

Paul cautiously personalized the conversation, "Don't mean to be rude, but weren't you hallucinating under the same insanity?"

I looked around and all eyes and ears wanted to know. "Just the opposite. I've never been saner. Never were my choices clearer, nor determination more focused. What I did wasn't cheating. I realized that keeping up the charade with my wife was a lie."

A collective sigh swept the room.

"Unfaithful? Meeting her for lunch wasn't unfaithful. Trying to meet her at the museum wasn't either. The museum is a place of beauty and history, a public place. And I invited her for a late lunch, not dinner."

Paul followed up, "But what if she had, you know, responded to you at the art museum? What then?"

"I don't know. But I'm sure it wouldn't have turned immediately into something we'd have to hide.

"Look fellows, I had four intentions. One for each part of my heart I guess.

"I wanted to know why we didn't make it as a couple.

"Another quarter of my heart realized I was fully alive with Alexandra and I wanted to share her warm and friendly company. We are in the same field, save the world environmentalists who succumbed to pulling forty hours a week making very little difference.

"Part of me wanted to make sure she was all right and that she saw herself as beautiful. I wanted to show her that a man could genuinely care for her.

"Lastly… yeah part of me wanted to see if we had a future together. I wanted to know that, too.

"If Alexa and I, wandering the artwork, recognized there was nothing but a one-sided infatuation, so be it.

"Look, I'm not an imbecile, there *was* something years ago and there *was* something there when we met at her office. I saw it in her eyes, her carefree smile, and I felt it in her hug. This was no wild goose chase!

"And *if* we went the way of exploring a relationship, it would occur after I was separated and divorced. I wasn't about to cheat on my wife."

The conversation turned to college days. A healing realization arose. Our combined memory pieced together the eighteen months that preceded my unceremonious dump on the tennis court.

Not long after the tennis court letdown, Clay and I ditched the apartment in Cary and moved to Raleigh's Boylan Heights neighborhood where we rented a house on Cabarrus Street. The house was ideal for college students. Ideal because only college students would rent it!

Clay threw out, "Remember the dilapidated garage? It became the genesis of residential recycling in North Carolina. If that old garage were still standing it deserved environmental homage! That's something you did after she dumped you, remember?"

I'd seen a news blurb about residential recycling in California and asked the rhetorical question 'Why don't we do that here?' The next day I opened the phone book and called the City of Raleigh. I remained undaunted as a sequence of phone numbers sent me in circles. Finally I was routed to a cheerful woman in the Department of Public Works who said, "Just call me The Trash Lady."

The Trash Lady and I spoke about recycling and confirmed there was interest at the Raleigh Public Works Department. "At a department strategy meeting a month ago my boss raised a similar question. Trouble was, nobody in the city has a clue how to proceed. Why don't you come to my office and we'll discuss it?"

Next day, I parked my trusty Chevette out of harm's way, made my way to a debarking driver of a massive trash truck, and asked if he knew the Trash Lady. His forehead crinkled and an eyebrow rose protectively. The Trash Lady was the director of this operation. He cautiously showed me her office which is best described as a matchbox on steroids – a special noise control cubical placed within the large service bay. From the outside it looked like a box car lost its wheels and slid into the work bay. Not much of an office, but it provided relief from banging and clutter of trash equipment and privacy for employee - supervisor conversations.

She welcomed me. Clutter choked. There wasn't much difference between the muddle around me and the mangled innards of a trash compactor truck. I wondered if she got her nickname from her job or office hygiene. Columns of paper and bound reports rose in stacks from the floor to shoulder height along each sidewall. Other piles originated from her desk, chair, and all flat surfaces presumably because the boost gave them a better chance to reach the ceiling. Like stalagmites, each formation looked old and off limits to human touch. A sneeze would send the precarious structure down like a house of cards.

The Trash Lady bade me sit but I hesitated without option to comply. She whisked a stack off a chair and motioned.

"I'm curious about your vision for residential recycling." She started, "Nobody around here practices it. Details are unknown. As far as I know it's in its infancy." She genuinely wanted ideas and began a series of questions.

"How do you propose we get started?"

I'd already thought, "Start with a pilot project. Keep it small, contained, but visible. A pilot project will give the effort the ideal stature. People will suspend judgment. Who'd be threatened by a pilot project? A controlled experiment will allow the city to learn, succeed or fail without political fallout."

"I see, right." She nodded. "We don't have to figure out how to start everywhere all at once. Just assess potential."

She smiled as she jotted notes. "Where should we put the pilot recycling center?"

"Has to be in Raleigh, not on the outskirts. The location should be downtown, a tight knit downtown neighborhood. A suburb location would give the wrong impression.

"We need a neighborhood with an identity, an owner's association and newsletter." I mentioned three viable candidates as she scribed.

"Wherever we site it, we need a local advocate-- someone to answer questions and give it a face."

"What should we recycle?"

At that time there was no market for plastic. But metal recycling had been big business since the days of Rockefeller, and paper recycling probably before Henry Luce put his name on so much print. Owens Corning and other glass companies might have need for glass. "Start with steel and aluminum cans, paper, and glass."

We hashed out details as the Trash Lady made one-line notes. I glanced at her as she annotated and wondered if she had the power to get something new started or was she a dreamer?

Finally, she looked up and asked, "OK, where do you think we ought to put it and whom do you think we could get to run it?"

Unhesitatingly I said, "I can do it. I live in one of the downtown neighborhoods, have a dilapidated garage, and had the passion to see it through."

"What will you need from us?" she asked.

"I can't get people to try residential recycling if they don't know about it. Give me advertising.

The Trash Lady was surprised that we'd framed the whole thing in a matter of minutes. It seemed pretty straightforward to me, ignorant as I was about the workings of a city and a little thing call budgets. She said she'd get back.

Sure enough, it wasn't long before she called and let me know that Raleigh, and maybe the whole state of North Carolina, would start residential recycling as we laid it out. Cool!

"Are you still willing to head up the effort?"

"Sure! But I needed to inform the landlord. He's pretty easy going. I'll get the owner's permission and we'll roll."

The Trash Lady said she'd get us the barrels and advertising.

When it came to our landlord, he was terrified of the damage four single college guys might cause to his dubious rental property. But he was too Southern to confront, too ill of health, or too weak of constitution to visit. He never looked in the front door in all the years we rented. Every time I went to his office he squirmed as if I was bearer bad news. The $400 security deposit and the rent we scraped together each month was a lot to us, but left him woeful. I comforted him that we were treating his house fine. It was the trucks shaking the foundation that worried me.

The landlord immediately approved my idea of the recycling center but said the garage wasn't on his property. It belonged to a neighbor. Hmm … I'd already rigged a basketball goal on the structure and reinforced and straightened up the leaning timbers! Still, it would make an ideal foster home for residential recycling.

I took it up with the renter next door. This time I started my negotiation with a plan. My neighbor brewed homemade beer. "Your search for clean empty Heineken bottles will be solved!" I baited. "You can have up to two cases of greens a month."

He quickly divided up the garage space. The newly swept dirt floor almost sparkled in anticipation for its moment of glory.

And that is how it got started. A high percentage of the folks in our neighborhood supported recycling. They showed great pride that Boylan Heights was given a chance to lead the experiment. Announcements went out. Drivers from other neighborhoods were easy to spot, aimlessly looking for a garage that wasn't visible from the street. They came in search of an environmental solution, backseats and trunks filled with stuff that a month before would have been entombed in a landfill. Altogether, the pilot site ran about six months. The Trash Lady thanked me and said they'd started a second site. Our pilot site was put to rest.

The guys toasted a beer to that early success. I thought I'd wasted all my spare time brooding over Alexandra but Clay reminded me I'd made a difference when I was at my lowest.

We turned to another harebrained and unlikely scenario that came on the heels of Alexandra's dumping. This dealt with the insane asylum that bordered our neighborhood.

Our neighborhood wasn't idyllic. We had a state prison two blocks west. The prison sat stone cold, separated from the community by a railroad line and the ubiquitous razor wire fencing. Like a welcoming motel, the prison kept its lights burning. On foggy nights, an eerie glow ricocheted like a ghostly gloomy presence. On the east low-rent offices and light industrial buildings offered no redeeming ambiance.

Western Boulevard, a major thoroughfare through Raleigh, took a hard left turn in front of our house just before it straightened out and became a four-lane highway. Folks hit the gas as they rounded the turn, emitting trails of tailpipe pollution and the roar of accelerating engines. No one whose house fronted the busy street sat in his or her yard. To do so would have given you a dose of noxious fumes and qualified you as a candidate for our other neighbor-- the state mental institution Dorothea Dix.

The Dix hospital was a treasure, a true gem on the south side of Boylan Heights. Amid the hustle and bustle of a mid-sized southern city, it was our little Central Park. There was a gentle creek that ran through it, and the trees – oh, the trees! Whoever laid out the grounds did a remarkable job creating a tranquil facility. The road from our neighborhood crossed a creek over a fieldstone bridge. All roads on the Dix grounds were unlined giving the facility a residential feeling and barely wide enough for two cars to pass. A procession of behemoth old trees flanked the roads. Each massive hardwood commanded as much crown as it did height.

The Dix buildings were glazed-yellowish brick, others red brick, and bespoke of an era when buildings were meant to last. The large tress and varied buildings made it look like a private school. All in all, there were probably fifteen or twenty buildings in the main hospital area.

The rest of the grounds— more than a thousand acres just west of downtown Raleigh—lay fallow. There were hiking trails and ponds. A two-lane road crept through the underused property southwest of the hospital. Spotted here and there were North Carolina State agricultural extension offices.

I took long jogs across the grounds. Some days a herd of young cattle joined me. I'd call to them playfully, my 'moos' answered in bovine as we hoofed through the fields. It was a perfect place to regain your sanity, whether you interred or just passing through.

The Back Row guys and I shared great times on the grounds. We'd leave college books behind and play like kids. We'd frolic in the hospital's manicured front lawn with dogs loping beside us as Frisbees and footballs crossed the sky.

After one such playful outing, the TV news announced Governor Jim Hunt was going to turn the grounds into a mega prison. Prison populations were going up and the people in the know saw incarceration as a growing business.

"Dorothea Dix a prison?" I asked Clay as we watched the news in our shanty living room.

"Doesn't seem right! The facility is ideal for its current purpose, and the front grounds so peaceful."

"Yeah" Clay chimed, "This is the state capital and already we have a prison!"

I borrowed Clay's Instamatic camera the next day and went back to Dix. While pictures were developed I wrote a letter to the Governor that wavered between opinion, prose, and poetry. My portable electric typewriter droned as I pecked a message years before word processors made the going easy. When the film came back, choice photos accompanied the letter.

Friends and family applauded my passion but shook their heads, "Sending the letter won't make a difference."

I shrugged saying I was motivated and had to share my feelings.

Shortly afterward, I received a letter in the mail from Governor Hunt's office. I skimmed the letter. The letter was appreciative of my ideas, blah, blah, blah… and invited me to a meeting. *Invited me to a meeting*? A careful second reading confirmed the letter didn't reject.

At the appointed time, I headed up in a high-rise office building in downtown Raleigh. My contact wasn't the Governor, but an official for Hunt. When I got to the upper floor I found his name and title on a door. He was Hunt's special political advisor who handled sensitive issues.

The door opened into a spacious suite outer office. A prompt and courteous secretary greeted me in an office's filled with upscale décor. This wasn't a lowly crony. Richly decorated wood paneling, plush carpet, and art spoke of executive stature.

He invited me into his corner office. The expanse of windows took in all of downtown. Numerous tasteful trinkets and items displayed his journey through life. Arrangements personified good taste. Not a single stack of documents in sight, everything was neat and organized.

He greeted me warmly, "The Governor would have liked to meet you personally except he had a very busy agenda today."

I nodded graciously. He said it so honestly and with the right amount of feeling it didn't sound like a practiced speech.

"I appreciate you taking the time to see me." I adjusted in the plush chair realizing here I was something more than a college student, I was a voter with a voice.

"Your letter touched the Governor. This subject matters to the Governor. So if it matters to him it is my first priority."

He lifted the envelope carefully removing letter and photographs. He unfolded the letter gently ensuring the pictures didn't fall and then spread the contents between us as if he was unraveling an ancient script of immeasurable value. We sat quietly reflecting on the letter and images.

The letter ran deep and emotions. That's when I realized he'd braced for a hostile confrontation not a meditative exchange. But we both sat quietly pondering the future of Raleigh's largest expanse of open space.

He spoke, "I see you are very passionate about saving the hospital and not keen on a prison. Tell me why."

"The hospital seems so relevant in the world we've created. The pace we've chosen erased the idyllic era of Andy Griffith and that era's three jail cells run by a dopey guard.

"We live in a city where one massive prison isn't enough and the state wants to build an even larger complex. We lived in a city whose planners turn quiet neighborhood streets into major thoroughfares in favor of commuting and commerce."

It was my turn to speak for the trees, my chance to be the Lorax. "In this ever-more hectic world Dorothea Dix stands as a bastion for all. It promises special care if any of us ever needs it. It tells everyone the state thinks enough of us to provide a place where we can recover in an institution not stuck off somewhere ashamed, but kept close, right here in Raleigh. Folks can convalesce on peaceful grounds filled with century old trees. Dorothea Dix with all its beautiful trees and green lawns is more than a place for treatment; it's an oasis, a symbol of hope, and a quiet buttress to the sane people of Raleigh. It's a sign of support-- before you needed it. I don't know what folks in other states do with mentally ill folks, but I kind of like the way we keep them within visiting distance."

I looked at the letter and felt a tinge of embarrassment. It included a poetic phrase so sensitive, so ethereal, that it might earn me a free pass into the loony institution. But my host overlooked the lyrical part accepting it as a sign of being fervent.

"What is it about the prison expansion you are against?"

"We already have a large penitentiary within an eighth of a mile of the hospital. I don't see the wisdom of expanding that business in downtown Raleigh. There must be a higher good for this land smack in the middle of Raleigh. The state capital is in some small way hallowed ground. And the Dorothea Dix is a green gem that must be used wisely. The land should not be metered out for a short-term spike in prison population.

"Don't you see it?"

He held his opinion.

I pitched, "Dorothea Dix contains vast tracks of undeveloped land behind and beside the hospital. Please don't look at this gem through a contractor's eyes. This land and Dorothea Dix is entrusted to us by past generations who showed wisdom and restraint. Let's not squander it."

I comforted, "We don't need to know its best use right now. Just save it until a higher use is identified."

My host nodded but kept his peace.

Silence descended. Directing residential recycling was easy, but this called for a vision I didn't entertain.

We ended our pleasant meeting with a handshake.

Later supportive friends asked with genuine interest how the meeting with the political emissary went. Some pointed out, "The Governor had a reputation for doing what he said he was going to do. All relevant thought is made before an announcement. The meeting might have been cordial, but the Governor would see it as political suicide to recant what he'd already publicly stated."

As evidence to the ways of politics, friends pointed out an earlier contentious issue. The Governor had made a statement when a waste hauler had contaminated miles of North Carolina's roadside. After he committed to digging it up and landfilling he a lot of questions arose so he appointed a Blue Ribbon Panel. This consortium of experts studied options and concluded the best course of action was contrary to the governor's stated plan. But the Governor's office said thank you very much to the Panel and went ahead as publically stated. They felt it was more important for a governor not to break his word.

Folks consoled, "If a Blue Ribbon Panel of experts couldn't change the Governor's mind; what chance is there for a college student armed with a portable typewriter and poetic letter?"

"I included photos!" I countered.

What happened? Did a huge supermax security penitentiary rise?

The Governor's office went silent on the subject and regrouped. No bulldozers showed up on the Dorothea Dix grounds while I lived in Raleigh.

A few years later, in 1984 a master plan was unveiled for the land that included the Department of Health's expanded presence. Dix survived. By far the biggest new occupant, 385 acres, would be NC State's Centennial Campus. The enormous building project was highly touted and marked the one hundredth anniversary of the university. The following year, the next governor, Jim Martin, earmarked another 485 acres to the Centennial Campus. Current accounts say the burgeoning educational facility has over 1,100 acres.

"Those were successes," Paul said. "You may have been down and out about Alexa, but you found time to do two things most people never would have tried, and look at the results!"

We toasted achievement.

I recalled months wasted, emotionally shattered grief over Alexandra, and had forgotten making a small but lasting mark on society.

Cream rises to the top, so do curdles. And good friends remember curdles. Part of their job.

"What ever happened to that male dancing thing?" Gary inquired. "Didn't you try and start some kind of male strip show about that time?"

Questions flew as Gary continued. "And wasn't that how you met that loser, the guy who eventually stalked me at work!"

"Oh shit!"

Gary's memory dredged up a beast long forgotten. Like a grotesque deep sea monster that hadn't seen the light of day in decades, a failed endeavor surfaced.

"Stalking you, who the hell are we talking about?" asked Paul.

"You're right." I told Gary. "I thought about forming an alternative to topless bars. It started when the 'Chippendales' came to town. I figured if the Chippendales drew a crowd… Imagined we'd perform for bachelorette parties."

"No way!" Paul exclaimed, "I never heard!"

The guys got fresh beers and mixed drinks as we launched in a new direction. It was late but between friends, time had no standing. New bags of chips were open and we bound into shameless discloser.

"The plan was to create a small dance group. We'd take gigs in three-man teams. One guy could come in with a construction worker outfit; another might have a more artistic approach. I picked three songs to start with and choreographed skits.

"It didn't quite get off the ground," I said sheepishly. "But Gary is right– male dancing is how we met the stalker."

Gary broke in: "What was his name? God, I've blocked it out of my memory!"

Gary stood, ran his hands through his thick, black hair and added in total disgust, "He was gross!"

Mark chimed, "He reminded me of the guy in *Silence of the Lambs*. Remember him? Remember the crazy guy who kidnapped the girls and stripped off their skin to make a dress?"

"Yes!" Gary knowingly exclaimed skin twinging.

Mark let out a howl and shivered as if his own flesh was being ripped off as sullied memory returned.

"It started when I put an advertisement in the paper; *male dancer available for private parties*. I gave myself a stage name, 'Nad.'"

"Nad?" Paul asked, knowing couldn't have heard right.

"Nad. As in gonad!"

We belly laughed.

"Well, I didn't want to use my real name!"

Mark tipped back in his bar stool crashing into a recliner, and laughed until it hurt.

When the noise subsided, I went on; "The first guy to call turned out to be the psycho with severe homosexual tendencies. The Jeffery

Dahlmer want-to-be offered to be my manager and suggested we get together over lunch in the next week or so. I didn't have enough sense to pull out a cross and silver bullet and chase him off.

"The ad brought another call. The second caller was the owner of a dance studio. He asked intelligent questions. I confessed we were clueless and just organizing the effort. He invited me to his dance studio. It wasn't far away from our Cabarrus Street house, in one of those bland city buildings east of our neighborhood.

"The guy was middle-aged and on the up and up. Young ladies eight in number warmed up for ballet lessons. The older ones turned head towards the only male on the dance floor. Their attention made my steps lighter."

It's a good feeling to be checked out by so many women all at once. It doesn't hurt the male ego one iota knowing your only chance is there because there's no competition.

"The dance room was neat. Mirrors covered the walls and a narrow balance rail fixed along the perimeter. An ornamental stamped metal ceiling sixteen feet high gave the place class.

"The floor was dark brown, like the well-worn floor in an old textile plant, except this floor was spotless; the color from years of wear and countless footfalls. The sprung floor gave with every jump.

"The owner joined me momentarily on the dance floor and we talked while the lesson got underway. He asked about my dance experience. "One semester of PE ballroom dancing." I said. "But I have passion in my heart and I'm in great shape."

The studio owner formulated a plan. He turned on his heel and I followed his gaze as he took in the room. "We… we need male dancers for my ballet and jazz programs. Plenty of girls," he said sweeping his hand. "But I'm woefully short of guys. Chronic problem."

"Here's the deal. I'll offer you free lessons. Free lessons for you and I'll extend reduced rates for each guys you bring in."

I remained silent following his pitch.

"The catch? You have to participate in the studio's dance performances as long as you take lessons."

"Seems very reasonable." I took another look around his studio. With girls festooning the place, I could *suffer* through some lessons! We shook on it and I told him I'd get back in touch.

The Back Row guys sat in shocked silence. Paul stated, "Buddy, I thought I'd heard it all!"

Paul asked shyly, "These other dancers you were counting on… did you pencil us in?

Mark inquired, "Did this have something to do with the wolf mask?"

I exuberantly slapped my hands. "Oh you *devil* of a boy!" Mark was right. Our claim to fame was going to be more than sensual dance; I planned over the top humor to lighten our performances.

"Yes indeed! At the start of the show we'd invite one of the girls off stage and give her a part. The show would start with a sheer curtain between audience and performers. We'd start behind the closed curtain with backlighting casting a shadow. The audience would watch the dancers in shadow relief. Gary and I experimented with reverse projection, or that's what I called it. We'd blend in real dancers with reverse projection images against the sheer screen.

"We'd have flashing lights illuminating the audience synced with the music and the whole room would be a whirl of color, shadows of dancers and images of erotic innuendo. The projection and dancers would blend seamlessly on the backlit shear separating us from the audience.

"We'd open with Pink Floyd's 'Time.' It starts with spacey drums leading into ethereal music and ends with that soulful, sensual, erotic female solo."

The guys stirred, we'd all been Floyd fans and remembered the song well.

"When the female vocal solo was raging, the dancers would circle around the girl we'd brought backstage and then oscillate away. Two guys would rise up and pretend to play hands down and around her body sensuously before drawing away. We'd encourage her to move her hands likewise down her body and it would appear like a tempest of sensual contact. The song would end, shear curtains would rise and the first lady would join her friends."

Dave summarized, "Cool! Cool start!"

"Yeah, we'd set the tone the way the James Bond movies start with the dancing nudes cast in silhouette. Our display would feature one of their friends. The sheer curtain would make it seem like they were peeping on their friend's sexual encounter. Clever, eh?

"Like Mark said we'd be more than sensuous bodies, we'd incorporate fairytales. The first was a takeoff on Goldilocks. We'd invite another girl from the audience to play Goldie. The guy dancers would be the bears. We'd feed the lady her lines from off the wings for all to hear. Real campy… no professional airs, just fun! The ladies would laugh hearing lines piped in and their friend in on the action. The Goldilocks scene would end with her lying in baby bear's bed and poppa bear mounting her. Of course the guy would keep one leg on the floor like the old time-movies!

"Even if we were close on the comic timing, it'd be a hoot! It would raise a ruckus among her friends and give the volunteering lady a good blush!

"And the coop-de-gra was going to be our Little Red Riding Hood spoof. With State being the 'Wolfpack' I figured this would inject local charm. I'd found the mask Mark talked about and a little red hood that draped in back to a low point, paneled front with wide front ties. Perfect cape for lady Red's part. The scene began with the wolf, that'd be me, and Red played by the central audience figure, birthday girl or bride-to-be. The wolf and Red would meet in 'the woods'-- a single painted tree prop. Again we'd call out Red's script from stage right.

"After their introduction, and some comical set-up lines, the Wolf would lope ahead of Red and onto the bed. And the scene would change to the farmhouse. Red would enter and stand at the foot of the bed. I'd powerfully rise off the bed in the wolf mask, wearing grandma's nightgown and guide her gently onto the bed, as we'd exchange:

'Oh what big eyes you have…'

'The better to admire all your beauty, my dear Red.'

'Oh what big ears you have…'

'The better to hear and listen lovingly to every word you utter, my darling."

"Oh what a big bulge you have between your legs…"

"The better to split you with my precious!"

"Oh what a long tongue you have…"

"The better to eat you with!"

"At that I'd dive head first on her abdomen and begin… well you know, pretend licking her in a most delightful manner."

The guys were howling with laughter.

Paul threw in, "Any uncommitted bridesmaids might have volunteered for an encore performance sans the mask."

"A distinct possibility!" I admitted with gusto brandishing the grin of a true carnivore. "We were quite willing to accept Master Card, Visa… and select forms of barter!"

With contagious grins my pals howled like a pack of wolves at the thought of easy pickings. Gone were doubts of joining the ranks of dancers! They could have made great performers. It's all about motivation!

"So why didn't you do it?" Dave quizzed.

"Remember Mr. Sicko, the spineless character of uncertain sexual orientation? We met a few times. He kept calling me Nad and I kept reminding him my name was Brian. He achieved nothing and we never lined up any gigs. It never dawned on me to get someone else to do the front work. I didn't have the time to be a student, take dance lessons and organize performances so we needed him to find gigs. Without a first show the idea imploded. I dropped the whole thing and hit books instead. Don't think I ever called the dance studio owner."

Mark said wryly, "I'll bet by now he knows you're not coming!"

"Heck, with all my save the world stuff *and* the male dancing, I could have earned the title Porn Star Saint!"

Paul said, "So you thought you wasted a year and a half drooping about after Alexa? Maybe. But you succeeded on two out of three of the most outlandish things I've ever heard a college student do!"

He lifted his St. Pauli Girl beer in a toast.

And what of Nad? I would have made a damn good male dancer. We'd have advanced the art by twenty years with dry ice, mood lights, reverse projection and interactive skits. R rated fairy tales would have pleased. By gosh, we'd have ushered in a new era of entertainment in Raleigh!

But your heart has to be fully invested. And the only real act; the only three-ringed circus I wanted to run, was a mature, spiritual, and intimate relationship with a loving and caring woman. The dance troop never made its first performance.

Today, if you live or travel through Raleigh, you'll see recycling going strong. Residential recycling occurs throughout the state and untold acres of farmland have been spared the indignity of being used as landfills.

My old neighborhood, Boylan Heights, stands. Western Boulevard was rerouted and the neighborhood reverted to a quieter place. The house we rented looks great, but the old leaning garage that gave birth to recycling is gone.

Dorothea Dix Hospital still stands with all its charm and most of its cherished hardwoods. A visit there is good for the soul, even if you're just passing through.

NC State's Centennial Campus shares the grounds where once a mega prison was planned.

As for male dancing, Raleigh is a bigger, wilder place. The female version still draws a crowd, but male dancing never caught on.

Framed

July-27

Celeste presented me with a gift upon my return. As I set my luggage down she brought out my Taj Mahal e-mail framed. Each page was displayed in a black wooden frame under glass.

"Here, you can have this back."

I reached for her delicate gift. Better I hold than wear splintered across my face. I accepted her offering from trembling hands.

I thought she would be relieved to hear me finally admit; "You've been right a long time. Our relationship is over and it's time for separation."

"No it isn't."

"What? You asked me to come up with a plan!"

"Not that plan!"

"I *will never* understand women!"

"I hoped we would try and make it."

"So what were the last few years about, Celeste? All the times you brought up separation? You made lists showing how we'd divide possessions? What's different?"

"It's different because you're saying it. You're the one calling it over. I did it to get your attention."

"What's left to say, dear? I expressed my undying love-- love that weathered hibernation for twenty-three years."

Celeste challenged, "You never wrote me such a moving love letter!"

"I cannot argue that. The only evidence stands silently enclosed beneath sheets of glass."

I looked down sadly and turned away presuming she was right. What was left to argue but terms of separation?

I sat deflated and tired, "Honey, I'm torn. I love you, but staying with you feels unfaithful to the woman I fell in love with years ago, my silent princess."

"Well, separation isn't much of a plan!"

Her tenacity astonished me. Later that night we redressed the fissure and she revealed a surprise that gave her hope. In my absence playing golf, Celeste had decided it was her turn to contact Alexandra. She'd organized a private investigator.

I didn't see that coming, but it is safe to say my blind love left much out of focus.

Celeste informed me about her PI contact with Sasha and I spun up with anticipation. I came alive beaming with joy and eagerly pressed Celeste to share what she'd learned.

"What did she say? Did she say anything about the way she felt? The way she feels?"

Celeste angrily crossed her arms, mouth froze with contempt. "Boy, I can't believe how your energy shot through the roof! You went from a normal tone to one of veritable ecstasy at the idea that Sasha had talked to *somebody* about her feelings.

"If you want to know what the PI found out, ask the PI." She clammed up cementing conversation.

Talk to the PI instead of Sasha? I felt marooned, a space traveler alone in a disabled craft a long way from home. Adrift with less and less chance of contact. Sasha was supposed to talk to me! But indirect contact was something, one last gasp, a last breath of life before all communication was lost. One last loving memory before the oxygen ran out.

The next morning I called the PI. "How did Alexandra sound, how did she feel?" I absorbed every word and inflection of this second-hand image of my beloved.

I told the investigator I wanted a transcript of their discussion, but one hadn't been made. I continued asking questions jarring the PI's memory and ferreting out every last gram of meaning like the lost space traveler searching for one last image of home.

The PI went over every detail twice. Sadly, none of my questions were answered and no glimpse into Alexa's feelings emerged.

I thanked the PI for sharing and absorbed the last oxygen. Power drained from the marooned capsule's control panel and the cabin went dark. Dark, starkly cold, and still.

Best of Friends

Late Summer

"I've lost the best friend I'll ever have." Black Sabbath

Celeste and I hung in there. Day-by-day, week-by-week, we hung in there the way human beings suffer searching for the right thing to do.

Time and again she lamented I hadn't conveyed my love to her in all the years we were together in such an eloquent and heartfelt way as I had for Sasha. "Where are my love letters?" was her echo.

Celeste pointed out, "It is futile, totally crazy living one place and loving someone else. A person can't live that way."

"Well, you can, but it vexes, ages you, it really ages you."

I realized that Celeste was the best friend I ever had. She might be the best friend I would ever have. I shared, "I feel I'm losing the best friend I ever had."

"Oh, so now she is your best friend too?" She asked incredulously.

"No, you!"

She calmed as I went on; "At the beginning of the summer, being just friends wasn't enough. Now I see how much our friendship really means. Months ago, comfort and convenience, security and reassurance seemed easy to replace. A wife, a marriage, a lover needed to be much more. But faced with the possible end of our relationship, I have a heightened appreciation for these aspects of marriage."

As we grew apart, each aspect of the relationship was drawn out so it could be observed – lines securing two ships at sea that only become visible when the ships diverge and the ropes tighten. The strong lines hidden beneath the surface of the everyday waves while ships were close now strained into view.

The value of a spouse being a near and dear friend came into view-- a friend who knows you better than anyone else.

Comfort was easy to overlook. Celeste was petite and delicate of frame making her cold natured. We often spent evenings snuggled beneath a blanket and watched TV or a movie. We shared more time like that before the boys were born than after but even after kids we carved out evenings to sit close. There was warmth and comfort in that closeness. Comfort was a line being cast aside.

Convenience was something easy to take for granted. We worked together seamlessly, unselfishly. We shared the shopping, cooking, and child rearing. Teamwork made it convenient to do everything our busy schedules demanded. If Celeste needed to rearrange her schedule at the last minute to accommodate work, I covered. When I volunteered for coaching activities we worked it out. Convenience was about to change.

The security of two incomes was reassuring. Our incomes made for a comfortable living in a desirable home. As the one who would move out, the looming change weighted heavy. When I'd been laid off for a year when a previous employer downsized Celeste's income paid the bills. Then, when contracting became stable, Celeste resigned her steady job and opened up her own office and my income reassured. Security of two incomes was ending as it was loosened from its hitch.

Release the line!

There is something to be said for the loss of intimacy, too. Mind and body flourish with a full 360-degree relationship. A full circle relationship includes intimacy. Whether it was a back rub or foot rub or more erotic contact, there are times when the need for contact is palatable. Sometimes the need is overwhelming. And I need that contact regularly. Intimacy was another line connecting us.

Casting off! Cast each line free and clear.

We were becoming two untethered ships floating free each other, slowly diverging.

Where will we go? We used to know the answer. It didn't matter where we went, we'd go there as one.

I'd lost the best friend I'd ever have.

UP!

October-03

"If you're not in it for love, I'm out of here." Shania
Twain

Lewis! There are those damn lyrics again!
Plans to attend a Shania Twain concert predated 'The e-mail.'
The week of the show Celeste asked "Should we still go or give our tickets away? Long drive and evening with your soon to be ex-husband."

"Equally long drive and evening with your soon to be ex-wife. We still together, not separated or divorced and we haven't done enough of this kind of thing, especially since we've had kids. You're a real Shania fan. Let's not throw this… weekend away."

The drive to DC was pleasant. We left early enough not to be rushed. Celeste brushed me up on Shania's music. I was impressed by how big a fan she was and how this music was an unseen conduit to her passion. It was neat to learn something new and observe a hint of zeal. We talked about my search for other living accommodations. Work had me on the road three days a week and I'd delayed the search for an apartment.

When we got to Northern Virginia we pulled into the Vienna Metro station and parked. The Vienna Metro is the farthest west Metro station and train cars arrive mostly empty at that hour. As we boarded, the few other folks getting on were headed to Shania. I struck up conversations about Shania's shows. A young couple had their first baby a month ago. This was their first night out since the birth. They snuggled close on the bench seat; love's halo encircling them. An older couple had attended many of Shania's shows. Directly in front of us sat a mother and her six-year old daughter. This would be the mother's second Shania concert and daughter's first.

We felt energized arriving at the MCI Center. A pedestrian complex was pleasantly humming. Restaurants, stores, and friendly folks manning customer service booths for arriving patrons.

Section 400 was upper bleachers center stage. From the bottom the section looked like a good venue. We entered through the ramp that fed the highest section and eventually got to the section and looked down. Now… where was row M?

We did an about face and headed up steep stairs. The letter M is smack dab in the middle of the alphabet and the row is darn near at the top. We got closer and closer to the back wall and exposed steel beams supporting the roof. As we turned and looked the stage had shrank considerably. Worse, I felt like a small cereal flake clinging to the rim of a breakfast bowl. I glanced up to see if there was a giant spoon hovering.

Looking down the steep incline, it didn't seem like a good idea to stand and cheer when the concert got underway. Vertigo might set in. "They ought to provide safety harnesses and tether occupants in these last few rows. Trapeze anyone?"

I felt Celeste chill.

I waited until the song was over and asked, "How are you doing?"

 She added, "We're not going to make it. But we can still be friends."

I gulped our unexpected 'goodbye without reply. I put my arm around her shoulder as she quietly cried. We held hands and leaned tenderly close. With silent tears in our eyes we stared bravely into the future.

After the warm-up band was done, I looked around and saw empty seats below. It was about twenty minutes after the advertised start time.

I excused myself and headed on a mission. This evening meant too much to sit in the nosebleed section. I tracked down a customer service representative and upgraded seats.

I quickly collected Celeste. She excitedly gathered our jackets.

Two young ladies who sat beside us gave Celeste a sly look and wink saying; "Leaving so soon? Have fun!" Their sexual innuendo and youthful energy refreshed us both! We left the two girls and the rest of Section 400 Row M.

Our new seats were in Section 117 directly in front of the first level box seats, just off center stage. We could cheer without tumbling. The concert was enjoyable and we made the best of it.

The Metro ride and our short drive to Ray's apartment were pleasant. Celeste nestled in my arms on the train, asleep, warm, and rocking to the gentle motion. We held hands as we walked to our vehicle and drove to Ray's.

Celeste crashed.

Ray made hot tea for two. "So how's your stumble, your mid-life crisis?"

Hot liquid singed my tongue before I could respond.

I cringed, "I certainly have more respect for trials and tribulations!

"I saw Alexandra in Lynchburg last night."

He blurted with effervescent curiosity, "You *saw* Alexa last night? Did she come to Lynchburg?"

"No, it was another Alexandra. The one that lives next door neighbor, remember? She's all grown now and baby sits."

Ray harassed, "You little shit!" You knew…"

"Yeah, I knew what you'd think.

"Know what? I realized the local Alexandra, the neighbor kid, is the same age as Sasha was when I met her. My kids love her she's sweet and cute."

Ray added, "By the look on your face she has a nice rack too!"

"These young girls must spray paint on tee shirts and sweaters. I swear to God, shirts didn't fit that way when we were younger!"

"You mean thank God they didn't fit that tightly when we were younger!" Ray corrected. "Otherwise we'd never gotten anything done, school-wise. We'd had a perpetual boner."

"I *had* a perpetual boner!" I confided. We both laughed, remembering the hormone-driven era. "You're right, shirts like that and belly piercing would have made concentrating impossible.

"Anyway, this young kid helped me reflect how immature we were, blissful ignorant. Seeing her helped me realize Sasha and I were both kids."

"Kids," Ray conceded, "But we knew what we felt."

"We were joyous kids that thought we were men."

Ray added, "That youthful boy needs room to grow, to love, and feel pain."

Ray nursed his tea, and then poignantly asked, "Did Alexa ever get back to you? Answer your questions?"

"*No!*" I said loudly in a comic tone. "Ahh, no… she didn't get back to me. But thanks for asking."

"So, you *still* didn't figure out why you never made it as a couple?" Ray probed.

"No."

"Well partner, I've got your answer, *dude*."

"You do?"

Had I stumbled upon a hidden oxygen cylinder for the marooned astronaut? I looked closely, reading his face to see if this was a ruse.

"Yes, I do!" Ray exuded confidence, "Brian, you were a fucking nerd as a freshman and sophomore! That is your answer.

"Hell boy, you were lucky the girl got in your car in the first place. Dude, you were helpless!"

Ray took a breath yielding a moment to respond.

My mind raced, "I recalled wearing glasses, enrolled in engineering. Those two traits alone are not damning! I'd avoided the nerd trappings of a pocket pencil protector, and never strapped a calculator to my hip. Well, I don't recall doing that.

"A nerd, you say?" I countered buying time. "What about all the other fucking nerds on campus? We were all nerds back then. If she was holding out for other than a nerd…"

"Not all nerds, man. We weren't all nerds." Ray continued, "Guys that had girlfriends through high school came across smooth and approachable. You and I were slow on the draw."

"You've changed!" I shot back.

"Don't dodge the subject, home boy!" Ray cornered me and wouldn't let up. "You were a died-in-the-wool nerd. You probably had big bug eye glasses."

"I did! Clay said bigger frames were better because you didn't have to turn your head to see!"

"Clay was your fashion consultant?" Ray flamed on. "Blind leading the blind!"

We both laughed at the stinging truth.

He continued, "Sasha probably didn't date too many engineers other than you *if* what you called going out was dating!"

I fiercely defended, "We dated!"

"She was on a mercy mission with you," Ray rocked with laughter. "You may have volunteered helping the blind, but she did her civic duty courting you!"

"O man!..."

"If nerds had a theme song..."

"An anthem?"

"A national nerd anthem! You and Clay would be in the video, veritably poster children. 'Mommas don't let your babies grow up to be engineers.'

"Don't get me wrong, you were always brave enough, about the biggest damn heart of any straight guy I know. But like you said, Sasha *was* a princess."

"Out of my league?"

Ray shook his head, "You wanted to be high up on her list. Well buddy, your kind deed driving her back to her dorm was your one and only ticket into the queue for her heart. It got you noticed, but that was the best you could hope for!

"If you'd driven a BMW... well that would have shown a bit more class than..."

"My Chevette! My little blue Chevette was a great car! It had a kick ass stereo. And the sheet metal on that car is the exact same thickness as a BMW!"

"Uh huh, right," Ray conceded. "That's a poster child response! The metal might be the same gauge, but to a fine young girl like Sasha, she'd fancy the import."

"Wow… I never thought of that!" I laughed.

"OK, I didn't drive a luxury or sporty car and I may have been, may have *dressed*, a little nerdy…" I repositioned to make a case.

"You were a great guy on all other fronts. She saw the little boy in you, the nerd, not the wholesome man you'd become. If she met you a year later after you filled out your frame, had some fashion sense, and were comfortable around women, she might have been interested. But she's a fifteen second impression kind of person. You started as a nerd. Never had a chance to erase that perception."

"Thanks for the insights. You're the first person to say anything about why I didn't measure up."

Ray continued, "Let me add this. Remember when you and Joyce met in Alabama, on your NASA co-op stint?"

"I don't remember filling you in on Joyce."

We met the last three weeks I was in Alabama on my work-study program. I was one month shy of my twentieth birthday. It was a unique time for me because Joyce warmed to me like butter on hot toast.

"Yeah, of course I remember Joyce." I confirmed. "Who could forget her sorority's Bahama Mamma Come-on I-wanna Lay-ya Party! It was an outdoor event one bright sunny Saturday. All kinds of events picnic events and team races were scheduled. Most had sexual overtones. The sorority did an amazing thing bringing sexual tension to the front and combining it with games. Among other surprises was a water balloon toss that used condoms instead of balloons. I remember a three legged race."

Ray looked at me for clarification about the third leg.

"No, it was a traditional strap holding participants legs together thing, but the girl wrapping legs made sure she secured one up high and brushed every guy's third leg! They had a sack race and that race when you carry the woman on your back? Chicken fight! Anyway, Joyce and I were both athletic and won the first three events. The organizer took us aside and told us to sand bag the rest of the day. We purposely fell down near the finish line laughing. Throwing events was more fun than winning!"

"Great day to be in Alabama." Ray enjoyed the image, "Bahama Momma what? Quite a pair you must have made!

"You told me years ago that Joyce had been sexually active since she was twelve, right?"

"Good memory!" I congratulated.

Ray responded, "Hey some facts that tend to stick in the old noodle!"

"Yeah, Joyce confided in me that summer started doing the wild thing long ago, before she entered her teens. She did it with guys in their twenties more than *twice* her age. She never gave guys her own age a second thought."

"So she ignored the guys in high school?"

"Correct. She was attracted to older guys that were more experienced and had cars and money."

"Cars and money." Ray resonated.

"Cars and money."

I didn't see where Ray was taking this. He surprised me with his recollection of Joyce. Ray had a special part of his brain allocated to stories about sexuality. That part of a man's memory doesn't degrade!

Then Ray brought his lines of thought together.

"Brian," he started kindly, "you were a virgin when you and Sasha met. You came across as a nerd with no confidence."

"We were all young." I countered.

"Joyce wasn't!" Ray sprang his trap. "Joyce wasn't as naive as you, even though she was a year younger."

I stayed quiet. I was getting tired and didn't see his intent. "All right, point made."

"Life is not fair, Brian. Like I say, if you'd met Joyce or Mary first, hell, by the time you met Sasha you would have exuded all the confidence you needed, you'd have dropped your nerdy ways. The two of you could have been a great couple. But Sasha's first impression of you was as a nerd who needed to be treated with kid gloves. Hell, I suppose most guys our age were in the same boat."

He added, "Joyce was a kid but she spent a lot of after school time wrapped in the sheets with guys twice her age. While you were playing baseball and football in high school Joyce was scoring in her own game. A whole slew of guys a decade older than you were scoring and dancing in her end zone."

I didn't feel a need to defend Joyce's honor. Ray may have added some color but he was accurate.

He paused to let me reply. Neurons and synapses didn't respond. It was late. I needed to recharge.

Ray stepped hard on my silence: "She was just a kid, but Joyce was more grown up in some ways at fourteen than you were at twenty-eight when you got married!"

"That's for sure."

I sat back, "My head hurts." I ran my hand through my hair pressing thumbs hard against my temples. "My brain hurts like I've run out of some chemical needed to think."

Suddenly I sensed where Ray was about to lead. My mind groped to regain composure. Flying in low across the bow, Ray's strafing run had my Taj Mahal in sight. My precious Alexandra was about to take a hit.

I preempted the character attack, "And maybe my sweet Sasha fits in the same category as Joyce?"

Ray showed great political tact leading me to the conclusion. He shrugged saying, "You put it together. She was a bombshell; guys crawled out of the woodwork to be near her. Hell, you crawled to her twenty years later!"

He sat forward adding quietly, "Don't you think she had at least one guy rock her world? Don't you…"

Ray wove his tale wisely. But I couldn't let it go on. "Forget about suggesting Sasha was already rolling in the sheets at that age. Jesus! My mind cannot take that Ray; my *heart* can't take that." I surprised myself. "Forget about the horizontal tango part.

"I played it careful with Alexa. God! What a terrible mistake if she wanted the opposite!"

My brain felt the hollow aching feeling again. The long drive, loud music, and now the conversation about my princess drained some key brain ingredient. Synapses coughed dry and sputtered. Mind clicked and whirled with a dull throbbing ache. The Bean was out of optimism java.

"You think Sasha was way ahead of me in the relationship building skills, in sex and all?" I asked in a helpless voice.

"Umm…"

Ray rapped his fingers on a table. "I don't know, Brian. I really do not know about the sex part. But do you think a girl that beautiful wouldn't get hit on every day of her life? Don't you think one of the early suitors caught her fancy?"

"She said she had a boyfriend back home. I'm sure she had more experience around guys than I had around girls."

"Yeah, well, a male hummingbird had more experience around women than you did.

I winced. Had I struck out because of my chastity? Had I struck out because Sasha wanted someone that exuded more confidence that took rather than asked?

Part of it made sense, but part didn't. "Joyce became very friendly in the three weeks we knew each other. As an adult she obviously saw me as a man mature enough for her tastes. If I was grown up enough for Joyce, I should have been grown up enough for Alexa."

Ray shrugged.

At some level I accepted Ray's idea. Like the salmon waiting to spawn, I' remained celibate in my journey through the whitewater up to that point. I waited for my princess. Only after Sasha had rejected me did I venture sexually into other, more accessible streams.

I implored, "I just wish she had given me a chance!"

"Well buddy, I wish she had, too!"

"I was a fast learner!"

"Yeah, a fast learner who hadn't been schooled," Ray said. "Some of us come out of the gate a little behind the rest of the pack."

"I would have made the point to help someone catch up. I wouldn't have turned a cold shoulder. I would have helped."

Ray supported me, "You did! You did with Celeste! You did a great job bringing your very shy wife along. Cheers to you on that, Brian."

"And I would have called if an old friend, and old girlfriend, had asked me those questions. I would have taken the time to talk."

My mind felt dizzy like the water spinning down a bathtub's drain.

We rose, "Thanks for talking, I appreciate your insights. You may be right about all this."

"I'm right about you being a *nerd*!" The smile on his face was genuine and brought back my sense of humor.

"About *us* being nerds… back then!" We both laughed.

Sasha would have been on a mercy mission, a veritable Doctors Without Borders mission on a date with me. I laughed at the realization.

"See you around." I said heading to bed.

"Chin up!" Ray encouraged.

"Love you, brother!"

"You too, man, you are a great friend and I hope you work through this thing and come out *strong*!"

Ray ended with a worried tone, "You sleeping with Celeste still, or want me to make the couch?"

"Goodnight, Ray!"

Last Call for Unicorns!

"Talk or tunes? Tunes or Talk?"

Donnie greeted as he ducked into to backseat flinging his casual briefcase and gingerly depositing an expensive video projector. He belted into the front seat eager for an answer.

Donnie was my associate. As the only other full time employee in my little company, we did our best keeping things afloat. Actually, we devoted the lion's share of our attention to enjoying life. We worked enough to keep the company solvent but neither would die from stress.

On long drives we challenged each other's imagination and spun wild yarns that encompassed current events. We'd buy each other's lunch if the tale was grand. I ate well this day.

The tale went:

I love the way we call ships "she." We seldom gender nouns in the English language, but it works for ocean going vessels.

Ever been around a large ship as she prepares to disembark? The crew issues a series of horn blasts warning impending departure. Blasts provide a sonic countdown. They tell other ships and the shore crew of the ship's immanent departure. And when a ship leaves the dock it is a done deal. Each onboard soul departs and folks on the docks remain behind. You're either on or not. Mid-sea retrieval of latecomers is seldom an option.

You've undoubtedly heard the Sunday school version of Noah and the Ark. Ready for the rest?

The Bible tells us that Noah accepted his assignment with vigor even though he wasn't a shipbuilder. Fact was, Noah wasn't a regular "person." Some thought he was a lesser prophet, others called him a seer, but the truth about Noah was more remarkable. Noah was a unicorn.

Unicorns had the ability to transform themselves into other physical shapes. Shape shifters they were called. These enchanted beings were highly spiritual creatures. They took their natural shape when they were at peace and one with the universe. In this rarified condition unicorns looked like magical ponies with a large horn protruding from the center of their forehead, narwhales on hooves. These creatures were highly regarded in the animal kingdom for their spiritual presence and their ability to transform into other bodily configurations. While in their natural state, they took many shades and tones -- black, white, gray, even spotted like an appaloosa. Noah was the latter variety, almost pure white except for his rear quarters were deep chestnut with intermingled white blotches.

Noah's alternate shape was human, a rarity among unicorns. He was a striking unicorn, but an average-looking guy. Some may have called him a nerd.

Unicorns selected secondary shapes depending on their personalities. Hot-tempered unicorns became dragons. Sea turtles and dolphins were the choice of easy-going gregarious types. Noah chose a human form because he had an industrious nature, and the human form is ideal for getting things done. Progress is all about language and opposing thumbs.

Noah got the call from God and worked hard managing the project. Building the ship was a huge chore, but even bigger was gathering animals. Flying ones, crawling ones, slithering ones, on foot, paws, and hoof were all on his "to collect" list.

Noah fenced in hundreds of acres of corral and sent the call out for a pair of some species and seven pairs of others. But what he didn't tell volunteers-- seven pairs would get on, fewer pairs would get off. Hey, lions and tigers have to eat! Noah knew the lengthy journey would thin out the ranks and he planned accordingly. The manifest allowed at least one breeding pair of every species would disembark.

Rounding up animals was a monumental task. Noah's saving grace was that all animals instinctively followed unicorns. I bet you wondered how in the world one guy could gather so many critters. It was his unicorn side, shiningly obvious to animals. Noah got so busy building and gathering he didn't have time for the most important collection of all, his unicorn mate.

Noah didn't want a dragon unicorn as a partner. Bad idea on a wooden ship. Phoenix versions were out too. Noah hoped to find a unicorn that would join him on board and share the subsequent journey. He was mighty particular whom he would invite-- after all, this would be his mate, and the two of them would play a big part in repopulating the species after the waters subsided.

Noah would only bring one unicorn to join him, foregoing the standard booking of seven pairs of herbivores. He would make sure his unicorn wouldn't become a carnivore's entree. One special female would do.

In a rare idle moment, Noah spied a prize. She was the perfect height, pure white coat; only her hoofs bore a trace of gray. Her eyes were the most serene place to wander he'd ever discovered. And they hit it off. Best of all, she wasn't a dragon. In fact, she hadn't chosen what secondary shape to take. She'd remained a unicorn up until now. Once a unicorn chooses a secondary shape that's it, they cannot pick another. But until they do, they're free to choose. Noah hoped this unicorn would join him and become human.

Days, weeks, months, and even a year passed. The ark was built, the stable filled, and then the rains came - slow at first, but steady.

Floods start so commonly-- just another rainy day. Precipitation dappled the ground. Just your average rainy afternoon. Then another day and another just the same.

The first sign of worry arose from the ground. On the third day of intermittent drizzle and downpours the soil became saturated. Puddles formed and wouldn't go away smirking of deeper waters to come. Drops of rain set off tiny circular waves dappling the muddy pools. Droplets rebounded skyward and collapsed back into bog. Kids, being kids, played in the rain despite parents' objections. There were puddles to jump in, and the youngest children joined puppies exuberantly splashing and dancing.

Giraffes and rhinos grew restless inside corrals. They paced and tested fences wanting an escape the deepening morass. Heavy animals became agitated staggering in unstable mire. Fear and great uncertainty traced many a furry face.

Noah issued the order to begin loading the animals and the first blast of horns was issued. It took backbreaking days to organize and board all. The ship's horn sounded regularly as beasts queued and moved in prearranged order. The sixth day ended very late at night for Noah and the crew. All animals were loaded and the crew was exhausted. Most of the crew staggered down the ramp to nearby dwellings for one last night on terra firma while a few remained aboard to take care of restless animals. Crew and animal passengers were anxious but exhaustion brought sleep.

By the seventh day, the town folk living near Noah had come to regard him in a different light. The neighborhood had gotten ever so quiet. The steady rain kept most residents inside and muffled noises, but those that ventured out discovered the animals had disappeared. No more baying, no more lion humping his mate forty times a day like there was no tomorrow, no more monkeys' slapstick routine. Some folks came up and peered one last time at the massive ship from the bottom of the loading ramps leading up above the ground fog out of sight. Still, no one demanded passage on the ark. Noah's neighbors just stood and contemplated the massive vessel and then sloshed back home.

The final boarding call bellowed. Noah's small shore party emerged from their homes as fierce gales descended. Rain swept hard as wind blew sideways. Large drops pelted with an uncommon sting knocking down crew as they struggled to the ship.

Noah's team finally was aboard and as he glanced down the list of passengers. Tired but ecstatic upon accomplished the mission without loss, they settled ready for Noah's order to cast off.

Then Noah stopped shocked by the realization he'd forgotten one ever so important member. He had not collected his unicorn soul mate! Instead of congratulating his team on a job well done Noah was on the brink of becoming unglued. He berated, "Unbelievable! I've been so busy that I forgot a critical addition!"

His first mate didn't appreciate the depth of Noah's dismay until he saw how brokenhearted he was. He took stock and told Noah, "Go! Go find the unicorn! We'll be right here waiting for you."

Noah ran to the side of the deck and scanned the distance to get his bearings. He searched the horizon for any sign of her but she was not to be seen through the dark morning sky that gave little light and less solace to his troubled eyes. He had braved the ordeal to build and the quest to gather without question. Now he was frightened for the first time. He shuddered at the harrowing task that faced him.

From the railing at the edge of the massive deck he looked down and saw only water. Virtually all the ground surrounding the ship had disappeared. A few higher grassy knolls defiantly resisted the rising tide. The base of the boarding ramp had vanished. Noah strode onto the ramp leading down. Suddenly a squall rolled down the starboard side and nearly blew him off the teetering incline. He braced himself and felt his center of gravity rock precariously. He threw out his arms and shifted his hips regaining balance.

The ship moaned with a creak that ran from stem to stern and then another emanated from the keel as the wood swelled. The wooden ship awoke ready to take on a life of her own, alive in the wind and rain. The ramp Noah stood on heaved and bucked, not at all like the sturdy structure that had supported elephants two by two. With keel covered by 18 cubits, the wooden ark groaned as she flirted with buoyancy. She was an ungainly sight in fine weather but now she faced the elements she was made for and was eager to rise with grace and certainty. Noah could feel the ship move up and sideways while he balanced his precarious perch and realized she would soon be free of her moorings.

He tottered a few steps down the ramp until he was out of his crews' sight then changed forms. In unicorn condition, he was sure of hoof and, more importantly, at one with the universe. He could feel the wind before it blew, see the squalls as they gathered and could even feel where the mate of his choosing was. Noah immediately gleaned that she was miles and miles away. He sensed her presence over mountains, over valleys, over rivers and far away over washed out roads without bridges. She wouldn't have heard the last call for boarding. Noah used his unicorn telepathy to call to her, but it seemed useless. He called and called but heard no reply.

He set his heart with determination. "Ain't no mountain high enough; ain't no valley long enough; ain't no river wide enough to keep me away from you." he brayed. He lowered his nose and leaped forward, down the ramp and into the flood-- away from the safety of his ark but toward his heart's desire.

He ran like the wind, only faster. He pelted the rain with his withers, not the opposite. He galloped through fields turned into quagmires. Past villages plagued with sorrow. People wailed at their doom, chickens took roost on tops of structures only to find themselves afloat with a gust, flapping wildly against their fate. Children cried and mothers died; yet Noah ran on. He tarried not at the trouble around him. There were but two to save and that would require a return trip through this turmoil.

The ground was invisible beneath his pounding hooves. He plowed through standing water slipped over rocks, caught a bush here, and smashed a submerged farm implement there. His forelocks bloodied as he ran a degree above blind.

There was no time to chart out the best path. There was no best path. Water rose in flood proportions, everywhere a moving sheet glistening. Yesterday's creeks were raging rivers; yesterday's rivers moving lakes. Yet Noah galloped, changing direction only to reach higher ground and stay on course to retrieve his love.

The mountains were no haven. Their height kept them from being flooded, but raging water ran between each peak.

The river he had to cross was frothing whitecaps. The current sent him nine measures downstream for every one he swam across. But on he went.

At last, his heart told him he was close. He surmounted the last impediment and saw her. She stood on a high plateau. Through pouring rain, no gloom masked her glory. Through a thousand gales, she remained unfazed. As Noah closed the distance he again called in the silent language only known to unicorns. She turned and saw him, but she did not call back. As she turned Noah saw another animal appear and take a post beside her-- a large, chalk-white stallion mottled and splattered with mud.

Noah drew close enough to hear the stallion whinny, agitated by the rising waters and Noah's approach.

Noah took in her eyes and he telepathically spoke again, inviting her to come now. He didn't have time to say how terrible the return journey would be. Nor did he have time to point out the certain peril facing her if she didn't join him on the ark. As he looked into her eyes his mind observed what his heart had missed. He gazed upon her forehead. Seeing his eyes fix on her flat brow she confirmed, "Hello, Noah. Yes, I've chosen."

To his amazement there was no horn gracing her forehead. What could this mean?

Befuddled, "You've chosen?" Chosen what? To die? To drown? To become a horse?

"My God, you've chosen one other than me!" He told her telepathically, "But I've already got seven pairs of horses!" I can't take any more horses. I *need* you as *you*!

The stallion reared up powerfully as if to make the rising waters go away or threaten Noah.

Noah was wide-eyed and totally at a loss. He stepped back and shook his head to clear his mind. Must be just an illusion from running, he thought. She read his thoughts and tilted her head with ears forward, as if to say: "Hello, aren't you following any of this?"

She turned her head slightly away from Noah toward her colossal stallion letting her body language speak. Noah shook his head again and grimaced. Involuntarily, he drifted out of his spiritual calm and reverted to human form. Just a man now, an average guy lost in a storm of epic proportions. He felt helpless standing there on the mesa with water threatening all around. He lifted his hands with his palms facing up and wailed, "But *we* were supposed to be a couple!"

She understood human words as all unicorns did and gazed back confident, beautiful as ever. But she did not speak. Her eyes were as warm and inviting as the first time they'd met and Noah locked on them for a sign. Rain danced down her neck and shoulders like a myriad of pearls. A calm smile was upon her face. Though the eyes invited, he could not read her mind. He turned his head puzzled at the awful twist of luck. Lightning split the sky releasing a terrible deluge.

Noah glanced at the two horses, felt his loss, and cried. His human tears flowed quickly, and as the first fell from his cheek, the water level rose immediately. Noah's tears were tied to the floodwaters, as was God's displeasure with man. With every teardrop, the sea around them grew. The stallion rose again, this time for no purpose except that is was all he could do against the rising doom. Noah's aspiration stepped sideways giving her stallion room to land.

The lonely heartbroken man turned slowly in a circle. Prayer and desperation mingled. His eyes locked between the heaven and horizon as he rotated around taking in the abyss.

When he stopped turning he faced his beloved and felt the effect of her choice. He was tired. Tired to the bone. His shoulders drooped and legs became unsteady. All the miles of running and swimming, the bruising caught up. Drained and wasted, the long journey back to the ark seemed-- impossible. It *was* possible only if your heart was in it. Now it didn't matter. It just didn't matter.

Another bolt of lightning spooked the stallion, which bucked and began running nowhere in a big hurry. Noah lowered his gaze and saw his love hesitate. Would she follow the horse or come to her senses?

Noah closed his eyes without thinking and said; "God help us. God help me! May the Glory of God help us all!"

His prayer resettled his condition and he resumed the shape of a unicorn. Slowly his eyes opened. He didn't see the stallion or his love. He held his heart at bay preventing him from sensing where she was.

She had made her choice. And he would make his.

A deep rumble broke overhead.

He turned, forced a gut check and felt rejuvenated enough to try. "They need me on the Ark!" He cantered back... back... back.

The river was unreal; trees with outstretched roots and limbs littered the surface menacingly. The upturned roots conspired to entrap. Stiff dead animals bumped quietly against his tired body, their cold hard bodies asking morosely when he'd join them. He avoided their lifeless stares to maintain hope.

He crossed the valley with great difficulty. The mid-afternoon sky looked like midnight triggering more fatigue.

Noah struggled up the mountain, the last major obstacle between him and the ark. Beleaguered and wasted, willpower alone propelled him. Consciousness left as he staggered for the only shelter he knew, the Ark. He faded in and out-- at times human, at times unicorn, always stumbling forward.

He was battered mercilessly, pounded against rocks, smashed against the occasional tree that remained rooted; all for the want of his love. Darkness shrouding the world.

He lost his balance and tumbled colliding to a painful stop. Without mental activity, his body's cells were the only source of self-preservation. His arm hung something permanent. His hand trembled uncontrollably but his bicep and forearm insisted this was the place to hang on, to make a stand. No central thought instructed his body, but the iron and carbon that comprised his temporal existence sensed what he clung to was alive, had form, and offered hope. His legs raised himself up one last time and, as he made vertical, his thigh touched a rigid tree trunk and hoisted his weary body to the lowest limbs and passed out.

Daybreak brought meager light, but the rain continued. He stirred realizing he was in a squat but hearty olive tree. Light gray clouds danced in a fog bank. He couldn't see beyond the limbs of his refuge. The lack of discernable form made him dizzy. Vague shifting clouds confused. It was impossible to tell if the gray veil was near or far. He batted his hand at patches enveloping his lonesome stand only to find them far from his reach. Tired and disoriented he stayed put. Day slid into night with only a little loss in visibility.

The next day the weather cleared a little. He felt the early morning sun, but could not rise. His limbs and torso had locked around the tree and his muscles would not release their grip. His flesh had groped tightly the deep recesses of bark as if he'd become an appendage to the tree. He focused all his effort but could barely move a finger.

As the day warmed, so did his body and he extricated himself. Cranking his stiff body one joint at a time loose, one bruised muscle untwisted every few minutes and he looked down the mountain. Floodwaters covered the valley and all foothills-- turbid water everywhere. He wasn't going forward. He turned and realized he was perched about 70 cubits below the summit. He climbed back to the top confirming a similar situation on the reverse slope. He wasn't going back.

Noah left the summit and returned to the edge of the water. Wondering what had happened to the Ark he changed into unicorn and felt the ship and its occupants safe.

His raspy unused voice squeaked, "Good."

He looked about and found spots of grass, wild flowers, moss, and lichens no worse for the storm. He hadn't eaten in days and grazed. Food in his belly gave hope and occupied his mind for a couple of hours, yet the steadily rising water forced him up the slope. He saw a lonely board float his way, changed into human form, and retrieved it. Board in hand he headed back to the tree.

Noah reflected on his one possession and laughed at how materially poor he was. "No making an ark out of this! Better sleep on it." He wedged the plank into the thick limbs and made a crude bed. He crawled up and lay curled fetal on his sole creature comfort.

He thought of his love and the foolish choice she made. His mind flashed to his love and her stallion and he rose to his knees and pounded the air with his fist and shouted, "Screw 'em!"

He repeated his outburst at the top of his lungs, as he'd never shouted before "Screw You!" His anguish didn't echo in the lonely soaked countryside. Waterlogged surroundings and heaven, a heaven as heavy as his heart, dampened the repeat. The sound of his voice was lost in the surreal landscape. The world had no room for the voice of man, like man had never been created, like man would never speak again. Lost forever.

A lonely shudder convulsed his body.

He collected himself and collapsed on his plank into a broken sitting position squarely facing his lot. No part of the determined optimism that had marked every waking moment remained. He offered a humbling realization: "Screw me!"

He smiled at the trace of humor and the voice of man in the air.

There in the air—voice… words. It broke his mood and mulled to what was left of creation, "What a desolate place to be heartbroken." Then he shouted, "You can be too much of an optimist in this world!" The congregation of barren twigs made no reply.

Forlorn, the rains came and stayed through the remainder of the day and into the night. He crossed his legs and remained still as conscious migrated deeper. Wet and cold, feelings faded away. His body absorbed all his thoughts and passed them through the board, through the tree and into the mountain. He became perfectly still. He saw nothing, felt nothing. He simply was. Quiet, still-- then asleep.

He awoke, stirred by the cool feeling on the tips of his fingers. His arm drooped over the edge of his board conveyed the presence of water lapping within inches of his resting spot. His face sorely deformed by the rugged board. The tree held firm, but now the trunk was submerged. Noah admired and appreciated the tenacious roots that had carved an existence in the rock and remained adhered to the mountain despite the flood. A sprig of his unquenchable optimism reappeared and he saw beauty and gave thanks. The roots that had defied the lack of soil and had coaxed minerals directly out of the rocks had given the tree a chance.

He stood giving thanks to his perch and slid off his board launching himself toward the peak behind him. After a few strokes he lowered his legs and found fractured surface and made his way to the summit. Now he would wait for daybreak or rising water, whichever came first.

Day arrived. Ominous clouds rolled by, enveloping him, and he could see rain in the distance, but his position remained dry. Water consumed the entire mountain except the reach of a man's arm around Noah.

"Looks grim!" he laughed calmly. A flock of geese squawked in flight overhead. They headed one way, and then reversed, only to reverse again. He laughed out loud, "I'm not the only one who doesn't know where to turn!" He watched their bewildered but rapid progress.

All around him leagues of water covered all but the highest peaks. He glanced to his left and right and saw in the distance higher peaks, none within swimming distance. Besides, he'd chosen this one… or maybe God had.

Noah spent his energy meditating and drawing deep calming breaths. As he sat on his disappearing rock, high in the bland sky the confused geese banked hard left a few miles from his position. He thought their destination aligned pretty much with the direction he would have traveled to find the Ark. The geese descended rapidly.

He muttered in wonderment at the only sign of life bolting away, "Strange for geese to drop like that… They'd do that only to take refuge… to land.

"To land!" he shouted.

He changed into unicorn and felt the Ark was indeed near. If it drifted nearby soon…

Hope rose and he scanned the horizon and shockingly spotted a small raft approaching his position. As it became more than a spec on the horizon he saw figures atop the raft made of a large gate and other sundry floating items. Noah changed into a person and hailed the small band of people aboard.

"AHOY!" He shouted. "AHOY!" rang full again.

He laughed surprised at the choice of words. "'I've never said 'ahoy!' but it is appropriate now!"

He lost his step and found himself waist deep in water. A few inches of rock remained of this once towering mountain. Noah strode back to the last dry perch, waved his arms broadly, and shouted for all he was worth, "AHOY!"

Four shapes on the raft rose gingerly looking with eagerness. He could see their elation at hearing a voice. They were close enough so Noah could also see their dismay when they saw he wasn't in a position to help. They exchanged the bleak smiles of the doomed. But they couldn't help but warm to Noah's excitement and each in turn waved back.

There were two men and two women haggard to wits end, quite tired of their adventure.

The raft headed nearly straight toward Noah and seemed as if it might actually come to rest on the small outcrop of rocks beneath his feet.

"Come aboard!" one man called.

"We don't know if the raft will hold," said the other guy, but then he added, "But come aboard anyway. Only one way to find out!"

"Looks like you guys are up a creek or something!" Noah said jokingly.

"Yeah, up a creek without a paddle!" said the first to greet Noah.

Noah laughed and said, "Well, maybe I can save you from that fate!" He immediately took two strides toward the oncoming raft entering the water with a shallow dive and disappeared.

The four on board waited a few moments and were perplexed when Noah didn't pop up beside their raft. They scanned the water, first on the side of the raft Noah had been closest to, then on the far side.

One man crossed his arms and said, "What the hell! Think the guy went crazy and committed suicide right here?"

One woman kneeling inquired at her broken reflection on the water's surface, "Can you do that? I mean, can you jump in the water and hold your breath and die?"

The other women spoke flatly gazing toward the horizon, "Let's not find out."

Ten seconds, then twenty, then thirty passed and the little band of agitated travelers peered intently around the edges of their raft. Startled noises about twenty feet behind them made them turn and see bubbles break the surface and Noah's head poke through.

The first girl gave out a loud sigh.

Noah laughed and began paddling toward them. He laughed again and the newcomers quietly exchanged questioning glances. As he approached the raft he slid his perch board onto the raft, saying triumphantly: "Well, you have been up a creek, but now at least *we've* got a paddle!"

The group bonded immediately and hauled Noah aboard. Moments later, the last of the mountain succumbed.

The raft drifted slowly, aimlessly with its five occupants. The mood slowly returned to a somber hue. There was nowhere in particular to row below the pewter sky that encased. The distant peaks of mountains would soon be covered and remove any reason to propel the raft apart from the tide's intent.

Within an hour, the bland sky turned dark and the rare patch of light was immediately snatched away. The quickness surprised all but Noah. The four original raft members were stunned how instantly the sun had dropped away. One woman said sarcastically, "God! Now what?"

Noah let out a loud "Ohmmm" shaking the raft with its unifying depth. The skin of his raft mates' crawled.

They were ghostly spooked when they heard the strangest bray reply.

"That… that sounded like an elephant!" one exclaimed.

As the castaways looked around they realized one side of the horizon was completely black, yet the other side reflected the sky's dreary light. Then they distinctly felt the raft pushed aside as if the water was making way for a large object. The call of wild animals filled the air as maniacal monkey screams and cheers of all sorts of birds and critters rained down.

Noah took the paddle and waved it above his head, pushed the blackness away from the side of the raft and called to the crew on the ark.

One traveler said disbelievingly, "Voices! Did you hear that! Voices somewhere up there!

"Angels!" said another.

In the darkness a voice was heard, but all they heard was "… bitter end."

One of the men shivered and cried despondently repeating the pronouncement. Loud splashes fore and aft unnerved the beleaguered foursome. Noah said, "Not that kind of bitter end! Quick-- find the end of the line! The lines… ropes man! Grab the ROPE!"

One of the women called deliriously: "Oh my God! There is a rope! My God, there is a rope hanging down from heaven!" She broke down in tears, stumbled overwhelmed, as did the others.

Noah laughed boldly with the joy that characterized his life, "Remember that thought after you get on board and muck stalls, my friends, remember that thought!"

Noah successively fashioned harnesses out of the lines and secured each traveler with a skillful double bowline knot. One by one they were hoisted up the Ark's formidable hull and each reflected upon the massive dark wall that separated them from certain demise.

Aboard, adventurous stories were shared. Noah's crew told how they had anxiously watched desperately for his return. When the Ark began to float, they harbored less and less hope of ever seeing him again.

His first mate took him aside and asked about the recovery of the unicorn. Noah shook his head, lowering it for a pause.

"Nope," he replied, finally looking up with red eyes. "Unicorn didn't… make it." He snorted a moment, clearing his watering eyes and sinuses in favor of a more cheerful demeanor. He smoothed the back of his head and rubbed his forehead unconsciously with his other hand, then shook his head one more time and exhaled slowly, "She didn't, uh… join me on the Ark."

Observing his sadness, his first mate cheered, "But look, you found others! How wonderful!"

"Yes, indeed, truly wonderful!" Noah perked.

As days turned into weeks, Noah grew especially close to one of the castaways. They worked well together and spent hours delicately holding hands on the boisterous main deck and below. Noah was thankful for what God had wrought.

The waters subsided and the Ark came to rest. Noah wound up marrying that raft mate and they had three kids, three regular kids. Noah's wife was not a unicorn so their kids knew not the separate reality of unicorns. Their children were people, just like all the other people around them.

Noah found delight and purpose ensuring they grew into fine young men.

He took the form of a unicorn inconspicuously a few times after they settled. He called out to other unicorns, but never heard a reply. All the unicorns that chose to be dragons would have drowned. Wasn't likely eagle unicorns would have found dry perch. There was never a unicorn or stubborn horse born that could swim forty days and forty nights. No way. He shook his head at the loss. But he was dumbfounded that dolphin and sea turtle unicorns didn't call back. They could survive the rising water, but for reason Noah never learned, they did not.

Noah accepted his fate as the last unicorn with grace. He honored daybreak and each sunset as the end of his enchanted line thankful for the gift of life and the chance to contribute to the wonderful spinning world called Earth. And he was thankful for the woman who joined him on the Ark, who trusted him to reach for a rope when all reason and logic told her not to trust. He thanked God many times for her as the years went by, many more times than he thought of Sasha.

Otter Lake

October-19

The guest room closet held an invigorating surprise. Pleasant aroma from leather and canvas jackets greeted. Jackets and woolen sweaters in various fashions seemed eager to see the light of day for the first time in six months. Shifting hangers conveyed a sense of adventure. A short hike around Otter Lake, tucked amid the Blue Ridge would be a day retreat.

With a gleam in his eye that sparkled as crisp as the autumn air, Ray said he had "business" in town, but managed to free his Sunday for our hike.

"Man! This mountain air!" Ray exclaimed. "Makes me tingle all over every on end!"

The morning warmed and sweatshirts yanked as our trek followed a trail speckled golden with leaves. My two older boys gallivanted leading the way while the youngest rode my shoulders. I patted his leg, "Won't be long before he refuses this perch and chooses to careen through the woods with his brothers."

The older two eagerly plunged into the creek that fed the lake. They frolicked wet up to their thighs, warmed by enthusiasm for life. A boy, a stick, and imagination equal entertainment at its finest.

Even the sky was carefree, free from gray clouds that might threaten our activities. I relaxed and enjoyed the possibility of learning to be carefree again, just like my boys.

By the end of our stroll, all three kids were wet, cold, and hungry. We'd planned ahead for this moment. Dry cloths and lunch awaited us in the parked Ford Explorer.

My two-year old thought nothing of undressing in the parking lot as he was quite used to people snatching his trousers to change diapers. My oldest thought it was a lark to strip down beside my Explorer, protected only by flanking open doors, as he donned dry threads. But my middle boy was in a shy stage and refused to change until he protected himself from view by climbing in the back seat. Now, each relaxed comforted by cozy dry cotton. Warm dry cotton; cotton is to the skin what love is to the heart. This planet just wouldn't be the same without it!

We stopped briefly, ate our packed lunches, and headed home. Ray and I hadn't talked about my stumble from grace all day and he remained quiet, even secretive, about his "business" that had brought him to Lynchburg. We held our tongues on the drive home.

As we pulled in the driveway to drop the kids off, it started to drizzle. Celeste said, "Good timing." The weather changed rapidly and Celeste would have the boys inside for the rest of the day.

Ray and I left and headed up the driveway. Ray had ridden the train down freeing up his return. Our plan was a long return drive to his place.

"So what was this business you had in town?"

He answered with a sideways smirk. His eyes scanned outside the car absorbed by his old stomping grounds. With nostalgic interest, Ray asked, "Drive through the neighborhood slowly." He nodded quietly at the familiar and eyes widened at change.

"Why did you jeopardize your marriage the way you did? The neighborhood, pleasant house, you fucked all this up. Your boys? Wife? Celeste still loves you?"

"I guess so." I responded starting with his final question. "But for years… you know I wasn't sure. It was like her love didn't reach me. I didn't feel it. Maybe my love for her was the same and it never got received."

There was silence as we navigated through the first stop sign and took a left out of the neighborhood.

"But why?" Ray continued.

We made our way through the next stop sign and turned left.

"This was for me. For me," I repeated. "This was for me when I was a young man, way back when."

I took a breath and continued, "And this was for each heart that ever squirmed in unrequited love." I added convincingly. "This whole thing was because it *matters*."

We found ourselves at another stop sign, and surveyed the traffic. I picked my space and turned right.

Ray led, "It matters…"

"Right, it matters." I continued as we accelerated. "My *heart* matters. Your heart matters. Each and every person who had their feelings spurned by another, each person that has had their feelings crushed, each person that was found too ugly, or too poor, or too nerdy. We matter!"

I continued with conviction, "By God, each heart matters!

"I couldn't just walk away from my feelings! Once I saw her again, I had to let her know how I felt. I couldn't internalize my love and let it pass quietly back into the misty void of memory.

"Well it does matter. I *matter*!" I said fervently with intensity that nearly brought tears in my eyes. I drove on autopilot paying enough attention to the road but not really seeing it.

Ray agreed, "Yeah, you matter."

My agitated state abated and I directed more attention to road and traffic. Ray relaxed as I devoted more awareness to driving and less to sermonizing.

"And you matter," I shot back, including him in my saga. "Everyone matters. If someone pours his or her bloody heart out, that *is* a big deal! That matters. You can't just say, don't encourage him… he doesn't matter." The windows rattled with my oversized voice.

"I mean what is the point of creation if we don't act our deepest, most sincere feelings…our feelings, for God's sake!"

"Only two things made me feel like a failure in this big world. The first time I couldn't nurture Alexa into opening her heart was the first failure.

"The second failure was to live through it again.

We were north of town. We'd driven through lights and heavy traffic I couldn't remember a thing about the last few miles except conversation.

We were going to Ray's place in Alexandria, Virginia. I was angling for a small overseas USAID project. Granted, the contract destinations were not honeymoon spots-- many had US State Department travel advisories in place. If the meeting went well, my little company would have a marble in a big game and I'd land a walk on part in a war-ravaged country.

Ray changed the subject, "You didn't bring much clothing."

The plan, following a successful meeting, might include a flight out of DC to do a quick assessment. The likely scenario included lots of red tape. But I wanted to be ready just in case. "If there's a fast track and I get on it, you'll be my ride to the airport, and my company for my last nights in the US."

As we drove through the rolling countryside, the gentle hills turned into mountains and I thought of Celeste. Ray seemed to read my mind, "We could turn around, drive home to Celeste and the boys and you could try again. Call USAID and renege. Have them find someone else to step into the void.

"I lost two dreams over the years. One was my Taj Mahal princess whom I lost twice. My other dream was to help people in great need. Without the first, I'm compelled to cling to the second."

"Well then, this could be our last night together." He caught himself. "For awhile… last night I mean… what do you want to do?"

"I haven't thought past a meal."

"There are other options, of course. Two guys alone in a city, one shipping out for overseas. Man too bad you're not dressed like a sailor. That always garners warm compassion from single ladies!" He broached the subject, "We could go to a stripper bar, if you want to. I *might* be able to find one."

I smiled and laughed, "You probably programmed the location of every nude bar your car's navigation system!"

Ray and I remained silent for a few minutes. He asked again, "So is that a yes or a no on the dens of iniquity?"

"I'll take a rain check."

"When you get back then," he comforted as if we'd have something to look forward to.

Ray's Place

October-19

Ray vaulted into his almost comically compulsively clean home-owner mode. Shoes slipped off at the door, he scurried off to attend a task out of sight. Left at the door I admired his spic and span dwelling. My bags looked foreign and out of place. His place took to my scant mismatched belonging like a healthy organism accepts a virus.

I tip toed to the guest room.

He boomed from his room, "Put them down anywhere." He said from the hall. I caught his involuntarily cringing as the first bag gave a dull thump ruffling the bedspread. Ray sauntered in, "What about supper?"

"Great idea, pick."

Ray focused on my smallest bag, a dense package of green canvas. A puzzled scowl transformed his face.

"It's a reserve parachute bag." Hoisting the larger than fanny pack size bag in the air, I twirled it rotating around its long axis and caught the bag before it fell. "It contains essentials for emergency purposes. Emergency exit bag, it stays packed and ready, just in case. If my situation goes bad I grab this bag and bug out without a second thought."

"Oh yeah—a bug out bag. Right. What's in it?"

I removed the D-ring retaining bolt and spread the top layer of contents neatly on the bed.

Ray picked up the heavy retaining bolt, "I've never seen a bag secured with something like this."

"Got the bag from a military pawnshop. It's an old reserve bag." I showed him how the bag worked. "That is the ring you'd pull to release your reserve."

"Cool!" He turned the sturdy metal fixture and settled it in his palm feeling the coolness and weight. He set the bolt down and inspected my stuff.

As he rummaged I said, "Bare essentials."

Ray handled the stuff eyeing each piece. Included were: a crushed wide-brimmed floppy hat, socks, a pint of water, a thin steel wire coiled, tiny bar of soap, equally diminutive compass, and a miniature folding Leatherman utility knife and a few other items.

The knife caught Ray's attention and he looked up, "Not much water in there. Planning on walking out of Iraq or Liberia with a couple of pints of water and no food?"

"No. I'm planning on flying in and flying out."

"This your defensive stuff?" Ray lifted the small utility knife and the tight coil of steel wire. "Is the wire for garroting someone? What, no handgun? And this little knife-- you better know the person pretty well before you try and stab them with that!"

I didn't answer. Ray ignored a few other items and his attention locked onto the most interesting content. He picked up a package in a clear zippered plastic bag. "Open it?"

"Sure."

"This your private stash of weed, or hashish in case it gets *really* bad?" He gently unzipped the bag. "Any special cyanide pill?"

A photocopy of my Virginia driver's license, blood donor card, a copy of my passport photo page popped into view along with a diminutive photocopy of dental x-rays. Cash caught his attention.

"Damn!"

"Greenbacks." I confirmed.

"How much you got here?"

"Enough to buy some hashish in case it *really* gets bad!"

We laughed. It felt great to laugh with my old friend. Glad he hadn't asked about the x-rays.

"There's $2,500. Some small bills, some larger."

Ray thumbed through the bills so neatly they remained a tight stack.

"The thing is I might need some money so anyone robbing or extorting me would expect American cash. Having no stash would be suspicious.

"There's another $5,500 sewn into the lining."

Flipping the empty bag over, I displayed a section that had a second lining. "The seamstress did a great job don't you think?"

Examining the bag closely he asked, "Here?" He stroked the smooth nylon panel. No visual sign gave it away, but he found it by diligently rubbing the lining and feeling for the bills' subtle outline.

"Yep, that's it!"

Ray traced the edge of the cash hidden in the false lining and smiled.

"Did you see her put it in there? Were you there when she finished sewing? Hate to think you might need it, cut it open with your little knife and find Monopoly money!"

I chuckled, "Me, too!"

He lowered the bag and let out a deep sigh. "Well, I guess you know what you're doing."

The uncertainty of my assignment was just that-- uncertain. Risk is a part of life. I assured, "The world is safer than the nightly news leads you to believe."

I repacked the bag quietly realizing the contents might never see the light of day until I was back in the States.

"I'm hungry, let's eat." I said.

"Wait, you're missing something!"

He trotted to his room. I finished backing my cramped reserve chute and waited. The soft sound of wood rubbing signaled one drawer opening, then another. Fingernails scraped the bottom of a drawer and a crinkle signaled he'd snatched something.

I shook my head, "There isn't room in the bag." I acknowledged with a whisper. But friends sometimes know exactly what you need. Ray might just have something that would save my ass, a sacred relic, a talisman that only a friend would think of.

Ray reappeared. "Here, you might need these."

He proffered his left hand, and a new deck of Bicycle playing cards sat in his palm. I took the deck. The seal was unbroken, brand new. The cardboard box portrayed the familiar blue image gracing the back of the playing cards.

"Great," I said, taking the package from his hand. I squeezed the box and felt its firmness.

"Thanks."

He offered his right hand. Clutched between his thumb and fingers were three condoms. Gripping the top, he let the strand drop and unfold.

"These, too!" he said, waving the intimate protection. "These might be better than a Kevlar vest!"

"I can't say I'll use them from what I've seen of Libyan and Iraqi women!" I joked as I took the condoms.

"You never know, you might get assigned somewhere the women don't look like camels!"

"Yeah, then I can break out the cards and play…"

Ray answered for me, "Strip poker!" We both laughed. We sat on the bed as we laughed. I tucked the final items into the bag.

We were grateful about the tender moment we were sharing. We both nodded and soaked it in. I'd taken big chunks of my life for granted. Not anymore.

"Got matches, a lighter?"

"Yeah, I got matches, I'm set. They're in there. These last two items completed my needs. My little ark is ready for sailing," I closed the bag and secured the holding bolt.

"Let's eat!" Ray said.

The Last Supper

October-19

"You may ask yourself… this is not my beautiful life, this is
not my beautiful wife." Talking Heads

Rain passed scrubbing the air clean for a city. A sharp quarter moon embarrassed city lights. Even stars dared appear as Ray and I hoofed it to the restaurant section of Old Town Alexandria.

As we navigated the streets on foot, I realized, dodging parked cars and throngs of people, I could enjoy city life again. Tight spacing between houses, the rare parking spot, people from all over the world shared sidewalks, some walked with purpose, others milled. The effect was a spectacle that vibrated with energy. I relished the change. Confidence set in. I could make it in the big town again.

"Might be our last night together… for a while." Ray said as we took our seats.

The host offered, "Care for a drink?" We both ordered water and I cherished each sip of the fine, trustworthy, American water. I worked the glass in my hand like a precious gift slowly rotating it, wiping condensation beads.

Ray got our earlier conversation back on track. "You know, you should write a pop-up book."

"A pop-up book?"

He became vibrant with the thought, "First page, you meet Sasha. You and your little blue Chevette. Pop! Out comes the car."

Ray raced, "The next page, she spies a knight on a white horse. No, better yet, a guy in a white Ferrari. Isn't Ferrari's trade mark a white stallion? Perfect. No, make it a *yellow* Ferrari. The princess's deep passionate cadmium yellow, interlaced with strands of deep red undertone."

I signed but couldn't slow him.

"Boing! She jumps in that car with glee!"

The image of the door opening and the little Alexandra figure angling for the plush Ferrari interior stuck me in neutral, but Ray hit the gas.

"Then you get a hard on and she cuts it off with a pair of shears!"

"Ouch!" I said, involuntarily repositioning myself in my seat and crossing my legs. I squirmed, still smarting from his storyboard.

We both laughed hard. I put my head against the wall behind me.

"So much for the kids' book," I said.

"Besides Ray, my woody wouldn't fit into the book. Not unless we make it one of those really *big* books."

"Yeah, like the kind at the library Reserve Desk!" Ray laughingly supported the manly notion.

We quieted down a notch lest we interrupt folks seated nearby.

I composed myself rubbing my head with my right hand, "Let's go with a protruding heart instead of a hard on. Let's have her cut my heart."

"Nicks your heart," Ray added.

I followed, "She doesn't cut me… "

Ray put his creativity in high gear. "No, she doesn't cut you, she slams her car door and it *catches* your heart."

I said, "Hence the scar tissue, the emotional scar tissue! Beautiful." I could see a cartoon figure with his heart protruding out of the Bean's chest being crushed in a paper foldout door. Alexa closes another guy's car door and pins my heart.

"Slam, open, slam, open. Kids will love opening and closing the door! Can you imagine slam, open, slam! Poor old dad reading the story might have a problem with it," Ray clowned."

We regained our senses and acted more like two adults sitting in a restaurant.

Ray chimed, "OK, we go with the heart, slammed in the door…"

We became quiet. We both knew why.

"What then?"

I answered rhetorically, "What then? What now?"

I hesitated, "Ray, how about I leave you all the creative power and authority and you write the ending."

I could say that about a pop-up book.

I was about to leave my wife for a week or two. The separation would have little chance to heal, given the distances involved. Or maybe a little distance would help our hearts grow fonder. I didn't know.

My leg jerked involuntarily triggered by the image of the paper door slamming my heart. I stuck my foot out to catch the door.

I excused myself and headed to the bathroom. I splashed water on my face and looked at myself in the mirror. Was this the same little boy that jumped out of helicopters as a kid? Was this the same little boy that "grew up" and had three boys of his own?

I applied a vigorous dose of water and rubbed hard. I turned, dried myself, and quietly intoned, "Hoka hey," as I reached for the door. The phrase cheered Native American braves in challenging times. Let's see how it worked for me. "Hoka hey," I repeated as I opened the door and rejoined Ray for dinner.

Salads arrived in my absence. Ray's fork waited.

He asked seriously, "Tell me Brian, if Alexandra called you today, called right now, would you go to her? Would you go to her or would you go overseas?"

I finished my bite of food. The cell phone tucked in my left front pants pocket came to mind. I listened for a moment and searched my thigh for the tremor of vibration mode, "Overseas. No question," I added without further hesitation.

"No question?"

"No question."

Ray continued probing, "If Celeste called…"

I took his question before he completed it, "If Celeste called, if my loving wife of fourteen years called, I'd still go.

"Ray, I feel I can make a difference. Somebody has to. That's where all progress comes from-- individuals rising to the occasion to care enough to give their very best. Face a little risk and do what's right. If Celeste called, I'd still go."

"So you wouldn't stay for either of the two women you loved the most? OK."

Ray relaxed. He settled back in his chair. Dinner arrived shortly and we started in.

"I'm refreshed by the return of your decisiveness."

"How's that?"

"Ever since I've known you, you've been a decisive guy. Thoughtful, yes, careful at times, but decisive.

"Sasha's got you by the short hairs. We used to call this 'whipped.' Know what I mean?

"But 'whipped' had a mighty significant preface you never got from her, so it's astounding you were over barrel so long."

"Had? Nice of you to put her in the past; she is still in my heart. But I'm trying. I mean hearts, lungs, and the body must go on, right?"

I forked a bite, reaffirming the necessity of carrying on.

"Ray, you asked me earlier about why." I stoked the fire again. "If I don't get it out now, I never share the depth of my attraction."

An indirect answer might prove to be the shortest distance between two points.

"Have you ever had a revelation?"

"What do you mean?"

"Ever have a revelation about the past?"

Ray tightened his forehead, "I don't know, Brian…"

"Remember my story about jumping out of the helicopter for the first time? The experience triggered a primal memory, a revelation of the past. In that instant of helplessness I had a primal memory of being born. I retained a 'feeling' deep inside from the moment of birth and connected that primal experience to the instant I hung suspended in the air beside the helicopter and gave a little kick into the air. My mind connection the two events as I dropped."

Ray added, "Umbilical cord and static line. The helpless fall… birth."

"Exactly! The feeling existed in my primal memory. The primal experience formed *before* I learned words or organized thoughts. And it remained out of mind because-- after I learned to think and speak-- I'd never had anything to connect it to. That is, until I experienced freefall from 3,300 feet. When I felt the helplessness rush of gravity tugging me back toward earth, the experience became instantly and indelibly connected to my earlier primal feeling.

"Well I had another revelation a few months ago. And this other revelation of the past answers your question of 'why'"

"OK. Go on, you've got my interest," Ray encouraged.

"I was lying in bed one night, just a day or two after I saw Sasha for lunch back in June."

"In bed? Hey asshole, don't tell me this was all just about *sex*!"

I consoled, "No, it wasn't sex, man. It's about pursuing… my spiritual destiny."

I stretched my back before continuing, "As I lay there awake, my body didn't feel like my body. My senses were distorted. My bed felt huge, like it stretched from one side of the room clear across to the other."

"I felt strange. Like when you have a fever; your body's swollen, disjointed out of proportions. My mattress was huge compared to my body size. And my legs weighed three times as much. My arms were heavy, massive. It was like I didn't have any strength. I didn't have any muscle to compensate for my weight, like I hadn't exercised in years. Then I realized I was reliving an infant's perspective - a primal memory.

"With no mobility, I just lay there.

"Then I heard my heart beat when I was in my mother's womb!"

I halted giving words time to sink in and sipped water.

"Ray I remembered first experience. I felt my heartbeat. And I realized there was another—my mom's—that was different than mine. I wasn't hearing it, I felt it. *Feeling it*! That was my first conscience realization as a human being!

"That memory formed way before words, before other experiences. As a fetus, hearing and feeling, and really everything else, was feeling.

See the brain hasn't distinguished sources of input yet. Everything is jumbled. I felt my heart before language and conscience. It was feeling, all feeling, before thought developed.

"Hearing was feeling, touching was feeling, thinking was feeling, everything was feeling; it didn't matter which sensing organ was stimulated. The feelings of sound were inseparable from other sensations. They were all vibrations of one kind or another that pinged the senses."

As I spoke I relived the moments. Slipping back as best as I could as we finished dinner, I was back to those tender moments of such an impressionable time.

Ray quietly followed my odyssey.

I shook and cleared my head. "In that moment I could tell the difference between my mother's heartbeat and my own heartbeat!"

I placed my fork down, concluding my meal.

Ray composed himself, swallowed and asked, "Well, what did it feel like?"

The waitress arrived and offered to fill our glasses. To that offer we agreed. We both passed on dessert-- the truth of story sweeter than anything on the menu.

After the waitress departed I said, "Hard to explain! See, I have to use words to tell you. And words and mental acuity came along after these feelings, much later than the event.

"My heartbeat felt three-dimensional. It felt fluted like a budding rose or a tulip. Imagine the shape of a flower bud about to open. Bulbous at one end, gracefully coming together in the middle, and radiating out ever so slightly at the other end. That's what it felt like.

"I realized in the womb my heartbeat had two parts, separate yet connected. It felt fluted; a round base ever so gracefully coming together, then it diverged. Somehow the first beat was the base and the second…"

Ray stayed quiet. We'd both leaned forward, drawn about as close to each other across the table as we could be. He saw I was in touch with the memory. We both slid back from the edge of our seats.

"And that's when my heartbeat took on distinct form, it took on a sound. I distinguished sound that instant for the first time separate from other sensory input. The sound came into focus, clear focus. I didn't have a name for the sound when I was a baby in the womb. But the memory came back into focus as I lay there as an adult."

"There was the slush-slush of blood through my body. But I discerned the actual heartbeat independent of the subsequent sloshing of blood flow. The heartbeat feeling, my heartbeat, had two parts. And *now* as an adult I could distinguish them as two beats!"

I stopped as the waitress brought the bill. We collected ourselves one more time. The waitress smiled and thanked us for our business. She turned smartly and departed. I glanced around the restaurant. Folks just like us, eating and finishing up their meals. No one else appeared to be recalling primordial memories.

Ray leaned in close supporting his weight on his arms.

"And I heard the sound of my heartbeat."

"And it resounded 'Sa-sha' Sa-sha' 'Sa-sha.'"

Love is Like a Yo-Yo
January-17

I thought half a world would separate me from Lynchburg by basketball season, but the labyrinth of red tape sets its own time table. No immediate trip overseas.

Eric's boy was on my basketball team. That fact seriously endangered our chances to have a winning season. Eric joked after missing the first three games, "Medicine is like the mafia -- once you're in, there's no getting out."

I dropped by Eric's home after bringing his boy there after a game. One of mine came on the same tow line. Undaunted by the intense game they'd finished, the boys ran outside to play.

Eric and I gathered in the kitchen while the kids stayed out. A wooden banister and three steps separated the kitchen from the sunken den. The TV at the far end of the den flickered a college game sound almost inaudible. It would have been hard to hear from the chairs and sofa in the den. From the kitchen, the announcers' voices bubbled a warm murmur like a tranquil fountain.

"How did it go?" started Eric.

"You should've been there! We won. Close and exciting, a real nail biter! Hey, your boy got his first bucket plus a free throw!"

"Great! Sorry I missed." His eyes lit up in fatherly pride.

Eric was genuinely interested in his son's activities. Most parents don't need reminding about being present in their kid's lives. Just the choices we make, the jobs we hold, and obligations get in the way.

"How'd your boy do?"

"About usual, if they gave out scholarships at this age we'd be set. But I'm having a heck of a time getting the rest of the kids involved in the offense. Our teamwork is great, but some don't have a prayer to score. Let's just say they have the kind of basketball skills that will give them a legitimate shot to make the marching band as they get older."

Eric offered, "What I've seen looks great even with the future trombone section! Those of us with kids that aren't stars appreciate the teamwork you instill. Glad each player is getting off a shot and the better kids give up chances to score in favor of passing to the brass."

I nodded accepting his assessment.

"Care for lunch?"

I hadn't noticed any hunger or thirst until Eric offered but it had been hours since breakfast. During the game coaches and players are too keyed up to think of food. Afterwards hunger presents itself like a full court press.

Eric visited the well-stocked refrigerator and began preparing sandwiches. I got plates and cups. We ate simply, like most lunches at home. Neither of us sat down while we polished off our food.

He made hotdogs for the kids. The boys came in long enough to eat, raise the noise and mess level.

The boys darted outside and I halted them; "Clean up!"

They cleared their plates without grumbling and headed out.

"So how is the love life going?" Eric asked as we stepped into the den.

"I should ask you. Might get a more sensuous answer!"

Eric just shrugged.

His couch felt comfortable. It was the first time I'd been off my feet in hours. The fabric was made of faded tan canvas printed with a mosaic depicting early Americana. Log cabins and woodpiles, a horse drawn carriage, a single-room schoolhouse, and a small country church repeating over and over in faded hues. It was an image that bound generations of forefathers and mothers. In physical toil and emotional upheavals it's nice to be reminded of the larger fabric of life.

The TV featured ACC top ranked teams oblivious of us. The incessant appliance offered warmth, but we didn't want to become boob tube prisoners so volume stayed low.

"What a long strange trip it's been."

"I'm joyous and frustrated when I think of Sasha. It gets me down, but I get back up again."

"Your mistake was you believed you'd get over her in *this* lifetime," Eric said with conviction.

He went on, "When you love someone, really love someone, Brian, you don't get over them, don't forget them. They're part of you. Healing is about dealing with all parts of you. Healing is about embracing each day fresh, learning how to live again, and then living for all it is worth. Sometime it's about moving on."

I sat back impressed.

But Eric's wisdom pointed to sadness in my heart. I seldom listened to the radio during my commute to and from work. Love songs sent me tumbling and my heart yearning afresh.

"Eric, I tried things to get Alexa off my mind. I tried over the counter Zantac last summer at the onslaught of trouble. Then red licorice."

"Really?" Eric sounded skeptical.

"Candy worked better! I tied each slender length in a knot before eating and it soothed my angst."

Eric quipped, "Makes sense, if your heart is tied in a knot, tying red candy into a knot will yield significant medicinal results!"

"Make fun, but I didn't need a prescription."

"Licorice is marginally medicinal. The modern candy, however, is void of the real thing, all artificial flavoring I'm afraid."

"About mid-fall, I grew impatient with my lack of progress, so I changed gears. Each time I thought of her I'd replace the thought with an instant congratulation.

"If I thought of Alexandra upon waking, before feet hit the floor, I'd redirect thoughts; 'Great job getting up as soon as the alarm went off!'

"If a thoughts of her resurfaced as I showered and I'd repeat my mantra; 'Great job setting the shower temperature.'

"Preparing coffee, the Bean returns to Alexa, and I'd check my thoughts; 'Perfect quantity of grounds. This will be a marvelous pot.'

"I gave little praises to draw thoughts away from Alexa."

"Did it help?"

"I began seeing my fixation as a strange form of self-abuse. Punishing myself for not getting the woman I wanted like there was something I could have done differently. By redirecting mental activity I silenced a negative script."

"How long did you keep it up?"

"Kind of slipped away, but it helped for a spell when I needed it. A few weeks ago I changed tactics. By early winter I started thinking happy thoughts. My strategy was to supplant an image of Alexa with a happy thought. Don't get me wrong, thinking of her was happy, just counterproductive. I trained myself to supplant my failure with a happy thought. Like if I was driving to work and I recalled a moment we shared, I'd force a thought 'What a beautiful morning! I am blessed and darn lucky to be healthy and alive today.'

"At work if my mind slipped back to her beautiful face, I'd switch supplant 'I'm so happy to have a chance to work here and make a difference!'

"I overwrote recollections of Alexandra with things from the present."

"And that helped?"

"I slowly realized it was up to me to create joy and happiness. The present is the only time available. Whatever her reasons, Alexa wasn't keen on opening her heart to me and sharing a joyous life. So I'm gearing up to create that joyous life on my own."

Eric slapped his thighs and said, "Good. You're trying to move on."

"You're a doctor. Did you ever read anything about a midlife crisis being precipitated by, I don't know… a change in hormones or something? Women go through menopause, right? Think men might go through 'womenopause'?"

"What?"

"When a boy enters his teens and starts the change from kid to man his hormones start racing. They race incessantly for years. The surge launches him on a quest for female company in a way he hadn't sought before. Instead of play friends, he starts searching for a mate. Instead of unleashing the urge to play Red Rover Red Rover or tag, he'd rather a girl come over and share a little one on one time. With hormones swirling he creates relationships and contact with girls as a response to these changing urges.

"Then… what if at some age the whole mental, hormonal, or other physiological balance changes again?"

Eric admitted, "I read a number of journals but I don't recall research along those lines."

"Guys get this rush of testosterone as teenagers and we begin fulfilling our adult needs. Decades later a guy in his thirties or forties has had all the kids needed to perpetuate the species. Hormones change again. For twenty or thirty years he's ridden on this stable plateau of high hormones. But now biological feedback says no more kids. Time for another change.

"And he slips off the stable hormone plateau. But see, the average guy only knows one thing about a change in hormone levels. Last time he had a change it instigated his search for a woman. So what does he do when he feels a change mid-life?"

Eric remained quiet.

I added, "He's a one trick pony—change in hormones and life situation equal search for a woman. Man reverts to the one and only pattern of behavior he associates with changing hormone levels-- he looks for new companionship."

Eric reiterated, "I see your point. Guys go through transitions at various ages. A huge change occurs between teen and young adult. At thirty we settle into the role of being 'working guys' and give up late night socializing. We leave a chunk of our rebellious energy and childhood behind and accept being dad. At forty I suppose we look around and see we're becoming a full-fledged adult. No hiding from the fact… and we realize we're done siring kids. Soon we'll be granddad. Later in life we'll face other societal clues like retirement and go through the next transition."

I supported, "It isn't just biological, it's social. We change and gradually adapt to the role society pens for us. But we rebel at those junctures if there's some part of us clinging to an earlier stage, a need not met. We hate to move to granddad if we left a big part of our heart in an earlier transition."

Eric echoed and nodded, "A need not met."

We exchanged glances and shrugged leaving sociological behavior for others to unravel.

He slapped his thigh and rose quickly, "Now, let's play doctor!" His tone was full of youthful enthusiasm and mischief.

Eric made his way to a desk in the corner of the room where he retrieved a thin notebook.

My eyebrows rose, "Don't know. The last time I played doctor I was in first grade in the basement of my neighbor's house. And Carol was an older woman by a full year."

Eric returned, opened his notebook, with his voice cloaked in an Austrian accent. "Hum, let's zee here."

"I vould like you to peeer into zees images and tell me vat you see."

Inside the folder were images his pre-school child drew. Scribbles and colors abounded. It would take some interpretation to decipher. The good doctor was about to use crayon images as a cheap stand-in for a Rorschach test. The clinically accepted black and white cards gave way to the readily available construction paper and colored wax squiggles entitled 'My Preschool Art.'

I laughed at his fake accent.

"Oh my, it is Terminator 4! Terminator has returned as Doctor Freud with the diabolical mission of confounding humanity and… "

"Yes, laugh now, but zoon all vill be clear!"

He took out the first sheet of construction paper and asked, "Vhat do you see?" He handed me a large taupe colored scribble. I inspected it with great care and consideration.

"Doc, I'm not sure, but you might want to *focus* the camera next time you take pictures! Nothing here but random scribbles. You still got the receipt for these?"

"This Carol girl. Did you play doctor just once?"

With a twitch of his wrist, Eric waved the first card away and displayed the next image.

"Ok, ok, it *does* looks like a splotch of colored wax." Pre-school drawings *are* hard to interpret, but I was willing go play along. I'd give him a straight answer if I ever discerned anything amid the random mutant shapes.

Eric asked with quiet professionalism. "OK, tell me what you see in this one?" He seemed a little more serious as he revealed the next drawing.

"Umm, a leaf."

The next page came out. "And this one?"

"Hey, they're getting better! That one… looks like a cloud. Definitely a cloud."

"Just a cloud? Does the cloud look like anything?"

"Looks a hell of a lot like a leaf, but I'm expanding my mind into the third dimension. I'm working here!"

Eric sat up and stretched his back, a little dismayed.

"Ok, they *are* getting better," I conceded. We made eye contact.

"Let's keep going," I suggested.

"Right!" Eric responded and raised the next card. This card had much more intriguing patterns. There was depth to the image.

"Looks like a tree, a large tree in full bloom… and…" My voice trailed off as I looked closely and was about to add interpretive depth. Eric changed tactics. He put the sketches back in the stack. His hands oriented the cards and he gently dropped the edges against the folder straightening all sheets. The drawings quietly went back in the folder.

"Those are some good cards!" I added.

"I'm going to stop before we get to the card everybody says looks like a vulva."

I sprang off the couch and looked at the seat.

"You must have had some sick patients in here, doc!"

"Let's just talk," Eric said.

I parroted. "Just talk."

"The fact that she never got back in touch, how does that make you feel?"

"Oh boy! Nobody asked how I feel! A bit sad.

"More than a bit sad. No closure of the past and no path forward with her. I feel like I have no present and no future that I want. You can't be in love with someone who won't call you back."

"I disagree." Eric looked down, stopped and waited, letting the silence become thick with anticipation. He looked squarely at me, "You've proven just the opposite. You can be in love with someone that really doesn't give a shit if you are alive!"

"Is that your professional opinion?"

"Psychology is not my field, but yes, that is my opinion."

Eric paused and I didn't know where he was going. He added, "How long are you going to crucify yourself?"

I answered surreptitiously; "Can't find much around here with less than a year lease. Let me tell you about 'Terrace Apartments.' That's a real estate term for a subterranean dungeon where mold and spores breed like a biological lab!"

Eric gave a knowing smile, "How'd Celeste take it?"

"Hell, Eric, it's been hard on both of us. Torture. She used to ask me why didn't I just go to Alexandra and talk to her. She says I should find out if there is anything reciprocal and make a go of it."

Eric replied: "She always had more sense than you. Sounds like one way out of the quagmire. Why don't you?"

"I never told anyone, but I visited her place twice. Even though I'd bravely asked her to pick a time and place entrusting our future in her hands, I couldn't stand the silence. I dropped by her house twice since she stood me up at the museum. It mattered way too much to me and I had tried each and every avenue, work every knob and lever.

"Went by her home once during the day, again early in the evening. But she had not been at home. Her car had been there the second time, but nobody came to the door. I waited at the curb a while before leaving. Raleigh is a long way from Lynchburg if you keep striking out. Two unlucky trips and her total lack of communication made me question the wisdom of a return trip.

"Probably should have tried prayer instead!

"Funny, before I visited her place I imagined where she lived, what kind of house, etc. I'd imagined her house on the right side driving into the neighborhood. She would live on a quiet street, in a quaint brick home. And she'd live in a well-kept, simple but elegant home. An elegant abode befitting my Taj Mahal princess. In my mind, trees covered the half acre lot, giving a shaded appearance. Splotches of sunlight danced through to the tall grass below. 'My roommate wasn't much help around the house…' I mentally added a scruffy element of grass a little too tall and shrubs in need of a pruning.

"When I visited her dwelling her home was on the left, and not brick but siding. So much for clairvoyance! But I'd imagined the trees and shaded correctly. A landscape crew would have had a productive few hours.

"Going to Raleigh unannounced again wasn't in the cards. The failure of all my communicative efforts and my lonely visits left me drained, vulnerable. I wouldn't travel to Raleigh anymore."

I answered hollowly, "We all have a right to remain silent.

"Her silence speaks volumes, don't you think?"

"Indeed, I do. But do you?" Eric asked.

I nodded yes. I felt like lowing my head in admonition of my failure, but I checked the impulse and met his eyes adding detachedly, "Yeah, I do."

Eric instructed, "Say after me B-I-T-C-H.

I added with zeal, "BIAAATCH!" bringing a smile to our faces.

Eric slapped my back, "One giant leap for Brian, one small step for mankind."

"So where do you go from here?"

"Love is like a yo-yo. Pretty easy to get hold of, fits comfortably in your life and hand, even has a 'ring' around your finger.

"Like love, a yo-yo takes time to learn. Patience is necessary. But unless you are really good you'll turn it into knots. And unless you are patient and enduring enough to untie the knots, it isn't worth shit. Hell, you'll probably throw it away."

"And start over?" Eric asked.

"Start over? Why? If you knot one, and you haven't *learned* what the hell you did wrong in the first place…"

I admitted, "I'll probably try again. I'm no hermit. Got a lot of love to give and I gravitate to sharing. I'll start over with some of the vigor and optimism that drove me as a younger man. I hope that love isn't just for the young!"

"Young at heart, love is for the young at heart." Eric affirmed.

"Celeste and I talk about it often, divorce I mean. Seems inevitable, but there's something childish in throwing in the towel and starting over, going for the easy love. You know?"

Eric countered emphatically, "No. I don't know. There is no easy love."

"Well, I mean the starting over part. In the early part of a relationship it's easy to be attracted and feel like you're in love. At the beginning you're forgiving, generous, kind, and endorphins and hormones swirl.

"If Celeste and I don't make it I hope love arises again. I hope and pray I forge enough love to *start* and *finish* the next relationship.

"See, if that's the challenge, if that is what I need to learn, then starting over is counterproductive. I wonder if I'm hiding from the truth. Can I build a relationship that can weather the tests of time?"

"Brian, you made it fourteen, sixteen years? Sounds like you passed the S.A.T."

I continued with great certainty, "Love is what you make it." In a lower voice I repeated, "Love is what you make it. Any love is what you make it. Friendship is what you make it; acquaintance is what you make it. And love for a woman, a wife, is what you make it."

"Love is definitely what you make it," Eric agreed calmly. He tapped his folder with the Crayola sketches. "Pretty much everything in life is what you make it."

I caught his point about the cards. He'd driven me there from the start.

He cleared his voice, "You know the world is a lot kinder to single women these days. Kay never remarried. A divorced woman has standing in society. Not like decades ago. No shame in it and I don't think there should be. A single middle-aged woman can date, even sleep around with hardly an eyebrow raised. Neighbors might see one boyfriend's car in the driveway this month and another car next month. Who would say anything?

"Separation and divorce often provide financial payouts that make divorced woman quite well off. They may have a disincentive to remarry.

"Kay got the house and the terms of our divorce bring her a monthly check while she remains single. She may fall in love again; I hope she does. But the terms of her existence discourage tying the knot. She can date, she can be romantic, even get a live-in guy. But she'd give up easy money by getting married. If she ties the knot, she gives up quite a chunk of guaranteed income. Income that increases with inflation no less!

"Could be the same with your Alexandra. She might relish playing the field and shy away from a guy that smells like love and commitment. And brother you sure came across serious from the get-go! Hooking up with you would shatter her little world. If she moved, she'd lose her government retirement and she'd have to sell the house. There could be a lien against the house. If she remarries or moves, her ex gets half of the sale."

There was a crescendo of quick pounding footfalls running closer to the house.

"Something to think about," Eric shrugged.

"Are we done here, doctor?" I asked.

Soon two rambunctious boys would be up the steps and bounding through the door. It was time for the two older boys in the den to put their dad faces back on. We were smarter for all the wear and tear. We didn't cry when our feelings got hurt or when we stubbed our toes. But we were still little boys in a lot of ways. Our session searching for answers and nuances of love was over.

"Yes, ve are done," Eric replied in his best Austrian accent.

"Good. Then can I see that fourth or fifth picture again?"

"Which one?" Eric opened the folder and got his hands ready to flip through the stack.

I joked, "The one that looked like an apple tree, remember? The one with Eve standing there in profile with her right hand tucked behind her head, fluffing her luxurious hair as it rains down mid-back, splayed by an unseen wind. Her C size breast jutting perkily proud before her."

Eric's hands flipped the stack with urgency, "Let me see that!"

"Boy, if the AMA knew you had pictures like that in the house with a growing boy…"

The door flew open. Our "quasi-mature" conversation concluded.

Priceless

February

Celeste's cousin getting hitched offered the most awkward vacation opportunity imaginable. That it occurred around Valentine's Day was salt for the wound.

It would be international-- invited to Costa Rica as part of the wedding ceremony by friends who no doubt fancied us a couple more than we saw ourselves these days. Lately we were doing great, buoyed in a sustained swell and optimistic we could live with joyous mind and heart.

Two days before our planned departure we hit rough waters. Celeste looked over the end of year credit card report and spied a ledger of summer flowers.

"Did you really send her flowers?"

"Yes. Such an offering was made. It seems decades ago and I've aged so much since last summer. I regret hurting your feelings."

Celeste played for an "I'm sorry," but I wouldn't desecrate feelings nor pretend it didn't happen.

A difficult terrain in every direction awaits the troubled couple. Somehow a singular connection still held taut between us. All lines had been cast off except one. That single line remained indiscernible a transparent connection we couldn't see, but both felt. And we respected it, as if that single unspoken tether of faith knew what was best.

We went on the trip more like bit part actors in a play performing the supportive in-laws role.

Costa Rica is a great place, well worth visiting and the resort exotic. Actually, the small resort was on the extreme side of exotic and I wondered if we'd ventured onto the set of the TV show "Survivor." It was remote requiring a hike from the village to get to our cottage.

People of this warm country were kind and trustworthy. Refreshingly, no prejudice separated locals from tourists.

During the stay extended family walked the beaches, rode horseback galloping full tilt along the sandy coastline, and swung through the tops of the rainforests. Celeste surprised me with her horse riding skills. Yep, we had fun and even held hands.

One morning we set out to explore the beaches, joined by Fred and his wife Tica. This was a great outing because Fred and Tica also had three young kids and seldom got away from responsibilities. We were giddy with freedom as we gathered in front of our bungalows. I started barefoot on the beach until sun bleached sand roasted my feet. A faithless firewalker, I turned and scampered back to the room for sandals. As I bolted for our room, the others clad in footwear eagerly wanted my attention but my burning mission occupied.

I ventured back. They shivered agitated like they'd been stung by an exotic spider. Finally Fred calmed, "You just missed a topless girl wearing a thong so skimpy it could pass as dental floss!"

What?"

Tica and Celeste burst out laughing, "You almost ran her over when you turned back to the cottage."

"I… I remember passing a young lady on the path but my feet…"

I snapped out of the heat induced tunnel vision, "I missed *that*?"

I shook my head, "God works in mysterious ways! I can't believe it!" I twisted my head down the path anticipating a second chance, but lush undergrowth and twisting trail prevented a view more than twenty feet.

I charged, "All right then. Press on!"

Fred's smile was only slightly larger than the two women's but his reached deeper.

One of the locals had clued us in that a nearby beach was frequented by sunbathers of many varieties. The beach welcomed nudes and modestly attired. The four of us surprised ourselves by willing to go… but in swimwear.

Visiting a beach shared by nudes changed what provisions we packed. My backpack overflowed with bottled water, a blanket, a book, and plenty of sun block. The sunscreen wasn't just for our quartet. I joked with our little party, "I'll lavishly apply the skin saving salve to anyone we meet."

Tica acknowledge, "You're so thoughtful!"

"Just that kind of guy!"

We journeyed along the narrow path that danced along the shore and inland depending on terrain. Finally sharp igneous rocks and coconut trees surrendered into a broad empty expanse of lava brown sand. In the distance a young lady without a top rested on a large towel. It was difficult to see if she sported a stitch anywhere.

As we approached Fred excitedly confirmed, "That's her! That's the woman you missed on the path!"

"I see you left out a little detail that she's been on the Atkins diet a little too long."

Tica soured the moment; "It wasn't the Atkins she adhered to, more like the 'Karen Carpenter' diet!"

The rail thin Aztec ignored the gringos.

We scoped two miles of beaches and didn't see more than a dozen folks. The only topless were the guys and the single frail goddess.

On our way back, Fred and I played island native and opened coconuts. The milk refreshed and the meat provided lunch. We carted a few coconuts back to our cottages and opened them for the rest of the wedding party.

The next day was filled with horseback riding and swinging on the slide-for-life atop the trees. On Friday, Fred, Celeste, and I chilled at the shaded pool with a few others. Celeste was absorbed in a novel. Fred wasn't done playing wilderness provider. He gathered coconuts from trees shading the pool poking at the hard-shelled fruit directly above Celeste's teak lounge chair.

I joked to Fred an indirect warning, "Hit near her with one I'll give you a twenty."

He continued the hazardous pursuit.

"Bring down two on her lounge chair and I'll give you a hundred!"

Fred finally understood the hazard of his pursuit concluding, "Bring down the whole bunch on her… *priceless*!"

We both cracked up.

A single guy pool side winched in dismay. I comforted, "It's a married guy thing."

Fred and I took joy in each other's company on those rare occasions we could dance outside the lines of civility. Thus comprised the lone degree of freedom reserved for the married man.

Celeste smiled and shook her head at our comedy and turned the page.

Later that afternoon the wedding was held outdoors, followed by a meal and a reception. The sun set quickly in the tropics and it was time for the reception that included dancing on an expansive round outdoor patio. Chairs were placed on the perimeter of the slate patio. Fred and Tica, Celeste and I, put our belonging on teak chairs in the center of the semi-circle and danced into the night.

As a conclusion the hosts brought out three guests not in the wedding party. Two lanky young men and one young woman appeared. The girls sported a marvelous tattoo on the small of her back. The tattoo was a first rate intricate image of a mystical dancer.

The three new guests comprised a "surprise" the host arranged. They were invited to perform a fire dance. The young American girl traveled the Orient and tropics learning fire dancing in her carefree year away from home. The team of dancers let loose. At times the three danced as a group other times they performed solo. Tica wore a loose fitting rayon dress and sat beside Fred. Celeste sat on my thighs sharing a chair. Had it been three male dancers she'd have found a different perch.

During the show the two guys used flaming batons. Fire sprang from both ends of the rod. The girl held a rope in each hand, about four feet long, and on the end of each rope hung small blazing containers. The men's batons got loose a few times skittered precariously close to the encircling audience. Someone asked; "Is this part of the show?" half worried, half entertained.

Throughout the evening the batons and fire goblets whirled through the dark night throbbing in synch to the music.

The girl's last act was the most impressive. She did limbo bends backwards as she faced Fred and me. Fred observed, "Nice to be front and center in a show like this!"

Back farther and farther, all the while the dancer twirled her ropes fiery trails streaked the jet black sky. She did some other impressive gravity defying bends before dropping down to a full split with the gyrating rhythm of the fire still circling and twisting.

Fred jabbered jokes but I reprimanded him never taking my eyes off the split dancer, "Not now, man! I'm busy!"

As the show concluded we gave the fire dancers a hearty round of applause. Fred turned to me and said "Dancing with family and friends, forty dollars. Watching fire dancers in the tropics, one hundred dollars. Having the fire baton land on your wife's dress… *priceless*. The married husbands and wives howled with laughter. The singles thought it cruel.

Departure time arrived early. By 6:10 we were completely checked with an hour and forty-five minutes to mill around the tiny but pleasant San Jose airport. Café Britt, a major exporter of coffee from Costa Rica, does its best to soothe travelers with complimentary coffee and chocolate-covered coffee beans at souvenir shops. Employees were quite knowledgeable, helpful, and friendly. With so much time to kill I sampled just about everything they had. Fortunately, the fine gourmet coffee grown on volcanic mountains is low in caffeine.

Celeste rested against a wall while I lingered in the shop. The store's shelves displayed numerous bags of Café' Britt's export coffee. And on display was, you guessed it, *Shade Grown Coffee.* Shade Grown Coffee was Café' Britt's brand, available in beans or ground.

The Bean strikes gold! With a captive audience of store clerks I uncovered the real shade grown bean's story.

According to Café' Britt a single coffee tree (you'd call them bushes if you stood beside them) produces about one to one and a half pounds of coffee a year. About 2,000 handpicked berries go into a pound of coffee.

A proficient coffee picker gathers ten baskets of coffee berries a day translating into 2,400 cups of java per day per worker.

And why is any of this germane? In dollar volume, coffee is the second largest commodity exported in the world, second only to oil. As claimed by Café' Britt, Shade Grown Coffee is Organic Coffee certified by an international agency called O.C.I.A. (Organic Crop Improvement Association). It is cultivated without pesticides, herbicides or chemical fertilizers. At first the "shade" part seemed a bit of a misnomer and I grilled the employees. The well-informed airport store attendant gently removed skepticism by pointed out benefits associated with allowing larger trees to cohabitate the same field as the coffee trees.

With so much time to burn the employees continued under my inquisition; "Coffee trees are small and wouldn't support the indigenous bird or monkey life. A country stripped of native trees, provides no homes for monkeys or birds. Wise coffee growers provide a more diverse ecological system allowing larger shade trees to share the slopes. So it is good for the environment."

From a cost standpoint, Shade Grown Coffee supposedly takes three to five times the labor, so it isn't just a marketing gimmick. Added labor is needed because coffee bushes aren't quite as resilient due to the taller poio and plantain trees shading them. Coffee growers don't get the yields they would otherwise if they planted monoculture coffee and used agricultural chemicals. Suffice to say there really is something to this. It is better for the environment and a colossal international market.

These days American grocery stores and special coffee houses have added environmentally friendly coffee in many wrappers. Give a monkey a home. Check it out.

We arrived in Greensboro North Carolina no worse for the wear despite the cold front that lingered around us even in the tropics. It was late afternoon as we made our way from terminal to car. I reached for the keys, hit unlock. At the same instant the door lock went 'thud' Celeste lurched into a tiff.

Emotional scars had remained hidden during our vacation waited patiently as if parked in our vehicle stateside. Open the door, turn the key and welcome to your old life.

Her stare burned holes through the windshield.

I shook my head unable to break her trance, reached over and held her hand. We drove north. To our left the sun vaulted its way chasing night from the oriental sky. Spectacular clouds filled the western sky. Optimistic peach/pink/purple colors danced on the sunny side of a cloudbank. And on the same cloud, the side away from the sun reflected cool pewter.

Closure

Midnight- Early June

Full moon illuminates a colorless hue. A sheet of gray cast lifeless glow through half-opened Venetian blinds. The ground looks like gnomes spread plastic sheeting as far as the eyes can see. Nothing moves. Yards, roads, air all still. The sterile landscape, a close relative of death, drills realization into my stubborn head. I realize my joy is not at all rooted in Alexandra's response. She can be stoic. I can move on.

The secret to joy is sharing love and expecting nothing in return. This message reverberated through my head as a nightingale opened its warble.

The secret of joy is to give love unconditionally. I diminish myself if I let society instruct me on what I what, what I need to be happy, what I must feel to be satisfied. My source of joy is giving. Frustration descends the tighter I hold other expectations.

Like Peter Pan's playful shadow returns needing mending, joy's homecoming needs celebration.

With a leap and a bound I headed outside. Basking in cold light warmed by wisdom I shouted, "The world put up with Brian running at half-speed way too long." I announced to a watchful owl and the now quiet songbird. "I've been a Lost Boy giving less love than I should. Exile is over!"

____

June 12

About 11:30 on a warm workday afternoon I took a break finding quiet refuge in an abandoned second story conference room that had a bank of south-facing windows. I'd been buoyant for weeks but peering south a strange melancholy haunted. Today? Why droopy today? I propped myself against the glass. Sky was overcast from horizon to horizon.

Gray slate windowsill cold on palms, I peered aimlessly at the southern sky.

A co-worker passed by the open door behind me, "Looks like a storm!"

I turned, sharing a half-smile with eyes as bright as I could force them, and nodded.

The visitor hesitated, "Spring shower, gloomy sort. Looks like it will be with us awhile."

I remained silent, mind rolling back to the gathering storm. Low hanging clouds jostled for position. A shuffle indicated that my visitor moved on.

It hit me why I was on edge. Today was the day-- the one-year anniversary of seeing my Taj Mahal princess.

I looked at my watch. This day last year—just minutes to a full year we reunited. Exactly a year ago I entered the lobby of her office and met with a hug.

My gaze swept the skyline looking south and slightly east. She was down there… somewhere in Raleigh. I exhaled in a weak chortle as I doubted she'd recollect anything special about the anniversary.

My hands playfully swept the slate window sill. I stroked the backs of my hands on the hard, cold surface and then my palms. I lifted hands and pressed them against the glass. It, too, was cool. I repeated the half-chuckle after realizing my hands pressed to reach her, to touch her. Hands raised and pressed to cold glass in search of my heart's desire.

"I'll love you for always." I smiled and took a seat, still fixed on the sky, realizing aloud, "I'll carry you among my treasured memories."

Of all the long-lost friends to see again I was thankful my eyes took in her beauty and our hearts touched.

I can live with that.

I said a little prayer and got back to work.

Father's Day

June –20

No time for e-mails this Father's Day! Another busy day-- shot right out of the cannon.

I loaded up the boys mid-afternoon with two of their friends tagging along for a trip to the pool. I turned the radio loud as we drove and sang with unbridled energy. Songs bellowed across the emotional landscape:

"A little bit of Monica… A little bit of Mary all night long… A little bit of me makes me your man."

Aretha offered a counter point, "R.E.S.P.E.C.T."

I asked boys too young to fathom the dichotomy, "What's a guy to think? The more the merrier or respect and cherish?"

The radio blared, "War… what is it good for, absolutely nothing!" The boys went wild repeating the chorus with throaty impact sounding like concussion grenades. When one kid got tired of singing the chorus another would fire up long after the song was over.

We squealed into the family oriented pool's parking lot, windows down and music blaring.

Lots of kids with middle aged parents in tow enjoyed the fine weather. Graying dads and moms, wonderfully resplendent in their own rights but not eye candy anymore, sunned themselves.

A beautiful lady and man arrived just before I slipped my specs off. The newcomers sat at the opposite end of the pool taking adjoining lounge chairs.

I abandoned the sedentary approach of most adults and joined my joyously screaming kids.

On this Father's Day my youngest made banner progress. In the span of a few seconds he developed from a child afraid and unable to cope in the water to a boy who jumped and swam back to the ladder. The older kids joined us and I took turns lofting them into the air. My middle boy was light enough to propel with a giant throw yet old enough to do a beautiful flip before he hit the water. I tried the high dive to prove I could still do it and bolster my boy boys' confidence to try. He was three inches too short for the high dive, so he spiked his wet hair to gain appearance and got in line. Nobody stopped him.

My little one invited me to throw him into the air to land in deep water. This was a first. I agreed and headed to an unoccupied part of the pool.

As we walked to the far side I heard, "Hello, Brian!"

Without glasses, I blurrily gazed at a man seated nearby tracking the sound of his voice.

He repeated his salutation and I responded, "Ray? Hello, Ray!"

Ray had chaperoned the attractive blond.

He asked, "Is this one of your kids? He's grown!"

Rug rats scattered like mercury before suffering introductions.

Ray's kids from his previous marriage weren't present. *Kind of sad for a Father's Day?*

I returned, "I'm here with my three boys and two of our neighbors."

Father's Day. One man with his family. Another with his new… date. I was happy with my unquestioned and unsupervised access to my children. Ray appeared relaxed and happy in his situation.

"What a surprise!" I announced.

"I met someone who calls Lynchburg home."

I nodded to the attractive woman, "So I see. Saw the two of you arrive but couldn't make out your face. Actually I saw her arrive and wished you out of the picture!"

They shared a smiled like they'd been together a while.

"Rachel, this is Brian, Brian… Rach."

She offered her hand from her lounge chair and exchanged a firm shake. She was radiant. Her blond hair had many highlights that ranged from fair to light brown and her eyes a remarkable shade of green.

"Sorry I didn't recognize you Ray. Did you lose weight?"

"Nope. Hair color."

Rachel looked sideways at him.

"Sorry you had to learn it this way honey."

"Looks good." I offered.

"That old friend of yours did some modeling with Revlon didn't she? I'm pretty sure I picked out the box with her picture on it. Midnight Madness, wasn't it?"

I smiled at his short dark hair, "Close! Real close. It was Clairol, and the color-- Brown Recluse! It's the only hair color that comes with a warning label plastered on the box 'Caution do not allow contact with your eyes or get it under your skin. May cause severe heart palpitations and irrational longing!'"

I addressed Rachel, "So you are the reason I get to see Ray. He'd never come to the pool with me!"

"That is because you'd expect me to play with the kids. Probably have to put lotion on your back."

"Did you complain about lotioning on her back?" I searched my short-term memory for her name but came up blank.

"Have a seat!" Ray offered. He threw a towel over his shoulder.

My kids saw I was about to do an "adult" thing when I should be playing and left me to my own devices.

I glanced around, all seats were taken, but Rachel shifted her prone position freeing up the corner of her lounge chair. The chair rocked slightly under her gorgeous torso as her tanned legs curled to her right offering me a spot. Rachael looked like time and/or money well spent.

I addressed Rachel sincerely, "Thank you."

Rachel leaned forward gracefully adjusting the chair up a notch or two. She lithely twisted her body like a springboard diver. The arch of her back accentuated her chest and neck as she arranged the lounger into a seated posture. Her genuine smile and grace made me quite unwilling to relinquish my small corner of her chair.

"Rachel is a nurse specializing in cardiac patients."

I internally questioned the situation. *Same girl fall through summer? A respectable job? Might she be more than a flavor of the month?*

I followed, "A heart nurse might come in handy around here. You stopped a number of the guys' hearts the moment you walked in." I pantomimed the use of a defibulator; "Clear!"

Rachel gave a huge smile and shifted her long legs in a delicate manner. Like a mermaid's tail, her legs moved together as she rotated slightly to her left side. Her right leg gently extended and touched my lower back appreciatively. Legs generated no sound as they slid one upon the other--smooth as a prepubescent dolphin.

Rachel said, "Ray's told me so much about you!"

I laughed having absolutely no clue where that put me in her mind. I smiled broadly but lips remained closed.

No words or glance needed toward Ray. I had way more on him than he had on me.

"I told Rachael you were one of those guys that would go to hell and back for the love of his life."

My head nodded affirming his appraisal. "There are some I'd have gone to hell for with no chance of return."

Ray confirmed, "That's true. Foolish but true."

Rachel entered the fray, "How ro… Why do you say it was foolish?"

"Because if he didn't have a friggin' chance to get out it would be kind of a waste of eternity, don't you think?"

I wasn't sure what Ray thought of eternity, heaven or hell, but my promiscuous buddy was full of surprises today. I answered flatly, "In matters of the heart, one instant is worth eternity.

"You know me, Ray, even with no way out, I'd find a way. Never give up. Never surrender. And if I couldn't get out… well hell Ray… I'd change the underworld into heaven!"

All smiled at the audacity.

I glanced at the kids. They frolicked in the blessed union of sun and splashing water.

I turned back opting to lighten the conversation but Rachel followed up first, "Oh, Ray, would you come to save me if I needed it?"

"Honey, if you were in hell I'd probably be there too. I wouldn't in a position to help!" They exchanged a laugh at the predicament.

I stretched my torso, signaling my lack of interest in the conversation and unconsciously touched the Band-Aid on my left arm. A large gummy mark tattooed my skin on either side of the bandage.

"So how is the heroin habit?"

"Family pool, Ray, family pool. It is horse here, or horsy habit. Don't mention heroine." I added with a serious tone.

A grandmother next to us raised her head from her slumber, glared our way, and then regained her docile posture.

"God, you two!" Rachel exclaimed.

"I gave blood yesterday. A nurse, not quite as pretty as you, took a pint."

Ray quipped, "See, there you go, saving someone from the brink of death, like I said. But this way you do it in a manner that makes the rescue seem so… mundane."

"Type O Negative, universal donor, they love me."

"I don't give blood," Rachel confided. "I know I should but I just don't. I'm around it all day.

"Ray doesn't give either." I led the conversation dangerously close to Ray's licentious past just to dangle a wheel over the precipice and signal it was a good time to turn the wheel and change directions.

A few moments elapsed as Ray hung in thin air. I added, "Ray may not save someone in hell but he traveled the globe, good spots and troubled places so much so that he can't give. Ray's been to most of the Exclusion Countries List on the donor questionnaire. The medical products he sold helped more folks than I'll meet in a lifetime."

I turned to Rachel and asked point blank. "Did Ray tell you about Alexa, my old flame in Raleigh?"

She was on the spot and Ray didn't answer. Rachel figured correctly that there wasn't any point in hiding the truth. "He mentioned you're going through a tough time."

I looked deeply into her green eyes. The moment stretched into a few seconds and she didn't turn away. I smiled and turned to Ray, "Yeah, yeah it was a tough year actually."

Tongue in cheek I added, "A year. Damn! Think I gave her enough time to call back? She may have been busy!

"What started out as a way to help clarify the past and express my feelings of love mushroomed." I motioned with hands expanding like a cloud as I turned checking the kids.

The kids played safely in the pool making new friends and leaving friends to play with others. No hurt feelings when they left one friend to jump and play with another.

"I empathize with that buddy, but here is a thought… next time you want female company to sort things out, pick someone that will talk and do stuff with ya'!"

Ray leaned forward confidentially adding in a whisper, "Rachel knows a physical therapist who'll wrap her legs around you as you do the wild thing, whip snapping her back and legs in a most opportune time so as to drain every last drop out of you *and* crack your back."

Ray repeated more loudly, "Crack your back…" opening up his hands in self-explanatory fashion. "So it is a legitimate medical treatment. You can even get insurance to pay for it.

"Well, they'll pay about half of it up to twelve visits a year. After that you're on your own. Don't know if you could take more than one of those a month, Brian!" Ray challenge with a grin and leaned back into his chair.

"I've always been fond of the healing touch and quite supportive of… alternative therapies. Sounds Swedish."

Ray added with the gusto he approached women "Sounds barbarian. Rarghhh!"

I glanced at Rachel to get confirmation but got no hint. Nothing exchanged so far rattled her calm.

Ray added, "And, Rach and her friend both live in your area, same zip code even. So you don't have to cruise down to Raleigh, bang on the door just to answer the questions that bother you so."

I lifted my knee up and grasped it with my hands and said flatly, "Appreciate it! I'll keep that in mind."

A quick scan towards the pool confirmed the kids splashed safely.

Rachel plotted a different direction, "I'm amazed. I never thought men cared so much for their women. I never imagined a man could love a woman that gave him so little. Most guys I've met are the take it and leave type. I sense little emotional connection after a few dates, sometimes there remains little after months." She glanced toward Ray wondering.

Ray asked her seriously, "Really?"

"Sorry you had to learn it this way honey." She mocked.

We drifted silently reflecting how unlike our experiences and expectations of intimacy.

Rachel asked, "Here's a thought-- did you ever consider that you already experienced her open heart? Maybe you saw was all there was."

"Huh. I believed she could open her heart, can't most? I could see love dancing in her eyes. I could hear it when she accepted my invitations. It was in there hidden deep but in there."

My smile wilted, expectation versus evidence weighing in, "I mean she had to… it was part of my plan!"

Rachael countered, "You dated fifteen months. Maybe you experienced her open heart, you know? Maybe that's all she ever opened up. When did you first sense she repressed her feelings, for you, maybe for everyone?"

I shook my head. I'd come to the pool to enjoy Father's Day. But my year of searching left me strong. Opening the wound was purely academic now, no chance of harm.

"Was there any one particular event that showed you where you stood?" Ray pursued.

"No. No. Not that I… Well, well, well, hello memory!" A new image fell in the slide projector of life. I saw Alexa and me standing in a crowd.

"There was one. I blocked it all these years! We'd been together a few months when we ran into my lobotomized roommate out on a date. It was at night club."

I talked quietly not wanting to disrupt the sunbathing parents or burn the ears of youngsters.

"My roomie's name was Scott, tall and blonde, strong shoulders. Scott had anger issues that made it awkward to share a dorm room. He'd wake at night screaming at his father. During the day he'd verbally disrespect women. Saw them as sex objects. To him a relationship was a one night stands. Afterwards he'd criticize his date's drunken performance."

Rachel shifted her eyes and adjusted her weight in the chair.

"Anyway, Sasha and I ran across Scott in a club and he's drunk. I later learned it was a common condition when he was out on the town. Maybe the only condition he could stand himself in public. I introduced Alexandra. A tiny droplet of spittle flew out of his mouth as he leaned toward her and jokingly asked, 'What are *you* doing with a loser like this?'

"I figured he was ribbing me in a friendly mocking way and giving Alexa a sideways compliment.

"Sasha just stood there. For a long moment she remained rigid. My God! She acted embarrassed standing beside me and finally uttered 'Well...'"

I shook my head at the pool, "I'd forgotten! I'd forgotten. She just stood there and never offered an answer.

"It was the deepest, emptiest 'Well...' rock hard on the bottom where her heart should have been, where some compassion and appreciation should have rebounded Scott's jab.

"Scott snapped out of his stupor. He apologized at opening a door that led to such an awkward moment. He backpedaled into the crowd leaving me to patch things up with Alexa.

"I didn't think anything of it at the time. I apologized for his behavior and forgot about it. Later that night, when I got back to the room Scott expressed regret for his performance."

Ray asked flabbergasted, "You'd been dating Sasha for a few months, getting nothing all along the way, right? And then when asked for one nice thing to say about you… all she can come up with is 'Well'…?"

I scratched my head.

Ray shifted in his chair, moving closer. He reached out touching Rachel's left shoulder. "Brian, you've known Rachel for what, ten minutes? I bet you could tell me a dozen charming things about her, about why you'd be delighted to spend time with her."

"Sure, she is vivacious, has a great sense of humor, is dedicated to helping humanity through her work, has beautiful eyes, a chest that makes plastic surgeons jealous, and such stunning looks men's necks cracked when you walked in!"

"Exactly. In a few minutes you see the beauty of her spirit and physical appearance. And you would be pleased to share her company."

I nodded in agreement and patted her smooth leg, "Absolutely."

Rachel sat erect and said fervently "If my date had treated me that way I'd have slapped him upside the head and walked out on him right *now*!

"No… first I'd dress him down chewing out his sorry ass in front of everyone, then slapped him and walk out!"

"I…"

Rachel added tersely, "Brian, there are no excuses to have nothing nice to say. At they very least she could have committed on your kindness for taking her to the party."

Rachel pondered a moment then added, "No… the more I think of her answer… it was a come-on to your roommate. That's how I read it. She didn't say anything nice about you because she saw something she liked in Scott!"

Rachel shrugged her shoulders and rearranged herself on the chair.

"Well, I later found out she adored big blonde guys, so you may be right."

"Bad call my boy. Rach is right. It sounds like she was using you to get to the party to *find* someone else. What kind of answer is 'Well?'

Rach is right, apart from the slapping thing of course, you should have pulled her aside and set her straight, told her not to dishonor you. Then you should have walked out on the bitch and made her find her own way home!"

"Think I should have dumped her right then?"

They both nodded.

"Wish I had you in my corner." I said placing my palms on the lounger behind me and stretching.

I glanced back at the water. My clan was rapidly approaching. The oldest insisted on money for snacks, the younger two wouldn't take no for an answer this time. They wanted me wet. My parking meter had expired.

I stopped them long enough to introduce them to Ray and Rachel.

My middle boy immediately began complimenting Rachel on her beauty, first her hair, then her eyes. My boy's compliments headed down her body. Rachel's breasts displaying a hint of nipples protruding through her scant two-piece.

He is too much like his father not to notice cleavage. Her full breasts and tight tummy were an alluring package. The navel brad gleamed in his eyes. Her stealthy smooth legs a mile long to a young boy standing at the foot of her chair.

But his discretion was right on the money and he knew what to say and what not to focus on. When done, his eyes bright with smile, looked expectantly for acknowledgment of his kindness.

Rachel rewarded him with a warm thanks and he turned with glee toward the pool. Young boys may pretend not to be interested in girls, but he beamed knowing the prettiest woman at the pool had noticed him. He splashed wild with glee upon entering the pool echoing.

I excused myself and headed to the pool's edge where my youngest, barely able to discern such things and no prudence to hold anything inside said, "She had nice titties." Boys giggled and one nearby dad lit up. Many noticed-- only the babe uttered the obvious.

"Chip off the old block!" Ray confirmed.

I turned, smiling at Ray and left a longer glance toward Rachel where I held her green eyes and said, "Pleasure meeting you. Don't be a stranger around here; I'm sure you can get a discounted membership. I'd give you a free pass if it were my decision just to enjoy your company. You, Ray, I'd charge double!"

"Rach says there're tennis courts up the hill. Maybe next time I come we can play? Get a foursome together?"

Tennis. I didn't answer.

Ray baited my hesitation, "You look like you've got the perfect build for tennis. And don't tell me all your coaching and dad duties leave no free time for old friends."

I glanced at the tree-covered hill that separated us from the courts. "Walked up there the other day. Six courts with lights. Good shape, very good shape."

I took a deep breath before I returned my gaze to Rachel and Ray.

"Yeah, I can play tennis. Need new gear. I'll have to take it easy on you!"

Ray answered, "Good, I might be seeing more of you soon. I'm thinking about reentering the Fortress."

A broad smile crossed his face.

Rach didn't catch react.

Kids tag teamed against me leveraging bodies pushing and pulling toward the water. It gives them such joy to get their old man wet! I am only too happy to oblige. But I make them work for it before relenting.

Before I fell in I turned to Ray and Rachel one more time and thanked them for the insight they'd given and asked them to stay in touch. They nodded and waved.

I pondered Ray's 'Fortress.'

The kids synchronized their effort and I hit the water as I realized; "Fortress of Wellbeing!"

When I dropped the kids off a chore awaited me. Celeste asked me to move her desk out of her bedroom. She'd removed all the drawers' contents while we swam. Though we both wanted her and the kids to say in the house, financially it seemed untenable in the long run unless I got half the equity. Painting the interior and sprucing up the bedroom would make the house more marketable. The oversized desk we'd lugged in years ago had to go.

Stairs and carpet creaked exactly the same as I remembered. Familiar bedroom but a new comforter festooned the king size mattress. That was about all the change I could see except smaller furnishings had been removed—like pictures.

"Looks great! You were right about the room needing freshening up. A paint job will do it good."

I approached the old desk startled by its size and institutional feel. "What were we thinking putting a desk like this in here? Just what the average young couple needs—work in the bedroom."

I shook my head realizing if I didn't shut up she'd take my words as derogatory.

"Might wind up with next winter's kindling at the bottom of the steps," I quipped. The desk's daunting bulk would be tricky to move.

"How did we get it in here?"

"Ray helped."

I looked closely without seeing a sign that she knew he was in town.

"How do you remember something like that? I forget a lot bigger things that who moved a desk a decade ago."

I glanced in the direction of our neighboring house where Ray used to live. When Ray and his wife split it was a foreign event, just an example of how *other* people's marriages disintegrated.

"You want to try it on your own?"

"Excuse me?"

"Do you want to move the desk or get some help?"

"Oh… let me get those lashing straps in the basement. I think I can handle it."

I glanced back at her cleaning effort. She'd emptied all the drawers and the top was free of clutter except a single letter. I cocked my head as I glanced at the folded pages.

"I found this while cleaning up." She touched the letter with her fingertips sliding it an inch toward me and then walked into bathroom.

I drew the letter near. Addressed to Celeste, it was written in neat block letters. I didn't recognize the handwriting. The letterhead was a clue. It was from a company I worked for in DC. The date was 1988. I looked more closely at the handwriting. The two-page love letter rambled a bit, vacillating from a young man's heartfelt emotions to his quest to understand the big picture. The author was none other than yours truly. I didn't remember writing it, but holding it in my hands brought a smile.

"So… I *did* write you a love letter!" I blurted.

We'd move many times during the first years of our marriage. Our trip overseas caused water damage to many keepsakes. We'd lost irreplaceable super-eight home movies from my mom and dad's collection of family treasures. We'd lost childhood memorabilia and items from the tender years of courting and marriage. This letter, squirreled in the back recesses of the top drawer had survived.

Seeing the note reminded me of cards I'd written Celeste.

She came out of the bathroom and, with a raptor's finesse, plucked the letter out of my hands.

She didn't look up.

"One of your dilemmas put to rest!" I pointed out jovially.

She shook the pages, "My letter composed only *two* handwritten pages! Alexandra's got three *typed* pages."

"The handwriting was small. The pages full," I contended.

We both laughed and sat on the sturdy desk that held our letter like a hidden treasure all these years.

Moving the desk could wait.

ABOUT THE AUTHOR

Gregory Eric Slominski grew up the dependent of an Army Officer when families moved on average once a year. The loving family lived throughout the United States and survived two overseas assignments. The author graduated from high school in North Carolina and attended North Carolina State University where he received a Bachelor of Science in Mechanical Engineering.

As an engineer, he worked as a consultant in the Washington DC area and overseas in Israel before moving to Lynchburg, VA. Mr. Slominski attended Lynchburg College where he received his MBA. He ran his own company and worked as a consulting engineer and for international manufacturers.

While his children were young and the novel written, his volunteer passion was youth sports. He coached and ran youth sporting programs.

Father's Day is his first novel of the tetralogy that follows the exploits and adventures of Brian Whitlash.